Tomorrow's
Memories

Tomorrow's Memories

A Journey Beyond Fear

Norman O'Banyon

iUniverse, Inc.
Bloomington

Tomorrow's Memories
A Journey Beyond Fear

This is a work of fiction. All of the characters, names, incidents, organizations, and dialogue in this novel are either the products of the author's imagination or are used fictitiously.

iUniverse books may be ordered through booksellers or by contacting:

iUniverse
1663 Liberty Drive
Bloomington, IN 47403
www.iuniverse.com
1-800-Authors (1-800-288-4677)

ISBN: 978-1-4620-4422-1 (sc)
ISBN: 978-1-4620-4423-8 (ebk)

Printed in the United States of America

iUniverse rev. date: 08/12/2011

Contents

CHAPTER 1
SEATTLE
The introduction to fearless living

Kathy hated being the last one out of the office. It was just spooky quiet when everyone else was gone. She had stayed late finishing an accounting report. "Wouldn't you know it," she murmured to herself as she made her way down the dimly lit hallway to the supply room. "One last print job to complete and I run out of toner! Why now?" She hurried around the corner and opened the supply room door. It was very quiet with no one else around. She was tempted to leave the last part of her work until tomorrow morning. But she knew there would be a sense of satisfaction when the report was finished.

She was at the metal cabinet in the corner when she heard the door close behind her. Spinning around she was startled to see Martin, the office technician, standing there staring at her.

"What'cha lookin' for?" he asked with a bit of a smile. "I can help you find what you need." His gaze was fixed on the buttons of her blouse, as he shuffled into the small room toward her.

"No, that's O.K. Martin. I just need toner." Kathy felt a wave of panic that warned her, this was not a safe situation. She took a small step to move toward the door.

Martin shifted his direction to block her. It was done with the smile still on his face, but she suddenly felt very trapped, and not a little afraid.

"I know where everything is kept in here," he said moving even closer to her. His eyes swept over her again. She could smell the odor of sweat and stale clothes. His breath was like an old coffee cup. "Let me help you there." He leaned closer, reaching past her, an attempt to accidently stroke her breast.

"Martin!" was all she could say as she spun away from his touch, and pirouetted around him. She held fast to the wall as she slithered toward the door. Once in the hall, she ran to her desk, grabbed her purse and coat, and continued running to the elevator. Only when she was safely in her car could she release the tears that expressed her outrage. "Damn him, damn him, damn him!"

Norm O'Banyon studied the green eyes looking at him from across the table. She had said very deliberately that old vine Zinfandel makes her feel weak in the knees. Now thoughts of a somewhat playful nature frolicked in his mind.

He had met Kathy, and her children, two years ago in Victoria. Since then she had become a very important part of his life. They worshipped together at St. Andrew Presbyterian Church, attended Scott and Jenny's school activities, had occasional social evenings with his son and daughter-in-law, Bruce and Annie; and most of all, he looked forward to their dine-out evenings twice a month, although he refused to call them "dates," as she did. He insisted that they were not courting, whatever that meant. Tonight, their dinner at Salty's had been perfect. The food was as outstanding as the view of Seattle across Elliot Bay. Their conversation had been focused on Kathy's job at Starbucks. With an approaching audit, her responsibility in acquisitions would be evaluated, and her work proficiency reported. She had shared that this is the most stressful time of year for her.

Her steady gaze alerted him to the importance of the question she was asking. "Are those your words, or did you hear it somewhere?" The topic was a familiar one to them, and they both understood how complicated it could be. "Do you really believe the future is ours to mold any way we choose?"

"Yes I do," he replied, just as direct as she had been. "In fact, I believe that is the way we shape it, one choice at a time. That's why I said 'We are making tomorrow's memories today.'"

She was still for several moments, looking out at the ebbing tide. "I don't think I can completely agree with that." She still thought about the close encounter in the supply room, even though she had told no one about it. "I feel so small and inadequate in such a huge place," she said softly, and wanted to say more. "I don't see how my choices can amount to much more than a hill of beans;" then cracking a little smile she added, "and do you know this year we are purchasing almost two hundred million tons of beans? I'm just a little minnow in a great ocean of choice." Across the bay, a ferry boat slid silently out of the Coleman dock, headed for Bainbridge Island, or Bremerton. "Others are making the choices that mold my life."

"Starbucks is huge," Norm answered in understanding, "and getting more so by the day. Do you think you would like to have a job in a smaller company?"

"Oh no," Kathy responded with surprise. "I love working there, and it makes me proud. I just don't feel very safe, or believe I have a bit of control over its future." She was as still as the gull sitting on the piling outside their window.

"But how about your future," Norm asked gently. "I think we're talking about the way we can build memories that we treasure."

Kathy sipped the last of her glass of wine. "You know, I have a lot of very happy memories. But they seem to be the little ones. The memories that stand out for me more are the painful ones that have reshaped my life."

Norm nodded in understanding, "Are you thinking about your dad, and your marital history?"

She nodded her agreement. "Dad's been gone for seven years. It still feels like yesterday, and I didn't have any choice in his long bout with cancer." She straightened her shoulders and sat more upright as though adjusting a heavy burden she was carrying. "Greg left us nine years ago, and I didn't see it coming, or have a voice in it either. He just wanted to be gone from us, and I just had to scramble to keep us afloat."

Norm reached across the table to hold her hand. Once again he was surprised by its warmth and softness. "This is going to sound like we are arguing, and I really don't think we are. What you are saying is that both in the abandonment from Greg, and in the death of your dad, you made the choice to carry on. That was your decision.

The how of it was more a matter of problem solving. Does that make sense?"

"Yes, I suppose it does, but I'm not sure if I see how that allows me to mold my future. There is still the possibility of cancer or . . . ." She didn't want to suggest the failure of a precious relationship.

"Yes, in our family we talk about those terrible things over which we have no control as, 'being hit by the pie truck.' When I think about it, I've never seen a pie truck. It would be terrible to be run over by any truck, but very sweet if it was the right flavor pie." His warm smile was an obvious attempt to bring some levity into a serious conversation. "I think the point I am trying to make is that in the event of some calamity, we still, if we are a survivor, have choices to make. It is our faith that shapes the positive choices, and our fears that shape the others."

"Let me ask you," he was trying to get their conversation into a more comfortable mode. "Can you identify some of the fears you have that are keeping you from making positive choices?"

She studied her empty glass for a moment. For just a moment there was the reflection of the supply room incident; she hadn't said a word to anyone about it. She gave a tiny shudder, then answered, "I'm afraid for my kids; you know, that I won't be able to provide for them the way they deserve. That probably causes me to be pretty conservative, playing it safe. I'm afraid I won't be able to help my mom if she needs care. That keeps me from some serious conversations we could be having. I suppose I'm afraid you might want more from me, and at the same time I'm afraid you won't." She took a deep breath and looked steadily into his eyes. "I'm not sure what that is preventing." Finally that warm smile returned to all parts of her face.

He thought he could ask one more question before this started sounding like a counseling session instead of a choice dinner. "Would you say that fear in general is a negative enough reality in your life that it keeps you from being happy?" It was a probing question.

Kathy took a big breath, as though coming to a decisive moment. "You know what I'm really afraid of," she asked. "I'm afraid if I don't have another glass of that Zinfandel, I'll be sorry, and if I do, I'm afraid I won't be able to find my way home." They both giggled at the easy way she could deflect a serious conversation. They also both understood that it was a conversation that must be revisited. The evening lights from Seattle cast flickering reflections across the bay for them to enjoy.

She settled for a cup of coffee accompanied by the white chocolate raspberry cake the restaurant is known for. Their table conversation had turned casual. He asked about her weekend plans, and she wondered how it was working to divide his time between parish work and the counseling center. Yes, the kids were looking forward to the summer vacation, and her mom was going to take care of them, as much as they needed. The question was asked if he had firmed up his vacation plans aboard *Dreamer,* his sailboat.

"Are you still going up to Desolation Sound?" Kathy tried to make the question sound casual, for she understood he would be gone for at least a couple of weeks.

"It's funny you ask," came the easy response. "Bruce was interested in the same thing yesterday. You might remember that I was headed that way when he and Annie first came aboard *Dreamer.* So, I may have company again." He didn't know how to interpret her raised eyebrows and the "Hmmm," that came with it.

Moments later they were beginning to make those motions of leaving the table when Kathy reached across for his hand. "I've been thinking about your earlier question, about fear. Yes, I have a lot. More than average I'd guess, and it does get it my way a lot. I just want you to know there is no fear about us. I think everything is right about you." Releasing his hand she once again giggled, "I really, really like you!"

He came around the table to help her up, delivering a tender brief kiss on the way. "I really, really like you, too."

The drive out to South Cove, on Lake Sammamish, where Kathy lived with her children, Scott and Jenny, took only a few minutes. Those were uncharacteristically quiet minutes, however. Finally Kathy asked, "Did I do, or say something that irritated you?"

Norm turned to look into her searching eyes. "Oh, Love, no!" He was always glad for her willingness to open a conversation. "I'm just really thinking about the conversation at supper." His smile bloomed. "You know I can drive and talk. But I can't drive and talk and think at the same time." Her giggle was a comforting assurance that his silence was understood.

He continued to share his thought with her, "You know at Resolutions I see five or six couples or people every day. They are all in conflict, of course. Why else would they be there, huh?" He wanted to keep this conversation light and easy, but had the feeling that like an iceberg, there was a huge discussion under the surface. "They are all deeply afraid."

Letting just another quiet moment pass, he continued, "It's not that they are stupid, necessarily; in fact, just the opposite. Some of my clients are brilliant women and men. They didn't go into their marriage intent on ending in a divorce in just a few sad years. They didn't decide to have a family, intent on having estranged, angry, or screwed up kids, or a devastating custody struggle. They certainly didn't build a beautiful home just to tear it into pieces in settlement disputes. They didn't go into business with the plan to go bankrupt, or cheat on their taxes, or go to jail. And those are just the ones I'm going to see tomorrow!" He shook his head for emphasis. "So I wonder what's going on in people. Why do we choose to fearfully self-destruct?"

Kathy understood, with thoughts that large, why it might be difficult to drive and think and talk at the same time. She watched the approach of the familiar intersection that led to her home. "Would you like to come in for a cup of coffee, and talk about this a bit more?" She felt that familiar tug of separation that was increasingly difficult for her. "I'd be glad to fix us a cup."

"It's a tempting offer," he answered with a weak smile, "but how about a rain-check? I have three killer files I must read yet tonight. The first appointment is early in the morning, and I've got to be either bright or shiny." He chuckled at his attempt to be clever. "And the afternoon is going to be challenged by our State of the Union report from the regional Finance Director. If it is anything like past reports, I'll be hard pressed just to stay awake. Hey, how about Thursday or Friday evening? I could cook a light supper, and you could bring a dessert. Do you think we could?"

A brief hug, which they both wanted to extend longer, and a soft kiss, ended the evening for them. There was, however the promise of a Friday evening dinner at his place on Queen Ann. The prospect of being together again was something welcome, and very positive.

Norm showed a surly couple into his office at 7:15 a.m. the next morning. He had introduced himself in the waiting room. Their stiff bodies and stern faces reflected a mood of aggravated resistance. It was not going to be an easy session.

"How long is this bullshit going to take?" the man asked as he slumped in a chair at the end of the table. Norm had taken a chair at the middle of the conference table, and then the woman sat across from him. The seating selection helped Norm understand who was going to be a problem.

"Mr. Clawson," Norm began gently, "the court has asked me to write a recommendation on the fair distribution of assets in your pending divorce. The inventory of assets you have shown me indicates that there is a lot of value on the table, your business, home, investments, properties, and care for the children. To do this carefully might take a while. Don't you think it's worth taking a look?" It was a standard opening for him in these negotiations.

"For Christ's sake! It is not going to change a thing! This is just a cluster mess," he said with a frustrated gesture. "I'm going to get screwed, and that's for sure." He was not willing to look at his wife, but directed his outburst toward Norm. "Just get it over with."

"Mr. O'Banyon," the wife began. "Robert and I have been married nineteen years, a quarter of which might be called 'happily.' He has a prosperous design company, loves golf, drinks a lot, and travels as often as he can, without me or the family. We have two daughters who are in high school. He scarcely knows them. He doesn't eat with us, and when he is home, he's in front of the TV. For the past ten years I have asked him to go to counseling with me, but he refused. I think he is cutting corners in his business too, because in the past three years we have been sued five times by unhappy customers, all of whom won their case. When I finally filed for divorce, Robert seemed surprised, but I had warned him repeatedly." Her face seemed empty of emotion.

"What a bunch of crap!" was the only response from the end of the table.

They wasted several more minutes trying to place fault or excuses on the failed marriage. Finally Norm refocused them on the task at hand. "Listen folks, the court has asked, without a prenuptial agreement, for an equitable division of your assets before your marriage can be dissolved. Let's get to work on that." Looking at Robert, he asked, "I suspect that you have given this some thought; what do you think would be a fair division?"

"I don't want to split anything, damn it! I just want to leave everything alone." He seemed to sag a bit lower in his chair.

Looking across the table at an ashen lady, he asked, "Linda, what seems fair to you?"

"I've been thinking a lot about this. I don't want to destroy Robert, but I don't want to waste any more time on him either. I think the girls and I should have the house and furnishings. He can use some of his stock to pay off the mortgage. The girls should have financial assistance until they are out of college. I think I should have the Lexus and they should get the Honda."

Before she could say any more, a burst of profanity erupted from Robert, ending with, "For Christ's sake, just put a gun to my head!"

There was no mirth in her weary smile as she responded, "For goodness sake, Robert! You have a lucrative business worth ten times what the house is worth, two vacation homes, a boat, the club membership, your portfolio and retirement account. Get your head out of the sand. I'm trying to be nice to you just now. Do you want to play dirty?" Her level gaze made him finally look down.

Norm wanted to maintain the tiny progress he felt had happened. He asked, "Sometimes, to check if a division is fair, I ask if folks would like to exchange asset lists. Robert, would you be satisfied if Linda got the business, and accounts? Would it satisfy you to get the house, and cars, and custody of the girls?"

There were several moments of quiet before Robert responded, "No. I knew this was going to be a bunch of bullshit. I'm lucky to get out with my skin." Slowly getting up from his chair he headed for the door, saying over his shoulder, "Just write the God damned thing the way she wants it. I'll sign it." There was a bit of a sob that lingered as he closed the door behind himself.

Wiping a tear from her eye Linda said, "You do this every day? How do you maintain your sanity?"

As she offered her handshake in parting, Norm answered, "We both know this is not sanity. It's the necessary pain in parting a precious thing, a family. I'm sorry for all of you, and hope this is the beginning of a healing process for you."

His 9:00 o'clock session was much the same, with the exception that Florence Daniels, the divorcing wife, was accompanied by two attorneys, who did most of the talking. Her husband was in prison for embezzling nearly two million dollars from his insurance employer. Most of the stolen money had been recovered prior to his trial. The bonding agency had made up the balance of the restitution, and was now in litigation to get that loss back from her before her pending divorce.

Her attorney was arguing, "Be reasonable! A sum of forty seven thousand dollars may not seem much to a large corporation, but it is more than a year's salary to this lady. You are asking her to liquidate everything she has left in order to pay for a crime she didn't commit!" The negotiations were intense but not heated. Only Florence showed emotions, and they were intermittent between tears of sorrow, and trembling grief. She was terrorized by the notion of having everything taken away from her, and only a little aware of gratitude for no children who would be going through this nightmare too.

At last, Norm entered the conversation as an advocate of Resolutions. "It seems to me," he began, "You can put a lien on this lady's house that will pretty much guarantee that she will never sell it. She won't be able to get out from under the debt. An alternative to that might be a reduction of the collection for the amount she might be able to receive in a refinance, which would allow her at least some wiggle room, and you would get some cash to close the collection. It beats waiting fifteen or twenty years for a possible pay-off."

The insurance attorney wanted to know how much of a reduction she could pay. And the obvious answer was, "Let's get the house appraised and see. Who knows, if rates are low right now, and prices are fair, she might be able to pay half, or maybe more. At least she will be able to pay some."

Florence looked at him with relief. It wasn't a full smile, but the terrible dread of losing everything was relaxed. It was a life-raft in a troubled sea, one which the attorneys could accept and offer their companies. There was a bit of further clarification over timetables and expectations. Then finally, handshakes all around and the session was complete. Norm was reminded again of how exhausted he felt with so little physical exertion. His was not an easy job.

His 11:00 o'clock session had to be rescheduled, with more representation present. The case involved a family with a teenage son, who while under the influence of alcohol, had slammed his car into another filled with students. Several of the passengers had been injured. The parents of the most severely hurt had filed suit for personal and punitive damages for their son. Their seventeen year old son had received a shattered left hand, elbow, arm, and shoulder, which would allow only limited movement for the rest of his life. He had also lost his left leg at the knee.

Norm's challenge with this group was the defendant's attorney, who seemed bent on provoking conflict by using insensitive inflammatory language. His point in the proceedings was that the insurance company had met all the medical expenses, and that a terrible accident did not deserve punishment. "It was an accident for goodness sake." Then, throwing fuel on the irritating fire, he added, "Oh was he really an athlete, or just someone who likes to play with a ball?" "Do you have reason to believe he would have been a runner if he hadn't lost his leg?" "You know, most kids are couch potatoes anyway."

Finally, when the session turned into angry confrontation with the threats of physical violence, Norm ushered the angriest out first, then asked the others to return with sensible counsel, who could be more rational. "What a morning!"

He walked to the ship canal for lunch, which amounted to a hamburger and diet coke at the Nickerson Pub. Yes, a beer would have been preferred, but there was still that State of the Union report to get through. He cut the lunch break short, choosing to get back to the office a bit early.

Selecting a chair near a window was a good strategy, Norm thought. If the session was as boring as he feared, there would be people-watching on the courtyard below. The thirty five or forty employees, who gathered in the big conference room, anticipated a business as usual meeting. Sharing in that notion, Norm had no idea that the information he was about to receive would make a complete change in the direction for his life.

The Chief Financial Officer was introduced, and welcomed with the usual courtesy. To Norm's surprise the finance report was printed and handed out, so all could quickly see that Resolutions Inc. had done well in the past twelve months. Revenue was up, expenses down. It was an open and shut report lasting less than five minutes. Then Sydney Branch, the Corporate Director, took the microphone.

"I love coming to Seattle," he began. "Of the seven cities in which we have centers, it is the most beautiful I get to visit, and the traffic is absolutely mystifying. How do you all put up with it? I asked the cab driver this morning to bring me into town the back way. He said there wasn't one, but he'd charge me for it if I wanted him to. The freeway was bumper to bumper all the way. That's hardly free." There was a murmur of laughter. It was a good beginning.

"This morning I told my wife I was either going to talk about money or sex. She asked if I knew enough about either to try. (pause for groans.) I'm here today to share with you my concern over a serious matter in our company. No, it's not our compliance with new regulations or hiring qualifications, and our finances are great, as you have just heard. Are you aware that our recruitment process has been increased three fold this year, and our training series has doubled? We have increased our placement costs because we are bringing in fresh personnel from all over the country. What I'm really in the dark about is the turn-over we have had this past year with our Resolutions counselors. Are you aware that we have lost 47% of our most important frontline people? Out of one hundred and seventy seven men and women, we have had to replace eighty three! Think about this. None of them were retirement age. Only two left to do graduate work. A handful went to competing agencies, even though our compensation package is the best in the industry. Another small group took advantage of their MBA to accept management positions in other companies. But another significant group left with no new position secured at all. Apparently they would rather be anywhere than here! That is a sign of something very wrong. We are bringing in an analyst agency to determine if we have a systemic problem in management. Of course it's expensive to replace that many employees, but the bigger picture is that they are far too valuable as an asset to our company to lose."

"In my mind's eye I see some man or woman getting ready for work in the morning. They are rested, happy, chatting with their family. They are singing or laughing, refreshed and eager to get on the freeway." He raised his eyebrows in mock surprise. "Ten hours later they return home beat up and bruised by a day of work here at Resolutions. They are grumpy, and not fun to be around after that sort of day. They are unhappy, and looking for any other job. They came out of school highly prepared. And suddenly the realities of a conflict Resolutions situation wear them down and out. What is wrong with this picture?"

"As a manager, I know that no other occupation offers as many ways to help others learn and grow, take responsibilities and be recognized for achievement, and contribute to the success of the team, as mine does. Where have I been missing the boat? I believe that the powerful motivator in our lives isn't money, which is awkward because that's how we reward hard work. The motivator is the opportunity to learn, to contribute to others, to make a difference in our business, and in our world. To accomplish that we need more than a brave troop of beat up counselors who are looking for a way out!" He paused for a moment as though choosing carefully the next few words.

"I believe it's up to me to find an antidote for the poison of corrosion that is eating away our ranks. I need to find some way of preserving our frontline people. Harry Truman knew where the buck stops when it comes to making big decisions. To that end I have instructed HR to build a new field to our leave system, to give every counselor one mental health day a month, to be used, or accrued, up to twelve working days per year. No, this is not simply giving you a greater vacation schedule. I want you to use it however you are best served mentally, emotionally. I want you to find a way to replenish the energy used in Resolutions negotiations. Take a hike, dance lessons, go fishing, or to the library, do a service project, learn yoga, I don't care. I want you to have a therapeutic break, to stay mentally bright, so you will love your job." His eyes swept the room to be sure that the first point had been received. "Yes, it is that important!"

"Secondly, I want you to create, or have in place, a mission for your life. Build a strategy to live out that mission, and then set goals to achieve that strategy. A company's strategy determines the types of initiatives that management invests in. If a company's resource allocation process is not managed masterfully, what emerges from it can be very different from what management intended. Because companies' decision-making systems are designed to steer investments to initiatives that offer the most tangible and immediate returns, companies shortchange investments in initiatives that are crucial to their long-range strategies."

Taking a big breath he continued, "Here's where it gets really frustrating to me. One quarter of our lost counselors last year left because of divorce. They didn't keep the mission of their lives front and center as they decided how to allocate their time, talents or energy. Two dozen families split up because somehow they forgot a vital principal, to create and keep a strategy for their life. Something needs to be done."

"To that end, I am willing to invest in you, if you are too. I am willing here and now to grant every employee a one hour early closing on Monday, Wednesday, and Friday, if you will pledge to match the hour on Tuesday, Thursday, and Saturday. Please hear me. This is so crucial we are adding ten percent to our support staff, and an extra counselor in each center. We are not asking you to do all your tasks in less time. I am not offering you an early afternoon happy hour, or shopping trip, or tee time. The purpose of this offering is that you pledge to spend the hour with your family, reading, talking, and discovering ways of clarifying your purpose. If you are single, use that hour a day becoming the sort of person another would be delighted to spend their life with. If you think you can better benefit your life by learning some new technique for mastering the problems of autocorrelation in regression analysis I'm afraid you may be part of next year's casualty report. You may apply the tools of econometrics a few times a year, but I guarantee, you will apply the knowledge of the purpose of your life every day. It is the single most important thing I can urge you to learn. Clarity about your purpose will trump knowledge of activity-based costing, balance scorecards, core competence, disruptive innovation, the four Ps, and the five forces." The folks from the accounting department broke into applause. "The choice and successful pursuit of a profession is but one tool for achieving your purpose. But without a clear purpose, life can become hollow, or drift like a rudderless ship." This was not only their CEO, he was a motivation manager, and cheerleader all in one! The room was under his powerful influence. "Will you contract with me to spend one hour out of every day on your life strategy?"

After a long pause, allowing the impact of his words to sink in, he went on. "There is one more thing I would like to talk about this afternoon. Thank you, by the way, for your courteous attention. I think this can be dry stuff." No one in the room held that notion. "In graduate school there was an important model in one class called the 'Tools of Cooperation', which basically said that being a visionary manager isn't all it's cracked up to be. It's one thing to see into the foggy future with acuity, and chart the course corrections that the company must make. But it is quite another to persuade employees who might not see the changes ahead, to line up and work cooperatively to take the company in that new direction. Knowing what tools to use to elicit the needed cooperation is a difficult skill."

"One style of community building we can call 'power tools,' which uses coercion, threats, punishment and so on. It's the military way, and many companies begin in this quadrant because it is easier, and involves the founding executive team in an assertive role, defining what must be done, how and why. As you might guess, there is another style of community building we can call 'discovery tools,' which depend upon the training, intuition, and skill set of the workers to understand the desired outcome, once defined, and work cooperatively toward it. The first form often produces division in the work force, and competitive conflict as a subsidiary of the task, and the second develops positive growth, and surprising proficiency. If employees' ways of working together to address those tasks ultimately succeed over and over, consensus begins to form. MIT's Edgar Schein has described this process as the mechanism by which culture is built. Basically, people don't even think about whether their way of doing things yields success. They embrace priorities and follow procedures by instinct and assumption rather than by explicit decisions, which means they have created a productive desirable culture."

Norm's mind was replaying the thought: "a power culture produces conflict, and a discovery culture promotes community," That's not exactly what was said, but it made such good sense.

Sydney was concluding his presentation. "We're taught, in finance and economics, that in evaluating alternative investments, we should ignore sunk and fixed costs, called incremental analysis, and instead base decisions on the margin costs and marginal revenues that each alternative entails. We learn that this doctrine biases companies to leverage what they have put in place to succeed in the past, instead of guiding them to create the capabilities they'll need in the future. If we knew the future would be exactly the same as the past that approach would be fine. But if the future is different, and it almost always is, then it's the wrong strategy to use."

"Unconsciously, we often employ the marginal cost doctrine in our personal lives when we choose between right and wrong. For example, a small immediate gain, even from questionable behavior, is weighed much greater than a potential future gain. A voice in our head says, 'Look, I know that as a general rule, most people shouldn't do this.

But this is an extenuating circumstance. Just this once, it's OK for me to do it.' The marginal cost of doing something wrong 'just this once' always seems alluringly low. It suckers us in, and we don't even look at where that path is taking us, nor at the high cost it entails. At base, justification for infidelity and dishonesty, in all their manifestations, lies in the marginal cost economics of 'just this once.'"

"So, again to this end, I have asked all area managers and supervisors to begin immediately a survey system I'll call the 'Discovery Culture.' I'm asking them to give me a quarterly evaluation of every employee's level of enthusiasm for their job." The silence in the room grew deeper. "By that I mean I want to know about their level of cooperation, innovation, and attitude of community. Are there signs of leadership or evidence of discouragement? I know this sounds subjective, and it will be. In the past your productivity has determined your rewards. Now I am adding a system that rewards your positive leadership. It could sound threatening as an invasion of your privacy, or some sort of secret file on everyone. It is not. It is for my eyes only, and I do believe as a powerful positive tool, it will create within Resolutions. a new climate of health and productivity, which is my only endeavor. At the end of the year a bonus gift will appear in your paycheck to affirm my belief in this new plan."

"There they are, my holy trinity: one day a month for mental health; one hour a day for family core purpose; and a new culture of integrity and discovery. I believe in them enough to put resources behind them. I believe this will usher in a bold new attitude for our company and its future. If you would like to comment or expand on my principles, I invite dialogue. Give me a call or send me an email. I promise to answer every one. All this will be printed for all seven centers to examine and digest, and I hope that individual centers will design some sort of discussion process about it."

"Once again, thank you for your valuable time this afternoon. I'll be happy to tell my wife that I didn't need to talk to you about either money or sex." Laughter and applause concluded the most helpful State of the Union report Norm had ever heard. He reviewed the three pages of notes he had taken. He was eager to chat with Kathy about it.

She had suggested that they could get some fresh shelled crab at the Pike Place Market. It would be an enjoyable trek before supper. "How long has it been since you explored the market?" she asked.

"I love the summer produce, and flowers," he answered. "But, I have never ventured down to these levels."

The Pike Place Market was a pioneer effort to make a commercial outlet for local farmers and craftsmen. Opening in 1907 with Klondike gold money, it is one of Seattle's specialty tourist spots. Norm and Kathy had made a turn off the main floor, and found more shops on the lower level. To their surprise there were two more levels yet to be seen. A shop featuring wind-chimes and bells was of particular interest to him. In a tiny space, shelves were filled with hundreds and hundreds of unique brass items.

"Hey," Kathy exclaimed, "my Grandmother had a bell like this." She shook the handle of a small carved brass bell that immediately sang a clear note. Several other customers in the cramped shop turned to look, and smile. "She used it to call us in from play, and to announce that dinner was ready." Kathy was beaming with the happy recollection.

"Why don't you get it?" Norm asked, also with a contented look.

"Well," she began in a way that always made him smile more, and know that her answer would be politely negative. "At least I know where I can buy one if I ever need it." They heard a mellow hum that grew in intensity. It was bell-like, but the note lingered in the tiny shop.

"What do you suppose . . . ?" Norm turned toward the source of the ringing.

The shopkeeper heard his partial question, and answered, "It's a meditation bowl used by the monks as they go out begging. They stand in the roadway either ringing it like a bell, or stroking the outer rim, and it gives a sustained sound." The note that they had heard first was still growing in volume.

The two people who were in the aisle looking at the bowls seemed oblivious to the addition of two more shoppers. But looking over their shoulder Norm noticed that they held a short wooden rod, one end of which was covered with leather. By rubbing the outside of the bowl with the leather end, the sound continued to increase. "Wow!"

Kathy reached around them to hold a small bowl. The intricate carving on the side was definitely eastern. When she flicked the side with her fingernail, a crisp bell sound emerged, and lingered pleasantly. The other couple in the aisle turned as though only now aware of their presence.

"Aren't these cool?" the husband asked. He moved a bit so Norm and Kathy could get a bit closer to the display.

"I've never seen anything quite like them." Kathy answered. "They are not exactly a bell, and yet they seem more."

Norm was reaching for the large one on the lower shelf. "Let's see how this guy sounds." He used the wooden tool as a drumstick and heard an even more mellow sound that resonated long after he had hit it. "Wow!" The outside of the bowl had an elaborate design of over-lapping lotus blossoms. The inside of the bowl depicted a praying Buddha. The shop-keeper edged in between them, aware of a possible sale.

"Let me demonstrate that one. It is really cool." He held the bowl in the hollow of his hand, and stroked the outside with the leather end. A deep resonance began. The more he stroked the rim, the louder, more prominent the sound became. It was the combination of a chime and a musical instrument. "Wow!"

"I believe," the shopkeeper continued, "these are also used in their meditation activities in worship. Its sound helps them to go deep within their prayer experience." He continued to stroke, and the bowl continued to sing its mellow harmonics.

Kathy leaned over and whispered, "Why don't you get it?"

"Well," Norm grinned, "at least I will know where I can . . ." She jabbed his ribs with her elbow.

"You're such a kidder. Come on; I'm serious. I can see that you would like to have that bowl. It might not be here when you come back later." Again she gave him a little nudge with her elbow. "I'll tell you what. If you say 'yes', I'll get it for an early birthday present for you." Once again she nudged him, but this time more tenderly. "Just say 'yes'!"

All the way home she held the bowl in her lap, occasionally making it sing softly. It really was a unique find.

Their dinner was over, the table cleared to the dishwasher. Now Norm, once again, sat across the table from that sweet familiar face. He had carefully chosen a bottle of old vine Zinfandel to sip. They sat quietly for a bit watching the shower clouds drift over the city. The meditation bowl was proudly displayed at the center of the table.

Kathy had listened to his excited recount of the report from the director of Resolutions. She was glad for the announcement of some gratis time off his work week, and the hint of an annual bonus. But she was struggling to follow his thoughts about how this connected with their conversation about fears. "I can tell you are pretty enthused about the meeting with Mr. Branch, but I'm having some trouble seeing the connection with more than Resolutions." She was aware of facing him so he could see her honest confusion.

"I know I have had all week to think about this, and it just seems to be getting bigger. If we can change the inner climate, or as he called it, 'the culture,' of our corporation, how much easier would it be to change the inner attitude of a person?" Norm took a sip of wine before he continued. "If this is the formula to modify the company, I believe it will work even better on a person." He had an expression of discovery. "It all seems to fit together for me: positive mental attitude, core values, and a culture of discovery. That is such a winning formula! If we can, and as we do, immerse ourselves into these principles, our perception and appreciation of the world around us will change. It changes anything." Giving it a tiny bit more consideration, he thumped the meditation bowl, which gave a sweet ring. Then he added, "No, it changes everything!"

She had not seen this animated cerebral side of the complicated man she admired. "But weren't those business principles? I don't think he was talking about more than that."

Norm was enthused enough he could have spoken loudly. Instead, he took a breath and said in an almost hushed voice, "They are not business principles, but life principles applied to business. I think these will work in any situation, if they are applied."

"Do you really think he meant for the report to be seen as this big?" Kathy was still wrestling with the scope of the report. "I don't think he intended to reach beyond Resolutions."

"I know you are right. He only meant it for us. I can though, make an analogy to show you how it does affect us. When some first grade teacher helped you learn the A-B-C's, she didn't know where it would take you. She just wanted you to have the basic skill and principles to read and write. She just wanted to be a good first grade teacher." Smiling a crooked grin he added, "She didn't know about, 'How do I love thee? Let me count the ways.' But tucked in the basics were the incredible possibilities that led to poetry, novels, and great works of the masters." His smile seemed to grow with his excitement. "Mr. Branch's report didn't intend to affect anything beyond the improvement of our company. But I'm convinced it certainly will."

"I've been thinking about our conversation about fears that keep us from happiness or redefine our world. It's amazing that the word 'fear' appears several hundred times in scripture, with synonyms like 'reverence', 'awe', 'dismay', 'dread', 'trouble', 'terror.' Three hundred and sixty six times the term, 'Be not afraid,' is spoken to God's people." Norm smiled as he said, "That's one for every day of the year, and an extra for leap year. We are wired to 'love the Lord with all our heart, and mind, and soul, and strength.' But at the same time we never are separate from the awareness that absolute love means total surrender, and the 'fear of the Lord.' which is the beginning of wisdom, according to Job."

Kathy shook her head in confusion. "I really don't follow that heavy thought."

Norm was still pressing a point that seemed pretty clear to him. "I thought of a picture of a truly fearless couple." He looked steadily at her until she asked, with arched eyebrows, "Who?"

"In the Genesis story of the garden of Eden, Adam and Eve were completely fearless. They didn't need to work or worry; life seemed ideal." Letting his smile twist into a bit of a naughty one, he added, "They didn't even worry about clothes. There was nothing to disturb the tranquility of their life," he paused to make his point, "until their disobedience about eating the forbidden fruit. Then guilt and shame and fear took over and their idyllic world ended, and they needed to hide. In the Church we have the Doctrine of Original Sin which explains our natural propensity to sin. I just think it is wonderful to remember that in the initial design, we are wired to be fearless."

"But . . ." she started to say something about always wanting the comfort of clothes. Instead she thought it wiser to say, "You are a theologian, and can think those lofty thoughts."

Norm nodded in a casual agreement. "I do have the advantage of four years of graduate school to fill my head with books, and tools for the task. All of us, however, want to study, to know more about God. We want to have a stronger faith, a more stable understanding. That's all theology is. It has always amazed me that only about one fourth of our population attends a church, but about ninety percent believe in some sort of higher Being or power, and we want to be more connected." The lights of the city were twinkling in the growing dusk, playing happy games with the shadows of evening.

Shifting in his chair, Norm said, "This is a trying topic. I'm thinking, as a good host, I should change the subject, maybe put on some music, or talk about the kids. Would that be good?"

"Whatever you'd like," she answered in that lilting way. "But remember, in our house we say, 'If it's not country, it's not music.'" She made a fake grimace of apology, knowing that his preference was classical, or jazz. "But seriously, I want to hear more of your thoughts about what we have been going over. I still feel a little lost. I don't follow how the annual report relates to Adam and Eve. How does it fit together?" She still had that relaxed smile that assured him this conversation was just that, a happy conversation.

He refilled their glasses, and pondered where to begin. "There is only one kind of fear, even though we have bazillion different shapes for it. Have you ever wondered why not all of us are afraid of spiders?" He knew her phobia of spiders was nearly pathologic. "Or why some of us are afraid of large crowds and others are not?" She didn't know about his loathing of crowds. "Why are some people afraid to speak in front of a large crowd and others of us cherish that privilege? The only kind of fear is the one we create!"

"I think I remember from my first psych class that only the fear of falling is instinctive to us, no others. If a baby is dropped onto the bed, they will instinctively extend their arms. But we have to learn what is hot, or painful, or dangerous to us as we grow up." He thought for just a moment before adding, "I suppose we all seem to experience separation anxiety the first time we are placed in a nursery or preschool. I'd say that is pretty universal."

"So, part of our fear is learned from a global or external world. We were raised in a threatening age of war and uncertainty, where nuclear attack was possible and 'duck and cover' under our desks was the response. Since 9/11 we are afraid of mindless terrorist attacks. Many would echo A.E. Housman's words, 'I, a stranger and afraid, in a world I never made.' There are more sources of external fear than we can list."

"Like layers of an onion, there are deeper sources for our fears, those that are internal. Because we each had personal experiences that created fear in our lives, we are our own worst enemy. Fear is a self-created adversary. Over one half of marriages today end in divorce. Three quarters of those families have one or more children, who somehow feel responsible for their parent's inability to stay together, which creates a host of fearful entities. We manage to take a terrible situation and compound it sometimes to an unmanageable state. This is a technologic age, but we still have horrible crippling diseases, and occasionally death that cause even more fear within us. Those are just some of the internal causes for our fears."

"Then there are those which are much more private and terribly destructive. Child abuse, neglect, bullying, and abandonment, all play havoc with our thoughts, memories and imagination, and all of which create the condition we call 'fear'. We will wage a losing battle with alarm over the world's problems, and our immediate circumstances, until our inner fears are somehow overcome. Fear is not primarily caused by the world around us, but is generated and perpetuated from within us. This is the realm of our most private self, known only to us and to God. It is where the taproot of all our fear really exists. It is where our fears will be healed. My excitement over the power of positive change tucked into Mr. Branch's three points is right here! He has shown us a roadmap that leads to new mental health and freedom from crippling fears."

He was aware of how one-sided this conversation had become, yet he didn't know how to help Kathy share more without asking some probing questions. "Does that make any sense to you? Or is it just an irritating buzzing to you?"

She answered more brightly than he expected. "No, I don't feel like it's a buzz. Why would you say that? I can see how engaged you are with this, and feel as though I can catch up with it. I still really, really like you!"

He pressed the question a bit more, "Can you see how these principles might change how you feel about some of those feelings about insignificance at work, or painful memories from your childhood? Were there times you felt afraid or hurt?"

"I was a very sheltered little girl," she replied. "My folks both worked, but mom was home early every afternoon. I only have happy memories about that. My three younger sisters accepted my care when mom wasn't home, and we lived in only a couple different homes during my childhood. I'd call that pretty safe. My dad worked for Puget Power, and treated me like a little lady. I remember once for my birthday he took me out for lunch. I think I was ten. When he told the waitress that 'the lady will have a milkshake with her hamburger and fries,' I felt just wonderful. That was one of the reflections I shared at his memorial service." She thought for a moment about the phrase, 'separation anxiety' that Norm had just used. A plaintive chord was sounded within her.

"There were times in the winter, however, when the storms knocked down a lot of trees over the wires, that he would be gone for days." Her expression became less cheerful. "I can remember thinking that he might never come back. That was horrible. After the Columbus Day storm he was gone nearly two weeks, which seemed like an eternity." As she recalled those memories and spoke about them, tears formed in her eyes and her chin quivered slightly. She was surprised by the wave of emotions they elicited.

"All of us carry those tender vulnerable memories." He reached his hand across the table to touch hers gently. "I think you just uncovered a shadow of the fear-root."

"Have you got time for a preview of next Sunday's sermon at St. Andrew?" He knew it might take more than a couple of minutes to explain his plans.

"Yes, of course I do. I'm always glad to have a better understanding of the message, and the kids are spending the night with mom." She wiped the stray tear.

"Well, next Sunday is the third Sunday of Lent, so the Scripture lesson is Luke 12:15-21. It contains a breathtaking announcement: 'Fear not little flock, for it is your Father's good pleasure to give you the kingdom.' The sermon is titled 'A Crash Course in Courage.'"

Kathy nodded with understanding and anticipation.

"I'll start by telling the congregation of the reader-board sign I saw outside a church. It said, 'don't let worry kill you off—let the church help.' It is pretty corny, but a way to remind the folks that scripture is a firm assurance that the Lord's presence is a faithfulness, a goodness, a loving kindness, or an intervening power in times of need. The 'Fear not' verses are particularly helpful in taking our first step to living without fear. They were spoken to people who felt abandoned in adversity, and needed both the assurance and the experience of the Lord's presence and loving care."

"For example, the first two of these 'Fear not' verses are spoken by Isaiah to the Babylonian exiles (41:10, 13). Into their discouraged sense of abandonment, the Lord says, 'Fear not, for I am with you, yes I will help you, I will uphold you with my righteous right hand.' The Hebrew word for 'fear' can also be translated 'dread.' A paraphrase then may sound like, 'Don't dread life because of your circumstances.' God is saying 'don't be afraid of your unfamiliar surroundings here in exile away from the securities of Jerusalem and the temple. I am your God, and I am with you in spite of everything.' I'll try to explain to the congregation what it is like to be face-to-face with God."

Kathy looked at him with a squint of confusion. "What do you mean 'face-to-face'?"

Norm reached across the table with his right hand. She accepted it, naturally, in her right hand, which brought them face to face. "When our fears so dominate our thinking that we shy away from trusting even God, He invades our self-imposed solitary confinement and reveals himself as our friend. 'For I, the Lord your God, will hold your right hand, saying to you, 'Fear not, I will help you.'" Looking into her green eyes he said softly, 'face-to-face'. He added a thought about next Sunday, "I wish I could get the congregation to take hold of someone's hand for that part of the sermon. It is pretty powerful isn't it?"

"Yes, it really is," she said, not releasing his hand.

"The third 'Fear not' I want to consider with the church was spoken by Jesus to the disciples when they were caught in a turbulent storm on the Sea of Galilee (John 6:15-21). They were terrified."

"A few hours before, they had witnessed the miracle of feeding five thousand, with just a couple fish and loaves of bread. Jesus had gone to pray, while they set off across the sea for Capernaum. When that sudden storm engulfed them the thought had to be in their minds; 'If the Master could do that with the loaves and fishes, he could save us now!' Or something like that."

"Then Jesus came to them. Through the howling wind he spoke words that filled them with wonder and worship, awe and fear. As I read it he spoke not so much a clap of thunder, but a sigh of relief, 'It is I; do not be afraid.' And when he got into the disciple's boat, they immediately made it to shore. The men never forgot those words. Nor can we."

"The English translation of Jesus' liberating words doesn't quite do justice to the true meaning in the Greek text. I think this was one of Jesus' twenty two 'I am' assertions. What Jesus said could more accurately be understood as, 'I am; have no fear.' He will not leave us helpless in the restless seas of our life. Sometimes the Lord rides out the storm with us, and at other times he calms the storms inside our deepest inner soul. And when he does, we can begin to face the fears that haunt us and our world."

"Last May, we were on the final day of our charter in the British Virgin Islands. We were headed back toward our home port when a very dark squall line developed right in front of us. The rain was so dense we lost sight of one island after another, until we were engulfed in the downpour. Fortunately, we had a compass course and diesel engines to push us through the tempest. Several anxious minutes passed before we found the harbor entrance. When our lines were finally securely attached to the dock, even though the rain was still pounding down and the wind was whipping about us, the whole crew breathed a sigh of relief, thinking, 'I am, have no fear!'"

"The final 'Fear not' verses for us Sunday morning are our text for the morning, Luke 12, 'Fear not little flock, for it is your Father's good pleasure to give you the kingdom.' Think about that for a moment. 'It is your Father's good pleasure to give you the kingdom.' I believe a full understanding of that to be the kingdom of hope-lifting, life-changing, faith-building fearlessness! And it's a gift for goodness sake! That's really hard to believe isn't it? All this talk about fearlessness sounds too good to be true, and yet, it is Jesus himself who proclaims it. Isn't there something within us that says, 'This can't really be for me! There has to be a catch in it.' This verse brings us into the presence of a God of Grace, whose good pleasure is to give us such an amazing gift."

"Some time ago a Time magazine article reported an extreme winter storm in Wyoming. Roads were closed; the drifts grew deeper and deeper. Rivers froze. People suffered. The mercury dropped to a record breaking low. The Red Cross used National Guard helicopters to fly in supplies. One crew had been working long hours for several days, pausing only to refuel and load fresh supplies. They were several miles from their base when they spotted a tiny cabin submerged in the snow in a narrow canyon. A thin whisper of smoke from the chimney told them that someone down there was still alive. The rescue team figured they were probably out of food, fuel, maybe medicine. Because of the steep terrain they had to put the helicopter down about a mile away. They put on heavy packs of emergency supplies and set off, trudging through the waist-deep snow. When they finally reached the cabin, they were exhausted, panting, perspiring. They pounded on the door, and after several moments a tiny gaunt woman opened the door. The lead man gasped, 'We're from the Red Cross.' She was silent for a moment, a scowl on her face, finally she said, 'Hit's been an awful hard winter. I jest don't think I can give anything this year.'"

"These 'Fear not' verses are a knock on the door. We open the door and miss the reality of the situation. We are lonely, he says, 'I am with you.' We are weak or weary, he says, 'I will hold you in my righteous right hand.' We are in the grip of a terrible storm, he says, 'I am; be not afraid.' We see the resources we thought would bring us happiness and security dwindling away, and he says, 'Fear not little flock, for it is the Father's good pleasure to give you the kingdom.' We can open the door to a liberating, empowering presence that leads us into a new future."

"Jesus said, 'Behold, I stand at the door and knock; and if anyone hears my voice and opens the door, I will come to him and eat with him and he with me.'"

Norm took a long sip to finish his glass. For just a minute the room was still as they both looked at a sparkling Seattle night skyline.

Kathy interrupted the silence by saying, "Whew! I love getting the sermon first hand! This is a lot more inspiring than when I have to share you with the congregation." Her grin was an appropriate benediction.

A week later, Kathy was with Norm again. They were joined by Bruce and Annie, Norm's son and daughter-in-law, at Maggie's at the Bluff, a fun grill at the Elliot Bay Marina. As soon as they were seated, Annie said, with sparkling eyes, "Goodness, this brings back fun memories! We were right here the day Bruce proposed." Looking at Norm, she asked, "Didn't we have Shipwreck Sundaes?"

Kathy giggled, "Did he propose here in the pub?" She could imagine a romantic moment here, but only after a lot of more romantic places.

Annie joined in her mirth, "Oh no. He proposed on *Dreamer*, the sailboat. We just came here to celebrate as soon as we got to the dock." She had liked Kathy extraordinarily since they met in Victoria. She would have said more about their trip two years ago, but Bruce cut her short with a question.

"Hey Dad, I'm glad to be here too. Tell us the reason for the invitation. Have you two got an announcement to make?" A playful smile accentuated his raised eyebrows. He was glad for the close relationship that had grown between Kathy and his dad. And he was hoping.

Norm leaned over the table in a confiding way. "In fact, I do." Kathy sort of choked on her sip of coke. "A couple weeks ago, we had our annual report. Mr. Branch, our CEO, inspired me with a new principle direction we are going to take at Resolutions. It's too big to tell you all about it here, but in short, I think he has shown me a pattern of modifying our basic attitude about fear and faith. I've been thinking some special time aboard *Dreamer* is in order to work on that. I'd like to finish the plans we interrupted two years ago, and go up to Desolation Sound. I could do it alone, but think you guys would do at least some of the work, if I brought you along." The other three all started talking at the same time.

"When are you planning to go?" "How much vacation time shall I ask for?" Kathy asked, "Am I invited too?"

Finally Norm restored order by telling them, "I've learned that the best plans are the ones we make together. So I don't have any details. I thought I would just find out if you are interested, and, yes Sweetie, I would love it if you would join us." Again there was a flurry of simultaneous talking.

"Wait a second." He was nearly laughing. "I'll take that as a positive response. Here's the only plan I have so far; I'll move *Dreamer* up to Campbell River, where you guys can drive up and meet me. I think you can drive it in about six hours, depending on how careful you are with the ferry schedule. It will take me about three days to get the boat there. Then we can hop from place to place for about a week before heading home. If we go in June the salmon fishing will be at its peak, and if we go in July, the weather might be warmer." Norm noticed that Kathy had become very quiet. "Are you alright with this?" he asked her.

She cast a quick glance at Annie, then Bruce, before answering. "The trip sounds wonderful. I'm wondering what your family would think, however, if I came on vacation with you." Her meek smile told them all that she was struggling with a moral dilemma. "Well, I mean, to be real blunt about it, where would I sleep?" The other three burst into laughter.

Annie was the first to explain. "I know just how you feel. When these guys asked me to come along for the first trip, I worried about the same thing. I even offered to sleep in the salon, or in the cockpit." She wrapped Kathy in a hug. "*Dreamer* has three staterooms. Bruce and I will share one, this time. There's one for you. Norm, who we can call 'the Skipper,' has the aft one. There is a potty off the salon that we would share, and he has another little one in his stateroom. It will not be completely private, but it is proper enough." She cupped Kathy's head between her hands before she let go. "The fact that you raise that question first means a lot to me." There was another quick hug.

Bruce asked, "Will we be at a resort or marina each night, like before?"

Norm shook his head. "There are nice facilities at Campbell River, and, as I recall Hariot Bay is nice too. Gorge Harbor is a toss-up, depending on current ownership. It seems to change hands a lot. Refuge Cove has a store of sorts, and a potty and showers; but for at least three of the nights, I think we'll be on the anchor."

Kathy asked, "Is that safe?"

"If we stay in areas designated for anchorage there will be good holding, and protection from the wind. That's all we need for safety," Norm said reassuringly. "*Dreamer* will be snug as can be."

They finally ordered their food, but the highlight of the evening was the growing excitement for another journey aboard *Dreamer*. Norm said that he would add a small radar unit for their safety, and put the inflatable dinghy on some brackets to keep it out of the way. Consensus was reached that July would be the preferred time for the trip. Scott and Jenny would be out of school, and could stay with her mom. Perhaps by then, Kathy would get a grip on the anxiety of such a huge adventure.

Bruce said, just as they were getting ready to leave, "Dad, do you have an idea of what we will be doing, along the way? We are still talking about the stuff we learned on our first trip."

"Bud, we still have a lot of details to work out, but I'm thinking we can have an opportunity to concentrate on creating what the boss called a 'culture of discovery.' It has to do with meditation refocusing our inner geography. We can talk more about that when we get started."

"Well then," Bruce continued, "I have oodles of vacation. I'd be glad to take *Dreamer* up with you. Would you mind?"

"Let's think about that for a while, Bud. I would, of course, want, and welcome your help. We could even do it non-stop. But, since they will be crossing the border into Canada, and catching a B.C. ferry, I think you would be more help to the girls than to me." There were a lot of issues to consider.

"Hold on a second!" Annie's voice was playful, but a serious expression pursed her lips. "Are you suggesting that two competent, well-educated, and independent women need help in driving a few miles into Canada?" Nothing more actually needed to be said on the subject. Bruce would accompany the Skipper north to Campbell River, where the girls would rendezvous, thank you.

There were three more planning dinners, all at Kathy's house, and numerous emails and phone conversations working out the plans. At 9 o'clock p.m. on July 7th, the crew made their way down the C dock at the Elliot Bay Marina, where *Dreamer* was moored. The girls wanted to provide a cheery, if difficult send-off. All the preparations had been carefully made. It was nearing high slack tide, and time to go. None of them were aware of how significant this voyage of discovery would be. There were tender hugs, flavored with the excitement of the unknown. They just knew it was time to cast off!

For those who enjoy sailing open water, twilight is an exhilarating time. The near topography loses its sharp focus as shadows grow deeper. Finally, only the silhouette of distant mountains remains visible, deep purple against a fading orange. Stars become bright chips of light in the gathering darkness. For those less comfortable with the open water, twilight is really scary. The sailor loses all landmarks and the sea becomes an invisible plane. It's easy to feel off balance and disoriented. At latitude 48 N, at this time of year, there are only five hours of darkness before dawn; but it is a deep darkness on open water.

"Dad, are you sure about this?" Bruce asked. They had enjoyed a gorgeous sunset for the first hour of their journey. But then it got dark. He had been quiet for almost an hour after they rounded Point No Point. On the diesel they were making about eleven knots, with the help of the tide, now at full ebb. "I can't see a thing in front of us, can you?"

"I'm real sure, Bud. We have the radar monitor; on the nav station we have a GPS, and charts. My goodness if we had anything more, this old girl could do it herself." He reached across the cockpit and gave Bruce a tender shove on the shoulder. "It is darker than a skaditch out here isn't it?" After a moment, he said, "It just takes getting used to looking at our navigation aids. You know there is nowhere in the world as carefully marked as Puget Sound?" Pointing a few degrees off the starboard bow, he said, "That flashing light is Bush Point. It flashes every 10 seconds. And back there," he turned to point off their starboard quarter, "is Double Bluff. It flashes every 5 seconds, so we can tell the difference." Pointing to the radar monitor mounted beside the companionway, he added, "And see that line coming down from the top of the screen?" Bruce noticed it for the first time. "That's a channel marker sending us a radar signal. We'll pass it off our port side by a half mile or so. The radar is on a six mile range right now. You can sort of see the outline of the shore most of the time. We can't get lost and we won't get too close. We'll just read our way through the night. O.K.?" Once again he reached over to ruffle his son.

"Yeah, that sounds good, but what if there is another boat out here in the dark?" Bruce had not completely accepted the idea.

"Bud, this new radar is cool! We will see the big ones at twenty miles; but within a half mile, we can even pick up a kayak. The rules of the road make sure that northbound traffic stays to the right side of the strait, inbound traffic stays on the south side. We can be comfortable, even though we can't see as well as in daylight." He wasn't sure he had explained it well enough, but Bruce nodded his understanding.

"I've been thinking about some sleep for you, Buddy. It's almost midnight, so let's do two four hour watches. I'll take the first one until 4. It will be getting light then. I'll wake you and you can steer for the next four. Jeeps (GPS) has all the waypoints we need already programmed. During the day tomorrow we can do two hour watches. By suppertime we should be in Nanaimo. Does that sound like a plan?" Bruce was already making his way down the companionway heading for his bunk. Over his shoulder he said with a sleepy voice, "I think we called him 'Jeepers' before. I'll see you after my nap." Norm smiled to himself, "Must be an O.K. plan, I guess." He loved night on the open water.

Eight hours later, he returned to the cockpit with a glass of Crystal Light tea, and a pop tart. "Morning Moose," he tried to sound cheery. "How are we doing?"

Bruce had several highlights from his four hour watch to share. But first he needed a potty break. "I'll tell you in just a jiffy," he said squirming a bit. When the Skipper took the wheel Bruce ducked below, saying, "Just in the nick of time!"

When he returned, he had a coke and a pop tart. "This is my idea of a balanced breakfast!" After an enjoyable bite he said, "I had no idea it could be so much fun running with these aids. Jeepers guided me between Cyprus and Blakely, and made the turn around Lawrence Point on Orcas Island. Since then we have been on one course." He motioned his arm in a wide arch. "And this is tremendous!" The expanse of water had opened like a vast inland sea. "Is this still Rosario?"

"No. In Canada it's called the Strait of Georgia. Have you seen ferry boats?" Norm looked around for surface traffic.

"There were a couple crossing into and out of Anacortes. You know, you're right, this is fun!" They both finished their pastries.

"Dad, I've been thinking about our agenda for the trip. The first one was pretty much for Annie and me, and you know how much we still think about that. You seem extra enthused about this one. Can you tell me more of our plan?" Bruce was ready for a serious conversation. The strait was as calm as a lake, with very little traffic. It was an ideal time.

"Brother, how would it be to be able to customize your core values and primary allegiances? How would it be to tailor-make your interior landscape to be a blessing to you and others, and a joy to God?" He waited for an answer.

"Well sure. Anybody would be delighted with that. But you are implying that I'm not able to do that now. Is that what you're saying?" *Dreamer* surged over a bow wave from some distant passing boat.

"You know, what I'm saying is that we are all probably settling for something less than our ideal self. We are making compromises at work. We are getting by with stuff that could be called 'good' but is not our finest. We're working with ingredients for our life that we have inherited, or borrowed from people we want to be like. We work at making changes and wonder why we fail. And we wonder why we feel drained by the effort. It's like all the times we try to lose weight, and don't." Bruce nodded with some understanding.

"When I heard Mr. Branch talk about changing our company, I realized that his model could be interpreted in a different way. A Christian understanding of his formula could actually get us off our own hands, and make change a wholesome and natural thing with us."

"Do you really think it is possible for us to be some kind of perfection?" Bruce had a questioning grin that also implied some hesitance.

"Not perfection, Bud, but process. We can kick-start a process of change that can affect everything, and the key to it is that it is not something we do, but something we allow God to do within us. This sounds almost too good to be true, but we are changing the 'culture,' Mr. Branch called it, of our interior world." The morning sun had burned away any of the marine deck haze. Now, except for a few wispy clouds, it was a bright warm morning.

Bruce asked, "But what if I'm content with my 'interior culture'?" There was no disrespect implied or interpreted.

"Terrific, Bubba! That means you are delighted with the missions of your church, and your involvement in it; you're excited about worship and look forward to each opportunity; you're in a supportive fellowship of growing believers. It means your marriage and business relationships are founded on a solid spiritual foundation."

"Hey! Hold on," Bruce said with a huge grin. "I said I was content; then you describe a super Christian."

"No, I think I described someone who has a positive and loving relationship with God, and who is in a growth mode to become even more involved in a culture of discovery."

Bruce was still bright, and glad to be in this conversation, but he was feeling more than a little defensive. "I just think a person can be content with less than that. It's like I love to play catch with you, but I don't need to try out for the Mariner's baseball team."

The Skipper wanted to keep this non-confrontational, so he agreed, "Yeah, me too. But one is a game and the other is a lifestyle, a core foundation." Thinking of another way to express it he asked, "Do you remember the Marlee Matlin movie entitled 'Children of a Lesser God'?" When Bruce shook his head, Norm continued, "I always thought that was a provocative title. Recently I read about a fellow in California who described our current generation as 'Children of a Looser God.' He contends that those words describe any of us who want to pare down to our size, the majesty, and righteousness of God. His holiness and justice unsettle our easy ethics, and challenge our fluctuating values. At times we all want a lesser, or looser god. We might even create our own. And as a result we lose our sense of awe and wonder in our relationship with the Lord God; we forget about adoration, praise and especially obedience."

Bruce had a question to ask about that, but first he wondered, "Dad, are we going to put the sails up this morning?" The sun was defining this as a perfect early summer morning.

"You know," his dad began in an amusing slow drawl, "we could do that, but the tide is coming in at about two knots and the wind is also following us at about five, so the best we could make is only about three knots, and then we would be late for supper." Looking around, there were very few boats in sight. "I think we'll just stay on the diesel, and make good time." Bruce said he needed another potty break, a glass of tea, and "Did you call it pirate pastry?"

When he returned to the cockpit, still munching the Pop Tart, he was ready to resume the conversation, which was a relief to his dad. "Honestly," Norm began, "I've been thinking I'm a little off the mark on this one. I seem to be the only one who sees the significance of this model."

Bruce nodded in understanding and agreement. "You know, Dad," he was brave enough this morning to speak the truth. "I love being on *Dreamer*. I've always felt like Desolation Sound is the adult table after all the years of eating at the kid's table. You have spoken of it almost reverently. So, I am jazzed just to be here. But I'll admit that so far I haven't caught what you see in the business report from your boss." He quickly took the last sip of tea from his glass hoping his dad would not be angry with his selfishness.

Norm's smile only widened. "Brother, can you imagine living in a black and white world? We could still see shapes and depth and distant objects, but totally without color. We could get around, but how drab!" His arm swept toward the glory of the morning around them, sunshine sparkling off the water, severe blue sky, and distant blue and purple mountains still wearing a mantle of winter snow. Can you imagine what we would lose if this was in black and white?"

"It would be both creepy and sad," Bruce said shaking his head.

"Children of a looser god have a black and white, or shades of gray faith. Do you know what 'idolatry' means?"

"Well yeah, it's like the Golden Calf story from the Bible." Bruce was really glad to have such a quick answer.

"You are right on!" Looking around to check traffic, Norm continued, "But it is also a lot more than that old story. The first commandment is, 'You shall have no other gods before me.' Think about it." Bruce smiled at hearing his dad use that familiar phrase again. "Idolatry is giving to any object, person, purpose, or plan the ultimate allegiance and control that really belongs to God."

"Unfortunately, we tend to elevate the things and people we fear, to the status of the graven image, a false god. When we fear certain people, and need their approval too much, we seek to please and placate them as though they were the source of our worth. They become little gods in our lives." Bruce would have asked a question, but Norm continued, answering it for him, "The same can be true for our families, careers, money, pleasure, accomplishments of the past, or dreams of the future. We become children of a loose god when we kneel at any of them, and give them power over our lives."

"Hey wait, Dad. I've got a question, but first, is that a B.C. ferry?" He pointed off the starboard bow.

"I believe it is," the Skipper answered. "I think it is the Tsawwassen ferry. We are making really good time." Even at a distance the ship looked more graceful and weather tight than the familiar Washington State ferries.

Bruce admired his dad for a moment, and thought he had never seen him as relaxed and healthy as he seemed today. "Dad, I'm a little confused. First you say that God tells us to fear not, and then you say that what we fear is what we worship. Did I get that right?' He had a puzzled expression that was a bit comical.

"Right, as usual. In the Bible there is a definite distinction between dread and reverence. The problem is that often the same word is used for both. The most common Hebrew word for 'fear' is 'yārē', which signifies godly reverence, a lifestyle of obedience, or just plain human terror. The same word is used, so we need to be sharp enough to get its meaning from the context to see which sort of fear we are encountering."

"When I got to seminary, the first important word I learned was, 'mysterioom.' He made a mock scholarly face to over-emphasize the word. "I was told that everything, scripture, worship, Church history and Church architecture contained mystery. It was larger and more significant than

45

plain or usual stuff. Our job, as young scholars, was to find, explore and appreciate the mystery that surrounded us. That's still the way it is with the 'fear of God.' The important thing to discover is the crucial part that reverential awe, or wonder, or mystery, plays in bringing us into a right relationship with our Holy God. It is in this relationship of complete trust and submission that we receive the power to overcome our fears, and find vivid color in our world. Everything flows from that healthy relationship. Without that relationship, we will have to deal with a gray world, where we wage a lonely battle with fear on our own." Looking directly at Bruce, he asked, "You do remember that we said the two bookends to everything are fear and faith?"

"I do," Bruce answered immediately. "Annie and I have had a lot of conversations about that. I think it has deepened our faith a lot." A satisfied smile flickered for a moment. It was fun to talk like this with his dad. "I work with a couple of guys, though, that I don't quite understand. They were both brought up with lots of Church. One of them wants nothing to do with the Church, or the faith. He says it was crammed down his throat. Not even Christmas or Easter gets any attention from him. The other guy is always talking about the stuff he has to confess. He is so aware of the infractions of his life it sounds to me like he only sees God as an extreme judge." He looked at his dad as though a profound answer was going to be given to him.

"I'm always sorry to hear about a parent that missed the chance to teach a child properly. That's why I said a right relationship with God is foundational. I think the emphasis of much of contemporary Christianity is off the mark too. It seems to me that if only God's acceptance is taught, with little or no mention about our accountability to God, we wind up with a feel-good experience with no mystery."

"Have you got time for one more story?"

Bruce snorted with delight. "Well yeah, where do I have to be this morning?"

The Skipper's eyes twinkled with the humor too. "O.K. I have a friend who is a part-time pastor to a dying congregation. They have pioneer roots, but in the last few years they have completely lost sight of the mystery. They are comfortable, with few needs. They are entertained by a few good stories on Sunday morning, and a selection of favorite hymns. Most definitely they are not about to change the way they have worshipped all their lives. If a newcomer should chance upon them, it doesn't take long for the grayness to become apparent. Having forgotten whose Church it really is, and maybe never seeing the mystery, they have a puny God, and are dying. They are like the story of the two boys who were playing on a bicycle—both of them riding at the same time, neither enjoying it very much. Finally, one of them said, 'You know, one of us could have a lot more fun if you would get off.' Think about it, if that little church was on a bicycle with God, who said let me pedal, let me steer, and you just grow and follow me, they wouldn't be dying any more. I think that is the essence of the culture of discover."

Bruce felt that the subject had been covered enough for him to ask a completely different question, but one he was not sure should be asked. For a while he listened to the throb of the diesel. "Dad, could I ask you a personal question?" He looked into direct clear blue eyes.

"Well yes, you should know you can always ask me a personal question."

Bruce chuckled as he said, "Well I . . . Annie and I wonder how you feel about Kathy. You guys seem pretty happy together." He waited for the answer.

"Well brother, that's complicated." He saw Bruce's head turn slightly as he raised his eyebrows in opposition to the avoidance. "No I mean it. I really like her, probably even love her, although I've never used those words. She is a pure delight. I love her laugh, her faith, her sense of humor, her delight in her family, and ours. I love the way she makes me feel when we are quiet. I like the wine she likes. Hey, I think she is tops."

"Then what's complicated about that?" Bruce wanted more information.

"Well, she's ten years younger than me. She is still raising her family. We have completely different lifestyles." He would have continued but Bruce interrupted.

"I'll buy the first two objections, sort of, but what differences do you have in lifestyles? You like her kids, and they think you are wonderful. Her mom likes you. The church thinks she is marvelous. We think she is terrific. What's so complicated about that?" He was delightfully blunt, with an emphasis on delightfully.

There was a lengthy quiet in the cockpit, the throb of the diesel plowing a straight course through the morning, leaving a long graceful wake. Finally taking a deep breath the Skipper answered, "Well, I guess I'm pretty comfortable with things the way they are. She has her life; I have mine, and we enjoy our time together. We really don't need more."

"Sounds to me," Bruce said softly, "a lot like that little church. Hmm."

There was another prolonged quiet. Perhaps the Skipper was choosing his words carefully, or maybe they were just difficult to speak. "O.K., I'm having trouble imagining the two of us as a couple, because I remember how painful it was to know that love was dying between your mother and me. I knew our marriage was over years before it was final. At first I tried to deny it. Then I tried to fix it. Then I just let it go, neither of us really cared. But now, the memory of that divorce is an obstacle to me. I don't want to repeat that in any way. I really don't want to be that vulnerable again." His voice was tense with the emotion that was still underneath it.

Bruce was aware that he was walking a narrow path. He didn't want to pry, nor be his dad's counselor or confessor. Finally he just said, "Those were painful days. I remember being in school and wondering how you both were making it through." He got up from the cockpit bench, and stood beside his dad, giving him a partial embrace. It was the most eloquent support he could think to offer. He was a bit sorry he had asked probing questions in the first place; but he understood they were in a fresh place, a really good place. Now would be an excellent time to change the subject. "Hey, how about those Mariners?" It was the classic shift.

"You've been on the helm for more than your two hours, how about me taking over for a while?" Bruce was glad to have the change, but also glad he and his dad could share the stuff that might not be so comfortable. "Are we still on course 283°?"

About an hour later, his dad came back into the cockpit, carrying plates with sandwiches and chips. Bruce had been aware of a growing hunger for quite a while.

"Did you feel us bump over the line?" the Skipper asked.

Turning around to examine their wake, Bruce fell for the opener. "Was there something in the water?" He halfway expected to see a string of fishing nets trailing after them.

"Naw," the Skipper chuckled, "it was the 49th parallel, the Canadian border. Officially, we are in Canadian waters." They both chuckled at the small humor, but Bruce's attention was switched to the plates.

"Are those deviled ham and cheese?" Once again he was connected with memories of delightful lunches they had shared aboard *Dreamer*.

"Not only that," the Skipper grinned, "we even have Molsons to go along with the celebration." When Bruce turned a questioning glance, he went on, "We're in Canada, eh! We should be drinking Canadian beer." Setting the plates on each side of the helm, he pointed aft off the starboard quarter. "That's Point Roberts, the last part of the U.S."

Bruce motioned to the port side, "and what are these islands. I have never been up here, so they are all new to me."

"Well, let's think about it. These two big ones," the Skipper pointed to the island they were passing, and the adjacent one just to the north of it, "aren't really big. If you could see the chart, they are just long and very narrow. They are the results of the glaciers scouring down from the north, and pretty heavy tidal erosion. They are Galiano, and Valdes Island. And the headland just peeking out above them, where you can just see the ferry sliding out of sight, is Gabriola. Nanaimo is just around that. We're making such good time. We'll be in before supper, I'm pretty sure."

The sandwiches and chips didn't stand a chance, but did satisfy that hollow feeling. As they were finishing their beers, Bruce asked, "Dad, can you tell me about the ringing of the ship's bell to keep time?" It was one of those wonderful questions meant to consume a wedge of time out of a long trip.

"Yeah, I think I can remember. Are you thinking of keeping us on bells?" When Bruce just shrugged, Norm continued. "The twenty-four hours is broken into six watches, each four hours in length. That's pretty simple. The mid watch is from midnight to 4:00 a.m. When I was in the Navy, I hated that one because it is dead dark the whole time. I really like it now. The morning watch is from 4:00 to 0800," he shifted into military terminology. "That one has dawn and sunrise in it. The forenoon is from 0800 to 1200 hours; the afternoon watch is until 1600 hours (that's 4 p.m.)" Bruce grinned his understanding. "The Dog watch is until 20 hundred hours, and in the old days it was divided into two two-hour parts so the crew could have a chance to eat supper. It has sunset and twilight to add interest. The First watch, which I have never understood the name, is from 20 hundred hours to midnight. I would have called it the last watch, but then, there is one after it so . . . ." He shrugged at his weak attempt at humor, again.

"The bells are an announcement of the passage of time. Remember that in the early navy, very few sailors even had a watch, let alone knew how to read one." After a moment he went on, "A half hour into the watch, one bell was sounded; an hour into it two bells were sounded. So, every half hour another bell was added, with a pause after each pair. When the crew heard seven bells, Ding, ding, pause ding, ding, pause, ding, ding, pause, ding," he said in illustration, "they knew that they were either soon to be relieved, or soon to be on duty. At eight bells the new crew was on duty. Six times through the day that series kept their time. Does that make sense?"

"Yeah, but I had no idea it was that complicated. I'm impressed."

The Skipper continued his pleased smile with Bruce's response. "What else did they have to do on long boring passages? Remember, 'Sailing is hours of boredom . . . '"

Bruce joined him in finishing the familiar quote, "'punctuated by moments of panic!'" Both men laughed at the moment.

By eight bells of the afternoon watch they were at the Nanaimo Harbor guest dock, checked through customs, and secure for the night. The first long leg of their adventure was complete. Both men were eager for a hot meal, and a night's sleep. Their prayers were gratitude expressions for a safe journey of 223 miles, with the assistance of two out-going tides and one incoming, through a beautiful location, and fresh understanding of the process they were beginning. Oh, good the night!

The phone startled Kathy at 10:15. "Who would be calling this late?" she wondered, and almost immediately dreaded the possibility of trouble for the guys.

"Hi Kathy, it's Annie. I hope this isn't too late to call."

Actually Kathy was glad to hear her happy voice because it meant she wasn't calling with bad news. "Not at all. I'm all packed and just wondering how I'm going to get to sleep. I haven't been this excited since I was a little girl going to camp." They both giggled because it was a mutual feeling.

"I'm glad to hear that you are ready to go. Are Scott and Jenny already at your mom's?" When she heard the positive response she asked, "Would you like to leave a little earlier than we planned? I know Norm suggested that we drive up Sunday. I think that was to give them a chance to refuel and clean the boat for us. But I'd like to be with them as soon as possible. If we left in the morning, we'd probably be able to help them dock the boat. What do you think?"

Kathy was a total rule follower. If the plan was for them to leave on Sunday they should . . . but wait, she wanted to be with the guys, or at least one of them, sooner too. "When do you think we should leave, 9:00 o'clock?"

"Well," Annie's voice sounded playful, "that would put us at the outlet mall by 10:00 o'clock, and we might be tempted to shop for a while. Could we go a little earlier, like 8 or maybe 7?"

There was a bit of a pause as Kathy wrestled with the desire to be a rule follower and the desire to be on the road to an adventure. Finally the latter won. "I can pick you up by 7:00 o'clock if there is light traffic."

Annie sort of squealed with delight, "It's Saturday; there won't be any traffic to worry about. I've got a basket of nibble stuff so we don't need to worry about breakfast." Her excitement was causing her to speak higher and faster. "Oh thank you. I really hoped you would say 'yes'. I'll see you in the morning."

As Kathy hung up, she pondered at the reluctance she felt. What was holding her back from feeling that joyful burst she had just heard in Annie's voice? Why did she so often choose the low safe boring road rather than an adventure? "Well, this will be anything but boring," she said to herself, not knowing how very true it was.

As Annie put her bag in on top of the boxes of food, she asked, "Can you think of anything else we might need?"

Kathy chuckled, "How about the kitchen sink?" She was actually surprised at the small bag of clothes and stuff that Annie brought. "Do you have a warm coat?"

"Yup, and a spare sweat shirt, maybe to sleep in, and another pair of soft soled shoes," Annie answered.

Kathy said, "I'm glad you gave me so many good hints about what to bring. I think my bag is still twice as big as yours, and I could have stuck more in."

"You'll be surprised at what we will learn to do without," Annie quipped. "In a day or so we won't even worry what our hair looks like, or if we have much makeup on. It is really amazingly fun to be like a boy." They both chuckled until Annie concluded, "Not!" Then they laughed out loud.

Kathy was grateful for her Chrysler minivan, grateful because Norm drove a Chrysler too, and grateful that, almost new, it was easy to welcome folks into her car. They made a plan that she would drive up to Bellingham, then Annie would take it out to the B.C. ferries. They didn't realize that they had just made up the same schedule of two on, two off that the boys were using. Along the way, they talked about their families, jobs, Kathy talked about the kids. Annie said they would love to have a family, but not for a while. There were some goals they wanted to accomplish. Bruce was thinking about going back to school. He really liked his job, Annie shared, but he would like to teach, too.

She reminisced about their first trip on *Dreamer*, how helpful Norm had been with their marriage plans. "I'll bet the two of you have great conversations about the future." She looked carefully at Kathy.

"Not really," she answered. "Oh, we talk about the future of our jobs; or the future of the church. We talk about the kids, but we are just real good friends."

"Oh, I don't believe that!" Annie said in mock alarm. "I've seen the way you guys look at each other, the way he likes to touch you, and listens to you. That's more than good friends."

Kathy said, "He is a very special man, and you are right, I do care for him, more than a friend. But our worlds are miles apart."

"No way! You guys are perfect together! What makes you think anything but good thoughts about that?" Her question was spoken as one sweet friend to another.

"Well, you know, he's a wonderful pastor, even though it's only temporary. At least that's what the church keeps telling him, but they are not interested in finding a permanent one. He has a super big load at Resolutions. I think he does a fantastic job there because he so cares for the people he's trying to help. His kids are grown," she opened her hand in expression, "while mine still have a ways to go." Thinking a bit more she added, "we both have a complicated marital past. I don't think I want him to go there."

Realizing she could help Kathy through this dilemma, Annie asked, "Do you think he doesn't want to go there, or is it you who doesn't want him to go there?" Only the sound of the tires on the highway filled the van for several seconds.

Kathy finally said, "I think if he knew the extent of the whole mess, he wouldn't care for a person like me."

Annie reached over to touch her friend's shoulder. "You still feel pretty bad about that, don't you?"

"Of course," Kathy replied, "I think about what I could have done differently, if there was anything I could have said, or been differently. I think about it a lot." She didn't want to go much farther, afraid of the tears that were getting pretty close to the surface. "It was a mess." She tried to brighten her voice, and sat more erect.

"Girlfriend," Annie declared in a mock street voice, "You should have been with us on the first *Dreamer* trip. I was amazed at how gracious he was to my painful past.

I had been hiding my guilt for so long. He made it very clear that yesterday is just that; it is past tense. We were told that there are no mistakes, only lessons. If we don't learn the lesson the first time, it repeats and repeats, until we do learn it. We were told how to love and forgive ourselves, and then others. I still think about that trip a lot. It was a major experience for me," smiling broadly she finished, "and that was before Bruce proposed." She looked out at the lush green fields of the Skagit Valley. This was such a beautiful time of year. Finally, she turned to Kathy and asked, "You've been alone for a long time, haven't you?"

"Well, if you mean unmarried, yes, for almost ten years. But our house has been a very busy one with two happy kids. I don't feel alone at all."

"Well, have there been any special guys in that time?" Annie just wanted to keep a conversation going.

"You mean, 'Have I dated?'" Kathy said with a weak smile. When Annie nodded, she answered, "There were a couple dates set up by girls in the office. You know, 'a colleague who has just gone through a painful divorce and wants to meet people.' There was one guy I met at the office Mariner baseball game who thought he could claim me for the afternoon. He invited me to the Pyramid Brewery, across the street after the game. That's when I found out that he was still married, but going to end it any day." She gave a shudder. "No I haven't dated."

Annie was curious now. "But you and Norm go out all the time. Bruce is always telling me about another fun restaurant you've found. I'm a little envious of your good times."

Kathy looked over, determining if Annie was just joking, or serious. When she saw that there was no teasing smile, she said, "We dine together regularly, but he is careful not to call it a date. I did for a while, but I think he wants me to understand that it isn't courting. It's purely plutonic. We are just friends.

"Seriously?" Annie asked. "You just said that, and I had trouble seeing how that could be. You are just perfect together." The car was quiet for several moments.

Kathy finally said, "We both like it, just the way it is, uncomplicated." Quickly changing the subject she asked, "Would you like to stop for a Starbucks in Bellingham? I'll bet there is one on our way. Then, if we get through the border as easily as the guys promised, you can drive to the ferry dock." Norm had told them to take the truck route through Sumas to avoid the crossing line at the Peace Arch. It was a bit further to drive, but avoided all the downtown traffic of Vancouver. They would simply be on Canada 1, until Horseshoe Bay, and the ferry would be waiting for them there. It was such an easy plan. Kathy wondered why she had more anxiety talking about her relationship with Norm than with the unknown boating adventure that she was beginning. It was an overcast morning, but one full of discovery.

Dreamer's crew was awake before six a.m. The harbor was still, but the call to complete their journey was insistent. They could have walked to a nearby café for a hot breakfast; instead they opted for a shower, and the opportunity to get underway as soon as possible. The ebbing tide would be against them for a couple hours, but they needed an early start to reach Campbell River.

They loosened the dock lines and slid out under a low marine layer with about a half mile visibility. Once around the harbor marker, Norm said he would take the first watch until 10 o'clock. Bruce thought that was generous, since he could read in his stateroom, or enjoy a morning nap, lulled by the melody of the diesel, and the wash of the bow slicing through the morning chill.

Sometime after the second bell of his watch, Norm wrote in his notebook, "Hour by hour, league by league, we measure our way through the way we tread; minute by minute, yard by yard, we open the prize that lies ahead."

By nine-thirty the girls were through the customs crossing, grateful for the careful details of preparation. There had been no waiting line, as expected. Clear signage directed them to Canada 1 westbound. When they arrived at the ferry dock, they were delighted to learn that the Nanaimo ferry was to sail in just about 15 minutes. They would have no wait at all. "Let's get some of those yummy chocolate Nanaimo Bars to take with us."

Once again Norm brought dishes of food to the helmsman. This time he served ham and cheese sandwiches on rye that they had purchased at the deli last night. "The food is day old," announced Norm, "but the Molson is fresh."

Bruce eagerly accepted the offering, saying, "If I knew the service was this good for the helmsman, I would have been on duty all the way up." Both men giggled at his humor. When the food was consumed and they were finishing their beer, the Skipper took the helm steering 288°. They would pass just to the south of Lasqueti Island, with still about 40 miles to go. "Hour by hour, league by league . . ."

Bruce asked, "I've been wondering about the idea of changing our 'inner culture,' I believe you call it. If it is easy, why don't folks do it any other way? Does it need a major trip, even though it is worth it, to make the change?"

"No, it doesn't take a major trip, or anything else." Grinning broadly, Norm said, "I just needed a good reason to get you all up here." After a moment to enjoy his own joke, he said, "I think it only takes one thing: intention. I think someone must envision the possibility of change and then begin the journey, with intention and determination."

Bruce picked up their dishes and bottles and set them by the companionway for later. "Then what holds people back from making the switch if it's that easy?"

"I'm not sure I said it was easy. That might be your word. I think when someone has established a culture for their life, it might be difficult to change. Habit, comfort, timidity all play their part in keeping us just the way we've always been." He overemphasized the words. "The biggest obstacles I can imagine are procrastination and over anticipation."

Bruce had a squint on his face. "What do you mean by those, we drag our feet or what?"

"The obvious," the Skipper began. "We put off doing something that needs to be done today, or we refuse to deal with a problem that is plaguing us now. Procrastination is a thief of time. Things that need to be done, and could be done in order, begin to pile up on us. They become a heavy burden that we just can't possibly carry. So we end up mentally flogging ourselves, seeing ourselves as unable to do the work, inept in every way. The fallout of procrastination isn't laziness, it's anxiety and stress. This is bad enough when we're talking about cleaning the garage or painting the fence, but when it comes to our most precious relationships, procrastination is serious. If we think we can't handle it, or it is beyond our comfort level, we ask, 'why take the risk?' and put it off. As long as we procrastinate, we keep life in our own hands."

He would have said a bit more except Bruce asked, "Do you think you might be procrastinating with Kathy?"

"Yeah, probably so," Norm said quietly. "I've told myself there is plenty of time for that serious stuff later. That sounds like procrastination to me." He was quiet for a bit more. "You know, I've come to believe that lying to myself may be more deeply engrained and more insidious than lying to others."

"Sure, I tell myself that I'm a better golfer than I really am," Bruce agreed. "But I don't think of that as lying to myself, because I really don't believe me." He was still trying to be humorous and light.

Norm asked him, "But don't you sometimes tell yourself that you're going to get something done, wanting full well to do it, but knowing that you won't?"

"I guess we all do that, don't we?" Bruce didn't feel like getting too personal about this. "I think everyone says that they can get to a certain task, when they know how jammed their calendar already is. I've got work on my desk that should have been done weeks ago, that I just haven't gotten around to. Is that procrastination or overload? Probably both," he answered his own question.

"The other side of the coin," Norm continued, "is that we get so full of anticipation for tomorrow that we get lulled, seduced, away from today. It may seem so inviting, alluring, and challenging that we forget to give this day our best effort, or we think of tomorrow as an escape. You know, if I can just muddle through today, I can get to the good stuff."

Bruce was quick to agree. "I know I agree with that. I keep thinking that the girls will be on their way tomorrow. That's the good time I want to get to." His smile was too wide to misinterpret.

"But for the sake of this discussion," Norm tried to refocus his son, "there is another side of anticipation that is not so pleasant. Rather than seeing something as an inviting escape, or a challenge, we may see it as morbidly dreadful. That's what we call worry, and most of us spend far too much time fretting about stuff that never happens."

The Skipper smiled. "I once had a pastor friend who said he was a 'therapeutic worrier.' If he worried about something it hardly ever happened; he could carefully plan to worry about all the things he wanted to avoid."

Bruce just said, "That's lame."

"Yeah, it is," the Skipper agreed. "But no more lame than folks who choose not to change their inner culture to one of discovery, because they are afraid of what it might bring them, or do to them, or what other people will think. There is nothing redemptive about borrowing tomorrow's problems. Neither is there anything generous about future promises as a substitute for living and giving ourselves to this present day." Little did he know that at that very moment, just nine miles west of *Dreamer*, the girls were hurrying north on Canada 19, toward Campbell River, and a surprise rendezvous.

"Hey Dad," Bruce wondered, "do you know what town that is?" He was pointing off the port beam. "It seems pretty good size. I thought we were going into the wilderness."

"I think it's actually two towns," came the reply. The nearest one on the point is Comox, and at the far end of the bay is Courtenay, which we can hardly see because of the hill. And you better be careful around the Canadians up here, talking about the wilderness. This part of Vancouver Island is known to the locals as the 'Gold Coast;' it's a vacation spa for them. They get tons of sunshine because they are in the rain shadow of the mountains just to the west, which block most of the storms. We've only got about twenty miles to go. And we still have a bit of the flood tide helping us along. We're making great time."

Bruce offered to take the helm for a while, if he could ask one more question. "Annie expects me to have a handle on the stuff we are going to be working on. I'm still a bit behind." He smiled warmly to add, "I appreciate all that we have talked about. I'm kind of getting the picture. My question is what needs to happen to begin the shift of an inner culture?" He had said it very well they both thought.

"Well, think about it, Moose," one of his favorite nicknames for his son. "The thing standing most in our way is our ego. We need to put it to sleep. I sort of think of a hypnotist that says to our ego, 'your eyes are getting heavy. When I count to three you will be sound asleep. One, two, ego is relaxing, eyes closed, three.' It's sound asleep, no longer nagging us. It's probably a poor analogy, but we are responsible for the decisions we make, and at the same time, life is ultimately in God's hands."

"Are you saying it's like me disabling a default switch on my computer?" Bruce asked.

"I like that image better than mine," Norm said with a nod. "It's what Paul meant when he said in the letter to the Romans: 'I appeal to you therefore brothers and sisters, by the mercies of God, present your bodies as a living sacrifice, holy and acceptable to God, which is your spiritual worship. Do not be conformed to this world, but be transformed by the renewing of your minds, so you may discern what is the will of God.'

"If we can't disable that ego default, we think we have the total responsibility and bear the total burden of our living. We think more highly of ourselves than we ought to think. It is hard work. Think about how much time and effort goes into doctoring up our image. We want to look good, say what is right, do what is most acceptable, trying all the time to appear only in a way that will make us admired, and trying to maintain that publicity campaign that says we are more, do more, and have more than the average person. That is purely exhausting!"

"Ego may be open or subtle," he continued. "It may be worldly or Christianized. It may require us to walk over our competitors, or take advantage of our fellow employees. It may mean taking over enough companies to wow the corporate world of business. Or it may mean getting enough new church members and building a bigger budget to impress the bishop; whatever it takes to make the others say, 'wow.'" Norm was surprised at how strongly he felt about this discussion.

After a sweeping look for other traffic and to check the GPS for their actual course and speed Norm concluded, "Ego keeps us forever tense and dissatisfied, forever in anxiety that someone else might appear better, smarter, and richer, more liked, more successful, more admired, more spiritual, more blessed. Ego is a terrible, terrible burden. That is why Jesus promises us in Matthew's Gospel, 'Come unto me, all who labor and are heavy laden, and I will give you rest.' We can be just weary of trying to carry ego's burdens."

"How do we disable that ego default? We acknowledge that only our Sovereign God is worthy of the throne, so we quit pretending and striving; we quit competing with God, and we bow down. We give Him and Him only, the glory. We let God be all and do all within us, and for us. We acknowledge that the One who created us has a full and perfect plan for our lives, and promised abundance if we follow faithfully."

After a lengthy pause to reflect on all that his dad had said, Bruce responded, "Wow! I wish I had that recorded. Do you preach like that to the church? I want Annie to hear that because it makes such good sense. Wow!"

"No, I don't preach like that to the church," the Skipper answered. "I could never call them 'Moose,'" He reached over to ruffle Bruce's uncombed hair. "And as much as I might try, I could never care for them the way I care for you." After a moment, he asked, "So, are you having a good day, Buddy?" He didn't know it but he had just quipped a question that would be repeated dozens of times in the next few days.

The Skipper asked, "Are you O.K. on the helm for a bit? I'd like to go freshen up, and check the Cruising Guide. I'm pretty sure the marina is right in the middle of town, easy to find. If their number is in the guide, I'll give them a call." Pointing to a distant headland off the starboard bow, he added, "I'm pretty sure that is Cape Mudge, the south end of Quadra Island. Just to the right of it is Discovery Passage and Campbell River. How appropriate is that name?"

Forty minutes later Bruce's cell phone rang. Checking the caller ID, he answered, "Hi Love, what's up?" He was delighted to hear Annie's voice.

"I just wanted to check in on you guys and see how you're coming along. Is everything O.K.?"

"Yeah, it's great! We've made real good time. I think I can just about make out the waterfront of Campbell River. Dad and I are still friends. In fact, he has helped me get more excited about our trip plans. I'll be eager to tell you some of our stuff."

"How did it work to have no sleep? Did you guys really go all night long?"

He could hear the concern in her voice, and loved her more for it. "Well, I got some sleep; about four hours before dawn, and the Skipper got some after dawn when I drove. I've had a couple naps that were pretty welcome, too."

Annie was smiling because Bruce had called him the "Skipper." "Did you stop in Nanaimo?"

"Yup. That's where he checked us through customs and we had an easy supper, and early bedtime. This has been a big, but very enjoyable, trip so far."

"I just wanted to check in with you, and tell you I love you." There was a little pause before she said, "And I've been praying for us all. I'll talk to you later. O.K.?" They both hung up smiling, for different reasons.

CHAPTER 2:
CAMPBELL RIVER
The new beginning

I t was easy for the girls to find the marina, because it was beside a huge parking lot. Several vehicles with empty boat trailers were parked at the far side of the lot, by the boat ramp. Campbell River had the typical look of a fishing town. There was ample space for them to park, and get to the fuel dock. The challenge was to patiently hang out with Smitty, the harbor master, until *Dreamer* arrived. During that time they got lots of information about the best restaurant in town, the Lodge. "They have the best chef in town" they were told. The best pub would probably be the Lodge. "They have the only pool table and six TV screens to watch soccer," their unofficial guide added. "The Tackle Box would be good for lunch, if you can't get into the Lodge." Then they discovered that Smitty's sister, Dot, is the bartender at the Lodge.

Kathy and Annie eagerly watched the channel for the first sign of *Dreamer*'s arrival. Finally that tall mast appeared over the docked fishing boats. "It's got to be them," Annie said.

Dreamer entered the Marina in a graceful port turn. The bumpers were over on the starboard side, and Bruce was standing on the foredeck with the bowline. The girls stood still in the shadows of Smitty's office. The harbor master, on the other hand, hopped out to help with the dock lines. *Dreamer* came to a full stop about a foot from the dock. Quickly Bruce handed the bowline to Smitty, and the Skipper stepped off with the stern line. It was a practiced maneuver that seemed effortless.

"Whew, it is good to get here" the Skipper sighed, with a big stretch. "That's a long haul from Nanaimo."

The girls couldn't hold the surprise any longer. They popped out of the office, both giggling their welcome, and hugged their men.

"Hey sailor," Annie said in a playful voice. "Want to take a girl out for some fun?"

Kathy said nervously, "I hope you're not mad at us for being here a day early."

She wanted to be playful, but that old rule-keeping business got the best of her.

"If I'd known I was going to get this nice welcome," the Skipper answered, "I would have shaved this morning." He hugged her to him, then looked over at Bruce, and asked, "Did you know about this?"

"Believe me, I didn't have a clue, and we just talked on the phone an hour ago." He ruffled Annie's hair and said, "So, are you having a good day, Sweetie?" When she nodded, he nearly burst into laughter, and added, "What a fun surprise! Now you can help wash the boat." Laughter filled the dock. The crew was gathered.

They put in 38 gallons of diesel. "Not bad for 31 hours of push," the Skipper said with a satisfied smile. "Now let's get her to a visitor space for a couple of night's rest." They emptied Kathy's van, got everyone situated and then pondered, "Shall we have a Molson here, or go have one with supper?" It wasn't a question of would they have a Molson, just where. "Let's go to the Lodge, I hear they have the best chef in town."

An empty table by the window seemed like the perfect spot, although the noise coming from the adjacent pub was pretty loud. As they were seated, Annie called to the bartender, "Hi Dot!" with a cheery wave. When she received a questioning look in reply, she added, "Smitty sent us; said you were the best." Dot waved back in understanding and appreciation.

The pool table was only a few feet from them, and the site of a heated game of Stars and Stripes. "Damn it, Patrick, we're playing pool here, not slop!" "What do you mean? I hit the shot I called, I just got lucky with the other one." It was a fun Saturday night crowd. Dot took their drink order, and apologized for the noisy game.

"Did you have any trouble coming up?" Norm asked. He was pleasantly surprised at how happy he was to see Kathy. It had only been two days since Seattle. Perhaps being in a whole new setting was making this extra special. He reached for her hand.

"Nope," her happy response was echoed by a squeeze of his hand. "It was just as you said it would be. We had our passports ready, and didn't try to make jokes, or say more than we needed to. Annie wanted to laugh when he asked if we had more than ten thousand dollars cash. I wanted to say 'in my dreams,' but we just said 'nope' and he waved us through. It was freeway right to the ferry."

From the pool table came another outburst of mock anger, "God Almighty, Patrick will you knock that off?"

Dot immediately said, "Brian, this is no time for prayer! Now clean up your mouth or I'll have you go tell Father Daniel that you can't control it."

"Jesus Christ, Dot! He just beat me four times!"

"I told you this is no time for prayer, Brian. We have guests here from the states. They'll think you are just unwashed fishermen." Then, after just a moment she added, "Wait, you are unwashed fishermen. If you swear once more, you're out for the evening. You can bring me a note from your mom to get back on the table. She still knows how to wash your mouth with soap." A warm smile softened her angry threat.

Brian also had a smile, but his words were sincere enough to avoid further problems, "Sorry, eh?"

Annie ordered a hamburger, and Bruce said he would have one too. Kathy ordered fish and chips, and, smiling, Norm said that's what he also would have, and vinegar with the fries. A large discussion followed about the proper condiments for food. The meal was lengthened by Bruce's recap of their conversations aboard *Dreamer*. "I think I have a better grasp of why we are up here," he asserted. "The Skipper is inviting us all to get out of our regular routine to do some interior reworking of our values, and foundational premises." Bruce looked at his dad for confirmation.

"And," Norm said with exaggeration, "we get to enjoy the most beautiful cruising grounds in the world. I want us to have a terrific vacation, with great memories." He had no idea how precise his desires would prove to be.

"God damn, Patrick, you must be cheating me!" they heard from the pool table. Instantly they all noticed Dot move from behind the bar.

As she began gathering the pool balls in a rack, she said sternly, "I told you this is no time, or place for prayer. I warned you, and now you are gone! Goodnight, Potty-mouths!"

Brian turned to defiantly argue, but withered under Dot's grim glance. He knew when he was out-gunned.

"Sorry, eh?" he said to anyone in earshot, slowly heading for the door. "Can I come back tomorrow night?"

"Can you control your mouth?" Dot didn't hear the answer from outside, but she grinned affectionately.

Annie was applauding. "Way to go, Dot!" She clapped a bit more. "You took charge! Does that happen very often?" She was still clapping her hands.

"Oh, just about once a week. He knows better, but is just too stubborn to quit. I have to get his attention, and then he says he's sorry." She smiled. "He's really a good guy." Coming over to their table she asked, "Can I get you anything more?" It was all pretty matter-of-fact.

They took the long way back to *Dreamer*, which meant they walked the block back to the marina, another block to the fishermen's terminal where there were several closed shops, a café that advertised a 4 a.m. fishermen's breakfast, and the Quadra Island ferry terminal, then back to the boat. All the time Norm held Kathy's hand, and she liked it a lot.

Back aboard *Dreamer* they sat in the cockpit while Bruce gave highlights and recaps of the conversations they had shared on the way up. "I learned a lot about idolatry, and procrastination, and ship's bells. I'm really excited about finding the mystery in tomorrow," he concluded.

Annie said, "Wow, Brucie." Kathy said, "That's a lot of conversation." And the Skipper smiled with admiration. He really was a wonderful son.

When it was finally obvious that this day was as full as it could be, Bruce asked his dad for an evening prayer.

"I can recall one from the early church," the Skipper answered. "Before the Book of Common Prayer, there was a collection of prayers called the 'Sacramentary' that was used in the worship service. One of the prayers, based on St Augustine was this." They all bowed their heads in the evening solitude. "'Eternal God, the light of the minds that know you, the life of the souls that love you, the strength of the wills that serve you; help us to know you that we may truly love you, so to love you that we may fully serve you, whom to serve is perfect freedom.'" The Skipper then added his own prayer.

"Lord, for safety in travel, for wonder and joy, for this night's pleasant restful slumber, we give you thanks and praise, in Jesus' name. Amen." There wasn't a ripple on the surface of the marina, all was calm, and right with the world. Oh, good the night!

Kathy was awakened by the plaintive call of a nearby seagull, or was it a small lurch of the boat, or perhaps it was the fragrance of low tide. Perhaps she hadn't been that sound asleep, yet she felt rested. She eased out of her covers, and dressed; ran a quick comb through her hair and opened her stateroom door. Bruce and Annie were seated at the salon table, apparently reading a Bible together. "Morning you two," she said in a husky voice that surprised her. "What time does it get light?"

Bruce chuckled, "Dawn is at four o'clock; I can tell you from personal experience on the way up. Sunup is about

5:30," he looked at his watch, "which is in about forty minutes."

Kathy feigned a whisper. "It's not even five o'clock yet? Is Norm up?" She couldn't remember the last time she had been up before five o'clock a.m.

"He just stepped up to the shower," Bruce said, "and I think he will shave today, probably because he has a friend on board." A smile played on his face. "You know, he doesn't do that for all of us." There was a shared smile of understanding.

That must have been the lurch of the boat she had felt. She was grateful for the potty facilities, and a bit more personal grooming, a better combing and some lipstick. She stepped into the galley and asked, "Where will a girl find a teapot?"

Bruce demonstrated the operation of the propane stove. "There are tea bags in the drawer, and if you prefer coffee, there are some Starbucks Via. If you use one of these bad boys, You need to . . ."

Kathy interrupted his demonstration with a pat on the shoulder. "I know all about them," she chuckled. "And I am really happy to see that we aren't roughin' it." She was looking in the cupboard for a large mug. "Can I fix a cup for anyone else?" It was going to be a great day!

When she had fixed her morning cup, Bruce beckoned for Kathy to join them at the table. "On the way up," he explained, "the Skipper had me read this passage from Philippians 3. He said it would introduce what we were going to be doing this week. We were just reading it again."

Annie offered to read it aloud, rather than cranking necks to see the print. "*Not that I have already obtained this or have already reached the goal; but I press on to make it my own, because Christ Jesus has made me his own. Beloved, I do not consider that I have made it my own; but this one thing I do: forgetting what lies behind and straining forward to what lies ahead, I press on toward the goal for the prize of the heavenly call of God in Christ Jesus. Let those of us then who are mature be of the same mind; if you think differently about anything, this too God will reveal to you. Only let us hold fast to what we have attained."*

After a moment of thought, Bruce told them, "On the way up dad explained that he was excited about the possibility of transforming the way we relate to everything around us. He says that's what Mr. Branch implied as a culture of discovery. It's a process we can do together; it's a way of seeing the mystery in our world." Listening a bit more intently, he added, "I think I can hear him whistling down the dock." They all listened to a familiar hymn tune, cheering the morning.

Kathy asked, "Does he always whistle?"

"Yup," Bruce smiled. "When I was little I thought he did it to warn me that he was coming. Sometimes I think he does it just so we will know where he is." Breaking into a big grin he added, "Then again, it could be that he is just happy in the morning." *Dreamer* rocked slightly as the Skipper stepped aboard.

The companionway hatch slid open and a head with curly gray hair, still damp from the shower, smiled in. "Hey, are all of you up so early?" he asked with obvious delight. His eyes met Kathy's, and she knew he was speaking just to her. "Let me get a glass of tea, and join you." Kathy had gotten up to get another cup from the cupboard. She stopped in front of the refrigerator to get the container of Crystal Light, and pour a glass.

Bruce was trying to explain the scripture they had just read, but knew his dad would do a better job. "Tell me again," he asked the Skipper," what Paul meant by 'perfect.' Isn't that what he says he hasn't quite attained?"

"You know, Bubba, it's awfully early to be getting into this heavy stuff," the Skipper grinned, "and especially since we haven't had any pirate pastry yet." They all chuckled. "But since we're all in attendance," he slid into the table with them, "let's think about it."

"What some translations call 'perfect', or 'complete', or others call 'mature,' Paul explains a couple verses earlier as, 'My object is to know Him, and I mean by that, to know the power of His resurrection, and the fellowship of His sufferings.' Paul isn't talking about gathering information about Jesus, but having the most personal intimate relationship with him. The Hebrew word used is *'yada,'* which in the Old Testament meant intercourse." He took a long sip of tea. "Paul's aim is to find the mystery, the deepest meaning of Jesus. He says the path of that intimate knowing is the power of His Resurrection, and the fellowship of His suffering."

Bruce raised his hand, like a third grader getting the teacher's attention. "Isn't that just the gruesome parts of Jesus' life? What about the miracles and lessons? It seems to me that we know him by those too."

"We do, for sure," the Skipper answered. "Paul understood that the Resurrection, and the fellowship of suffering, enlarged the meanings of those teachings and miracles. Because He lives, we shall live also. His conquest is our conquest, and His victories are ours. It is His promise to be with us always. The Resurrection is the guarantee that nothing in life or death can separate us from Him. To know Christ is not to be skilled in theoretical or theological knowledge, but to experience with Him the fullness, the abundance, of life."

"To attain this culture of discovery in Jesus, using Mr. Branch's terms, we just need to forget what is past, and press on to what lies ahead." The Skipper took a big breath, "I love the terminology Paul uses; he says it's like a runner who is straining, leaning, even reaching out for the goal. I guess that means the believer can't rest on laurels of accomplishment; never relax our efforts, or lower our standards, until we know Jesus completely." The interior of the boat seemed perfectly still. Finally the Skipper said, "You know, if we just sing a hymn, and take an offering, we'll have our sunrise service." They all enjoyed the moment.

"What are we going to do today, Skipper?" Bruce asked as a way of bridging a new moment.

"It feels like a bonus day, doesn't it" the Skipper replied. "I'm thinking folks might like a few minutes to shower, then let's hit the 'Tackle Box' for a fisherman's breakfast. After that we can chat, or maybe drive up Campbell River a ways. There are some great hiking paths along the bank we could explore. We could even take the ferry across to Quadra Island, and visit Hariot Bay, where we will be tomorrow night. I'm open for any suggestions."

There were only two available tables when the crew arrived for breakfast. A quick inventory revealed that Kathy and Annie were the only women in the crowd. It was a fisherman's breakfast. Coffee or tea was served as soon as they sat down. Apparently they were fresh out of Crystal Light. Everything on the menu looked inviting and caloric, and the service was designed to get eager fishermen out quickly.

The table next to them had several men who didn't share that opinion. The service was not speedy enough for them.

They asked for Tabasco sauce, more coffee, needed more creamers, asked for their check twice, and finally became abusive. "Hey lady, how about our God damned check," one finally grumbled, loud enough for the room to hear.

Annie leaned over, being the nearest one to him, and said, "This isn't a time for prayer."

The speaker glared at her and finally said, "Mind your own God damned business. I wasn't talking to you."

Annie was taken aback by his blatant rudeness. But before she could further respond, a familiar voice said from the other side of the complainer's table, "Yeah, it is her business, and all the rest of us who have to put up with your noise." It was Smitty, the harbormaster. "She only said what Dot says all the time." He took a breath to make sure the conversation was going to stay under control. "Hey, aren't you the guys in the tan Bayliner, in line for the hoist?"

"Yeah, so what?" the grouch murmured.

The answer was the one Smitty had hoped for. "I'm the harbormaster, in charge of the hoist. That's my business too, and I think I can get to you guys by noon, maybe 12:30." He paused for effect, "Unless you want to apologize for the cursing."

"Oh for Christ's . . . ."

Before the oath could finish, Smitty was getting up with a shrug, and walking toward the door. "See you at noon, or you can take it to the hoist in Comox." he said over his shoulder.

"No, wait, hey, I'm sorry. It won't happen again. I'm sorry." There seemed true contrition on the part of the man, and an awareness, if he wanted to get out fishing this morning, he had no other choice.

The Skipper leaned over their table, and said in a voice just loud enough for the crew to hear, "Don't you just love Campbell River?"

On the way back to the boat, the Skipper's cell phone began beeping. He looked at it as he was saying, "No business calls, and especially at 7:20 on Sunday morning." But when he identified the caller he answered cheerily, "Hi Kurt." After a slight pause, "Yeah, we are already in Campbell River." Another pause, "He was a great help. We made the run from Seattle to Nanaimo in one jump." "Yeah, we made it yesterday." "Nope, we were on the diesel all the way." "Yeah, about 31 hours." "About $150." Obviously his caller was very interested in the details of their trip. There was a lengthy pause as the Skipper listened. "Really? That would be great!" Another long pause, while the crew pondered the content of the call. "We'll be back here in Campbell River on the 20st." After another short pause, he affirmed, "Yeah, Wednesday." There was one last pause as the Skipper listened. "That would be outstanding. You can make reservations here at the Campbell River Lodge. It's about a block from the marina. We'll come see you when we get in." The call left the Skipper visibly delighted.

Bruce was the first to ask, "What was that about? Are some other folks going to join us?"

"No, nothing like that," the Skipper answered. "Kurt and Donna Warden from the church want to take *Dreamer* back to Seattle for us. They have two boys, and two weeks of vacation. They want to go back through Victoria."

Annie asked, "Do you mean they are chartering the boat?" She seemed surprised that someone else would enjoy their special space.

"They aren't chartering, but we are going to barter a bit," the Skipper answered. "They have a timeshare on Maui that they can't use in January. If I can get away for a week, I can use it in trade." It was surprising new information that the crew took in, each with a different perspective.

Bruce suddenly realized the implications. "Do you mean we have to drive his car back to Seattle?" A scornful expression covered his face.

"Bubba, he has a new $75k Cadillac CTS V Sedan. I think the proper question is who gets to drive it back? And I like the idea of being with these ladies all the way home; instead of hoping they don't meet other sailors along the way." He got punched in the ribs for that.

The subject came up again later as they were enjoying a walk on the gravel beach by the ferry terminal. They watched the Quadra Island ferry come and go a couple times, plying its short transit across Discovery Passage. "Will the Coast Guard know that they have the boat, and not us?"

"Yes, we've got the proper documentation; it's not unusual for the Coast Guard to see this sort of situation."

It was mentioned again as they made their way alongside the Campbell River trail, beside quiet pools filled with spawning salmon. "Do they know how to operate the boat?"

Finally, when they had returned to *Dreamer*, and were relaxing in the cockpit, Bruce said, "I was kind of looking forward to another all-nighter." It was the segue the Skipper needed to introduce the major subject.

"I've been thinking about this switch for some time with the Wardens. They made the offer when they first learned I was coming up this way. I like them, I trust them, and I think it will be mutually satisfying. But you guys just now have the information, and the idea is strange. That's how I feel about Mr. Branch's report. I've had some time to think about it and now I can see how it will be mutually beneficial." Looking at Kathy he said, "No, we won't talk about Adam and Eve. That was a bit corny. It was a bad start to a right plan. Let's go into the salon where we can talk."

A few moments later, he handed each of them a sheet of paper. "Here's our itinerary of ten destinations, ending back here. We won't need to travel far each day, unless we want to sail the long way. There will be plenty of time to read, or talk, or explore the most beautiful country you can imagine. I'm anticipating a marvelous vacation."

"That will take us out of our routine and hectic habits for the next part of the experiment. I've made a worksheet for each day. It is an outline that offers time for quiet prayer in the morning, complete with a meditation phrase." The Skipper went down into a galley cabinet and produced his meditation bowl. "Kathy gave this to me for my birthday, and I am fascinated by it." He rubbed the outside of the rim with the wand, and the boat was filled with a soft deep hum. "Here's a sample of a worksheet I made for today." He handed them each another sheet of paper. It read:

Day 1.)
Morning Prayer:

Dear and Loving Lord, thank you for a good night's rest, and the blessings of a happy crew. Thank you for the opportunities hidden in this day. Let me have eyes to see the wonder, and a heart to give you praise. Lord, today I would rather attempt to do some great thing and fail, than attempt to do nothing and succeed! With your help, and in your Grace, I'll try! Amen.

Meditation, read three times:

My fear is faulty wiring, not the way God designed, or desires me to be. God's grace will restore me to a joyful, righteous, and fearless life.

Discussion:

1). Face it
2). Retrace it
3). Displace it
4). Erase it

Conclusion, read three times:

I can overcome my fears with a creative reverence for God, expressed through awe, wonder, adoration, and obedience. Only God needs to be pleased.

The Skipper read each meditation aloud, slowly, phrase by phrase. He rubbed the rim of the meditation bowl as he did it, then again, and once again.

"I'm convinced," he said earnestly, "that if I saturate myself with these good thoughts for a week, there will be a shift in my total attitude and outlook. And it will be more about my orientation to life than any theological understanding. Does that make sense?"

Kathy and Annie sort of nodded, but not with great enthusiasm. Bruce asked, "Is it like feeling better if you spend a week getting a great tan, or bathing in a hot springs? I think you are saying the effect will be a general improvement."

"Well, Sort of," The Skipper answered, grateful for any response. "I'd say it is like healing us in ways and places we didn't even realize we were hurting."

Going on he said, "Let me make an analogy. I remember when you were about three years old. When I came home in the evening, it was a highlight of my day, because you would shout, 'Daddy's home!' and come flying from wherever you were playing, to grab my leg, and hug me like crazy. We both loved that."

"When I think about how much God loves us, it is tons greater than we could ever love even an adorable son, daughter or spouse. As much as I love you, God loves us millions of times more. As happy as I was to get your hug, God must get supreme pleasure when we greet Him with enthusiastic joy."

"But here is the rub. Instead of childlike abandon and freedom, I suddenly recall things I've said or done, or not done, that keeps me from letting Him embrace me with loving acceptance and assurance. I remember deeds of greed, or lust, or anger that have curdled that sweetness and caused me to pull away. I feel that God should meet me with concern rather than open arms, judgment rather than joy. I project onto God my own self-condemnation. Suddenly, when I need Him most, I feel estranged and distant from Him. But when I feel that separation from God, who moved? Did God? Not at all! I changed; I moved. God's love toward me still wants the hug, but sadly, I feel estranged, cautious, secretive, and empty."

"In that emptiness, my heart becomes a campground for every transient tenant that wants to pitch a tent. Fear takes up residence and begins to act like it is entitled to the whole place."

"I'm convinced that this deep, inner emptiness-caused fear is the root of all the rest. It gets focused on frightening situations, alarming circumstances, and troublesome people. At its core, this basic emptiness is the universal and inevitable human reaction to being separated from God, and it's all self-generated, and can be corrected."

"Wait," Bruce cut in, "are you saying that we can fix this ourselves? Where is Grace in that?"

"That's a perfect question, Bubba." The Skipper smiled warmly at him. "Let's look at a scripture reading from 1 John 4:18." Opening a Bible he had on the table, the Skipper read, *"There is no fear in love. But perfect love drives out fear, because fear has to do with punishment. The one who fears is not made perfect in love."*

The boat was very still, no sounds inside or out. After several quiet moments, the Skipper asked, "So, how is your day going?" Bruce snorted out loud, and the girls grinned at the incongruous question.

Bruce asked, "Are you wondering if we are in perfect love, or has it cast out our fears?"

"I think I'm asking," the Skipper, replied, "when we know that the Lord will never forsake us, or leave us; and when we know that God will never take second place in our lives, are we ready to allow God to remove the empty-oriented fear from our lives?" The crew nodded their heads together.

"Then I think the next step is . . . you might want to write this down . . . I will face my fears, retrace them to their source in my heart, displace them by making my heart Christ's home, and erase them with his perfect love." He said it again slowly, phrase by phrase. "Let's repeat that a couple of times to let it sink in."

Bruce pointed to the middle of the sheet of paper in his hands. "These four phrases are just what we repeated. Is this the outline?"

"You got it, Bubba," the Skipper answered. "First action is: face your fears; don't try to deny them or hide them. There are two undeniable things about our fears. They are real to us, and they won't go away by simply wishing them away; so we ask, 'what is it that makes me feel insecure, or alarmed, or uncertain?' I think our external fears fall into one or more of the 'P' categories, people, problems, possibilities, or perplexities. Face it simply means to step up and look it squarely in the eye."

"The second action is: retrace your fears, replay the tape in your mind's eye to the source of your present fears. Is there some person who injured you, or some past failure that is causing you to fear your future?" His eyes caught Kathy's for a long heart-beat. "Remember, if we don't deal with our past, we will compulsively repeat it. And the important thing about retracing our fears is that our gnawing guilt is not because of things we have done, but because we willfully avoid intimacy with our Lord."

Annie quickly asked, "Can you say just a bit more about that?"

"Think about it," the Skipper said with a grin. "If we feel that the most horrific part of our past has been completely and forever forgiven, how can it generate fear in our lives? We may regret the fact, or wish for some other response, but we do not fear what God has washed clean. Does that make sense?" All three nodded in understanding.

"Next on our list is to ask Christ to move into our hearts and displace our fears. 'Perfect love drives out fear.' We can't evict fear on our own. Only Christ can do that. The secret is to focus on him, hence the meditation phrases and our bowl, and to 'defocus', if that's a word, our fears. If we can do that we can deliberately refuse to spend time rehearsing our fears."

"I have a sweet friend who expresses it this way, 'fear is the dark room in which we develop our negatives into frightening possibilities.' But when we allow the Lord to flood the dark rooms with the brilliance of His presence, our fears are dispelled completely. Instead, we picture ourselves as the person Christ wants us to be."

"That brings us to the last act, because only Christ can erase our fears. It's his miracle we embrace. Our part is to pray, 'Lord, I don't want this fear anymore. I don't want to hang onto it as a false security any longer. I ask you to erase it, and clean it off the blackboard of my memory.' How the Lord will answer that prayer is the agenda we are going to share in the next ten days. We have wondered together what we are going to do. Have I said it clearly enough?" There followed a cacophony of questions and comments, but nearly all of them were positive. They were beginning to understand a 'culture of discovery.'

For just a moment the Skipper smiled. "Hey," he asked, "who wants to go up to the Lodge for a Molson, and whatever goes with it?" They hadn't even noticed that the sunset was well advanced behind the western horizon, from muted colors to gathering shadows.

As they walked into the now familiar dining room, Dot's voice was clarion clear, "Brian, this is not a time for prayer! No more cursing, do you understand?" She waited just long enough to get a grunt reply. "Brian," she nearly shouted to hold his attention, "what color is this card?" She held up a yellow piece of paper.

"Sorry eh, Dot? It just slipped out. I see my yellow warning card. It won't happen again, I promise." Brian was in true and predictable form again. The crew had to chuckle at his obvious discomfort.

By the time they had nearly finished their Molsons, and received their food, it was too much for Brian to contain."

"Jesus Christ, Larry, you are cheating the hell out of me!" The burst came from only one source, and Dot was on her way.

"Brian," she scolded, holding a red card in front of his face, "this is no time for prayer. I have said it for the last time, you are off the table. Bring me a note from Father Dan, saying that you have done penance, if you ever want to get back on the table. I mean it!"

Brian quietly put away his pool cue, pulled on his green jacket, and headed for the door, saying, "Sorry eh, Dot. See you tomorrow night?"

The crew felt that this was dinner with a floor show, at Brian's expense.

After dinner they were enjoying the balmy evening. They decided to walk the long way back to the boat. Somewhere after the closed shops and the ferry terminal, Norm slipped his arm around Kathy's shoulder. A few steps further, he turned her toward him so he could kiss her gently. She made no move, nor had any desire to end the kiss, which lingered long enough for them each to realize they were in a new and welcome place in their relationship.

Back on *Dreamer*, Bruce said, "So, Dad, are you having a good day?" With an enormous smile he continued, "I can remember a lecture I once received on the public display of affection." The shared laughter belied his feelings.

"That was not a public display," Norm objected. "Besides you weren't supposed to be watching." Kathy was only a little embarrassed by the conversation, but still relishing the moment.

When finally the teasing and easy conversation was winding down, the Skipper ended the evening by reminding them that tomorrow they were on their way to Hariot Bay, their first port of call. "We won't need to worry about the tide, or a very early departure. If we want to fish at all, we'll need to get a temporary fishing license."

Bruce asked, "Can we fish on the way, or do we need to go somewhere special to catch supper?"

Pointing back the way they had approached Campbell River, the Skipper explained, "We need to go back around Wilby Shoals, the south end of Quadra Island. It is the absolute finest salmon fishing grounds in the area." There followed small questions of clarification. Finally Annie asked, "Can we share a prayer before bed?" She held out her hands for Bruce and Kathy.

When they were in a circle the Skipper softly prayed, "Lord of Great Compassion, we come to you at the end of this day with gratitude, seeking your blessing of rest. Master, what we know not, teach us; Master, what we have not, grant us; Master, what we are not, make us. Help us to find rest and fresh strength this night, that we might rise in the new day so to reflect your goodness that others might see the grace and mercy of the One whose we are, and whom we seek to serve, in Jesus' name. Amen"

When the lights were out and the boat was still on a quiet marina, Bruce whispered to Annie, "Did you see that kiss? That wasn't someone who is kissing her friend. Do you think they are serious with each other?"

"I think," Annie replied, "that you should not leap to a conclusion." In the darkness there was a suppressed giggle. "And besides, he kissed her." They both buried their faces in the pillows to muffle the laughter.

Kathy's head was on her pillow, but her thoughts were on the man just a few feet away in the aft stateroom. "People say you can tell a lot from a first kiss," she thought. "If that was our first real kiss, I think I'm a pretty lucky girl." A warm smile curled on her lips as she recalled the kiss.

The Skipper was thinking, "She really kissed me back! I didn't expect it, but wow that was nice!" Oh good the night!

When Kathy awoke, she listened for any sound that would indicate someone else was already up. The boat was as still as can be. "Guess I'll just stay under these comfy covers for a bit," she thought. It gave her time to think how very happy she felt.

The Skipper eased off the boat, headed for the shower. Sunrise was still a few minutes away, but the sky was blooming with pink and orange clouds. As he hurried up the dock he had time to think how happy he felt.

Annie felt Bruce's arm cradle her a bit closer to him. She whispered, "I love you, and I love being on *Dreamer* again. Are you having another great experience?"

"I love you, too," he whispered back. After a couple moments he finished his answer, "I'm not sure if it is the boat, or what Dad does with it, but yes, I am having a fantastic time. Dad says that when we have everything in tune, we see the world in more vivid colors. Do you believe that?"

"That's a great way to describe it," Annie answered with a contented sigh. "Since the first trip, I feel more alive, more of everything, especially more in love with you." She snuggled deeper into his embrace.

By 5:30 the sun was peeking over Quadra Island, bathing the marina in warm summer sun. The crew, all scrubbed and coiffed, with cups of tea, were together in the salon. Annie had wrapped her blanket over her lap, with her feet snugly tucked under her. Kathy was happy to be seated by the Skipper.

"O.K." the Skipper began, "we have a great start on a fantastic day. Shall we do a morning devotion before we get in line with the fishermen for breakfast?" He was already handing them another sheet of paper. "Let's take a look and see if it works." It read:

Day 2.)

Morning Prayer:

Good morning Heavenly Father; thank you for the rest of night, and the glorious promise of a summer day. You are already painting our world with surprising colors. Thank you for the surprises you have tucked into the minutes and hours ahead of us. We know that faith stimulates discovery; hope sustains discovery; and love sanctifies discovery, so we cannot venture through this day without your power, your peace and your presence in our lives. We can already feel the energy of your healing power, in Christ Jesus our Lord. Amen.

Meditation: repeat three times.

I can overcome my fears with a creative reverence for God, expressed through awe, wonder, adoration, and obedience. Only God needs to be pleased.

Discussion:

Troublesome memories:

> Secret memories;
> Memories of my failures;
> Memories of what others have done.

(Sing to the tune, "O for a Thousand Tongues to Sing.")

> Jesus the name that charms our fears,
> That bid's our sorrows cease,
> 'tis music in the sinner's ears,
> 'tis life, and health, and peace.

> He breaks the power of canceled sin,
> He sets the prisoner free;
> His blood can make the foulest clean,
> His blood availed for me.

List twelve good, happy memories.

Meditation: repeat three times

I will release every painful memory of the past, and forgive everything and everyone who caused them, including myself.

As Bruce read the sheet of paper, he looked at the Skipper with a guarded expression. "We're not going to go back over the painful stuff we did before, are we?" It was obvious he had little intent to do that.

"Not at all," the Skipper answered with a big smile. "In fact I only offer this for our morning prayer, and the first meditation. I hope you will think about the other stuff until this afternoon, when we will share all of our secrets." When Bruce bolted at the suggestion, the Skipper laughed out loud saying, "Relax, I'm only teasing. We're not going to share anything uncomfortable. I only want to guide our thoughts this afternoon, if we have time." He reached across the salon table to ruffle Bruce's hair.

They prayed their morning prayer, and repeated the meditation phrase, while the bowl hummed its lovely melody. Annie said, "I remember how fun it was to sing on our first trip. Now that we have Kathy to help cover the wrong notes that you guys seem to add, could we sing again? Do you have any song sheets?"

Looking in his briefcase, the Skipper discovered a couple wrinkled sheets from a previous retreat. "I really like these around a campfire. The one on the bottom was written at the Young Adult Conference of the South Pacific. We were on Rotuma Island, Fiji." He handed one to Annie to share with Bruce, and one to Kathy.

Bruce asked, "Are these legal to have printed like this?"

The Skipper assured him, "Public domain by common usage makes the first two appropriate, and there was never a copyright on the third one. I think we are safe from detection." They sang them all, at least once.

Table Graces:

> *Sung to the tune of the Doxology, Amazing Grace, Joy to the World, or Hernando's Hide-away*
> "Be present at our table Lord;
> Be here and everywhere adored;

These mercies bless, and grant that we
May feast in fellowship with thee."

Sung to the tune "O Tannenbaum":
"We thank thee, Lord, for daily bread,
And all thy mercies 'round us spread.
We thank thee for thy love and care,
For guidance in our daily prayer.
For Christian friends, faithful, true.
For love's unfinished work to do.
In all we think and do and say,
Thy Kingdom come in us today. Amen"

Fellowship Songs

We are part of the family, that's been born again,
Part of the family, whose love never ends,
For Jesus has saved us, and made us his own,
We are part of the family, that's on its way home

Chorus:
Sometimes we laugh together, sometimes we cry.
Sometimes we share together, heartaches and trials.
Sometimes we dream together, of how it will be,
When we all get together, God's family.

When a brother (sister) meets sorrow, we all feel the
grief,
When they've gone through the valley, we all feel
relief,
Together in sunshine, together in rain,
Together to greet them, in God's holy name. (Chorus)

After the crew had enjoyed another breakfast at the Tackle Box, and walked back to the boat holding hands, Kathy wondered if she had ever had a more enjoyable vacation. "And to think," she smiled to herself, "it's only beginning!"

When the Skipper said they had one last chance at the potty before getting underway, Annie assured Kathy that it was only a polite announcement, and not a warning. She showed Kathy where to curl up in the front of the cockpit, so they would be out of the way, yet enjoyably close.

Annie was interested that the key was always left in the ignition, and when the Skipper turned it, there was a buzzing alarm sound. "Is it supposed to do that?" she asked.

He replied that in fact it was working perfectly. "That's the glow plugs heating up. With a diesel engine the start up is a little slower. The plugs get hot for about ten seconds or so," then turning the key a bit more, the engine purred awake, "and she starts right up." It was important information to have, Kathy thought.

She watched as the Skipper untied the bowline, which Bruce pulled in and dropped in the anchor locker up front. Wait, she should have said "on the bow." The Skipper untied the spring line, but held a wrap around the dock cleat, handing the end to Bruce to hold until the stern line was loosened, and the Skipper stepped aboard. It was so coordinated and yet so easy. With an, "O.K. Moose, you can bring in that spring line. We're good to go," they were underway. Kathy noted that the small black knob on the left side of the binnacle was pushed forward, that must be the gearshift; and the red one on the right was eased forward, that must be the accelerator. It was important information to have, Kathy thought.

Dreamer slid out of the marina with no wake. A tiny northeast breeze had hardly a ripple on the water. It was going to be a glorious warm day. The Skipper cautiously checked for boat traffic before turning south toward Wilby Shoals.

Since getting his fishing license, Bruce had been more and more excited about doing some morning fishing. He had chosen a silver flasher, trailing a black plastic lure about four feet behind it.

"Dad, are you sure this is how this all works?" Obviously there was latitude of opinion.

"Looks good to me," the Skipper quipped, "but I'm not very hungry after those hotcakes. I hope the salmon like it better." When he got no laughter from his humor, he continued, "I think the way that works is the flasher sort of darts from side to side, which gives the Apex a fish-like motion. If that doesn't work, put on that other thing. I think he called it a 'blu'oochy.'"

A what?" Bruce asked with glee.

The Skipper replied, "They're called 'hootchies' here in Canada. I think they are supposed to look like darting shrimp or small squid. Blue ones are called 'blu'oochies, eh?' They are the favorite. I'll bet you hook a whopper." The crew enjoyed the morning banter.

By the time Cape Mudge, the south end of Quadra Island was off the beam, they could see at least half a hundred small fishing boats plying the shoal. "This has got to be a hot spot to attract all these fishermen," the Skipper mused.

Kathy joined in, "Either that or someone told a very good story at breakfast."

Dreamer stayed to the west of the crowd for almost a mile. Then the Skipper started an easy port turn. "Kathy", he asked, "will you watch that fathometer." He pointed to the instrument with a digital readout. "If the number get less than fifty, would you tell us?"

Bruce moved to the stern, leaning over the chrome life rail. He had to reach over the inflatable to get his fishing lure in the water, as *Dreamer* slowed to a gentle trolling speed. "How far down do you think it should go?" he asked no one in particular.

Annie answered, "I think it should go all the way down to where the fish are." Laughter from the cockpit warned Bruce that there would be little help on the subject.

He was ready for some action for the first quarter hour. He let out a little more line, then after another quarter hour he pulled in a little line. "I think I'll try the blu'oochie," he said in resignation. *Dreamer* had made a slow turn to the south, and was now returning up the east side of the shoal. A bit further south they saw a couple of fishermen battling catches.

In the cockpit Annie was looking through the binoculars, studying the rock formation behind them. "Norm, do you know the name of that little island?" It was a bit startling to hear her use his name instead of "Skipper."

"On the chart it says that is Mitlenatch Island, and reports it has colonies of nesting Seagulls and Guillemot, those little diving ducks." He pointed to the chart book, "It also says there is a legend that the island is really an Indian princess who was turned into stone and placed here to remind the Cape Mudge people of a time when their wealth and power caused them to be arrogant and lazy."

"Oh, no it doesn't," Annie argued. Looking at Kathy, she said, "He does that stuff all the time. I just quit believing his stories." The smile on her face showed not a bit of malice, however, just playful banter.

Kathy leaned over so she could see where the Skipper was pointing, and read the fine print. "Actually, that's just what it says, along with some other stuff about the geology of the island."

Annie was not about to give up easily, "No way! He is always coming up with a scary story or some old folk lore. You really need to look out for him. He'll trick you." Kathy said she would be on guard. The morning sun had burned away any lingering haze, and the water was as calm as a pond. It was time for shorts and sunscreen. The girls went below to change.

"Are you doing alright back there?" the Skipper asked Bruce, who had been quiet for some time.

"Yeah, I thought I had a bump a little bit ago, but nothing serious. Do you want to do this for a while?" There wasn't much spark in his voice. "Did you see the guy in front of us just catch one?"

"Yeah, but I'll pass. If you want to roll it up, we can try tomorrow again. If I stay on this course we will be in Hariot Bay in about an hour."

Bruce asked, "Is that real time, or your way of saying 'sort of soon'? I'll hang in here for a bit. I think I have a hot flasher, eh?"

"O.K. and remember, there are no barbs on these hooks, so if you get something, don't give much slack, or they'll throw it for sure." With no action yet, it was a good idea to talk about a fighting procedure.

Kathy came back into the cockpit wearing tan shorts and a short sleeve matching shirt. She was as cute as Norm had ever seen her, and she was delivering a glass of Crystal Light.

"I am such a lucky man, and the day isn't even half over." Lifting his glass, he said, "Thank you." He wanted to say more about her attire and appeal, but restraint was stronger. "You look great," was all he could say.

She smiled back, and was about to say how comfortable *Dreamer* was to lounge about, when a shout accompanied by shuffling feet came from the back.

"Jeez Louise! I've got something!" Bruce's voice was alive with excitement.

The Skipper pulled back the throttle and moved the gearshift to neutral. He turned the wheel to starboard so *Dreamer* would make a safe turn, and try to keep Bruce in a comfortable advantage.

Annie said playfully, "Brucie, you almost were praying. Now is the time for catching."

The drag on the fishing reel growled out some line as the salmon made a run for deeper water. Bruce kept the pressure on. Then they could see the line moving further from the boat as the fish rapidly approached the surface. "He's going to jump!" Bruce grunted. On cue the water erupted about thirty meters from the boat, and once again Bruce was ready to keep a tight line. The salmon tried to go deep once more, but was obviously tiring. Bruce brought in line, held the rod higher, then brought in a bit more. It took several more minutes before the weary fish gave up.

The Skipper advised, "Annie, there is a gaff hook in the locker under you. It's probably way to the back and bottom. We'll need it to bring that lovely catch aboard." She hurried to find the tool. "Just look for the wooden handle."

Bruce finally lifted the rod high enough for the Skipper to reach down and position the hook right under the gill cover of the fish. With one tug, the hook penetrated and came out the top of its head, a sure and lethal stroke. "Good job, Bubba. I think you just caught a superb supper. Good job!" "Kathy, could you go down under the sink and find a tall kitchen garbage bag? We'll put him in the cooler with the Molson until we get in." "Wow, great catch! "So, are you having a good day, Buddy?" *Dreamer* was standing still on the tide.

CHAPTER 3:
HARIOT BAY

Overcome fear with creative reverence

Bruce was still telling about the epic battle with his estimated nine or maybe ten pound salmon when they made the turn at the light on Rebecca Spit, outside Hariot Bay. Even though it had been more than a decade since the Skipper had been here, it was suddenly, and pleasantly familiar. "I think the harbormaster is at the fuel dock. Let's put out bumpers on the starboard side." That was easy, since they were already tied there and needed only to be dropped over.

Once *Dreamer* was securely moored on the fuel dock, they were greeted, and told about several options for them to tie up for the night. The easiest, and quietest, would be on the end of the long dock. They were shown a cleaning table to care for their fish, and advised to place the "left-overs" on the pole with the sign "Cave Canem."

The Skipper did the honors with the filleting knife from the galley. Two very large and very delectable fillets were placed in another bag for the ice chest, enough to feed several folks. When he placed the carcass on the pole, he noticed a number of nearby boaters turn their attention toward him. A couple even had cameras at the ready. "What in the world do you think . . ." Before he could finish, the harbormaster said, "You might just step back a couple steps."

At the same time, the Skipper heard the rush of air behind him, and bent down in defense. The thump, thump of heavy wings was directly over his head. An enormous eagle swooped in to pluck the snack off the pole-platform, great talons reaching for the fresh meat, and carried it back up to his perch in a nearby tree.

The harbormaster chuckled, "Yup, Canem was really hungry this morning. You're the first ones back. By this afternoon, he'll be more picky, and we'll have to coax him down."

Bruce asked almost breathlessly, "Who's Canem?"

The harbormaster giggled, "The sign says 'Cave Canem,' 'Beware of the Dog!'" He laughed as he turned to leave. "It happens eight, ten times a day. He is the laziest, and best fed dog on the island."

"Look at the size of this place," Bruce exclaimed as they toured the shore facilities a few minutes later. "The pub has to have fifty tables, and the bar is enormous." Looking back at the marina, he added, "There can't be more than twenty or twenty-five boats. Why is it so big?" He would be even more surprised when they got upstairs in the dining room. "Holy cow! This is twice as big as downstairs! How come, Dad?" The resort at Hariot Bay was prepared to welcome a very large crowd indeed.

"I think you are only looking at the marina, Bubba. Let's walk around front." When they strolled through the lobby and out the front door the answer became clear. There were more than a hundred RV's parked in the campground. A parking lot beside the lodge indicated they also had guests staying inside. It was truly created to serve a large number of folks.

Kathy offered to pay for an early lunch, if folks were interested. She said, "I've been smelling those French fries since we came in. I'm starving!"

Annie agreed, "I went sort of light for breakfast. I'm thinking fish and chips." Elbowing Bruce, she asked, "How about you Mr. Fishkiller?" It was such a fun day!

When the baskets of food were nearly empty, and four glasses were drained, the Skipper suggested a hike around Drew Harbor. "It's about a mile long, and the only sand beach we will see up here. There are lots of interesting stones on the outside of Rebecca Spit."

Bruce, always interested in the details of an adventure, asked, "What sort of stones?"

The Skipper, wanting to be a bit glib, answered, "Hard ones." Then, after a groan from the others, said, "Cape Mudge has been a developed site for the coastal people long before the explorers came through. There were large villages on both sides of the island, old cooking utensils, and arrowheads are still found. There are lots of fossils on the beach, petrified wood, and my favorite, quartzite." When the other three looked at him for the rest of the explanation, he said, "Quartzite is a very hard material that the glaciers brought south out of the interior. When we find them they are perfectly white stones and smooth, and so hard that if one is shattered, the edges can scratch glass. But if they are polished in a tumbler, they are clear like agates. I've heard some folks call them 'sugar stones.'"

Kathy was quick to offer, "I think mom still has a rock polisher in the shop. No one has used it in years, but my dad did that a lot when I was little. Let's find some." There was a fresh eagerness to explore the beach.

An hour later Norm and Kathy sat in the lee of a large driftwood log, watching Bruce try to skip stones on the incoming tide. Annie was busy searching for good flat candidates for him to hurl into the rippled water. The warm sun had a tranquilizing effect on them all.

"I don't remember a time recently when I have felt this peaceful," Kathy murmured. "I haven't worried about the kids, and haven't even thought about my job. This is just wonderful." She leaned a bit closer into his shoulder. "May I ask a question about something that is none of my business?" She turned to look into his eyes. After Norm had said softly, "Of course," she pondered, "I've been wondering about the place in Hawaii you are trading for time on *Dreamer*. Will you go there . . ." then she revealed the source of her hesitance, " . . . alone?"

Norm chuckled, saying, "I don't know. I think I was just interested at first to have Wardens return the boat to Seattle. They are great friends in the church, and were eager to offer the trade. To tell the truth, I haven't given it much thought. January seems a long way off right now."

"Is that when it will be available?" When he nodded, she answered in a way in which he was becoming familiar, and more than a little fond. "Hmmm."

By the time the happy troupe returned to the boat, their pockets were full of white quartzite stones.

"There are two things I'd like to get done before supper," the Skipper said to a crew obviously ready for a nap. "Let's find out if five or six folks around us would like to share our salmon this evening, and then let's revisit our conversation started this morning."

Bruce and Annie volunteered to go knock on a couple boats nearby. Kathy, who felt like she should have some job at the moment, volunteered to pour a couple Crystal Lights. Neither job took long.

"O.K.," Norm began when they had re-gathered. "Let's look at the sheet we had this morning."

Kathy said, "First can we sing that 'Joy to the World' tune again. I get a kick out of singing Christmas tunes in July."

When the song was over Norm smiled to himself. "This is harder than herding cats," he thought to himself. "Repeat with me our meditation phrase at the bottom of the sheet:

'I will release every painful memory of the past, and forgive everything, and everyone who caused them, including myself.'"

"In Victoria at the timeshare, there is a room for 'left luggage,' he began again. "The first time I saw it I thought they meant 'lost luggage.' But it is for stuff people want to leave until their boat or plane back to Seattle is ready. They just park it for awhile."

"Reflecting on that experience makes me think about the place in our memories that might be called 'left luggage.' It's filled with the troublesome memories we wish we could forget, but can't. Instead of resolving them, we simply park them for a while. They are still there to haunt us, cost us sleep, and create that empty feeling we were talking about yesterday. The worst part is they cripple us from moving into the future with freedom."

"All too often," the Skipper said, not realizing that he was about to lead them into a pretty tender place, "our problem is that we remember what we'd like to forget, and forget what we need to remember. One of the main causes of turmoil in our lives is holding on to the past. The panic of discovery for what we have been, or done, combined with memories of the hurts others have done to us, produces a feeling of uneasiness about the past, and a fear of the future."

"Let me say very quickly, that I do not imagine this to be a therapy or counseling session, but a liberating moment when we realize that the Lord can do for us what we can't do alone. I believe we can be more empowered to overcome whatever has held us back from being fully present to the world around us, and able to reach out to others who are still restricted by fear." Looking at Annie he asked, "Will you read the meditation on the bottom of our sheet?"

Nodding happily, Annie read, *"I will release every painful memory of the past, and forgive everything, and everyone, who caused them, including myself."* She repeated it two more times.

"I think we can take a momentous step if we hear the words of Isaiah again. Let me read from the 43rd chapter." The Skipper turned to the marked place he had chosen. "Isaiah is speaking for the Lord God. *'Do not remember the former things, nor consider the things of old. Behold, I will do a new thing. Now it shall spring forth; shall you not know it?'* I have used that text a lot, always emphasizing that God was doing a new thing, and overlooking the rest of the words. He says, *'I, even I, am He who blots out your transgressions for My Own sake; and I will not remember your sins. Put me in remembrance; let us contend together; state your case, that you be acquitted.'*"

"We are to forget the past by remembering the Lord. We are to remember He has forgotten our sins and failures.

At His command we are to march through the prison of our memories, leading out each painful captive for display before Him, and we hear the verdict, 'Acquitted.' All our mistakes and all the injustices that have wounded us are already in His understanding. Confession means that we finish our judgment on ourselves and others. At that very moment He whispers, 'I forgot that long ago; now you are free to forget it also.'"

It was obvious that this was something the Skipper had worked hard to understand. "No one," he said firmly, "can take Grace lightly. God's promise to forget has been sealed by the sacrifice made on the Cross. When Jesus gave his life for us, He forgave our sins and freed us once and for all from bondage to destructive memories. Our challenge is to discover how to cooperate with the Lord in the dynamic process. He will not force us against our wills. I think that's why our recollections work against us. We do to ourselves the very thing that harms us so. The burning question is how can we become willing participants? How does the healing of memories take place?"

"Genesis 37 gives us a glimpse of an outstanding spiritual ancestor who illustrates the importance of forgetting destructive events from the past. Joseph, frequently identified by the many colored coat, was the son of Jacob, who actually named one of his sons 'Manasseh,' which means, 'The Lord has made me forget.' Do you remember the story?"

Annie shook her head, as did Kathy. Bruce just sort of shrugged, not admitting his lack of recall.

The Skipper gave them the condensed version of the story. "Joseph was the youngest of twelve sons, and thought that dad loved him best. He frequently shared that opinion with his brothers, to their dismay. Finally they reached that breaking point, where they wanted to break his neck. Instead they threw him in a cistern, and told their dad that he had been killed by wild animals. Joseph was rescued, sort of, but then sold in Egypt to the captain of Pharaoh's guards, who had an awfully playful wife. When Joseph said that he wasn't that kind of boy, he wound up in prison on her trumped up charge. How many hurts and bad memories has he collected so far in the story?"

"Joseph had a unique way of holding on to his faith. He was sure that the God, who had established the stars, still had a course for him. In prison he meets the palace butler and baker, who were wondering about their dreams. In casual conversation, Joseph explained the dreams so well that a couple years after the butler is released, he remembers to tell Pharaoh about Joseph's insight. And when the Pharaoh has the dream about seven fat cows and seven lean ones, you might know who is called to interpret it for him. Joseph told Pharaoh that God would show him the meaning of his dream; there would be seven prosperous years, when granaries could be filled, followed by seven years of famine. The Pharaoh was so pleased with the practical advice that Joseph was put in charge of all of Egypt. That seems like a big payday for such little work. But it's good for the story."

"Now the famine was so wide spread that back home, Jacob and his other sons had pretty much cleaned out the pantry. They heard there was ample food in Egypt; eventually his family came into the presence of a powerful official, whom they did not recognize as Joseph. He had the option to get even with all the terrible things they had done to him, but instead, he remembered that while they had intended evil, God had a bigger intent. They were reconciled, Joseph's memories were healed, and Israel was spared from famine and perhaps, extinction."

"If we are to forgive ourselves and heal our memories, we need to assume the name of Manasseh, 'the Lord has made me forget.' We also need to discover how to cooperate with the Lord in the dynamic process. God will never force the issue, so the burning question is how can we become willing participants? How does the healing of memories take place?"

"Here's how it worked for me." The Skipper took a big breath to calm his emotions. "I had gone through the motions of confession a lot. My goodness, every worship service called for a prayer of confession. While those prayers were wonderful, the problem was that they just weren't encompassing my sins, my hurts, my memories completely. One evening I decided to take God at his word. I sat down with a sheet of paper and asked God to help me to dredge up anything that I had consciously or unconsciously buried. Because I had not done this before the list was long. It was hard, and more than a little uncomfortable."

"I had divided my list into three parts: Secret Memories that I was sure no one else knew about; Memories of my failures, which were partly known by others whom I had hurt; and Memories of what others have done to me, beginning with my earliest memories. Sometime I wrote only one word that reflected a great deal of memory. My list became super long, but it finally came to an end. Then I went back, word by phrase, went back over each event as completely as possible, and made a specific surrender to the Lord, claiming his forgiveness and healing. In the case of the list of hurts from others, I asked for the power to forgive. Then in a special time of commitment to the Lord that I would remember to forget, I burned my lists in the fireplace. I sang Charles Wesley's hymn 'O for a Thousand Tongues to Sing.' Look at those words on your sheet, and see how special they become if you are erasing hurtful memories." The crew had been very still, listening to a revealed moment from someone special to them.

Bruce finally asked, "I'm pretty sure I know the answer, but are you asking us to do that exercise of confession?" There was no sign of resistance.

"Of course I'm not," the Skipper replied. "It is something to hold for a time when you have an inclination, as well as an ample opportunity, to give it a lot of attention, and prayerfully be deliberate." Again there was a pause with a deep breath. "What I am saying, however, is that keeping a short list with the Lord is crucial because we become what we remember."

"Unresolved guilt, unconfessed failures, or unforgiven injuries from others make us fearful and cautious. Our obsession with negative memories short-circuits positive memories, and causes us to forget God's goodness, mercy, or guidance in the past. It is, by the way, important to keep short lists with the ones we love as well, because it frees us to resolve problems quickly. With a liberated memory, we are able to focus on our blessings; rather than compulsively repeating the mistakes, we can expect a repetition of the good stuff."

"A while back, I found a poem written by George Kenyon. It has been a favorite book mark for a long time. Listen to these words:

> Lord, make me deaf, and dumb, and blind
> To all "those things which are behind."
> Dead to the voice that memory brings,
> Accusing me of many things.
> Dumb to the things my tongue could speak,
> Reminding me of when I was weak.

Blind to the things I still might see,
When they come back to trouble me.
Help me press on to thy high calling,
In Christ who keepeth me from falling.
Forgetting all that lies behind—
Lord, make me deaf, and dumb, and blind.
Like Paul, I then shall win the race
I would have lost but for Thy grace!

"I hope that you will also take some time soon to write down a dozen good, happy, creative, faithful memories, because today's actions become tomorrow's memories"

Kathy quietly smiled, hearing again a phrase Norm had spoken to her at Salty's. That seemed like so long ago.

The Skipper was trying to tie up their brief session. "Let's repeat that meditation phrase again a couple times." The meditation bowl serenaded their combined voices.

"I will release every painful memory of the past, and forgive everything and everyone who caused them, including myself."

Bruce and Annie got up to leave. Kathy, however, remained and asked the Skipper, "Do you think if we forgive, we will forget, too?" When he didn't answer immediately, she added, "I've always thought that when I have inner injuries, I need healing. And when the hurt is forgiven, or healed, there is just a scar left, which has no feeling. So I always remember, but there isn't any hurt to it, just an old scar. Does that make sense, or am I just wishful thinking?"

The Skipper smiled warmly, "You are not wishful thinking. But you are the only person I have ever talked with who used that scar analogy, just as I do." He reached over and held her hand. "Of course I think you are right on." Her hand gently squeezed back, and did not let go.

They were still enjoying the moment, recapping the stroll around the bay, when Bruce's head popped through the companionway. "Hey Dad, did you know they have a big gas grill that is available to us for cooking the fish?" There was obvious glee in his announcement.

"I did remember a grill," the Skipper replied. "But the last time I was here we had to provide the charcoal briquettes." The sun was nearing the western tree line, suggesting that supper preparations were in order. "Let's see how we can toast that huge salmon."

Bruce smiled at the exaggerated size. "We told folks to plan on a discretely late supper, like 7:30. Does that sound O.K.?" Before the Skipper could reply, Bruce blurted, "And we saw Canem again! He is so huge up close!"

"This is really a fun spot," the Skipper answered, "and we even have enough time to marinade the fish for about an hour."

The plan was to place the fillet on a sheet of foil, fold it and crimp the edges and pour on some white wine and add lemon slices. Then carefully rolling the edges together, he made a tidy, fairly secure package that would go right onto the grill to cook. The Skipper was confident that this dish would be worth sharing.

Kathy asked from the table, where she had been watching the preparations, "Is there anything I can do to help?" When the Skipper answered that it was pretty well done, she asked, "Can I take you for a walk then?"

They strolled up the dock, hand in hand; but going up the ramp to the shore, she held onto his arm, cuddling even closer. As they stood on the grassy knoll overlooking the marina, she asked, "So, Skipper, are you having a good day?" She didn't wait for his response before asking the rest of the question. "Is it always this much fun with you? I feel like it is one happy chapter after another. I'm really excited to see what happens next."

He gave her hand an extra squeeze with his arm. "Maybe, because you are looking for good things to happen, you find them all around you."

"Well, that's a kind thing to say, but I know what it's like when I'm not with you, and I can't find much fun in that."

"You know how to turn a boy's head," Norm said with a bit of a blush. He bent to give her a little kiss and was surprised, and very delighted, when her free hand hooked behind his neck and pressed their lips into a much bigger kiss. "Wow!" He wasn't sure what to say next, so he playfully asked, "So, Kathy, are you having a good day?" They both laughed, remembering the warmth of the kiss.

"I really, really like you," she said quietly.

"And I'm really, really glad, and I really, really like you too!" he responded. Then more seriously, he said, "You may be the most forthright person I've ever met. You make me feel like a schoolboy again."

"Is that a good thing or bad?"

"From my point of view, it is wonderful." Once again he held her in a warm embrace.

Finally, she answered softly, "I'm feeling a bit like a schoolgirl too. Thank you."

It was about time to get supper going, so they strolled back to *Dreamer*, holding hands.

When the foil pouches had cooked for about seven minutes on a side, Bruce carried them to the dock on the cutting board from *Dreamer*. As the Skipper opened them, appreciative "ooohs and aaahs" gave signs of approval from the eight neighbor folks who had gathered for supper. Surprisingly, folding tables and chairs had appeared to make this a fun dock party. There were even real wine glasses, instead of the plastic stuff the crew was used to. Bowls of salad, chips, and pasta rounded out the menu, with several bottles of refreshments. Bruce's big salmon was seasoned, and cut into serving sizes.

Folks began to introduce themselves, pointing to their boats to show where they were from. "Hi, we're Art and Bonnie from Sea Deuces." It was the big Bayliner parked right across from them. Art had been eager to help with dock lines when they arrived. "Hi, we're Jim and Mary Ann from Mahalo." He pointed to the only other sailboat on the dock. "And we want to say 'Mahalo' for the party." "Hi, we're the Coopers, Barry and Fran, from Good Times." He pointed to a beautiful Tollycraft. "We're Tom and Cathy Dixon, from Edmonton actually. We're here on a chartered Sea Ray from Vancouver." The wine was poured and appreciated. As the sun slid behind the western mountains, laughter and conversation underlined the success of Bruce's fishing experience.

"Hey Norm," Jim from Mahalo asked, "What was that brown jar you sprinkled on the salmon? It was terrific. I'm not sure I've ever had a better meal." Tom and Cathy also wanted to know the secret condiment.

"Would ye believe, now" the Skipper was trying his best Irish brogue, "that it's a wee bit of Leprechaun dust?"

"Come on. Is it an old family secret?"

"Actually," the Skipper confessed, "I'm a haphazard cook. I combine some sea salt, red pepper, not much of that, with some ground black pepper, some thyme, rosemary oregano, onion powder, and garlic powder. Usually I guess at the quantities. One container typically makes it through the whole season. It is best used for cooking shrimp in beer and butter."

"Oh, my gosh! That sounds good!" someone nearby exclaimed. "Are you going to be here tomorrow night? I'd like to make reservations!"

"I'm afraid the restaurant will get after us if we steal their dinner guests," the Skipper chuckled. "We're going to see if we can make it all the way over to Gorge Harbor."

There followed a splintered conversation about itineraries, and new ports of call. Several questions were directed to the Skipper about his recommendation for cruising sites.

"Hey, who wants to play poker?" someone called out. When there were no positive responses, the invitation changed. "Do you know how to play pinochle?" Only a couple of responses, so another suggestion followed. "How about a hearts tournament?"

The consensus finally determined that for the gamblers present, everybody should pitch in a dollar. The three power boats would host, having good lighting, and snacks. Play would be four hands at each boat, with the lowest two scores moving to the next boat. After three rounds, everyone should have had an opportunity to be with all present; lowest score would win $5, second lowest would get $4, and third place $3. "Let the games begin!"

It was dead dark when the *Dreamer* crew finally gathered in the salon. Kathy was the only one of them who had won some cash, with the second lowest score. Bruce was lamenting, "I'll bet we hear about this for days. She said she wasn't very good at it, and then she 'shot the moon'!"

Kathy finally responded to his taunts by saying, "O.K. I promise not to say anything more about the card games, if you stop telling your fish story. The last version I heard it had grown to nearly twenty pounds." Everyone chuckled.

"And I did offer to buy lunch somewhere tomorrow with my big winnings of four dollars."

Before the bickering became earnest, the Skipper suggested that they revisit the discussion of the afternoon. "So, guys, are you having a good day?" It was a question that, by now, brought instant smiles. "We are what we remember." The Skipper was really glad for their attention, as late as it was. "What memories are you going to save from this day?" he asked. His eyes and Kathy's met for a meaningful moment.

Spontaneous words and phrases tumbled one upon another. "Sunrise," "fishing and catching," "this fun resort," "new friends," "fantastic salmon," finally, Kathy said, "*Dreamer*." It was time for the Skipper to share a prayer with them, and bring this wonderful day to a conclusion.

"Sure, I want us to pray together." After a moment to gather his thoughts, he prayed, "Good and Gracious God, as night wraps its gentle arms around us, help us discover in our hearts, gratitude for your abundant gifts, sorrow for any sins we have committed in this nearly perfect day, and trust in your powerful guidance. Lord, help us to find forgiveness for the past, strength for the present, and confidence that the future can bring us nothing that in your mercy, we cannot meet. Let us rise refreshed in the morning, eager to reflect your goodness and love to all whom we meet in Jesus' powerful name. Amen."

There were hugs to each, and within just a moment or two, with lights out, *Dreamer* became nearly motionless. But on each pillow, memories of other highlights from the day frolicked happily, and added their own prayers of gratitude. Oh, good the night!

Kathy opened her eyes to find that darkness still held the early morning. Had she felt a movement, or heard a sound? She pulled the covers up around her chin and closed her eyes again. "I'm going back to sleep. It's just too early," she told herself. Regrettably, her mind was already in gear. "Was Norm already up, and getting ready for the day?" she wondered. "Would they move to another wonderful place like this one?" "Would she be kissed again today?" "Oh dear," she thought as she slid out from under the covers. "It's too late for more sleep."

As she stepped out of her stateroom, the salon was dark and empty; but when she had freshened up, and stepped out of the head, both Bruce and Annie were seated at the table. The lights were on, and a tea pot was heating on the stove. "Good morning."

Kathy whispered, "Is Norm awake?" Since it was still dark, she felt like respecting folks who might still be sleeping.

Bruce answered quickly, "We all walked up to the showers together. He is just taking more time to shave and look pretty for someone aboard." His teasing smile was a terrific way to begin the day.

Annie wanted to be part of the humor. She added, "The Skipper takes a lot more time getting ready in the morning than he did on our first trip. I think he's trying to impress you." They all chuckled at the prospects, but Kathy's smile went much deeper. They heard a happy whistle coming from the dock.

Moments later, the companionway hatch slid open and a smiling face peered in. "Hey, we're all awake! Fantastic! This is going to be such a good day!" The Skipper made his way to the galley and a glass of Crystal Light. "We are on our way to a super low tide, a minus two feet," he reported.

"I don't think there is much hurry to be anywhere else for a while." He went to the barometer and tapped the face of it.

Bruce asked, "Why do you thump it? Is it not working?"

"No, it's fine. When I want to know which way the barometer is moving, up or down, I tap the face to release any tension on the spring inside."

Annie asked, "Is it important to know about the reading? I thought that was only about storms, and it is pretty obvious that we don't have to worry about a storm today."

The Skipper thought for a moment before answering, "Even in July we get showers. The barometer tells us what to expect tomorrow. If there is little change on the dial, we are pretty sure to keep getting the good stuff we enjoy today."

Bruce replied, "Barometers are our friends!" in a sing-song voice. "I wish there was a stock market barometer that would tell me the right time to buy or sell, twenty four hours ahead of the change in value."

"We would be so rich!" Annie giggled. "We could retire early and go on more trips."

The Skipper finished the thought for her, "You could have a bigger *Dreamer* of your own!"

He went on to ask them all, "Since we are up and nearly awake, how about our morning devotion and then outline the day?" He was already at the cupboard where the papers were kept.

Kathy asked, "Could we sing that Doxology to Hernando's Hidcaway? I think that's a perfect way to start my day."

Day 3.)

Morning Prayer:

God of Wonderful Gifts, like a burst of sunshine that dissolves the morning fog, and sparkles on the tide, so Lord, you have come into our mind at the opening of this new day, assuring us that life is going to be beautiful. It's going to be one of our greatest days ever.

Through the deepest, unexplored sea of silence within us, beautiful positive thoughts are given to us. We are waiting. We are ready. We are listening. We will move, in Jesus' name. Amen.

Meditation: repeat three times.

I will release every painful memory of the past, and forgive everything and everyone who caused them, including myself.

Discussion: Who Needs a Hug?

What we are apart from Grace;

Humble Praise;

We are liberated to heroic service.

Meditation: repeat three times.

What I fear in others, I first fear in myself. In God's unqualified acceptance of me, I embrace myself as worthy of my own affirmation and encouragement.

When they had finished the second meditation, the Skipper began their discussion. "I recently heard about a third grade Little League player who slouched into the kitchen, where his mom was making dinner. He slammed his baseball glove on the floor and stood there on the verge of tears."

"'What's the matter,' his mom asked, 'did you lose the game?'"

"'Worse than that,' the little boy whined, 'I've been traded!' His chin quivered with despair."

"Trying to lend at least a bit of comfort the mom advised, 'That's all part of the game, honey. Remember when A-rod was traded to the Yankees, and Felix went to the Phillies? Sometime the very best players are traded.' She thought those were words of wisdom."

"'Yeah, but I was traded for Harry's six year old sister,' he answered miserably.'" There were groans of understanding from the crew, because everyone knows just what that little league player was feeling.

The Skipper nodded. "We said yesterday that we all need hugs of affirmation and acceptance. More than that, we need the embrace of total acceptance. That's the theme for today. Let's get it started by giving a hug to every other crew member." Gleeful giggles surged after a moment's hesitation. Norm and Kathy held their hug a bit longer than others.

"O.K. we're awake, the day is started, now let's go find some breakfast," the Skipper suggested. "I think we have one more morning of good service support, and then it will be granola and pirate pastry for breakfast." They marched up the dock toward the dining room, two couples holding hands.

Standing in line to be seated, they were delighted to find Jim and Mary Ann from Mahalo. Jim greeted them and asked, "Didn't I hear you say you were headed over to Gorge Harbor today?" When he was assured that was correct, he gave them some very good information. "There has been a shrimper pulling up pots by Smelt Bay. It's almost on your way into the Gorge. We stopped by his boat and bought a bag of fresh shrimp for supper. For $10 we had more than we could eat. We even used a few of them for bait for another supper. Look for a white boat with a bright red top. 'O Canada', eh?"

An hour later *Dreamer*'s diesel was singing baritone in the morning choir. Several boats had waited until the tide change to leave. Peering down into the clear water, it was pretty easy to identify anemones and starfish. There was an abundance of clam shells, evidence that either folks on the dock had discarded their shells from supper, or the denizens under the dock had fed well recently. There was enough depth to safely get underway, but not by much.

Bruce was removing the main sail cover, while the Skipper rolled up the shore-power cable. Once again they were operating as a functional team. The girls were curled, port and starboard in the front of the cockpit, out of harm's way. From the dock, the Skipper passed the bow line to Bruce, and then asked him to attend the spring line. Once the stern line was loosened, it was brought aboard by the Skipper. Bruce spun the spring line off the cleat and brought the line aboard, along with the bumpers; they were underway. "Oh, a sailor's life's for me," the Skipper sang, "upon the rolling sea; the sun and the breeze and my sunburned knees . . ." Bruce and Annie joined him as Kathy clapped with glee, "another Kubra Libra if you please. A sailor's life's for me!" Before they were clear of the harbor, the main was hoisted into the morning breeze, and the jib unfurled with a "thump." It was only about a five or six knot breeze, but enough to play with for a while.

The Skipper called in a clear voice, with as much accent as he could apply, "First Officer O'Banyon has the helm! Make your course due east until we clear the marker, and then take us south by southeast. I'll tend the 'riggin'.'"

Annie whispered for Kathy to hear, "Just like little boys; but the show is for us, you know."

Kathy was impressed again with how still the sailboat became as it gently heeled away from the wind. For just a moment she thought how much Scott and Jenny had enjoyed their experience aboard *Dreamer*. It was the first conscious thought of them in two days. The Skipper was explaining again how the boat functioned in the wind.

"This is called a beam reach, with the wind coming from the starboard quarter." He gestured off the back corner of the boat. "There is an optimal sail set for almost every angle of the wind. If we are beating into it," his hand moved toward the bow, "we must have the sails in very tight and flat. If the wind is off our beam," once again he pointed, but now squarely to the side, "we must loosen the sails more full and round. If we are running before the wind," this time he pointed astern, "the sails must be completely full, and I can even support the jib with a whisker pole, holding it out to catch the most wind. We just cannot go directly into the wind. If we want to go in that direction, we must zigzag, or tack back and forth into it." There were dozens of boats in sight, but *Dreamer* was the only one under sail.

"Hey Moose, do you see that boat a bit off the starboard bow, in pretty close to the shore?" He illustrated his question by pointing in the general direction. "Do you think that might be the shrimper?"

"I'll ease us that way a little more, and we'll have a look." Once again the boat was still except for the gentle wash of their bow wave.

About fifteen minutes later the Skipper said, "O.K. Brudah, take us up into the wind and I'll drop the main." He was rolling in the jib as he spoke. As Bruce swung the bow of the boat into the wind, the Skipper turned the ignition key, and after just a tiny pause, the diesel rumbled to life. Down came the main into the lazy jack lines, he unhooked the halyard, and fastened it to the ring on the mast. Bruce pushed the shift lever forward and eased some throttle. *Dreamer* was under power and responsive.

"I'll take us alongside the fishing boat, Bruce." The Skipper didn't know how comfortable he would be at close quarters. As they drew closer, two fishermen turned their attention to the uninvited visitors. One of the fishermen was recognized by his vocabulary.

"What the hell do you want? You're yanks, eh?" It seemed that Brian didn't recognize them.

"Hi Brian," the Skipper greeted him. "We were in the Lodge a couple of nights ago." The Skipper didn't want to finish the report ("when Dot kicked you out for profanity.")

"Big God damned deal," he began, and then his memory kicked in. "Oh yeah, I'm supposed to stop cursing. Sorry, eh?" He looked obviously uncomfortable.

Finally the Skipper said simply, "If you guys are shrimping, is there any way we could buy enough for supper?"

Recognition of the opportunity before him dawned on Brian. "You want to buy some of our catch? Cool! We usually get $5 per pound at the packers." There was a big hesitation as the rest of the plan formulated in his mind.

"But if you will write a note to Dot for me, I'll fill a bag for $10, O.K.?" *Dreamer* was standing dead still about three feet from the side of the fishing boat.

"Good deal," exclaimed the Skipper. He left the helm to go below for a notebook and a ten dollar bill. He wrote: "Hello Dot. We chanced to meet Brian while he was fishing. He was a pleasant person with no profanity. He even remembered to get this note for you seeking permission to get back on the pool table. I hope you will agree, he is a good man." Then he signed it "Norm O'Banyon on board *Dreamer*, a sailboat."

He hurried back into the cockpit to find that *Dreamer* had drifted close enough for Bruce to place a couple bumpers over the side, protecting both boats. The Skipper handed Brian the two pieces of paper and received a plastic bag with five or six pounds of fresh shrimp.

Brian asked, "Is this enough for supper?" He read the note to Dot, and then looked at the Skipper. "That's really nice of you to say." Turning to the other fisherman he said, "It says I'm a good man. Jes . . ." he hesitated, "Da . . ." he stammered for a proper word. "I don't think anyone has ever said that about me! Thanks folks. Thanks a lot!" There was a fresh look of joy on his stubbly face. He would show the note to Dot, but for sure, he was going to keep it. "See you, eh?" *Dreamer* was in gear, and pulling slowly away.

"Good luck Brian. Say 'Hi' to Dot for us. Take care." They were quickly beyond speaking range.

Bruce was holding the bag of shrimp. "Look at the size of these. They are more like lobsters; they are so huge!" You just never know what a morning is going to hold.

CHAPTER 4:
GORGE HARBOR
Rebuilding the inner culture

A few minutes later, Bruce called from the bow, "Hey Dad, do we go between these two islands?" He peered down into water that was beginning to look pretty shallow.

Annie was concerned with their destination as well. "Skipper, (she actually started to call him 'Norm' because of her growing confusion) is there a harbor entrance somewhere nearby? Maybe this is like the Hole in the Wall at LaConner. Is it just going to appear?" A concerned frown wrinkled her forehead.

Kathy was quietly looking for anything that might shed light on a new situation. For the most part she was content to trust the Skipper. That had sure been a good plan so far.

"Dad, it's getting pretty shallow up here! I can see the bottom!" That announcement was tinged with some urgency.

The Skipper had that mischievous smile that hinted at his lack of concern. "Then let's come almost about." As he said it he began to swing Dream's bow in a sweeping starboard turn. Bruce hurried into the cockpit, not real certain what else to do.

As the turn continued past 90°, a narrow passage appeared in the sheer rock cliff at their quarter. They had to go past it to have a clear depth to the entrance. "This is why it's called 'Gorge Harbor.' The only way into it is this very dramatic crack in the rock." The towering walls had to be three hundred feet high, minimizing even *Dreamer's* tall mast. The incredible surprise was so great no one could speak for a moment. Then they all began at once. Only Kathy seemed to have a plan. She hurried below for her camera to capture this delightful entrance.

"The Coastal People's village inside the harbor was one of the most secure in the area. They posted guards with piles of large rocks up there on the rim. If any unfriendly visitors tried to muscle their way in, they were bombed. It was a formidable defense." The entrance was just wide enough for two boats to pass, carefully, and about a hundred meters long. The crew craned their heads around, appreciating the novel feature.

As they cleared the entrance, and entered the harbor, they were struck by the cozy size of it. To their right were three anchored floating docks, and another to their left. "Those are oyster farms," the Skipper said. There are chains with colonies of oysters hanging under each one of them. They may also have some muscles growing there too." On the far shore they could identify a small marina in front of several low buildings. "Here's our home for the night," the Skipper announced. "Let's get ready for a starboard side tie-up." Now Bruce knew exactly what to do.

Once *Dreamer* was securely tied and ship-shape, the crew wanted to explore the harbor. They returned to the office, where they learned that Sean ran the fuel dock, the marina, and after four o'clock, he was the happy hour bartender as well. "We get quite a few boats in this time of year," he explained, "but not enough for a person to do each job. So I do them all. I like it." His happy smile revealed a happy spirit. "If you have fish to clean there is a table right at the top of the dock. Put your scraps up on the pole for the eagle, and make sure you watch your fillets. There's a pretty sneaky family of otter under the dock. They come up the drain hole on the table, and rob you blind."

"How big is an otter?" Kathy asked. "I thought they were pretty good size."

Sean shrugged and answered, "I guess they must be two, or three, feet long and weigh twenty five pounds." He held his hands a couple feet apart.

When Annie asked about a store, Sean pointed to the largest building. "That's the long house. We have groceries on one end, and the pub on the other end, with the patio. In between is the dining room. Mom serves fresh pastries in the morning, and dinner after 5 o'clock. Happy hour is all the time." Realizing that he was giving an orientation tour, Sean concluded, "You can hike up to Whaletown, which is about a mile and a half, or you can hike to the end of the harbor and follow the trail around to the left, up to the entrance lookout. There's not much on the east end of the harbor except a few Indian shacks." His bias was painfully obvious. "If you want to have some fun with the deer, get a package of soda crackers from the store. They'll eat out of your hand if you let them. But be careful cause they get some pushy."

He nodded as though satisfied with his instructions. "Oh yeah, the shower house," he pointed to the nearest building to the marina, "has good showers, but they take a token, which I sell at the dock. A five minute shower is a buck, one token. This time of year we start running short on water. Mom's been talking about getting a desalination machine, but darn, they are expensive. It would be great to have enough pure water though." Before he turned to go back into the fuel office, he concluded, "There are three gas grills by the ramp. They take a token for each ten minutes. You know, we have to bring the fuel in by truck."

The Skipper asked, "Is it just you and your folks that run the resort?"

Sean turned back to say, "Just Mom and me. Dad went fishing about four years ago, and didn't come home. I think he's in Baja, maybe Margaritaville, getting his tattoo." There was no mirth in his smile now.

"Are you here year-round?" The Skipper was interested in how this resort could be open all year.

"Yeah, we have folks stop in until about October. After that it's really dead until April or May, but we have to stay here to protect the property. I'd love to have a wife, but haven't found a woman tough enough to stand the winter isolation." Sean was about four answers beyond his comfort zone. "I got to get to work." This time he turned, and walked away.

Bruce clapped his hands, exclaiming, "We've got lots of fun stuff to do. I want to play with the deer, and maybe hike up to the entrance." He looked at Annie for agreement. "But I'm wondering, Dad, if I should do something with the shrimp. I've never cleaned, or whatever you call it, a shrimp. Do you know what we need to do with them?"

"I'll bet the two of us can figure it out, while the girls go up to the store for some crackers," the Skipper replied with a grin. "If you'll bring the bag of shrimp and the filleting knife from the galley, I think we can make a two-man process."

It took a couple tries, but the team won out. Bruce removed the meaty tails, and made a slice across the back. The Skipper removed the shell and deveined the meat. Within just a few minutes there were more cleaned shrimp than they would need for supper. "Now let's get them on ice and go find the girls," the Skipper said. Realizing how eager he was to share the rest of the morning with Kathy, he added, "I'll even buy lunch."

As they were rinsing off the cleaning table, flushing any refuse down the large hole in the center, they heard a commotion from under the dock. There was splashing much heavier than the water from the hose. Suddenly, a whiskered fuzzy face popped through the hole, seeking the source of the shrimp parts that had just been offered.

"Crying out loud," Bruce murmured. "That scared the heck out of me!" The face had disappeared when it saw the two startled people at the table. "That must be the otter that Sean told us about. Have you ever seen one?"

"Not that close, or outside the aquarium," the Skipper answered with a delighted grin. "Now we have something else to tell the girls."

They found Annie and Kathy seated at a picnic table. There were three young deer, held spellbound by the crackers the girls were nibbling. Occasionally they would offer a bite to an eager mouth. There seemed to be some happy pushing and vying for position to get the next nibble. Kathy waved as the guys approached. "This is more fun than going to the zoo!" From the edge of the trees across the meadow two more deer trotted to join the picnic.

Bruce took a cracker and walked briskly away from the table. To his delight, two of the deer followed him, hoping for a treat. Bruce returned for another couple crackers, and this time he jogged away. Once again the deer stayed with him. The third round, he sprinted away and was giggling as the deer bounded after him. They were a spectacle of eagerness, and surprisingly quick.

The Skipper cautioned, "Be careful. They may get a bit aggressive."

The girls moved from the seat to the picnic table top, and the deer pressed closer for more crackers.

"I've never been this close to a wild animal," Annie breathed with delight. Bruce sprinted away again with the two bounding behind him.

As Kathy was opening the third container of crackers, one of the deer tried to climb up on the table for an advantage. Annie gave a tiny scream of alarm, and Kathy simply threw the fresh crackers over the heads of the hungry animals, and spun off the other side of the table. Annie immediately followed, finding instant comfort and safety in Bruce's embrace.

Kathy said with a trembling voice, "Oh sure, we're all having fun with the animals until one of them forgets that we are visitors, eh?" Arm in arm, the four made their way quickly to the long house and lunch.

"Sweetie," Norm said as they gratefully left the deer, "that was quick thinking. Your distraction saved the day!"

She pulled his arm closer to her, and replied quietly, "I like it when you call me 'Sweetie.'"

Lunch was on the pub patio protected from the deer by a plastic wind-break, but within easy viewing. After the crew's hurried departure, the herd had settled down to easy grazing. One had curled down in the shade of the big maple tree.

There was a bit of a debate among the crew as to who would pay for lunch. The Skipper claimed the right, until Kathy said, "But please, I haven't paid for a meal yet. I offer but always get aced out." It was that "please" that settled the discussion. Bruce and Annie ordered Burger Baskets, and Norm opted for something a little more sensible. "How about a Chutney Chicken wrap?" he asked. Kathy agreed that a light lunch would be a proper thing for her too, as long as there were Molson all around.

The name of their serving person was Sarah, who lived in Whaletown. Her folks ran the store, she said. When Annie asked if Sarah was still in school, a happy smile responded, "I'll be a senior next quarter." Her youth suggested that she was referring to high school.

Bruce asked if there was a school on the island, or did she have to go into Campbell River.

Happy for the attention, Sarah answered, "No, we're lucky to have the internet. I get to do most of my class assignments on line. Once a month in the fall and spring I go into my Grand Mom's place in Campbell River for a few days to do testing. It's a lot better than home-schooling, eh?" She had a delightful smile, and a very friendly appeal.

Once again Annie asked, "Are there many classmates who live here?"

"Here on Cortes there are three other girls. Quadra is bigger; I think there are eight or nine there now."

Bruce was still feeling playful from the deer experience. "That might be tough on dating. Do you have much of a social life?"

Sarah gave a tiny giggle, and said, "I'm hoping to go to Vancouver UBC next year. There will be time enough for boys. Until then, I get to put up with all our yank visitors, eh?" She nearly sparkled with her own humor as she turned to place their order.

When the plates were emptied, and before the warm sun made the afternoon drowsy, Bruce said that he and Annie wanted to hike around to the entrance. "Want to come along? I'll bet it is a terrific vantage point."

The Skipper declined, saying, "I have some stuff to read and get ready for our afternoon conversation about hugging." A boyish shyness was exchanged in the glance he traded with Kathy. "Can we agree to meet back at the boat by 4:00 o'clock?"

Kathy quickly added, "Do you have a camera? I'd be happy to see what you bring back." The implication was clear that she would remain with the Skipper. The two couples left the long house in opposite directions, each interested in the secrets of the afternoon.

Norm had worked for over an hour in the salon of *Dreamer*, making notes and reading "Healing for Damaged Emotions" by David Seamands. He was so focused on his task that he didn't hear Kathy come below, until she spoke to him. Then with a start he asked, "Hi you, are you getting dozy in the warm sun?"

"Yeah, I'm having trouble with my eyes," she answered. When he gave her a concerned look, she continued, "I can't seem to keep them open to finish a whole sentence." They both enjoyed her humor. "I don't want to interrupt you; I thought I'd lie down for a bit."

"You are never an interruption, Sweetie." He was glad to know that she welcomed the endearment.

Kathy continued to the door of her stateroom. "Perhaps you could put on some music when you are finished with your work. I'd love to share a glass of Chardonnay to fight afternoon dehydration." Her smile was intentionally flirty.

Norm thought to himself as her door closed behind her, "Pressure! That is pressure I welcome!"

The boat was still for nearly another hour. Finally, he slid a Jim Brickman disk in the player and adjusted the music level so it would be pretty soft. He really didn't want to awaken her if she was napping. Almost immediately her door opened and Kathy joined him. She had changed into a pink print top and white shorts with white deck shoes, Wow, she was cute!

"Hey," he said in greeting, "I think you are raising the dress-code standard for the boat. You look lovely."

"Thank you," she replied shyly. "I heard you say we were going to chat about hugs, and I wanted to dress for the occasion." She went to the ice chest and pulled out a chilled bottle of Chardonnay, set it on the counter, an unspoken invitation for him to open it, while she found two glasses in the cupboard.

"Have you had enough sun for the afternoon?" The Skipper wasn't sure where best to enjoy their glasses. "We could go up into the cockpit, or stay down here where it's cooler."

"I'll vote for down here. I have become pretty comfortable in this boat, which is a fun surprise for me." Kathy made her way to the other side of the salon table and eased into a pillowed corner. She seemed relaxed, and without guile or agenda. After taking a sip, she picked up the bottle and read, "This chardonnay is scented with pineapple and mango. Luscious flavors of pear, caramel and butterscotch intermingle with tropical fruit leading to a decadent finish." She giggled, "Wouldn't you love to have the job of describing the wine? I can imagine writing some blue prose about the exotic contents."

Norm reached across the table to hold her hand. "And when you think about how many different varietals there are, each of which would require a full tasting experience, it would be a job with benefits," he completed her thought. They both laughed at the leisure of the afternoon.

"Seriously," she said, "I'm really surprised at how comfortable I've become on the boat. I had no idea it could be this relaxing, . . . so," she thought for the word, "so natural to be here with you." She gazed steadily into his eyes.

"I would say the exact thing," Norm said with insightful surprise. "I wasn't sure how it would work to have you aboard. Of course I wanted to share the time with you, but you are not a sailor, or the daughter of a sailor." It was his attempt to get back to a comfortable humor.

"I am not," she said thoughtfully. "But then, I've never had a chance to be, and this is a marvelous gift to get. Thank you." She gave his hand a squeeze, but didn't let go. "I really, really like you."

"I really, really like you too, and have been wondering when that becomes something more." He held her eyes in that firm gaze.

"I think it's when we admit that we want that other person in all of our life; head, hide, horns and all." It was a saying her dad had used to be funny.

"I don't know about the horns, but I do know that I care for you in just that way. In these four days I have realized how important you are to me. I can gladly admit what I have not been willing to say for some time. I do love you,

Kathy." She shuddered a little gasp as he got up to come around the table to kiss her. She raised up from her corner to welcome it.

"Ahoy *Dreamer*!" The call from the dock could not have been more poorly timed. Norm started to ignore it, and moved a tiny bit closer to deliver his kiss, then reconsidered with a groan, and moved to the companionway. "Ahoy *Dreamer*; is anyone aboard?"

Nearly inaudibly behind him, Kathy whispered, "I love you too. I have since the bus ride in Victoria two years ago." A happy tear danced in her eyes. "I love you too!"

Standing on the dock was Art and Bonnie from Sea Deuces. "Hey Norm, we promise we are not stalkers. When we heard you were coming here today, we just wanted to find out about those beer butter shrimp. We were supposed to be here tomorrow. I hope you don't mind. Hi Kathy." She had joined Norm in the cockpit.

"Heck no, we don't mind." As Norm said it, Kathy gently stepped on the side of his foot. "We bought some fresh shrimp from the fishermen this morning. Maybe we can cook them at the top of the dock grill about 6:30 or 7:00." He was trying to sound enthused, but his spirit was somewhere else.

Bonnie said softly, "We feel like old tagalongs; I'm sort of embarrassed. But we did get a couple pounds of shrimp at the store before we left Hariot Bay. Can we come for a cooking lesson?" Her manner hinted that it may have been more Art's idea to follow them than hers.

"Sounds like a continuation of a fun dinner last night," the Skipper concluded. "You know, we got some outrageous fresh bread at the store this afternoon. She baked it fresh this morning. That's all you'll need for a scrumptious dinner. Check it out and see if she has any left." Was it very obvious that he wanted to be alone with Kathy? Art and Bonnie strolled up the dock toward the long house.

Maneuvering Kathy under the dodger, Norm asked, "Now what do they say about mailmen? 'Not snow, nor hail, nor dark of night, or nosey neighbors will keep them from their appointments.'" He was moving close enough to smell her perfume. From the top of the dock a familiar whistle called for his attention. "Ahoy *Dreamer*!" Bruce and Annie were back! "I can't believe this!" he said in frustration. He leaned in and kissed Kathy softly. "I mean it," he said sincerely.

"Me too," she answered, and kissed him back. They watched the happy couple walk down the dock toward them. All four wore happy smiles, but not for the same reason.

When they all had fresh "dehydration prevention" and were seated around the salon table, Annie gave a report from the entrance. "You wouldn't believe how high it is. We could see Hariot Bay easily. There were eagles galore. I think we were near a nest, because we could hear that high pitched chirping they do. There were seals sunning themselves on the rocks down below, and we counted more than fifty boats fishing on the shoal."

Bruce cut in, "And two of the young deer followed us all the way out. I didn't have any more crackers, but Annie gave me a granola bar to feed them. I think they could be great pets. Is that legal?"

Norm and Kathy exchanged a happy smile. He said gleefully, "I knew this was going to be a fun trip, but who knew we would take back a contraband deer?"

The meditation bowl was on the table. After several more minutes of sharing highlights of the day, the Skipper softly rang the bowl; its reverberation lingering inside the salon. "Let's repeat this morning's thought: *'What I fear in others, I first fear in myself. In God's unqualified acceptance of me, I embrace myself as worthy of my own affirmation and encouragement.'*" He rang the bowl again, after they had repeated the quote.

"Kathy, would you read for us the section of Ephesians I have bracketed?" He almost called her 'Sweetie,' but thought better of it, for fear he would introduce another sidetracked conversation.

She turned to the bookmark and read: *"I have heard of your faith in the Lord Jesus and your love toward all the saints, and for this reason I do not cease to give thanks for you as I remember you in my prayers. I pray that the God of our Lord Jesus Christ, the Father of glory, may give you a spirit of wisdom and revelation as you come to know him, so that, with the eyes of your heart enlightened, you may know what is the hope to which he has called you, what are the riches of his glorious inheritance among the saints, and what is the immeasurable greatness of his power for us who believe, according to the working of his great power."* She paused to catch her breath, and murmured, "My goodness that was all one sentence!" She finished the reading, *"God put his power to work in Christ when he raised him from the dead and seated him at his right hand in the heavenly places."* (1:15-20)

The Skipper smiled his appreciation. "I once heard a talk show host say a very insightful thing. She said, 'My life seems to be one long obstacle course, with me as the chief obstacle.' I resonate to that, do you? Sometimes life feels like an obstacle course and I am the main obstacle of living to the fullest, as God would have it, and as the Lord offers it."

"I was just reading some words from David Seamands, a favorite pastor counselor, who said 'If we think we are nothing, we will live and act as though we are nothing.' I think that's why the words of Paul caught my attention. He says, 'so that, with the eyes of your heart enlightened, you may know what is the hope to which he has called you.' I think that means from the very depth of our personalities, we frame the attitude we live into each day. I mean if we see ourselves as 'the success' we will live and act like a success. In my case I have forever been the one in the family that was the strong one. In school that was difficult to define, but in the navy, and in college, it became more clarified, until after seminary, I thought I could carry any broken congregation, and did. In other cases folks are identified as 'sickly', and they have one ailment after another. Some people see themselves as 'victims', and never seem to get a fair deal. The list can go on and on. Some people see themselves as forever afraid, and you can guess the outcome."

"Remember the happy hugs before breakfast this morning? As I have reflected on it, I've come to see that we not only need the embrace of acceptance and approval from others." He glanced at Kathy who smiled in understanding. "We are in desperate need of being able to embrace ourselves. But because we look through 'eyes of the heart,' we know the real person inside our skins. Most of us have that haunting feeling that we don't deserve a hug from ourselves." He paused as though forming the rest of the thought. "Because we're convinced down deep that we are not very nice, or that we are failures, we tend to be super critical of ourselves. Even if we accomplish some deserved praise, we deny it, unable to affirm ourselves, unable to accept praise, because we are sure that we don't deserve it."

"Here comes the dominoes effect; instead of being our own best friend, we become our worst critic, paralyzing ourselves with all sorts of fear, fear of ourselves. No one knows our shortcomings, or overlooks our strengths better than we do. We are fearful of our need always to be right, of our feelings of jealousy, of our drive for prestige and power, of even our willingness to manipulate others to get what we want."

Bruce said quietly, "I've thought most of those things about myself, but had no idea others felt them too." The salon was still for a moment.

The Skipper continued, "Moose, if we treated our friends the way we treat ourselves, putting down strengths and repeating mistakes and weaknesses, we wouldn't have any friends left. That's what happens if we look with eyes of a sick heart, we get down on the person inside us. We risk losing one of the best friends we could ever have."

"Abraham Lincoln said, 'When I lay down the reigns of this administration I want to have at least one friend left. And that friend is myself.'"

"But Dad," Bruce broke in again. "We're hard wired to be the way we are, and we don't have reset ability. How do we reprogram our computer?" He pointed to his head.

"Good question, Pal," the Skipper replied. "There are two parts to the answer at least. First, obviously it is not something that we can do alone, but must rely completely on God's power. By grace we are made new. Secondly, we do have the responsibility to act like a new person when that transition begins. If we truly believe we are new creations, we will think and act as new creations."

"I think it is 1 Corinthians 15 that describes the change Paul experienced. You might recall that we first meet Paul at the execution of the first Christian martyr. When Acts tells us that Stephen was being stoned to death by an angry mob, the man who held their robes was Paul (actually Saul of Tarsus, who became known as Paul.) His success at driving the Christians out of Jerusalem was so widely known that he was given a letter of introduction to go to Damascus and continue his oppression. His personal conversion account comes in a section of soaring rhetoric about Christ's death for our forgiveness, His resurrection for our victory over death, His appearances to Peter, James, the other apostles, and last of all, to Paul himself there on the road to Damascus. That encounter was very important to Paul because it was his badge of apostleship."

"Understandably, there were a lot of critics who doubted his sincerity in claiming Christ Jesus. In verses 8-9, he speaks to their doubts in a wonderful way, 'Then last of all, He was seen by me also, as by one born out of due time. For I am the least of the apostles, who am not worthy to be called an apostle, because I persecuted the church of God.' Then he says what I am trying to get to this afternoon. He gives himself a big hug. 'But by the grace of God I am what I am.'"

"I am convinced that his healthy fearless self-acceptance in the context of the Lord's love for him explains why Paul was one of the most loving, forgiving, courageous heroes of the faith in century one. He outlines for us three elements of a Christ motivated hug."

"First Paul shows us that embracing ourselves begins with an honest recognition of what we were apart from God's grace. He talks frankly about that. His critics were saying that he was not an appropriate apostle, who had to be an eye-witness. Paul pushes the charge by saying he was 'born out of due time.' I've heard a lot of debate about what that meant. The word literally means 'miscarriage' or 'untimely birth.' He may have meant it to indicate that he was called to follow Christ long after the other disciples had been called. He could have meant to say that as a trained

Pharisee, a scholar, he was a miscarriage of understanding. As a lawyer of their heritage, he was a miscarriage of justice. As a follower of God, he was a miscarriage of the faith."

"What he had been, before he received the Lord's grace, is of no importance to Paul. But through that regenerating process he had become a new person. He didn't disclaim the past, but embraced it as a sign of what God can do. During the fourteen years of prayer and preparation, after his conversion and before his first missionary journey, the Lord worked within his mind and heart to produce a miracle. That's why he was able to say, 'Therefore if anyone is in Christ, he is a new creation; old things have passed away; behold, all things have become new.'"

The Skipper was quiet for a moment, deciding whether he should personalize the discussion. "Does it matter that I was a less than perfect person growing up? Does it haunt me that I was a less than ideal parent?" The Skipper looked into Bruce's eyes. "Or that I was a no-show as a husband?" His gaze shifted to Kathy's. "Yes, my spirit reflects that I would do it better if I had the opportunity; but the eyes of my heart know that God has changed me into a more compassionate man. Listen again to Paul's words, and decide if you deserve a hug. 'Old things have passed away; behold, all things have become new.'"

"Secondly, Paul could give humble praise for the person he had become, and all that had been accomplished through him. That praise made it possible for him to say, 'By the grace of God I am what I am, and His grace toward me is not in vain.' That word, 'vain' means 'empty.' God's grace was full and overflowing, more than enough. And as a part of the overflow, Paul couldn't stop praising the Lord for all He had done. Even in a dark prison cell Paul was singing songs of praise. Doesn't that sound like a hug?"

"The surest test of a personal hug, of 'I am what I am by grace,' is involved thirdly, in heroic service. Paul said 'I labored more abundantly than they all, yet not I, but the grace of God which was with me.' Talk about a world-changer; through the Lord's leadership Paul had three successful missionary journeys in Asia and Europe, Jerusalem, Ephesus, Athens, Rome; the centers of human religions, commerce, philosophy, and power. All felt the impact of the transformed Pharisee who knew Christ's embrace, embraced himself, and was free to embrace from the least to the mighty."

Looking at his watch, the Skipper was surprised he had taken so long to tell this account. But there was one last part to share. "I just have to tell you about a man I had in one of the churches I served. I was the new appointment, the fresh pastor. He and his wife were less than regular in attendance, always sat in the back, and never stayed to greet any other folks. One Sunday I maneuvered myself after the benediction to intercept them at the back door. I introduced myself and gave her a little embrace. I turned toward him and he was as rigid as a concrete pillar. I hugged him anyway, and they hurried away. The next Sunday they were in attendance again, and we repeated that scenario. The following Sunday they waited in the line of folks who were leaving to get a hug, and ask me to visit in their home. That had never happened in the memory of the old-timers who remember such things."

"That man became an outstanding leader in the church. They became active in study, in fellowship, and generous in their support. He and I became such good friends that on one particular Sunday I felt like I had to disentangle myself from his embrace for fear someone might misunderstand him, or us. He was a great friend, and it all began when he allowed himself to be embraced, by me, but more importantly, by his Lord."

"There is a direct relationship between our daily experience of God's grace and our willingness to communicate His grace to other people. The more we accept ourselves as loved by God, the more we are free to let go of our fear of ourselves. Pretentious pride and false humility are both unnecessary. We can say with Paul, 'I am what I am by the grace of God.' God knows our failures and has forgiven us. He knows our potential and affirms us. We dare not do less for ourselves."

Late afternoon sun flooded the companionway, indicating time to think about supper. "Before we leave this topic, I'd like to ask you to write five or six times on the back of your sheet of paper the words, 'I am . . . .' Then finish the phrase. How do you see yourself?" The boat was very still for a couple of moments.

The Skipper finally said, "Well, I am . . . . thirsty for a tiny bit more of that dehydration protection." He was immediately joined by the other three.

They took their glasses up into the cockpit where Annie asked an important question. "Didn't Paul say that we are not to think of ourselves more highly than we ought?" The notion of self embrace was a bit foreign to her.

"The trick to understanding that is in the how much is 'more than we ought,'" the Skipper replied with a wry smile. "The challenge is that we get tangled up in false pride, or the effort of humility, which is often only compensation for inferiority thinking. I once heard an evangelistic speaker talking about race relations. He asked us a direct question, 'What right have you to belittle or despise someone whom God loves so deeply?' You can understand where that question might lead us if we were talking about ethnicity.

He was challenging us to confront some painful prejudice. It can just as easily be applied to our afternoon conversation, but maybe a little more tenderly." Annie nodded, grateful for more understanding.

"We can't say," he continued, "'Well, I know God loves me, but I can't stand myself.' That's sinful for it insults God and His love. I don't think we can dislike the creation without implying that we dislike the design, or don't much care for the Designer."

"Said another way, we could ask, 'What right have you to belittle or despise someone whom God has honored so highly?' We can read in 1 John, 'Consider the incredible love that the Father has shown us in allowing us to be called 'children of God!'"

"Or we could ask, 'What right have you to belittle or despise someone whom God has planned for so carefully?' If Jesus went to the cross to demonstrate God's gracious love for us, the issue is not that we think too highly of ourselves, but that we rarely see ourselves in the matchless light of God. It is an abrasive way to say a really wonderful truth."

Kathy was watching Art and Bonnie from Sea Deuces make their way towards *Dreamer*. Art was carrying a large frying pan, a bag of shrimp and a bottle of beer. She apologized for interrupting saying, "I'm sorry to break in like this, but I think supper is on its way." She pointed to their approaching friends.

"Good deal!" the Skipper exclaimed. He reached over to touch Annie's shoulder. "I hope that wasn't too abrasive. The challenge of not thinking of ourselves more highly than we ought to is balanced by not thinking of ourselves any less than God's unrepeatable joy and precious treasure. I think the latter is the greater offense."

She reached up to pat his hand. "There has never been any offense. I love the way you make us think and stretch our ideas." She paused for a moment before adding, "So, Skipper, how's your day going?" They all burst into laughter.

From the dock, Art commented, "That's the sound of a happy crew."

Bruce answered immediately, "It's a Happy Hour crew. Come aboard, I think we have another glass or two." As Kathy went below to fill the glasses with hospitality, she smiled, thinking how very much Bruce sounded like Norm. He said the same words with the same inflection. What a pleasant gift.

Moments later the six sat in the comfort of the cockpit, shaded from the late afternoon sun. Art asked, "Now tell us about this Leprechaun dust. Is it your own concoction?"

The Skipper smiled as he answered, "Yes, and it changes all the time. I usually make up a batch in the spring and have it on the boat instead of a bunch of small seasoning containers. I may even split the batch so I can use it on the barbeque at home."

Bonnie asked, "Is it an old family secret? It sounds like a very practical way to cook aboard ship."

"Nope, no secret, and I don't mind sharing it with others, because it is always changing just a bit."

"Will you tell us?" she was eager to know.

"Well sure, if you can remember SPOTOG PRA, you don't even need to write it down." The Skipper was chuckling with their confusion. "Here's a sheet of paper if you want to record it."

"I use a tablespoon measure for the nine seasonings: two each of sea salt, pepper, onion powder, thyme, oregano, and garlic powder (SPOTOG); then one tablespoon each of pepper (cayenne), rosemary (ground), and allspice (PRA). Sometimes I think more salt would be good, but it has a nice flavor balance this way. You can experiment."

"To cook the shrimp, I melt a cube of butter in the frying pan, pour in about a half a bottle of beer, drink the rest, and add a good splash of Worcestershire sauce. As soon as it starts to boil, in go the shrimp for two or three minutes, just until they start to turn pink. I usually try to get them out of the liquid promptly, or they will continue to cook until they are tough. Save the liquid to dip bread in, and have at it. I'm sure this is the easiest cooking I'll ever do."

Looking at Kathy, Bonnie asked, "Did you teach him to be a chef? Usually a wife is lucky if her man will help in the kitchen."

"I'm not . . . we're . . ." Kathy was surprised at how hot her face suddenly felt.

Annie came to her rescue. "Bruce and I are married. We're," she gestured to Kathy, "guests of the Skipper, whom I usually call 'Dad.'"

Once again Kathy felt flustered at wanting to clarify her relationship to the Skipper, but decided to leave it at "guest."

"I usually don't cook fish in the galley, unless I absolutely have to", the Skipper explained. "There are gas grills up near the shower house. I'll bet we have plenty of tokens."

The six friends watched the sunset from a picnic table. Their meal could hardly be more convenient, a large pan with butter, beer, shrimp and seasoning. They each had a fork to claim tender sweet shrimp, and a hunk of bread to dip in the sauce. Art said, "A meal this delicious should not be this fun to eat." The only difficult part of the meal was any significant conversation, each was too busy dipping and crooning the praises of the pan. They managed to get another bottle of Chardonnay, and another loaf of French bread from the store before it closed. Art said, "I remember the Bible story about Jesus changing the jars of water into wine. We did what most folks are guilty of doing; we drank the good stuff first and then went to the cheap. That was such a great wine that you shared with us."

Bonnie said, "I don't remember a more pleasant evening with such great food and friends." The wonder of vacation had her in its grip.

By the time the crew returned to *Dreamer*, there was a sky filled with stars. The moon had yet to make its grand entrance, so they could clearly see star formations and find Polaris. Kathy was sure it was time to turn in. However, the desire to be in his company for just a bit more was greater; perhaps an opportunity would present itself for another hug, or kiss.

Bruce was almost to the companionway when he turned and asked an uncharacteristic question. "Dad, I've been thinking a lot about the topic you shared with us this afternoon. It really sparked some stuff we've been talking about at home." He looked affectionately at Annie. "I'm wondering if, maybe for our evening devotion, you have some scripture to support those ideas?"

It was the perfect question for an extended answer. Kathy sat down next to the Skipper.

With a chuckle, the Skipper began, "Yeah, I wouldn't start something this big without a lot of back-up. I've just finished reading Maurice Wagner's book, 'The Sensations of Being Somebody.' In it he reminds us of three essential components of a healthy self-image. Now these are close, but not exact quotes: One, a sense of belonging, of being loved; two, a sense of worth and value; and three, a sense of being competent. He goes on to say that there are major factors at work for and against us over which we have no control. The genetics we inherit at birth, the ethnicity, gender, social and economic factors all affect our opportunities. Blessed indeed is the person who has significant others who love and accept, forgive, support, guide, and affirm them into a healthy self-image. His point is that at best, these are limited. We need Christ Jesus. There is something we can be, but will never be apart from him."

"Then he gives references to Jesus' relationship in these crucial components of our identity. For the sense of belonging he points us to the fact that one of the incredible dimensions of the Christian faith is that we belong to Christ. Unlike every other religion in the world, we abide in Him, and He dwells in us. John 15 says, *'I am the vine, you are the branches. Those who abide in me and I in them bear much fruit, because apart from me you can do nothing . . . As the Father has loved me, so I have loved you; abide in my love.'* " Bruce nodded in understanding and agreement.

"As for the sense of worth and value," the Skipper continued, "we have to know that we count, that we are a treasure to God. Can you believe that Jesus values us so much that even the cross is not too great a price to pay? In 1 Peter we can read these words from J.B. Phillips: *'You are a chosen generation, his royal priesthood, his holy nation, his peculiar people; all the old titles of God's people now belong to you. It is to you now to demonstrate the goodness of him who has called you out of darkness into his amazing light. In the past you were not 'a people' at all: now you are the people of God. In the past you had no experience of his mercy, but now it is intimately yours.'* And as for a sense of competence, just think of the power Jesus adds to our lives. With Paul we can say, *'I can do all things through him who strengthens me.'* "

"We may not get to choose the family of our birth, the time or place of it, but we have enormous control over the important factors of our sense of belonging, of being loved, our sense of worth and value, and allowing that relationship above all others to enhance our sense of competence." The Skipper was about to continue when he said, "Hey, I just thought of something you may never have seen. Brucer, will you take three of the empty wine bottles and fill them with water from the hose bib on the dock?" The other three were completely baffled by the sudden shift in the conversation.

Moments later Bruce returned with three bottles of water, and a puzzled expression.

The Skipper instructed them to take the water to the starboard side of the boat, away from the light, and sprinkle a bit of water out. To their amazement, where the water hit the surface of the harbor, illumination happened. A soft green shimmer accompanied the tiny splash. "Be careful not to throw in the bottle." All three were delighted to cast arches of water and be rewarded with tiny explosions of light.

Kathy asked in a whisper, "Is it reflections of the stars?"

Annie, much more excited, "It must be some sort of static charge in the water."

Bruce was more guarded. "I think it's . . . . magic!" He laughed at his own humor. "I think it has to do with fresh and salt water mixing."

"Actually" the Skipper finally explained, "it is phosphorescent alga. When disturbed or excited, it emits a glow. It's like a mini light show. Fun, eh?" Bruce was on his way to the dock for a water refill.

"Hey, look at this!" Bruce exclaimed with his fresh bottle. "You can almost write your name in lights."

Standing right behind him, Annie giggled, "Didn't you say you could do that in the snow?"

"Yeah, but not in lights," he shot back. They all were like children with a new toy.

Finally the Skipper said that in respect for the neighbors, they might want to quiet down a bit; but tomorrow night there would be no neighbors, and plenty of opportunity to experience the summer alga. "How about an evening devotion before we turn in?"

When they were seated in the cockpit, the Skipper said, "There's a little fellowship song that is just right for just now. Sung to the tune Swing Low, it goes, 'God's love, is deep within me, ever satisfying my soul (repeat)'" They sang it together, 'God's Word . . . God's Joy . . . God's Peace . . .' The drapes of night pulled around *Dreamer*, quietly embracing them all.

"Bruce, what was a highlight for you today?" the Skipper asked.

"I think," he paused to make sure, "It was sprinting with the deer. One of them was playfully leaping, and passed me, almost over my head." He chuckled with the memory.

"Annie?"

"There have been a whole bunch of highlights. I'm still loving the Bible study discussions, and getting the shrimp from potty mouth Brian." She also paused to consider, "But the best was probably the lookout at the top of the entrance. That was magnificent."

Bruce gave her a little elbow shot for giving three answers.

"Kathy, what has been your highlight?"

"Can't I have three like Annie?" Her little chuckle was a delight to them all. "My highlight is spending special time with you." She looked lightly at the Skipper, and then quickly at Annie and Bruce. "This is one of those experiences that will become larger than life for me."

The boat was motionless and silent for a moment before the Skipper shared his highlight. "I think I am so very delighted at how enthused you all are to be on this trip. When we came in the entrance we were all spellbound, and that is just the way it should be. We were in the presence of mystery!"

"Here's a prayer before we release this day." They bowed as he prayed, "Gracious Lord, grant us a gentle night's rest, a clear dawning, followed by a cool morning. Let us find a warm noonday, a golden sunset, and a starlit night. And if clouds should cross our skies, grant us your sure faith to look for the silver lining. We are grateful for this day and eager for tomorrow. In Jesus' name we pray this. Amen."

As the others began to make their way below, Kathy said she thought she would walk up to the shower house one more time. She thought that Norm might join her for a stroll; instead Annie said she would come along.

They were quiet for a bit as they started up the dock, thinking about what to say first. Finally Annie whispered, "Did we interrupt a kiss this afternoon?" She was afraid the question was too bold, and really none of her business. "I'm not prying," she touched Kathy's shoulder, "I'm just really happy if that is the case. Bruce and I are glad for you, and for the Skipper, for Norm." They walked on in silence.

Finally, Kathy said, "Yes, my heart was racing. I'm not sure how to feel. I love his attention, and gentleness, but I'm terrified it means something more. I'm glad you guys came back when you did."

"We were going to turn around, and come back later." Once again Annie stroked Kathy's shoulder in an effort to clear any confusion.

"No, no," Kathy protested. "You guys mustn't let this become an agenda issue. I just want to go along with the trip, and not let romance get in the way." She shook her head for emphasis.

"But maybe," Annie said with a warm smile, "this is the main reason we are here. It could be just like our first trip on *Dreamer*. That was meant to help Bruce and me get through some problems."

Kathy didn't want to reveal the tumbling emotions going on within her, so she answered with more difficulty, and not a little deception, "You know that I really like him, but not romantically. I just can't accept that idea." Again she shook her head to make the point.

Annie realized there were some strong conflicts going on in Kathy's heart, so she just leaned against her friend in understanding. They were pretty quiet all the way back to the boat, each reflecting on the unspoken part of their conversation.

Oh, good the night.

The lone plaintive cry of a seagull woke the crew. It was still pretty dark. A second time the gull's call echoed across the marina.

Norm thought, "I'm sure I can go back to sleep, if it just doesn't shout again."

Annie thought, "If I don't move, Bruce won't know I'm awake."

Bruce thought, "I wonder if there are fresh pastries in the long house?"

Kathy thought, "I wonder why I was afraid to tell Annie about my feelings. Is it true that I am not interested in matters romantic? Is it that I'm afraid to be hurt like that again?" She was too far from sleep to turn off her thoughts. Yesterday's meditation came to mind, '*In God's unqualified acceptance of me, I embrace myself as worthy of my own affirmation and encouragement.*' "Oh I want that to be true!" she whispered to herself. The boat was absolutely still, with all those thoughts swirling within it.

After a while, she heard Bruce's hushed voice. "'Morning Dad. Did that seagull wake you, too? It sounded like it was right outside our hatch."

The Skipper grinned. "I think he must be the duty rooster whose job it is to wake up the farm." After a moment he added, "I'm going up to shower, but I have a couple extra tokens. I'll leave them on the table. You might see if Annie or Kathy needs one, otherwise let's make sure we give these back to Sean as a gratuity. They won't do us any good after this morning."

Kathy heard the companionway hatch open, and *Dreamer* gently rock as the Skipper left. She loved this boat, and being here with the crew.

By the time they were all dressed and groomed, the sky was a brilliant reflection of the rising sun, even though no warming rays had reached *Dreamer*. The dew on the cockpit seats made the salon an attractive alternative for morning devotions. When everyone had either a cup of fresh coffee or a Crystal Light, Kathy said, "I love singing in the morning. Can we sing another fellowship song?" The Skipper was already handing out the sheet for day 4.

Day 4.)

Sung to the tune "O Tannenbaum":

"We thank thee, Lord, for daily bread,
And all thy mercies 'round us spread.

We thank thee for thy love and care,
For guidance in our daily prayer.
For Christian friends, faithful, true.
For love's unfinished work to do.
In all we think and do and say,
Thy Kingdom come in us today."

Morning Prayer:

Lord, we are rested, and revived by your goodness. Thank you! You have put the whole world together beautifully and placed us in it. We believe with our whole heart that you want to say something to us today, and through us today. We ask that the serenity of your peace fall gently, softly, sweetly, and beautifully upon our mind today. Even now, we are ready to listen, and eager to move ahead with dynamic faith. Lead us through this day, Lord, in Jesus' name we ask it. Amen.

Meditation: repeat three times.

What I fear in others, I first fear in myself. In God's unqualified acceptance of me, I embrace myself as worthy of my own affirmation and encouragement.

2Timothy 1:6—7

Discussion:

God's gifts:
A sound mind
A spirit of love
A spirit of power

Conclusion: repeat three times:

When I feel inadequate to meet life's opportunities, I will pray for God's Holy Spirit for guidance, love, and power. I am equipped to be successful.

When they had finished, the Skipper said, "I have one more item before we head up to the long house for breakfast. The theme for today is 'gifts,' so it seems appropriate for us to each get one." He opened a small bag with envelopes bearing each person's name. Deliberately he began with Bruce. "Here is yours, Bubba. Don't open it yet." Then Annie and Kathy; finally he had one for himself. "I found a shop in Campbell River that had Coastal People art. These seemed like appropriate tokens of our trip together. Now, let's look at them."

In each envelope there was an image of a creature carved from wood and polished. Bruce had an Orca on a leather string necklace. Annie had an eagle, on a fine silver chain. Kathy's leaping deer was framed in a graceful oval, also on a silver chain. The Skipper's gift was a detailed mask of a man, on a leather string like Bruce's. Each person admired their gift with appreciation, wondering if there was a message in the choice.

Sensing the possibility of confusion, the Skipper explained, "I wanted to choose different gifts for each of us, so we would remember how special and unique we each are. We haven't seen any Orca. They are, however, great symbols of the Northwest. The eagles have been entertaining, and when we fed the deer crackers, I was delighted with your reaction, Sweetie. I had no idea when I first saw the deer how special that would be. I hope you like the gift, and understand the motivation. It will be more evident when we get to the discussion this afternoon."

Bruce asked, "Dad, was there a reason you chose a mask?"

"Well, no big reason, Buddy. I had a bunch of choices, and by the way, the shop-keeper said you could come back when we get in, and exchange yours for something you would rather have. I liked the Raven, which is the symbol Coastal People used for the Creator; I liked the otter, the seals, and a gorgeous bear. But the mask was used in their celebrations. It was always a happy thing, even if it didn't always look happy. I just liked the idea." He looked at Kathy.

Together, the other three declared how grateful they were for their unique gift, and how insightful the choice. Kathy said, "I wouldn't think of exchanging mine. I love it!" Both Bruce and Annie nodded in agreement. It was time for breakfast.

Stacks of pancakes, a walk in the meadow with the deer, and the bright morning sun made it a memorable beginning to the day. Finally, one last stop at the store to get just a few more things to complete their menus, left them with about three hours of ebbing tide. It was time to be on their way.

As usual Bruce was at the spring line, and the girls were in the cockpit, watching the action. Instead of stepping aboard with the stern line, the Skipper asked Bruce to release his. "We've got a bit of breeze blowing us onto the dock, so I can give us a little help maneuvering." He pulled the stern line in; *Dreamer*'s nose eased away from the dock, then he came aboard, put her in gear and eased forward. Smoothly they were away without more than a brush of the dock. "Oh, a sailor's life's for me!" the Skipper sang as they turned further toward the harbor entrance.

"There's going to be a minus tide of two and a half feet by noon, so keep a watch for rocks that we haven't met yet, eh?" Bruce moved forward to keep an eye on their progress.

Annie had a question, "Norm, I've been wondering about the name of these islands. Yesterday we were at Quadra, and this is Cortes; those don't sound like Native American names. Do you know why?"

"If you will go down to the nav station," the Skipper answered, "you'll find a book of charts called 'Exploring Puget Sound and British Columbia.' I was reading about Tenedos Bay, where we'll be tonight. It really is interesting."

When she returned with the book, the Skipper advised, "It clearly states that these pages are not for navigation, and do not take the place of U.S. Coast Guard charts, but they are good enough guides for roaming around. I think I was on page 75, which will show where we are going to be at anchor tonight." Annie opened the cockpit table so she could examine the pages, and Kathy moved over beside her.

"Do you see a little island named 'Kinghorn'?" When she nodded, pointing it out to Kathy, he went on, "Follow the line up the page and see how many explorer boats there were in here the summer of 1792, both British and Spanish. They seemed to have a cordial respect for each other and shared hospitalities." Both Annie and Kathy nodded, and kept reading.

"Now look over to the right edge of that page and see why this place is called 'Desolation Sound.'"

"Hey Brucie, listen to this," Annie chuckled. "'Regarding the general vicinity', Captain Vancouver writes: 'this area afforded not a single prospect that was pleasing to the eye, the smallest recreation on shore, no animal nor vegetable food, excepting a very scanty proportion of those eatables already described, and of which the adjacent country was soon exhausted, after our arrival . . . whence the place obtained the name of DESOLATION SOUND: where our time would have passed infinitely more heavily, had it not been relieved by the agreeable society of our Spanish friends.' It looks like that was written on June 27, 1792! Wow! That is fascinating!" She continued to study other entries in the book.

"Hey listen to this," Annie said with fresh interest. She looked up to see who might be her audience, and saw the entrance to the harbor approaching. She closed the book, saying, "It will wait until later. I love this place!"

The fathometer indicated 22 feet, but the Skipper thought there were more rocks showing than when they had first arrived. He slowed *Dreamer* just in case. There was a cathedral stillness in the gorge as they exited. No one spoke, but everyone was filled with exclamations.

They watched the sheer rock wall slide past them, shadows of cracks and crevices, with only a sliver of blue sky high above. All too soon, *Dreamer* was through the gorge, and into open water, and the crew could breathe a sigh of relief, or farewell. "Bruce, would you be kind enough to haul the main?" the Skipper asked. "With this fresh breeze, we might as well conserve our fuel," The white wing of Dacron was gliding up the mast. When it was fully hoisted, the Skipper loosened the furler line and gave the port sheet a big tug. Slowly at first, then with a big "thump" the jib set on the port side. Carefully he trimmed the sheet until *Dreamer* leaned with the fresh power. He pressed the red shut off button, and the diesel hushed to silence. It was that magic moment of being in league with the wind.

Kathy asked, as she watched the jib sheet being trimmed, "Is that as tough to do as it looks?" She hesitated before going on. "Do you think I could be strong enough to crank it in?"

"Come over and give it a try," the Skipper invited. When she was standing beside him, he explained, "This is a self-tailing winch. You need not worry about cleating the sheet after you trim it in." Looking at her listening face, he felt another wave of affection. To demonstrate the winch, he tugged the sheet out of the groove at the top, and using his other hand as a brake against the barrel of the winch; he eased out a couple feet of line. Then, wrapping the sheet back in the self-tailing groove, he offered her the winch handle. "It's a two speed winch, so if you crank it clockwise, it will take in line more quickly. Crank it counter-clockwise when there is more power on the line, or when you want to trim slowly and carefully. Try counter clockwise first."

She was surprised at how smoothly she was able to crank in a few inches of sheet. When she tried the clockwise direction, however, she found it much more difficult, even when she used both hands. She went back to her successful side saying, "Tell me when it's tight enough." She was amazed at the tension on the line, and equally amazed that the Skipper didn't tell her it was trimmed enough. She cranked a couple more turns, looked at him, and cranked a couple more slowly. Finally, he said, "That looks pretty good. We'll be on this broad reach for about a half an hour and then jibe at the buoy. Would you like to steer?"

Kathy's head bobbed with just a hint of apprehension. Annie was quick to say, "They will be right here to help if you get too worried. I did a pretty good job the first time, until I almost put us on the rocks." She giggled in remembrance.

The Skipper also remembered the moment, and answered, "You did fine, and we were not real close to the rocks. It just seemed closer because you thought we were in an emergency. It was fine."

Kathy had moved to the wheel, peering forward along their planned line. The Skipper pointed to a distant headland. "There is a buoy just to the right of that point. Stay to the west of it." When Kathy raised a frown questioning what that meant, he added, "Just stay to the right of it. There are shallow rocks between the point and that buoy." She nodded in understanding. "Ms. Swanson has the helm," he called in his attempt to sound like a ship of the line. She wondered if he was always this playful.

"Hey, Bud," Annie said to Bruce, "come and read this account with me. It says that the explorers found a fishing village near here with large fish drying racks; they called them 'stages'. While they were looking around the village, which must have been deserted, they were attacked by fleas. It was so bad that some of the men jumped in the water to drown the buggers. Nothing got rid of them short of boiling their clothes. This is so cool."

Bruce joined Annie at the table, but said, "If you tell me what you are reading, I don't need to read it myself. I get the 'condensed version', which is a good thing."

Dreamer danced across the calm water on a beam reach with a fresh breeze. She was slicing through the bright summer morning, equal to the task at hand.

"I'm going below for a glass of Crystal Light. Can I get anything for you guys?" His eyes caught Kathy's, and she smiled. How could even a polite offer carry such strong meaning she wondered?

The rest of the morning was textbook sailing; 'hours of boredom punctuated by moments of panic.' Actually, there was none of either. Kathy was on the helm until the Sutil Point buoy, then Bruce took over. They jibed the sails over to the starboard side, and at the Twin Islands they trimmed a bit more north to affect a track that would take them straight into Tenedos Bay. They would arrive by 1 p.m. unless they chose to dally along the way.

CHAPTER 5:
TENEDOS BAY,
PRIDEAUX HAVEN
Refilling our emptiness

P rideaux Haven Marine Park has several available anchorages, but none as protected or accessible as Tenedos Bay. Annie and Kathy had switched sides of the cockpit so they could read the map and look at the indicated land referenced. They had properly identified Sarah Point to starboard and Kinghorn Island to port. "That one is Zephine Head, I think," Annie directed. She was feeling like a navigator with proper information.

As *Dreamer* eased into the wind shadow of Redonda Island, the Skipper said to Bruce, "Looks like we have used all the wind this morning. Let's roll 'em up." He began to crank in the jib with the furler. By the time it was a tidy roll on the forestay, Bruce was lowering the main. Kathy smiled as she watched the engine start-up procedure. She silently said to herself, "Out of gear," Norm's hand made certain the shifter was in neutral; "Little bit of throttle," the red knob was pressed forward. "Turn the key halfway, and count to ten," there was a bit of a pause, "then turn it all the way." The engine throbbed to life pulling *Dreamer* back on course. Kathy's smile was one of satisfaction. She understood a vital part of the operation of the boat.

Annie was still looking at the chart. "Is that Mink Island?" she asked the Skipper. When he assured her that it was, she continued, "Then that little dock to starboard must be Portage Cove." It was fun to be able to read the chart and see their location.

As they approached the small bay ahead of them, the Skipper said, "This area is called 'Prideaux Haven Marine Park.' There is good anchorage on both sides of this peninsula, but the most calm, and least used, is the back part of Tenedos Bay." They could only see one boat at anchor, and it was at the front.

"Brucer, would you flake out about seventy five feet of chain with the anchor? Remember, there's a red link every twenty five feet. We'll drop the anchor in about fifteen feet of depth, and since the tide still has about four hours of flood, we'll have plenty of rode out." Both girls looked at him with the same question.

"What road do we have?" Kathy asked. Annie quickly nodded.

This time Bruce answered their question. "All the stuff from the anchor to the boat is called 'rode.'" He even spelled it for them. "Some boats use chain, some use a combination of chain and rope, but it is all called 'anchor rode.'" He smiled at his nautical terminology.

The Skipper added, "When we lower the anchor, we use five times as much chain as the depth we are in so the anchor will hold securely. We will be our own snug little island for the night." *Dreamer* slowed to 'no wake.'

Kathy asked if there were any deck jobs that needed attention as they approached the anchorage. "Thanks for asking," the Skipper said with appreciation. "Bruce will lower the anchor, and if you would like to go up on the bow with him and point at the anchor chain as it's going out, I can keep us in alignment. That would be a big help." Gladly, she went out onto the bow for a real helpful task.

They were slowed to barely holding steerage. The Skipper took one more look all around to be sure they were at least two hundred feet from any rocks or shallow challenge. He brought *Dreamer* to a full stop, then said, "O.K. Bruce, lower the anchor to the first red link. Don't drop it, just lower quickly." He put the boat in reverse with just a gentle nudge, then neutral. As soon as the anchor was on the bottom, he asked Bruce to pay out the rest of the chain. *Dreamer* eased back a bit more; Kathy pointed straight off the bow at the anchor rode. They all felt the anchor set as the chain became taut and the boat rested still and easy. The Skipper gave one more nudge to make sure they were secure. "Who wants a Molson?"

The sandwiches and chips were gone in a blink; the glasses were emptied almost as fast. Bruce said he and Annie would like to take the dinghy over to the shore and do some exploring. "Just be cautious with pulling out over barnacles. They will cut right through the inflatable," the Skipper advised. Pointing to the nearby corner of the bay, he suggested, "There is a gravel beach over there. I think that would be a safe spot." Bruce was already lowering the dinghy and setting in the oars. "Here are a couple lifejackets too. Do you want any fishing gear?"

Bruce thought about it for a minute, then answered, "No, we can come back if we need that. We won't be gone long, or far." His big grin suggested there might have been more to that sentence that just got cut off.

Kathy watched the inflatable pull away toward the beach. "Everything just seems to work so easy," she reflected. "Is it always like this?"

"Well no," Norm answered. "Sometimes we have lots of fun." He stood beside her watching the oars move rhythmically. "So, Kathy, how's your day goin'? Are you having as much fun as it seems you are?" He put his arm around her waist.

"I thought it would be a challenge with you guys, but this is so much more than I expected. Yes, I'm enjoying every minute." She pressed against him. "Would you like another half a Molson? I'll pour."

When she returned to the cockpit, he met her before she could be seated. Putting his arms around her, he said softly, "I've wanted to kiss you since we were interrupted yesterday. In fact, I've wanted to kiss you ever so much on this trip. It must be the sailor in me trying to get out." Without waiting for more conversation, she pressed her lips to his; it was a long, lingering, wonderful kiss.

"Me too," was all she said. They sat down out of the sun, watching Bruce and Annie make their way along the shore, exploring. Their stirred emotions were eager for more of the other.

"Sweetie," Norm began a conversation he had rehearsed several different ways, "can we have a serious conversation?" Kathy looked into his direct gaze, "Of course."

He said, "This trip is a dream come true for me, too. I can't tell you how glad I am that you seem comfortable and interested in *Dreamer*." Without waiting for her to say anything about that, he continued, "We've been such good friends since Victoria. I don't know that I have ever experienced such a comfortable and satisfying friendship with a woman." They exchanged reflections on their happy relationship.

Finally he said, "I think you want something deeper than this, and I do too. I want us to be lovers." She held her breath while a shudder ran through her. He reached over to hold her hand. "You are tender and full of kindness. You are happy and quick to laugh. You have a great love of the Lord, all of which make me want to share my life with you. I want us to be together, always."

Before he could go on, she eased her hand out of his. "I want to show you something," she said, going below. When she returned she had a small paper. She unfolded it and said, "I wrote this last Christmas. Do you remember asking the congregation to write their gratitude to God for the greatest gift? I started in a different direction. This is something I wrote, thinking of you." Tears began to fill her eyes.

She read aloud, "I believe that I was meant to awaken every morning to thoughts of you." She looked into his blue eyes, then went on, "I believe that each day holds the promise of love's expression." She reached for his hand, squeezing it strongly. "I believe that only you hold the promise of all my tomorrows." Her chin quivered with emotion. Taking a deep breath, she read quietly, "I believe that my only purpose for all my tomorrows is to love and be loved by you, everything else is commentary." Looking at him directly, she whispered, "I wrote that six months ago, and my heart has only become filled more by those thoughts." She sighed deeply, still holding his affectionate gaze. "Yes, I want us to be lovers, too." She studied his face, then the sun drenched harbor, the distant rocks and trees, a soaring bird, and finally back to his eyes.

She said softly, "I remember a part of a sermon you preached, in which you said, 'Think about what you are about to do, and think about the consequences. Remember that when you choose the action, you are also choosing all the things that result from that action.' You told us to 'live our lives based on God's Love, and our own best intentions, because each action places us in a position to select the exact consequences that we wish to bring about.'" Her smile was genuine, she added a question, "Does it irritate you when I remember what you have said in a sermon?" Her smile was growing, and becoming playful. "You don't want to guess what my intentions were, and are."

Now it was Norm's turn to feel the rush of emotions. "My whole life has been spent controlling my heart," he said. "I have always guarded against careless actions. To do anything that would be less than honoring to you, or God, or embarrassing and problematic to the church, would be horrible to me, all of which doesn't change my heart's desire for you. It means that I need you as my partner," he took a deep breath, "in marriage. Kathy will you be my wife?" The air around them was warm and soft, still as a dream.

She began to weep, saying "Oh my, I've imagined this moment and it was never this wonderful." She rose to kiss him gently. "What would that be like?" She blushed adding, "I mean, how would that work?" Her voice trembled as she became more flustered, "Oh I don't know what to say. I can't say 'No,' but how can I say 'Yes' without talking with Scott and Jenny, and Mom?" Finally, she asked, "Have you thought about the details of a marriage?"

He almost burst into laughter, partly because of her turmoil, and partly because of his nervous energy. "Actually, no. Do you mean the details of where would we live?"

She shook her head. "No, I'm thinking of the complications of blending our families. Do you really want to become a parent to an eleven and a nine year old?"

Norm smiled gently, saying, "Those weren't my first concerns. But I do believe I'm up for the challenge. This is almost as new to me as it is to you. I'm thinking of the details like where we could be married, and when. We could be married at St. Andrew's; the congregation would love that. Or we could go to Hawaii next January and have a wedding on the beach. I think success is as simple as making a plan, and going for it. I'm just really glad we can talk about it like this. It is a sudden and totally new idea, but I welcome it. Do you?"

Kathy could see Bruce and Annie getting back into the dinghy. "Very much, I do," she sighed, "but here come the guys." She moved into Norm's arms for another kiss. Then she said a bit breathlessly, "Let's not mention this to them." Her look was unflinching. "Please? It's all so sudden, and such a huge decision. Please?" She sat back in the shade of the dodger and watched the approaching dinghy, but her attention was elsewhere.

Bruce handed the dinghy painter to the Skipper. "Annie needed more privacy than the bushes, and I wonder if there is an unclaimed Molson."

Over her shoulder, Annie said, "I wasn't going to take out an ad on Craig's List for everyone to know." She continued below toward the head.

Bruce made a grimace, realizing that he had stepped on Annie's feelings. "Maybe I should share some of my refreshment with her to apologize." He snapped the mooring clips onto *Dreamer*'s transom, and scrambled aboard. Together they pulled the inflatable back up into its secure position.

"We saw lots of great stuff over there," Bruce reported. "But nothing that looked like an old village site. I thought there might be some remnants of houses."

"I suppose this might have been a temporary or summer spot for them," the Skipper said thoughtfully. "There isn't enough protection from winter weather. They were probably only here to catch salmon, and harvest shellfish."

"Yeah, there are piles of oyster shells everywhere, and we could see tons of live ones, hanging on the rocks a little under water."

"By low tide," the Skipper nodded, "there will be a band of oysters three or four feet deep all along the rocks."

Bruce's appetite was suddenly interested. "Can we get some to eat?" Looking at Kathy he asked, "Do you like oysters?"

With a weak shrug, she answered, "Well, I'm not fond of the texture or taste, but if they are just little ones, real little, I would try some." Her voice faded away at the end of that sentence because what she was thinking was that Bruce might be her son-in-law! That seemed weird!

The Skipper reminded Bruce of the old adage of picking oysters only in months with an "r." "That probably protects us from bacteria that blooms in warm summer months. I don't think I've heard of anyone getting sick from shellfish taken up here though. If it's worth the effort, give it a shot."

Annie joined them in the cockpit. "I'm sorry I snapped at you," she apologized to Bruce. "It was pretty urgent. But everything is fine now. Did I miss anything?" She accepted his peace-offering of a share of his Molson.

The Skipper chuckled, "I think you took care of the most important thing." After a look around their quiet anchorage, he asked, "What would you like to do before supper? We could explore some more." His eyes found Kathy's. "We could have our discussion about gifts, or we could just sit here and drink in this marvelous place."

Bruce asked, "Did you say you had a special card game for us this evening?"

"Yeah, have you ever played 31?" he asked. When the other three shook their head, the Skipper explained, "It is a favorite because the winner is excused from any galley duty the next day. We'll go over the rules later."

Kathy spoke up. "I'm interested in the discussion of the gifts," which was suggestion enough for the others to agree.

When refreshments were poured and notebooks collected, the Skipper said, "I remember a Sunday School teacher who once asked a boy in her class if he had trouble hearing. The lad answered that he could hear fine, but he had trouble listening. That's a good point for us to begin."

"We like to be told that we are skilled, talented, efficient, or competent. We like to hear that we are a success in our challenges. I remember a lecture in seminary by Dr. Albert Outler, one of the heroes emeritus. He began by telling us he was impressed with the level of accomplishment represented in our graduating class, the awards won, and the academic achievement that was unequalled. He asked us if we had heard of the 'Peter Principle,' which is the theory that people rise in life to the level of their incompetence. It is a sad truth that many rise to a level beyond their abilities and bungle the opportunities they are given. Then he gave us his 'Outler Principle,' which declares that as Christians, we should constantly be rising to the level of our human inadequacy, for only then can we discover the amazing gift of Christ's adequacy. He then shared the secret of how to receive that supernatural power: (1) a total surrender of our challenges; they are his not ours; (2) an invitation for Christ to live in us; (3) an intimate dependent relationship with him, and; (4) a willingness to give him the glory when we surpass our own abilities or adequacy."

"That was a huge lecture for me. It has helped me deal with a host of fears and feelings through the years, as I was challenged to do the impossible. It has helped me apply scripture in a special way. Bruce would you mind reading from the page I've marked? They are words written to Timothy to help him overcome feelings of fear of inadequacy. Paul gives him these words to encourage and inspire his protégé to rise above his feelings."

Bruce read: "2 Timothy 1: 6: '*Therefore I remind you to stir up the gift of God which is in you through the laying on of my hands.*'" Looking up, Bruce asked, "What was the gift?"

The Skipper answered, "In Galatians, Paul writes, '*And because you are sons, God has sent forth the Spirit of his Son into your hearts . . .*' The Spirit of Christ has set a fire of vision, and conviction, burning in Timothy. Fellowship with Paul, Silas, and Luke had kept that flame ablaze as they traveled together, and encouraged each other in the ministry of spreading the gospel. But now alone in Ephesus, Timothy needed to rekindle something that was fading. Paul didn't tell him to try harder, or not worry, or pray more fervently. Instead, Paul told him to get back to the source of his inner power."

"Paul's advice to Timothy applies to us as well because we have a part in fighting off the fears that keep us from being on-fire followers. We can allow the fire of Christ's spirit to be smothered with neglect or resistance. I heard a colorful description of Paul's admonition by Clarence Jordan, who said, 'I'm reminding you to shake the ashes off the God-given fire that's within you.' In other words, shake the grate until the embers are exposed; use the poker to push the coals together; then use the billows to blow life back into those flames."

"Paul next reminds Timothy that God is not the source of fear of any kind, including the fear that comes from feelings of timidity or inadequacy. Bud, read verse 7 for us."

Bruce was listening to his dad so intently that he jumped at the suggestion to read more. After a tiny hesitation, his husky voice read, "*God has not given us a spirit of timidity but a spirit of power and love and self-control.*" Bruce looked at his dad and asked, "Is that what you want?"

"It is, and since Paul often puts the key word last after the conjunction 'and' I'd like to take just a tiny bit more time to look at these gifts in the order that they are usually given in our experience. A sound mind precedes the ability to love." He couldn't keep from looking into Kathy's eyes. "The commitment to love leads us to ask for spiritual power."

Bruce was completely into the conversation; he interrupted, "Do you mean this is a psychological gift, a mental health sort of thing?"

"At base, yes, but it is very much more. The Greek word that Paul used is descriptive of a Spirit-anointed, or consecrated mind, a disciplined mind. It's a mind capable of thinking Christ's thoughts, and seeing the potential of people and situations the way he does. In a sound mind the powers of imagination are whole and healthy, focused on the Lord's vision for the specific opportunities of life. A Christ inspired sound mind lifts our focus beyond what we can do in our own strength and ability to what the Lord wants to do through us."

"Let's face it. We need the Lord's help in every relationship." His eyes once again found Kathy's. "In each situation and problem, where life dishes out challenge beyond us, we need divine assistance. Wherever we feel inadequate—in marriage, with our families, on the job, in our opportunities to share our faith, and in the impossible tasks the Lord has given us to do—we need to confess, 'Lord I can't make this on my own. This is beyond me.'"

"To such a prayer I believe his response would be, 'Good! You were never meant to be adequate on your own. Together we can think this through. I can reveal my strategy, and show you how you can accomplish it with my strength.' A sound mind means we don't need to thrash about with uncertainty. The Lord will guide and provide, if we shake the ashes off our sound mind." The other three were listening carefully to information that would be vitally important to each of them.

The Skipper paused as though reflecting on notes or choosing his next phrase. Finally he said, "A sound mind is able to conceive, and transmit to our emotions, the assurance that we are loved by the Lord. It is not only information we know, but we have an enabling feeling of being loved. Christ's spirit of love flows into and through us. Most of the challenges of life that make us feel inadequate are those in which we are called to love beyond our human ability." When he noticed Annie's frown, he added, "Think of the people you find it difficult to love as much as they need to be loved. Reflect on the people who have hurt you whom you find it difficult, maybe impossible, to forgive. Focus on the people who demand more of your time and resources than you feel capable of giving. Or consider the situations in which you need to give yourself sacrificially and want to pull back. Again we want to protest, 'Too much Lord, the needs of people are greater than I can meet!'"

"And yet, the great need in the world is for Christians with passion, which is Christ's intense love burning in us for people and human suffering. I think it was John Henry Jowett a great preacher from the last century, who wrote, 'The gospel of the broken heart demands the ministry of the bleeding heart . . . as soon as we cease to bleed, we cease to bless . . . we can never heal the needs we do not feel. Tearless hearts can never be the heralds of Christ's passion.'" Again he paused. The late afternoon shadows were massaging the harbor into perfect stillness.

"I think," the Skipper said with a heavy voice, "a passion for the needs of people, a broken and bleeding heart really makes us feel inadequate. To see the suffering and realize what love demands, creates the most desperate sense of insufficiency. That's why a sound mind capable of thinking with the Savior's thoughts, and feeling with his heart the need for love for the people around us, leads us to accept the third of the gifts Paul listed for Timothy in his antidote to the fear of inadequacy." Bruce glanced back at the open Bible in front of him, rereading the words he had shared.

"Paul then tells Timothy that the Christian is not only to have the Spirit of a sound mind, and the Spirit of love, but also the Spirit of power. The Greek word he uses here for power is the root from which we get the word 'dynamite!' It is an enabling and dynamic power. We can be assured that the Lord never calls us to do anything for which he is not willing to provide the power."

"One of my favorite benedictions is Paul's words to the Ephesians. I'll bet you will recall hearing them. *'Now to him who is able to do exceedingly abundant above all that we ask or think, according to the power that is at work in us, to him be glory in the church by Christ Jesus to all generations, forever and ever. Amen.'* The key phrase there is 'according to the power that works in us.' As we experience that power, and learn to depend upon it, we will be free of the fear feelings or the sense of inadequacy."

"Let me ask you one last question. How would you feel if you knew you were given the gift of a sound mind that could think as Christ thought and see the solutions to our problems the way he sees them. How would you feel if you were certain that you had been given the capacity to love beyond our human limitations, and possessed the gift of strength beyond our own energies? It's what Christ does through us, not what we are able to do for him, that accomplishes lasting results. I can think of one thing you would not feel with those gracious gifts; you would not feel afraid."

Two Grebes were slowly making their way around the end of the harbor, occasionally singing their little two-part song and diving for supper. On the other side of the anchorage a solitary loon floated as still as if it were moored there.

Sensing that their discussion was concluded, Kathy was ready to ask for a song. "Have you got a favorite song we can sing here in the wilderness?" She giggled at her own humor.

"I'll bet you know this one," the Skipper answered, now sure that it was over, but not complete. He began a familiar praise song:

Father, I adore you. Lay my life before you.

How I love you.

Jesus, I adore you. Lay my life before you.
How I love you
Spirit, I adore you. Lay my life before you.
How I love you.

By the time they had started the song for the second time, they were singing in a round. How fun!

Finally, they were just sitting quietly in the cockpit, each with their own reflective thoughts. Bruce asked, "Are there plans for supper? I'd be glad to help." Then smirking a bit, he added, "Since I intend to win at the card game later, and have a free pass from the galley tomorrow. Actually, Annie and I thought we would take another trip to the beach and wander around a little more."

The Skipper glanced at Kathy, but answered, "I thought we would throw a quick salad together with that smoked salmon in the refrigerator, and some bread from the long house this morning. Then you guys could go over, after doing the dishes." There was good natured hooting from all four. But it was an acceptable plan.

Kathy eventually watched the dinghy rowing toward the gravel beach in the corner. She and the Skipper were finishing the glass of white wine they had enjoyed with the salad. "I'm not sure we had a chance to finish our chat this afternoon," she began, eager to explain a bit more. "I'd like to say a little more about my hesitation." She was feeling butterflies. "I don't think I have ever been in such an intimate situation with a man I want so much, and feel so confused about it."

"Does that trouble you?" he asked. When she gave a small nod he went on. "Does it trouble you that this situation is so intimate, or that you are feeling desire, or that you are confused?"

"Well," she began a bit embarrassed, "Greg wasn't very romantic, and he didn't care where we spent the honeymoon, since it was only the weekend after we got married. We were at Ocean Shores." She raised an eyebrow with a smirk. "This, on the other hand is exotic, and so very private. Yes, it is very intimate. I . . ." she hesitated searching for the right expression. "I'm uneasy with the jumble of feelings within me. I'm afraid of . . ." Finally, she just shook her head.

"Are you uneasy because you don't trust me, or is it that you feel vulnerable, and maybe don't trust yourself?" Norm asked gently.

"To tell you the truth, I feel like that animal on Dr. Doolittle; do you remember the 'Push-Me-Pull-You?' It didn't know which way it was going. That's me." Kathy had a sweet smile, but her eyes were filled with conflict.

"I hope you can enjoy the good part, and know that I will protect you from the other," the Skipper finally said. "Expressions of affections like hugs and kisses are wonderful, and will lead to nothing more, right now, I pledge you. I will be your champion in protecting us from embarrassment or deception, because I care for you, more every moment. You are a precious treasure to me, Kathy, and I will make sure that nothing I do will tarnish that." He leaned over to her; she thought he was going to give her a kiss, instead he pressed his forehead against her's, and said, "I am not afraid of the feelings you cause in me. In fact, I love them; it has been a long time since I felt this delicious, strong attraction for someone. Because this is so important to us, I will be all the more responsible with our feelings." Then he gave her a kiss, but only a little happy one. "I really, really like you."

She burst out laughing, barely able to say, "So Skipper, how's your day goin'?"

The Skipper said he was going below to catch up on some reading in preparation for tomorrow. Kathy didn't know if he was saying that she was not invited to join him, or if he was just being polite. She chose to stay in the cockpit and read from her notebook, reviewing the four days that had already been accomplished.

She was so engrossed in the notebook she didn't hear the dinghy approaching. She was startled when Annie called, "Ahoy. Can I give you the rope?" Kathy hurried back to secure the painter to the cleat.

"Did you make some discoveries?" she asked. "It looks pretty brushy over there."

Annie responded before Bruce could, "I was surprised how close we are to the other side. There are all kinds of trails leading over there, and we saw several boats anchored. I feel like this is our private secret spot." Bruce had secured the stern line to the boat, and the Skipper had returned to the cockpit to help lift and secure the dinghy.

"It feels mysterious to remember how long ago the explorers were here, and how little the area has changed in over two hundred years. This really is isolated."

Bruce agreed, since he was obviously enjoying the pure charm of the territory. Then just as quickly he changed the subject, "Are we too late for the card game?"

The Skipper laughed, "You're just in time to get something refreshing, and a potty break. Let's play up here."

When they had re-gathered, he explained, "The game is called '31', and it is pretty simple to learn, and daring to play." In front of each player there were ten pennies to be used as chips. "The rules are pretty simple. We cut for deal, low card begins, and then we pass the deal clockwise. Each player antes one chip, then receives three cards, the rest are the stack with one face up. The object is to get all one suit; aces count eleven, face cards are ten, all the rest are face value. When it is your turn, you can either take the top card off the discard pile or the top mystery card from the stack, and then you can discard one. When you have all one suit collected, you can 'knock.'" The Skipper rapped on the table. "The other three then get one more turn before the reveal. Perhaps there is more than one hand that is all one suit, so the highest total nearest 31 wins the pot. If there is one who has a higher total than the one who knocked, they get the pot, plus one penalty chip from the knocker. The first player to accumulate 21 chips wins, and will have no galley duty tomorrow. Any questions?"

Kathy asked, "What happens if we lose all our chips. Can we buy more?"

"You get one courtesy, or honor round to win a pot. If that doesn't work, you must drop out and watch."

"Sounds pretty easy," Bruce said with a challenging grin. "I think this is going to be a piece of cake."

"Then let's play a practice round just to make sure the girls understand." The Skipper chuckled.

Play began with considerable table talk, both questions and suggestions. Basically each player understood the game. When Bruce smugly knocked, declaring that he had successfully accumulated a full set, Annie had one more draw, then the Skipper and finally Kathy. Bruce rolled his three cards out for all to see; his three spades totaled a score of twenty two. Annie tossed her cards onto the pile, as did the Skipper. Kathy turned over her first card, the nine of hearts, followed by the six of hearts. She paused for a dramatic finish, and revealed the ace of hearts. "I think that's a total of twenty six." Holding out her hand she said in a gruff voice, "Pay me what you owe me!" They all hooted with happy surprise.

"Wait, that was just a practice hand," Bruce protested. "You sand-bagged me. I'll be more careful next time. I'm going to keep my eye on you!" He realized it might not be quite as easy as he had predicted.

The first four hands were pretty balanced; each player won once, so the piles of chips remained even. Then Kathy won another hand and declared it was just luck. Bruce won the next one, and then Kathy won again, after the Skipper knocked.

"Hey, what's going on here? Are you guys in collaboration or something?" Bruce was both suspicious and frustrated that the game was harder than he had expected.

On the next hand Bruce was very happy to knock early, sure that this would be another victory for him, and he gave Annie some strategy advice. But when the cards were revealed, once again Kathy beat him by two points. She counted her chips, victoriously, announcing that she had exactly 21. "Yippee! No kitchen duty for me tomorrow!"

The harbor had surrendered to the cloak of dusk. Stars were brilliant against an increasingly black backdrop awaiting the moonrise. Kathy couldn't miss the chance to goad Bruce a bit more, "Anyone want to go double or nothing?" It was a taunt that Bruce could not overlook.

"Yeah, I do! But we need to shift the seating arrangement. I think you have signaled dad to give you good cards." It by no means was a serious accusation, but part of the growing camaraderie of the trip. Kathy and Annie switched places.

The next game had the same results, except it took Kathy one hand less to win. The Skipper laughed at Bruce's disbelief. "How can you do that?" Bruce lamented, "It's not logical that you would win almost every hand."

She answered, "Maybe not logical, unless you consider probability. Here's what I did, and I've never played the game before; I looked at my three cards. Almost always they were different suits. If Norm discarded one of those three, that was my target suit. I only needed one more to have a set, and I knew that it was not one of his selected suits so I had a better probability by 33% that he would discard another. If he didn't, I went to the stack for a mystery card. One out of four would fill in my set. So I had two chances every turn to get my card. It didn't take skill as much as patience, with a bit of good luck." She was a gracious winner.

Annie said, "But you made it look easy." To which Kathy answered, "Today I heard Norm say that success was as simple as having a plan and going for it." She smiled warmly; "I just didn't make it complicated by over-thinking the game."

The Skipper used her words to segue into the close of a fun day. "It's time to turn in. Hasn't this been a fun and full day?" He held out his hands to form a circle with the others. He really didn't expect any answer, but each of the crew had a highlight to share. "I got to steer straight for the first time!" Kathy said with happiness. "I loved the raw remoteness of this harbor. I feel like an explorer," Bruce murmured. Annie said, "I could imagine being a homesteader here and building a wonderful place." "I found some old familiar places," the Skipper added, "and some new regions of the heart with each one of you." He gave Kathy's hand a little affectionate squeeze.

"How about a prayer to close the day," he suggested. "Thank you Good and Gracious God, for bringing us to the place where love can knock on our heart's door. Lord, help us overcome our fear. Help us release any hesitance we have so that we can have the spirit of a child who runs with open arms to greet you. We believe that faith stimulates success; hope sustains success, and love sanctifies success. With your presence, power, and peace in our lives, grant us rest for the night and discovery in the bright new day. We ask this in Jesus' wonderful name. Amen."

They continued to hold each other's hand, listening to the silence of the harbor; no lapping waves; no sighing breeze; no bird calls, only the echoes of conversations they were repeating in their minds. Oh, how good the night!

Kathy opened her eyes in a very dark stateroom. She wondered what had awakened her; the boat was as still as a rock, and silent. "Something is wrong!" she thought with alarm. Now wide awake, she tried to detect any signal that would indicate the problem. "Wouldn't it be funny to hear Norm snore," she smiled to herself. The feeling wouldn't go away, however. There was something not right with her world, and she would need to get up and discover what it was. She pulled on a sweatshirt, and a pair of shorts. As silently as possible, she opened her stateroom door. The salon was empty and silent, but there was enough moonlight to allow her to move to the companionway.

"The hatch is open; that's strange," she thought. Carefully she crept up the ladder to the cockpit, where she found Bruce and Annie. Their camera was on a small tripod resting on the table. They were trying to capture by timed exposure, a surreal sight with a huge full moon setting in the west as dawn began to break in the east. Rocks and nearby islands stood out in stark black silhouette against the glorious moonlight; the harbor was barely lighted with both rippling reflections, and gossamer strands of delicate illumination. She carefully sat down, realizing that they were right over Norm's stateroom. No conversation was shared as they watched the unusual fantasy scene.

A soft voice came from the companionway, "Did I miss the invitation?" The Skipper was also in a sweatshirt and shorts. As he joined them in the cockpit he continued softly, "That is the most spectacular moon-set I think I've ever seen."

Bruce whispered, "Shhh, we'll wake the Skipper." Yup, morning had broken.

They all sat quietly, engrossed in the gentle panorama before them. Finally, Kathy broke the silence, "You can actually see the moon's movement!" As the silver disk approached the tree line, its steady inevitable march west was evident.

"I've got to get some more clothes on, or back in bed," Annie said abruptly.

"I think I left a snooze or two in the covers," Bruce said as he picked up the camera.

Kathy also stood up saying, "I guess the show is over. I'm going back to my stateroom to pray for a while." She ruffled the Skipper's uncombed curls. "See you when I'm presentable."

The Skipper was left alone in the cockpit thinking, "Wimps! They just don't make sailors like they used to." He smiled at his own humor, and watched the moon silently slide behind the far horizon.

He was sitting at the salon table nearly two hours later when the crew returned from their naps. "Good morning, Sunshine," he whispered a greeting to Bruce. "The water is hot for a cup of tea, or Via, and I left a pirate pastry for you."

"Have you been up since 4?" Bruce whispered back.

"Yup, I have. There was some preparation for this afternoon's discussion, and I've been trying to keep a journal of our travels. It is always a treat to be on *Dreamer*." He asked if Annie was awake.

As if on cue, both stateroom doors opened. Kathy was wearing a fresh green t-shirt and matching shorts; Annie was in a yellow t-shirt with white shorts. They were both as cute as a vision, and headed toward the same place. Kathy told Annie to go ahead, she could wait.

"Why don't you use mine", the Skipper offered. "I think the old boar that lives in there sort of straightened the place this morning. It's not as roomy, but it works just the same."

Kathy was already closing the stateroom door behind her. Maybe she couldn't wait all that comfortably.

When she came back into the salon, she asked, "Do you always make your bed and tidy up so well?"

Feeling a bit playful, the Skipper answered, "You never know who is going to be in the neighborhood. It's like mom always advising clean underwear in case I was in an accident. I tried to tell her that if I was in an accident, they wouldn't be clean anymore." Then speaking to her question, he added, "Yes, I like to make the bed and straighten up when I get up. There is something positive about entering a room that is made up rather than one that is messy."

Bruce said, "Excuse me, I'll be right back." He disappeared into the forward stateroom, to the amusement of both the Skipper and Kathy.

The breakfast menu was a do-it-yourself selection of instant oatmeal, granola, pirate pastry or cinnamon toast, with juice, coffee, or Crystal Light. "It may not be the most healthy diet for us, but it is easy and available," the Skipper explained. They took their food up to the cockpit, which was bathed in bright morning sunshine. When the dishes were emptied, the Skipper suggested that they have their morning devotion. Once again, sheets of information were brought out of the storage cupboard.

"Dad, did you do all this before we left?" Bruce asked.

The Skipper looked at him to determine if he was making a joke. When it was apparent that it was a sincere question, he responded, "Well no, Brucer, I have a copy machine in my stateroom. 'Here's your sign', as Bill Engvel says. Seriously, yes, I did a lot of paperwork to help this trip seem more planned, and I didn't want to use a lot of valuable time once we were here. Besides, I wanted to impress Kathy." He directed their attention to the outline:

Day 5.)
Sung to the tune The Saints Come Marchin' In

> We bless the Lord! We bless the Lord!
> We bless the Lord for all we're worth,
> And we'll use the power that God gives us,
> To arouse this tired earth

> We bless you all. We bless you all.
> We bless you all for all we're worth.
> And we'll use the love that you give us,
> To arouse this tired earth.

> We'll shout with pride. We'll shout with pride.
> We'll shout with pride for all we're worth.
> And we'll use the name of Jesus,
> To arouse this tired earth.

Meditation: repeat three times.

When I feel inadequate to meet life's opportunities, I will pray for God's Holy Spirit for guidance, love, and power. I am equipped to be successful.

Luke 19:11-27

Today I will turn over the control of my life to the Lord.

I will trust His control over what I was never meant to control.

With His guidance I will take responsibility for what He has given me to do, for His glory, and by His power.

Conclusion: repeat three times

Today I accept responsibility for what God has given me to do for his glory. I will trust God to control what I was never meant to, and grant me the wisdom to distinguish the difference.

When they concluded their devotions, the boat and crew were in complete harmony with the harbor, still, at rest, yet ready for adventure.

Bruce asked, "What's the agenda for the day Skipper?" His voice was almost a violation of the serenity of the morning.

"In my memory, Refuge Cove, our next port of call, was further away than it actually is. We can be there in about forty minutes, and since there is very little breeze this morning we will diesel straight over there. So I'd suggest we read, or take another exploration on the island until about eleven o'clock. I might even waste some time with a nap. We want to let folks who are leaving the dock there have an opportunity to make a space for us. There is a little store, as I recall, and a small bakery, limited to what they bake the night before, but it is good!" He thought for a moment. "I liked the schedule we had yesterday, holding our afternoon discussion until just before supper. Did you all?"

They were each nodding their agreement. Bruce said, "It sure gave us plenty of time to do fun stuff on the beach." Then, thinking what that may have implied, he corrected himself, "You know, explore, discover, and behave ourselves." All four were chuckling at his discomfort.

Annie asked Kathy if she would like to go explore with them. "We might want to change into jeans."

As the Skipper watched the dinghy row toward the gravel beach, he thought again how comfortable his life had become with Kathy in it. He decided to take a little rest and enjoy the morning. It seemed his eyes closed for only a moment when he felt the crew return. Happy voices were beckoning him to join them.

He found Bruce and the girls hauling the dinghy upright behind the life lines.

Bruce was bubbling with excitement. "That was amazing! We found a place that really could have been the old village. There were lots of rotted logs all together like a foundation, or maybe a collapsed wall. There was something that could have been a totem pole, or a part of one. But the best thing is a stone tool of some kind that Kathy found."

She had wrapped a flat stone in her sweatshirt; it was smooth with use and had a groove ground all the way around it. One side looked blunt like a hammer, and the other tapered to an edge like a hatchet. "I may be fooling myself," she said, "but this looks like a primitive tool." She offered the stone to the Skipper to allow him a closer examination.

"It sure looks authentic to me," he said with obvious conviction. He turned to Bruce and asked, "Do you think you could mark a chart with the location of the village? There might be some folks who would like to do an archeological dig."

"Yeah, I think I can remember the spot. Do we have time to go over again? I think I can show you." He was eager to continue the search.

"I was just about to light the diesel, if we want to get to Refuge Cove before noon. I think if we have it on a chart, that will be useful information for someone else to search." A moment later the engine rumbled its willingness to be underway.

Annie was in the salon. Saving himself a trip down the companionway, the Skipper asked, "Annie will you flip a switch for me?" When she answered, "Of course," he directed her to the control panel by the nav station. "The next to bottom switch is marked 'windlass'; will you please switch that on?"

Bruce moved to the bow, and removed the protective cap to the windlass button. The Skipper said, "Ready on the bow?" Bruce gave a thumbs-up sign and the shift lever was eased forward. The Skipper said to Kathy, "The windlass is pretty strong to crank in the anchor chain; but it's not a good idea to ask it to move the boat at the same time. We will just slide up on the rode a bit." *Dreamer* began to ease forward; at the same time, Bruce stepped on the switch and the chain began to clatter in.

When Bruce saw the red link, he called, "That's 50 feet." Another red link brought, "There's 25." Norm took the boat out of gear so its momentum would carry over the set anchor, perhaps a bit more. Bruce called from the bow, "We're loose and coming up." The anchor was free of dirt or seaweed, so Bruce continued to roll it in until it was secure on its bow cradle. He snapped a keeper chain and returned to the cockpit. "All tidy up there, Skipper." Kathy had been watching the process, unaware how essential that information would be to them all.

CHAPTER 6:
REFUGE COVE
Ready to go, and let go

Dreamer held to the center of the harbor until they were adjacent to the west end of Mink Island, then an easy starboard turn gave them a northwest heading. Two distinct headlands were on their bow. The Skipper announced that the second one was Refuge Cove. "It's only about four miles away; anyone else want to drive?"

Annie said she thought it must be about her duty turn, but wanted Bruce to stay close, just in case.

Norm took an uncustomary seat, making sure he was close to Kathy. He placed his arm around her shoulder saying, "The breeze is sort of chilly this morning."

She giggled because there was no breeze, and it was certainly not chilly. But the warmth of his body next to hers was welcome enough to make the humor appropriate.

The Skipper explained that about thirty years ago a group of young couples had decided to try to start a business together up here. "They purchased the land on the point of Refuge Cove," he explained, "and started something I would describe as a commune, building the houses and docks by themselves. They lived in separate facilities, but shared cooking and dining chores. They portioned out the various responsibilities like fuel dock, bakery, store, and maintenance, and surprisingly, it has worked very well. Now their kids are running the place, or selling their shares to folks who want in on it. I've always admired their foresight and ingenuity," he concluded.

Bruce asked if it was a religious group.

"I've never heard anything about that, and there is no evidence of a chapel or worship routine. I think they were just folks who liked each other."

As *Dreamer* passed Martin Island, Bruce pointed out a number of harbor seals that were sunning themselves on the rocks. It was an idyllic morning.

When they could see into the cove, the Skipper said he would take over. "Let's get ready for a starboard moorage," which meant three bumpers on the starboard side, a bow and stern line attached to a cleat, and a spring line mid-ship. They were all set. As they eased into the marina, there were two available slips on the 40 foot dock, and one of them was a starboard tie. Smiling broadly, the Skipper mused, "Doesn't it feel good to be so well prepared?" It was obvious that there had been considerable additions made to the marina area since his last visit.

A smiling young man came out on the dock to catch their lines, and help them tie up. He introduced himself as "Lowell," the harbormaster. "How many nights will you be with us?" "Just one," the Skipper answered. "Do you need diesel?" "Nope, but how about water?" "There's a hose bib, on the dock, but we ask that you do not wash your boat. We are beginning to run low on water this time of year, and so we need to conserve." He told them the store hours, and the bakery had expanded to offer a full lunch menu. "You can pay for dockage in the store. Have a good one, eh?"

Bruce said, "I just love that guy! He was cheery, informative and brief. Who wants a Molson?"

The bakery was still on the side of the hill above the marina, just where Norm remembered it, but it also had been expanded tastefully. There were now six tables inside, and four on the deck. The crew decided on an outside table.

The serving person that seated them warned, "It is a bonnie day, but we do have a problem with bees. The yellow jackets, which are wasps, are pretty aggressive right now that it is so warm."

The Skipper looked around and could see no traps. "Why don't you put up some traps to discourage them?" he asked.

"Well, we don't . . ." he hesitated, "we don't have any."

"Is it that you don't have any, or that you don't believe in destroying the bees?" the Skipper persisted.

"We hate the bees, eh? But we would have to have a whole lot of traps, and they are expensive."

"I just read about a way to make your own that may even get rid of some of your recycling. Do you have a couple plastic jugs?" When he was told they had a lot of gallon milk jugs, the Skipper continued, "Get me three or four jugs and an apple juice, maybe a tiny bit of raw hamburger, and we'll have ourselves a bee-clearing, bug-ridding trap. O.K.?"

The young man disappeared inside. When he returned the cook was with him, interested in the process.

The Skipper took the jugs, poured a bit of the apple juice in, and smiled as he added some raw hamburger. He tightened the lid and gave it a shake to coat the inside with the sweet juice; then taking his pocket knife, he made three vent cuts shaped like an upside down "V" around the middle of the jug. "That's all it takes," he said, adjusting the pointed ends of the vent inside the container. "That will be the bee's door in, and they won't find their way out. It is especially lethal if there is enough liquid in the bottom to drown them. Let's see if it works." He placed the jug on a shelf in the sun, but out of the way.

He was working on the second one when the young man said in a whisper, "Look at that!" A yellow jacket was crawling around the jug until it found a vent and went in. "It works!" They watched with interest as the bee made its way around the inside, but didn't appear interested in leaving. Within a couple of minutes, a second jug-trap was at the other end of the deck. "By tonight, I'll bet we have a dozen of these around the marina. Wait 'til I tell the boss!"

When their food was quickly served, Annie said, "I don't think we are getting the regular service. This must be VIP, don't you think?" They ate in relative peace, observing a number of bees that were going into the one-way yellow jacket diner, while only a couple briefly visited their table.

"I'm thinking," the Skipper said, "that this afternoon, we might want to take a hike on this island. By the way, this is Redonda. It is one of the largest in the area. Or we could catch some sun, and read on the boat; or we could catch up on the sleep we lost moon-watching last night. No, wait, I've already done that." As usual, the banter and levity was enjoyed all the way around their table.

They agreed that a hike would be fun. "Maybe we can get some bottled water at the store," Annie suggested. "Maybe we can have a potty stop first," Kathy added.

"I need to take care of our moorage at the store, too," the Skipper reminded himself. As they got up to leave, Lowell hurried over to say, "You can't believe how many bees are in the traps already! I think we're going to control the problem. If you are going to be here in the morning, the boss wants you to come in for breakfast, on us. Thank you, eh?" They stopped by a trap to inspect a growing layer of bodies at the bottom.

The store was much expanded from what Norm remembered. It actually had the feel of a full service grocery store. Bruce pointed out the Haagen Dazs ice cream; Kathy saw Pop Tarts; Annie noted all the fresh fruit; and the Skipper saw night crawlers. "Ooo!" The other three spun around in shock. "Night Crawlers?"

As the Skipper was taking care of their moorage, he asked about the worms. "Are they alive, in the cooler?" He was assured that they were, and that they were used for sea run cutthroat trout in the lagoon. That was information that needed some explanation.

"If you follow the trail around the point and over the shoulder, you will come to a fork. Most of the locals stay to the right. About a half mile further the trail opens out to a rocky outcropping that is deep enough to fish, by just casting in. Worms on a small hook work best, but sometime, afternoon is a good time for a small spoon or lure. Sea runs are cutthroat trout that are hatched in fresh water, and then make their way out to sea with the salmon fingerlings. When they come back to fresh water they are called 'steelhead' if they are 'rainbow trout', or 'sea run' if they are 'cutthroat.' This is getting toward the end of the run, but there have been some pretty nice fish caught."

When asked how large a "pretty nice fish" might be, they were told, "Last Tuesday some kids brought back two sixteen inch trout, and one that was almost twenty inches. It weighed over three pounds." That was all the inducement the guys needed to purchase some light leader, split-shot sinkers and an assortment of hooks and lures, with no barbs, of course. It is marvelous how an unplanned day can suddenly generate its own. A quick trip back to the boat to change clothes, again, get the fishing rods, and the Skipper grabbed a canvas tote-bag, saying, "We need something to bring all our fish back." A stop at the washroom surprised them with its cleanliness and remodeled size; there were new stalls and four showers.

"I am so into this," Bruce declared as they found the trail head. "Dad, did you notice that there are no cars or trucks around?"

"With no roads on the island, I suspect they would be sort of useless. But I did see a little four wheel ATV." The trail headed up the hill and into the brush, causing the four to stay pretty close together.

The afternoon was warm, with hardly a breath of breeze, and the uphill trail was surprisingly tiring. They were perspiring before very long. "Here's the fork in the trail," Bruce announced. "She said to stay to the right, eh?" He was trying to sound Canadian. The trail went into thicker brush, and was difficult at times even to be seen. Then it began to angle down toward the lagoon.

Kathy asked, "Did she say anything about bears?" It was the first mention of the possibility of danger.

"Why no, she didn't," the Skipper answered from behind her. "But you know the rule don't you?" When

Kathy ask "What rule?" He said, "You don't need to outrun a bear. You only need to outrun the slowest member of our party."

"That's cold," Annie said from the middle of their line. "But I know I can run faster than Bruce." She giggled her challenge.

"Well," Bruce snorted in response, "it makes a difference if I'm running mad, or running scared. I think if we are running from a bear, I would be super fast." Fortunately, their trail wound into a stand of larger fir trees, which was much more open, and ahead they could see the shore of the lagoon. Within a few more minutes they came upon the rocks that provided an ideal place to cast their lines.

"Do you hear those eagles? They must have a nest up behind us." "See the Loon? And did you call those little long necked birds that whistle, Grebe?" "Look, I think that might be an otter." The Skipper was about to say that most successful fishermen are quiet in their efforts, when a sharp tug on his line caused him to grunt and set the hook. He could immediately feel the frantic efforts of his fish fighting against the hook. Slowly he retrieved his line until out of the depths he saw a bright flash. They all stared at the lovely torpedo shape that came to the surface, splashed a bit and then the Skipper carefully hoisted him around to the grass behind them. "That's one for supper." He examined a trout about a foot long, and as fresh as it could possibly be. Before he could get the hook out of the fish, Bruce declared that he had one too. Almost as suddenly, he said it had gotten off.

"There must be a lot of trout in here for this much action," the Skipper guessed. "I set the hook, but not too hard, and didn't give him any slack. With these barbless hooks, they can spit them out pretty easily." They both put on fresh bait and cast as far out into the lagoon as they could. Even as Bruce's line was sinking, they could see it jerk with another bite. This time he set the hook and held the rod tip high. The fish struggled mightily, but Bruce's careful persuasion triumphed, and after an honorable struggle, he too lifted a fish onto the bank. "That's two for supper." He didn't want to point out that his was a bit larger than the one his dad had caught. At least he didn't want to point it out quite yet.

They each had a couple more bites, but were not successful in hooking them. Then Bruce caught another beautiful fish, even bigger than the other two.

The Skipper pointed out that those three fish might be more than they could eat for supper. In spite of the fun of catching more, he was rolling in his line. "I have to admit that I don't remember a more successful trout fishing adventure." He clapped Bruce on the shoulder. "I think it's Molson time, and I'll buy!"

Annie asked if they could remain here for a while to enjoy the lagoon's beauty. It was a suggestion that all agreed was a great idea. Norm stepped down to a shallow spot to clean the fish before their trek back to the marina.

A bit later he was seated on the dry grass beside Kathy, looking at clouds reflected on the quiet water. Bird calls were the only sounds they could hear. "This must be wilderness," she said with a hushed voice. "I feel worlds away from traffic and job and everything." She was close enough to press against his shoulder. "What troubles, eh?" Bruce and Annie had found a sunny spot to stretch out some distance away. Because she was sure they were out of earshot, she was brave enough to bring up the subject of marriage again.

"Did you really mean it, when you said you want us to be married?" Her voice was soft, just above a whisper.

When he smiled at her and said, "Of course I meant it," she asked, "But how?"

He chuckled and said, "Just the way folks do it all the time. We should talk to our folks, get a license, and plan some memories. Does that seem so difficult?" He swung around to face her directly, and took her hand in his.

"No, that part is not difficult. But even my good imagination is not enough to get around the idea of sharing the house with you, the bathroom, or the bed." Her eyes searched his. "There seems to be a million huge questions that all boil down to one: why would you want to do that?"

He could see no emotion in her face except honest curiosity. "I can think of a line from the movie 'Sweet Home Alabama', when he says, 'so I can kiss you whenever I want to.' That would be a good place to start. For two years we have learned a lot about each other. I know you are tender, honest, generous, and have a wonderful faith. I think you are passionate, witty, and intelligent." Because he suddenly found his emotions racing, he decided to try to hide a bit in humor. "Because I have never met someone so much like me." They both laughed out loud, releasing some of that tension.

He said, "I can imagine sharing every day with you, helping around the house, getting to know Scott and Jenny better. Why would I want to do that? Because it makes perfect sense; it's the way to find happiness for both of us in a blended life." He reached for her other hand too.

"But," now her chin did begin to tremble with emotion that continued to build, "you would expect . . ." She couldn't finish the thought.

"I would expect you to brush your teeth every morning and have occasional check-ups. I would expect you to help with the household chores, although I really do like to mow the lawn." His smile was growing. "I would expect you to cook some of the meals and help with grocery shopping, and to be a great parent to Scott and Jenny. I would expect you to want to love me like I want to love you." His smile gave way to serious silence. From the treetop behind them an eagle's chirping call echoed over the lagoon.

Kathy said, "I love you, and. ." she stood up, still holding his hands, pulled him to his feet too, "and think we can talk more about this later." She waved at Annie, and turned toward the trail that would return them to the marina. Bruce and Annie scrambled to catch up.

The first stop in the marina was the washroom. The guys waited for the girls before returning to the boat. Bruce asked his dad, "Is everything O.K. with Kathy?"

"Yeah, I think so," the Skipper answered. "Why do you ask?"

"Well, Annie thought she might be upset the way she left the lagoon so quickly."

The Skipper gave a casual wave of his hand, saying, "I think she just had to go potty."

Bruce nodded. "I took care of that in the brush." They shared a grin as advantaged woodsmen.

It was hot in the boat, but not as hot as in the sunny cockpit. The crew had changed into more comfortable clothes and agreed that the salon, with some opened hatches, would be the best place for the afternoon discussion. "You have to promise me that there will be no napping," the Skipper demanded. "At least, no noisy napping."

When they were all situated, Kathy asked if they could sing that "Saints Come Marching In" song again. They sang with gusto.

"Before our discussion," the Skipper began a disclaimer, "I want to remind you that all of our topics were chosen before we left Seattle. There is nothing intended for any specific person or situation. The names have been changed to protect the guilty."

He smiled. "Have you ever been driving on the freeway and the car in front of you has their brake lights blinking on and off, flash, flash, flash?" He nodded with them. "You know what is causing that, don't you? They have their right foot on the accelerator, and their left foot on the brake pedal. Go forward; no, stop, no go. It's silly, isn't it? And yet, I'll bet we have all done it, maybe until we realize we are burning up our brakes and wasting gas. It is an analogy of people who fear losing control, and so they have a heavy foot on the brakes of their life."

"If you ask them why they do it, they would probably say, 'Over the years I've liked being the boss over things. I feel very insecure when I can't manage things like my home, my family, or my job. That may be wrong, but it's just the way I am.'"

"I think the need for control begins when we realize the awesome responsibility we have for our own lives. Early in life we discover that there is a direct cause and effect correlation between our choices and what happens to us. What we do and say brings both good and bad results. The hurt of failure makes us want to avoid pain. We determine that we must work harder to guarantee success."

"That's when we slam on the brakes. Avoiding failure becomes a high priority; our grip on life becomes tighter. The thought of losing control makes us panic. We keep life's challenges pared down to what we can handle without much risk of failure. Having been hurt we control how vulnerable we will become. Much of life is held at bay." Norm was careful not to catch or hold Kathy's gaze.

"But the process doesn't stop there. Even if we do nothing, we can be injured by other people's mistakes. The only way to prevent that is to control them too. By telling our families, friends, neighbors where to go, what to do and when, we hope to ensure our own safety. Besides, pushing someone else around gives us a feeling of power and competence. It soothes our secret insecurities or feelings of failure."

"Ultimately, the fear of losing control weakens the most important relationship of life; it threatens our relationship with Christ Jesus. It keeps us from experiencing the full joy and delight of the abundant life that He came to bring."

"Christ loves us and offers us his power. All he asks is that we accept his absolute control." When Bruce frowned, the Skipper repeated, "His absolute control. Anything else is conditional. He expects us to surrender our wills to do his will, and commit our total life—all that we are and have—to him. Anything less is conditional, and places us in a posture of negotiation. Then he promises us his wisdom for our decisions, his unfailing strength for our challenges, and his eternal love for our relationships. Think about it, that's not a bad offer!"

There was lots of discussion information there, but the Skipper continued. "In spite of that money-back offer, our need to be in charge of ourselves, others, and situations often makes our relationship with Christ, life's biggest power struggle. We are reluctant to relinquish our control and allow him to run our lives. We may believe in him and be an active leader in the Church, and Christian causes, but trusting him as Lord, that is Master, of everything in life can be just plain scary. Even though we pray about our challenges and problems, all too often what we are really after is the strength to accomplish what we've already decided is best for ourselves and others. Meanwhile we press on with our own priorities and plans. We remain the script-writer, casting director, choreographer, and producer of the drama of our lives, in which we are, of course, the star performer."

"Over the years of ministry, I've come to understand that life really begins with a total commitment to Jesus. I've also come to see that this decision is the missing dynamic in most Christians today. Sure, many began the Christian life with a hand-me-down belief in Christ as Savior. But the implications of accepting him as Lord of all life were either not made clear or, if they were, not taken seriously. All of which brings us to the next vital step of living without fear. Take that devotion page we used this morning. See the bottom meditation? Let's say it again together:"

Today I accept responsibility for what God has given me to do for his glory. I will trust God to control what I was never meant to, and grant me the wisdom to distinguish the difference.

"Let's say it again, this time add a first sentence: '*Today, I will turn over the control of my life to the Lord.*'"

"Now, Annie," the Skipper asked, "would you read again for us the passage from Luke 19 that we had for our morning devotion?" It took her a moment to find the page and begin to read in a clear voice:

"*While they were listening to this, he went on to tell them a parable, because he was near Jerusalem and the people thought that the kingdom of God was going to appear at once. He said: "A man of noble birth went to a distant country to have himself appointed king and then to return. So he called ten of his servants and gave them ten minas. 'Put this money to work,' he said, 'until I come back.'"*

"But his subjects hated him and sent a delegation after him to say, 'We don't want this man to be our king.'"

"He was made king, however, and returned home. Then he sent for the servants to whom he had given the money, in order to find out what they had gained with it. The first one came and said, 'Sir, your mina has earned ten more.'"

"'Well done, my good servant!' his master replied. 'Because you have been trustworthy in a very small matter, take charge of ten cities.'"

"The second came and said, 'Sir, your mina has earned five more.'"

"His master answered, 'You take charge of five cities.'"

"Then another servant came and said, 'Sir, here is your mina; I have kept it laid away In a piece of cloth. I was afraid of you, because you are a hard man. You take out what you did not put in and reap what you did not sow.'"

"His master replied, 'I will judge you by your own words, you wicked servant! You knew, did you, that I am a hard man, taking out what I did not put in, and reaping what I did not sow? Why then didn't you put my money on deposit, so that when I came back, I could have collected it with interest?'"

"Then he said to those standing by, 'Take his mina away from him and give it to the one who has ten minas.'"

"'Sir,' they said, 'he already has ten!'"

"He replied, 'I tell you that to everyone who has, more will be given, but as for the one who has nothing, even what they have will be taken away. But those enemies of mine who did not want me to be king over them—bring them here and kill them in front of me.'"

"Thank you, Annie," the Skipper said after a brief quiet to digest the scripture. "Let's do a tiny bit of Bible background before we dive into the parable. A talent was a unit of measurement, whether it was used for weighing gold or silver; in one talent there were sixty minas, pronounced 'mee-nah,' and in each mina, there was the equivalent of one hundred Greek drachma. A drachma was equivalent to one day's wage. What each servant was given was the sum of about three month's wages. Now every good rabbi knew there were four ways to understand scripture: there was the literal meaning, which was called 'pashat;' it meant just what it said. Then there was a suggested meaning, which was called 'ramez.' The third meaning was more vague because it was inferred, or deducted by investigation; it was called 'derush.' And the fourth and most difficult meaning was the allegorical understanding, called 'sod.' A rabbi would often refer to the form of understanding just by the first letter of the word. 'This is the 'r' meaning told his listeners they were hearing the suggested meaning; or the 'p' meaning was the literal one. If however, a meaning could possibly be all four 'p', 'r', 'd', and 's', it would be paradise. We may understand our parable today using all four meanings."

"The first servant to make his report must have been pleased to say that he had earned ten minas, or about three year's wage. He was praised and handsomely rewarded, given authority over ten cities. The second to report had earned five minas, over a year's wage, and although he was not given as much commendation, he was granted authority over five cities. The third servant, however, out of fear, rooted in totally false assumptions about the nobleman, had hidden the mina away for safety, and had no profit to show."

"A dramatic twist occurs at the end of the parable. Dismayed by the servant's cautious unproductivity, the nobleman took his one mina away and gave it to the servant who had multiplied his investment tenfold."

Bruce interrupted, "That's cold. Where is grace in that?"

"I think the disciples would agree with you, Bud," the Skipper continued. "Because I think that is the point at which the original story ended. In verse twenty five there seems to be a parenthesis which appears to be part of the parable. 'But they said to him, Master, he has ten minas.'"

"What if it was Jesus' own disciples, who interrupted him because of the sudden and astounding turn in the parable, when the timid servant's one mina was given to Mr. High-returns? The disciples were listening so intently, with such rapt attention, that they simply blurted out their protest at what had happened to the one-mina man. Can't we understand their strong reaction? Jesus has our attention too. One of his most disturbing statements follows with a laser thrust. It really is a warning to those who fear to lose control. 'For I say to you, that to everyone who has will be given; and from him who does not have, even what he has will be taken away from him.' He is once again turning over the tables of our values. 'To everyone who has . . . ' Has what? Let's think about this." His three listeners were hooked into the thought.

"What if, from the beginning we understood that there is an autobiographical tone to this story? Suppose Jesus is the nobleman going away. After the cross and resurrection, he would ascend to heaven, receive the Kingdom from his Father, and return as reigning Lord. Remember that his kingdom means his rule over those of us who have given our allegiance to belong to him as faithful and obedient disciples. We enter that Kingdom by the gift of faith he gives us, and we live in its full joy as we accept the responsibilities he also gives us. The rest of the parable is really about us; it's our story. Each of us is one of the servants. Which one best represents how you have invested the mina entrusted to you? And one more question; if we are understanding this meaning as 's', or allegorically, what of the other seven servants who received minas but are no-shows at the weigh-in?" It was obvious that Norm had thought a lot about this parable.

"All three servants had two things in common. All were given one mina, and all were given the same opportunity to invest and multiply the mina. What does the mina represent for us? I believe it is the gift of faith. All of us receive the basic gift of faith, that's where grace comes into the story, Bud. It is not earned or deserved. It is freely given to us to respond to the love, forgiveness and reconciliation of the cross."

"By faith we are given the power to believe and accept Christ as Lord and Savior and turn our lives over to his control. That is the beginning of the adventure of the abundant life, and the assurance of eternal life."

"The same gift of faith that reconciles us to the Lord also releases us to follow his orders in every area of daily life. He gives us—all of us—a new life to live for his glory. But it is in the response to that gift with power to know his will that often the similarity between Christians ends."

Once again Bruce asked for clarification; "You're saying that it is a level playing field for all of us. There are no special advantages for anyone. Is that right?"

"Correctabungo, Moose." The Skipper gave him a big grin.

"Just as there were two things the servants had in common, there are two radical ways they differed. There was a difference in what they did with their mina, and how they were rewarded."

"So what does that mean for our mina? How is our gift of faith affected? The most obvious answer is that our faith is given to us to help us grow in our relationship with the Lord. Trusting his control of our lives produces growth in intimacy with him, and in the transformation of our character and personality in his image. We invest our mina as we pray in the phrases of the old hymn, 'Have thine own way, Lord . . . Mold me and make me after thy will . . . Hold o'er my being absolute sway.'"

"Multiplying our mina of faith means bringing all facets of our life under his leadership. That includes our family, our marriage, our friends, our employment, our recreation, our church. Christ is the Lord of it all, as we surrender to him what we do, say, and seek to be, as his person."

"Now we are ready to look at the second thing the servants did not have in common: they were rewarded differently for their use of the mina. Two were rewarded to the extent that they multiplied what had been given to them," The Skipper paused to interject, "There has been so much really horrible theological conclusions drawn over what the rewards mean." Then he continued, "The one who hoarded his mina had it taken away from him, which established the basic rule of life, 'Use it or lose it!'"

"The cautious servant refused to take responsibility for the investing and growth of the nobleman's gift. I think he feared doing something wrong, and ended up doing nothing at all. I think it is Robert Schuller who says, 'I'd rather attempt to do something great and fail, than attempt to do nothing and succeed!' The one mina man attempted to do nothing and that is what he earned. He had developed a habit of control, with elaborate explanations, for running his own life. He ventured nothing and got nothing; he lost what he had. This servant who refused to serve, is the 'patron sinner' of controlling people of every age."

"So where does that bring us?" the Skipper asked, implying a conclusion was drawing near. "Clearly the fear of failure is beneath the surface of our desire to be in control. The memory of previous failures keeps us from taking risks. We accept our mina of faith and keep it within safe controllable boundaries. When life makes its demands and inflicts problems, we are too scared to venture beyond what we are sure we can handle. A vague belief in Christ provides little help; as a result, we can feel alone, defenseless, and filled with anxiety."

"We should not be surprised that the nobleman took the mina from the cautious servant and gave it to the one who had made ten more. Why should the Mr. No-Profit care? He neither claimed his mina gift, nor used it for the purpose it was intended. So, too, do those who have been given the gift of faith to believe, yet fail to appropriate it by insisting on absolute control of their lives. Opportunities to invest their faith come and go without any trust in the Lord for his strategy or strength to follow orders. That really explains the words, 'I tell you that to everyone who has, more will be given, but as for the one who has nothing, even what they have will be taken away.'"

"An untested, uninvested faith is no faith at all. When problems or challenges come to the self-dominated person, they endure them as before, under their own control. Should their faith be taken away from them? It is really a moot question, because it was never genuine faith at all."

Once again Bruce raised a question. "Dad, that sounds pretty grim. Don't you think there is a grey area, or some wiggle room to soften that a little?"

"The thing that keeps me from agreeing that there should be some slack in there, is that it places us back in the arena of negotiation and conditional surrender. Accepting our responsibility to seek and do God's will, requires complete trust in his Son, who is with us to show us the way and provide the power to follow."

"I just don't know if I agree that anything human can be 100% dedicated," Bruce offered, holding to his point.

"Let's test that thought," the Skipper replied. Turning to Annie, he asked, "Sweetie, I don't want to offend you. This is a hypothetical question. What percentage of the time would you like Bruce to honor your marriage vows?" They all knew it was a silly question with an obvious answer.

"I'd be devastated if it was anything less than 100% of the time." she answered. "And I believe that he would say the same thing."

"I would agree with you both," the Skipper reconnected with his thought. "Complete trust requires something else, which is humility. For this discussion's sake, let's define pride as simply the refusal to be loved, and to love in return. True humility is the opposite. A humble person is not a wimpy, groveling bundle of self-effacement, but a person who knows he or she is loved and gifted by God. Secure in that love, such an individual constantly points away from self, to the source of strength. There is no room for the thought that he has all the answers for himself and others. Humility leads us to a right estimate of ourselves. And that estimate includes the realization that we are not omniscient, that we don't know everything and never will."

"So just telling people who are afraid of losing control that they should stop being afraid won't work. They—we—need to face the deep inner cause: pride that is masquerading as a know-it-all sufficiency."

"Let me say just this one more thing. The fear we feel actually results from the confrontation of the Lord's Spirit with our own spirit of pride. Scripture tells us that 'God resists the proud, but gives grace to the humble'. (James 4:6) That resistance is registered in our souls first as fear. The Lord is invading our fortress of arrogance. Our defensive response is the fear of letting go. It is a sure sign that the Lord has singled us out for the breaking of our control over ourselves and others. The refusal to humble ourselves before him sometimes means that he must humble us."

"But I am sure of this: the Lord never humiliates us. He has a much more effective way than that. He simply allows us to go on thinking we are running things until our control breaks down and we see how ineffective it really is. Fearing failure, we are hit by even greater failures. The people we've tried to control rebel, and let us know that they are tired of our grip. Then life falls apart in some situation we've been ruling with an iron hand. But at such times the Lord goes right on loving us, and will help us, if we only ask him, to recover from our foolish assumptions of self-sufficiency."

"Each of us is different, and we all have our own ways of bucking the Lord's authority. What can we do about our fear of losing control? Here are six ways to accept Christ's control that summarizes what we have talked about this afternoon." He handed them each a sheet of paper.

1). Admit that the need to be in charge of your life has resulted in a fear of losing control. Acknowledge that this is rooted in pride and that you need to receive more of the Lord's grace in your life.
2). Humbly tell the Lord about your panic over losing control. Accept his healing love and forgiveness for the limits you have placed on yourself and other

people by always wanting to be in charge. Tell him exactly what has happened under your insufficient management.

3). Make today the first day of a new beginning. Commit your life to the Lord's authority.

4). Experiment with trust and experience the results. Move quickly to the problems and needs you face right now. Take them, one by one. Give them over to Christ's control.

5). Keep a logbook in which you record what you have committed to Christ, as well as the results. Write a few sentences each day about living under his control. Discover how he works and note what is happening to heal your fears.

6). Ask the Lord to assign you a challenge with people and situations needing his love and power. Trust him! Through you he will do things you never thought could happen.

When the crew had finished reading the six steps, the Skipper concluded, "I believe the Lord wants us to experience the difference. He knows that we will not give up the anxiety of being in charge, until we really feel the joy of living by faith in his control. Take your foot off the brake!"

The boat was completely still for several seconds. Finally Kathy said, "Thank you. That was a very large thought, with many conversations tucked in it. It's going to take a while to . . ." she didn't finish her sentence.

After another prolonged silence, the Skipper turned to Bruce and Annie and suggested, "How about a walk up the dock? I planned a rice side dish for our trout, with sliced tomatoes and cucumbers. I can stay here and get a start on supper."

Kathy asked what she could do to help, and was told that she had to stay out of the galley. "Remember who won the 31 game last night?"

"O.K." she relented, "but can I stay and talk to the chef for a while?" Her perky smile precluded any other conversation. Bruce and Annie said they would go up and check the bee traps, and find out about hours for the bakery in the morning.

The Skipper seemed very comfortable in the galley. First he laid out the box of rice mix, a container of butter, and his special seasoning. "We have a safety procedure for the propane," he explained to Kathy. "First, I need to open the valve on the cylinder in the aft storage." He was gone for only a few seconds. "We always turn off the tank so there is no propane in the system. It is heavier than air, so if it leaks out, it will collect in the bilge, and could become flammable. Then I switch on the solenoid that controls the gas flow to the galley stove, and finally," he turned the knob on the front of the stove, with a clicking sound, which she would learn was the starter sparking, "we have fire!" He said it proudly as if it were a marvelous discovery. "Two cups of water to a boil, two tablespoons butter, a teaspoon or so of our 'AP', and in twenty two minutes, we'll have rice. I'll slice the veggies, but cook the fish when we are ready to serve it. I'll show you how to get trout fillets without a knife. Interested?"

"I'm interested in everything you do, but what is 'AP'?" she asked with a grin.

"It's our All Purpose seasoning," he answered. "It can go in soups, rice or potatoes, on fish or meat. It is a great way to add flavor without adding too much salt. I think it would be good for everyone if they used more 'AP' and less salt." He bobbed his head for emphasis.

"Are you always this handy in the galley, or are you just trying to turn my head?" Her grin was growing playfully.

"I am comfortable here, because I really like to eat well. Am I also trying to turn your head?" He repeated her question. "I don't think I want to do anything that would be less than caring for you; but, yes, I would like to impress you a bit." He stepped over to the settee where she was sitting and delivered a soft, and welcomed kiss. "I would like to impress you a bunch." They both laughed at his humor.

There was a prolonged silence before she asked, "When you talked about people who need control, were you thinking of me?" Her voice had become small and quiet.

"Not at all," he replied immediately. "I tried to assure you that these thoughts were organized well before our trip. Does that mean I don't think you have control issues?" he asked rhetorically. "I think we all struggle with our safety boundaries. It is a slippery slope when we want to make sure we can handle what comes at us, and at the same time, realize growth, or achievement, adventure, or a deep and satisfying marriage." He didn't kiss her again, although that was his desire; he carefully stroked her shoulder.

Kathy's voice grew even softer, "It doesn't seem like a struggle for you. Have you thought about . . . you know, what we were talking about before?" Kathy was beginning to blush uncharacteristically.

"Do you mean marriage, or are you asking about the wedding?" Norm was realizing how far apart the two of them were on this process. When Kathy nodded her head indicating that both subjects were a struggle for her, he decided to try to speak about them in the abstract, rather than a personal way.

"Well, I suppose when two people realize that they would be much happier together than apart, they begin to make merger plans. When they realize how partial their life seems without the other, they choose to correct that by being together always. I'm old-school enough to believe that simply living together without marriage is a short-cut that prevents continued growth, and implies temporary status to one or both. Is that simple enough?" He looked into her green eyes, thinking he had not done that enough in the past few days.

She nodded in both understanding and agreement. "I've never been much in favor of folks just moving in together. My dad used to call it 'shacking up', and it seemed to be less than complimentary." Norm was glad he had kept the conversation in the theoretical. "But what would your idea of a perfect wedding look like?" she asked, making it personal.

"Well, let's think about that. I suppose I have done so many church weddings that I automatically imagine that venue first. The challenge is that those weddings are more for the many people who want to be in attendance, as well as the formality of the union. When a family is being blended, I think it should be more than a half hour show, with flowers, candles, and music. I think a vacation where children are able to see the couple at play, and be included in the bridge-building; where they all eat together, and form memories of being loved, would be ideal. It is a challenge to weave two different histories together. I suppose I am a bit excited about the prospect of spending a week in Hawaii with you, and our families. There could be time to dine and celebrate as well as do the tourist stuff that would make it stand out as a unique and special time. The beach, sunsets, playing in the pool or sunning by it all build great memories. Warden's place has a huge grassy lawn that extends right down to the beach. It sounds almost too good to be true. I think God could use a place like that to make inspiring memories."

Kathy rose from the settee quickly; looking out the companionway, she asked, "Is that the guys coming back?" When she turned back, shaking her head, Norm saw that her eyes were brimming with tears.

"Sweetheart," he said taking her in his arms, "this must not be a painful thing to think about. Let's put it away until it becomes a happy thing for both of us." He kissed her softly. "We have plenty of time for serious stuff later."

"Getting a grip on my silly fears may be the most serious thing I can do," Kathy said into his shirt. *Dreamer* rocked gently as Bruce and Annie returned. Kathy quickly wiped her eyes and said again, "Please don't say anything to them."

Bruce's smiling face appeared at the hatch. "So, Skipper, how's your day goin'?"

The largest trout had been trimmed of head and tail so it would fit on the foil covered pizza pan. A pouch of mayonnaise was smeared on the inside of the fish before it was placed under the broiler. "I'm having a world-class day, Pal, how about you?"

"Me too," Bruce answered. "But why are you only cooking one fish?"

"Patience, Grasshopper," the Skipper tried his sensei accent. "Your big fish will feed two of us, and more. We'll make sure he has a good bath in lemon juice and white wine, then cook him on one side; and when we roll him over, we will cook the other two on each side. That way, if I have calculated correctly, the three will be broiled through, and done at the same time."

"Don't you just love these little individual mayo packages?" Bruce wanted to shift the subject off anything that may have sounded like a question of the Skipper's cooking ability.

Kathy quickly offered, "He said he was going to fillet the fish without using a knife. Did I hear that correctly?" She had composed herself sufficiently to join in the banter.

When the trout were thoroughly broiled, the Skipper set the hot pan on the stovetop. He took a fork and carefully lifted the very browned skin off the largest fish. "It should come off just this easily." He placed the skin on a discard plate. "Now, take the fork and insert it along this line on the side. It is called a 'lateral line', and is a separation of the musculature." He pressed the fork in and lifted away from the line, neatly presenting the upper half of the fillet, which he placed on his plate. Moving a bit further down the line, he repeated the process, until he had removed all the top part of his fillet. "Now the lower half is a bit more testy, because we are using the fork to rake the flesh off the rib bones." Beginning again at the line side, he gently lifted the cooked flesh off the bones. It took three more sections before he had cleared the entire fillet from the skeleton, now bared on this side.

"So, that's my half of the fish." Grasping the front end of the spine, he gently lifted the entire skeleton from the bottom half of the fish, dropping it on the discard plate. "And there is yours, Bubba. I usually throw the skin away." Both of them had an extra large portion of boneless fish. "Do the girls need help with theirs?"

Both Annie and Kathy had watched the demonstration closely enough to get started. Once the skin was discarded, they found that the tender flesh could be removed and eaten with no problem, and no bones at all. It was a fun and very useful discovery. Their dinner was accompanied by a bottle of chilled Chardonnay, and a recounting of Bruce's success with the fishing pole, giving an animated account of his extraordinary struggle with the "big one".

When only empty plates were left on the table, Annie suggested that the O'Banyon team would take care of dishes if the cooks, (giving Kathy inclusion rights to the title) could take a walk up the dock. It was a suggestion well greeted by all but Bruce, who argued that it was his hard effort that had provided the fish. One glance from Annie, however, convinced him of the excellence of her suggestion.

Evening shadows were sneaking across the cove as Norm and Kathy made their way slowly up the dock. Holding hands neither of them felt like hurrying through this opportunity. There were compliments on the meal and the marvelous experience of another matchless day. Finally, Kathy tried to introduce the subject that had been at the front of her priorities.

"You probably think I'm a nut," she began. "I want you to tell me how you feel about us, but I get all twisted up when I try to think about how I feel. There are so many ways I feel pulled and pushed. I don't think it is a matter of control, but as you were talking I think I got the idea that control is my . . ."

The Skipper stopped, pulling her around in front of him and kissed her, full and firm. When their lips parted, he asked her, "Do you love me?" His voice was soft with intense feeling.

"Yes I do," she answered grateful for his strong embrace that had not let her go.

"Do you want us to be married?" he asked in the same voice.

"With all my heart," Kathy answered. She was afraid that she would not be able to control her breath if there was another question.

"Sweetheart, that's all we need to know. Everything else is just problem-solving and date-setting." He gave her another kiss, but this much softer and playful. Releasing his embrace they resumed their journey up the dock, but Kathy's mind was racing.

"How can it be that easy?" she asked quietly, as though there might be eavesdroppers along the way. "You make it sound simple but I feel like it is much more complicated." For the remainder of the stroll up to the closed bakery she tried to explain her fears to him.

Finally, standing on the deck, now draped in evening shadows, he said, "You know, that all sounds like the symptoms of a person who has struggled for a long time to be a single-parent, and a bread-winner, while being alone without a partner who can provide a deeper support than she has ever known. I think you could benefit from also thinking about the solution, rather than just the ailment."

Looking at the beautiful scene before them, he changed the subject. "When I look at this place, something magical happens to my spirit." They could see *Dreamer* resting quietly out on the 40 foot dock. Beyond the front of the cove, the Sound stretched into the gathering twilight, open to the limits of visibility. "I forget how renewed I feel from just being here." He once again placed his arm around her shoulder.

"I will talk with you about your fears and challenges as much as you need," he said softly. "At the same time, I hope you can be revived, or restored by the wonder of this trip.

That might put some of those problems in a fresh light. Then, when you feel like it is the right time to talk about the details of our future, let's do it together."

Kathy breathed a sigh of relief. She had felt the need to explain her inner turmoil to him, to help him understand her conflict. Now in a kiss and an embrace he had shown her that he loved and accepted her, and was willing to be patient while she continued to sort all this out. She tightened her hug because she knew she loved him even more.

"If we don't head back," he said, "Bruce will probably be making up stories about us, and our naughty behavior." They both giggled, grateful for the moment of affection, and the freedom to be in it together.

As predicted, when they entered the salon, Bruce said, "There you are! We were about to form a search party." He laughed quickly to make sure his words were not offensive. "I've got the cards out and am ready for another try at 31." The Skipper suggested a game of Hearts.

"No way," Bruce insisted. "I want a chance to win my money back. No wait, those were your pennies, but I still want another chance to get even."

Kathy slid into the salon settee, saying, "Bring it big guy. I did it once, and can try, try again." Her humor was infectious.

For the next hour the four played several hands fairly evenly, so when the tally was made, only Kathy had a slight advantage, having won one extra hand. But when she won another, Bruce protested. "How are you doing that? I know that Annie wouldn't cheat, so how are you so lucky?"

Kathy shrugged, embarrassed a bit by the recognition. "I'm just keeping the cards I like, and it sort of works out. I don't know any secret formula."

"O.K.," Bruce challenged, even though you have a slight lead on me, I'll bet I win this game. If I do, will you fix lunch tomorrow? If you win, I'll fix lunch, deal?" He held out his hand to shake on it, making it official.

"That's a deal." As Bruce shuffled the cards, she added, "I was planning on fixing lunch any way. It's my turn."

The Skipper took his turn, and discarded. Annie drew from the stack, and discarded. Then Kathy knocked! She apparently had been dealt three of the same suit!

"Oh, that's just wrong!" Bruce lamented. "No way could you get . . ." he didn't even know how to finish the sentence. "And you tricked me into a bet . . ." again he left the rest unspoken. The other three each had one more turn to fulfill their suits, but the conclusion was inevitable. Kathy calmly and very dramatically turned her cards over one at a time, all hearts! She won; and Bruce was going to fix lunch. It was a double victory!

"Before this turns into a fistfight," the Skipper chuckled, "I'm going to take a glass of tea up to the cockpit and enjoy the last of twilight. Shall we chat about our itinerary tomorrow, before an evening prayer?"

When they were seated in the cockpit, Bruce asked, "Dad, it seems like there are fewer folks in here tonight. Is there a reason for that?" The slips on both sides of *Dreamer* were empty.

"My only guess," the Skipper answered, "is that this is Friday night. Since most charters begin on Saturday or Sunday, chances are folks are either returning their boats back to Comox or Vancouver, or are on their way here. We are quite a ways north from a charter base."

Annie asked, "How much further are we going? This is more beautiful than I could ever have imagined." The other two nodded in agreement.

"Good lead in," the Skipper said appreciatively. "Tomorrow we are going just around the corner, staying on this same island, Redonda. There is something of a fiord called Teakerne Arm, with a waterfall at the far end. If we get there early, and we should be able to do that, we might get a spot on the government dock. There is room for six or eight boats, if no great big ones come in. We can hike just about a quarter mile to Cassel Lake, which is swimmable." Looking at Bruce he corrected himself, "We can watch the girls swim, as we protect them from wild beasts." It was good for a smile all around.

"Then Sunday, we can get another early start because of the tide, and go to Big Bay on Stuart Island. It's a little over twenty miles, which will take us about three hours unless we miss the high slack. There is a salmon resort there, with great facilities. Then Monday we will slide back to Read Island, and Tuesday we will be back in Campbell River. The Wardens will be here on Wednesday. We'll be back in Seattle on Thursday, after two weeks in paradise. I don't like to talk about the conclusion of a trip that I am enjoying so completely." He looked into Kathy's eyes with affection.

"I was having fun too," Bruce wanted one more jab at the card game, "until the card sharp, that you brought along, took all my money." His huge grin said it was all in humor.

"Well, Amigo," Annie broke in, "I need to correct three things. First, I brought her. The Skipper brought you, remember? Second, she didn't take all your money, you still have enough to buy Molsons all around when we get back to Dot's; and third, it's card 'shark', not sharp. And she did win, fair and square." Annie offered Kathy a high five, to emphasize the point.

The Skipper asked, "Did you guys find out what time the bakery opens in the morning?"

Annie replied, "The sign on the door has summer hours as 7:00 a.m. to 8:00 p.m.; their winter hours are closed October through March."

"Well," the Skipper thought for a moment, "we have been awake early every day, so far. Let's go up and help them open in the morning. I think we could be underway by nine o'clock and get a front-row space at the government dock. Tomorrow will be an easy day." Reaching out for their hands he said, "Let's share a prayer."

"Gracious Lord, we say 'good night' by giving you thanks and praise for this wonderful day, for bringing us into this cathedral where mountains wear clouds and the tall trees dance with the wind. Thank you for bringing us to a place where your love can introduce this truth in our minds: the most powerful force in the world is a positive idea that finds a welcome reception in the mind of a believer. Tonight, we happily say, 'into my heart, into my heart, come into my heart, Lord Jesus.' Give us the nerve to live bravely, and love dangerously. We may surrender our independence, but we will never again be lonely, in Jesus' precious name. Amen." The crew continued to hold hands as they relished the scope of the day. Oh, good the night!

Kathy opened her eyes to a stateroom lighted with enough dawn to help her find her watch. "My goodness," she thought, "it's already 5:15! I'm getting the hang of this boat life. I can even sleep in!" She was moving toward her clothes, pulling a comb through her hair. When she opened her door, she was not surprised to see Bruce and Annie at the table. And when she whispered, "Norm?" They just pointed toward the shower house, which did not surprise her either.

When she had freshened up a bit in the head, splashing water on her face and looking for any evidence of yesterday's make-up, Kathy shrugged and joined them at the table. Bruce had fixed her a cup of Via. She thanked him with a quick back-rub.

Annie asked, "So, Kathy, how is your day going?" After a chuckle, she went on, "Are you enjoying this as much as we are?"

Kathy nodded, "I am," she said with a happy sigh. "It seems like time is all off. On one hand, it seems like it is going by very slowly; there is so much in every day. On the other hand, seven days have flashed by in a wink. This is a fantasy vacation for me."

"For us too," Annie said before Bruce could say the same thing. "It is such a special boat, but mostly it's what the Skipper does with us all the way through. Can you imagine how much help he was when we were struggling with whether we should get married or not?"

"Yup," Kathy nodded again in agreement. "He just seems to know so much about everything, without making me feel dumb.

Bruce was nearest the companionway. He signaled them to listen. From some distance they could hear soft whistling. Bruce asked incredulously, "Who whistles Beethoven, and at 5:30 in the morning?" A moment later the boat rocked gently as the Skipper stepped aboard.

"Good morning, lights of my life." He gave each crew member a hug, with Kathy getting a bit longer one than the others. He found his tea glass in the galley and filled it with Crystal Light. Finding a place with them at the table he asked, "So, how's your day goin'?" They talked about how quiet the marina was, and how well they slept. Mostly they expressed their delight in the trip and wonder in the discovery of a place called "Desolation."

"Are we ready for morning devotions?" the Skipper asked. He had brought the worksheets with him from the galley.

Bruce scanned his sheet, and asked, "Dad, these are so helpful. When did you have time to do all this work?"

"Well Bubba, Mr. Branch told me to use an hour every day to work on family core purposes. I just spent some of those bonus hours to get prepared. It actually helped me focus on our discussions. I think this might be something I will use again at a retreat, or study series. I'm glad you like what we have done." He handed Kathy a Bible and said, "Shall we get started with day 6?"

Day 6.)

In moments like these, I sing out a song.
I sing out a love song to Jesus.
In moments like these, I lift up my hands.
I lift up my hands to the Lord.

Singing I love you, Lord. Singing I love you, Lord.
Singing I love you, Lord. I love you.

Morning Prayer:

"So faith, hope, love abide, these three; but the greatest of these is love. (1 Cor. 13:13)
Gracious God of morning and evening, we praise you for this, another day.

Grant us the faith which is sure and certain of what it believes; the faith which unhesitatingly believes in your promises; the faith which is loyal to you in any situation.

Grant us, we pray, the hope which will never despair; the hope which no disappointment can quench; the hope which, in spite of failure, will never give in.

Grant us the love which is always ready to forgive; the love which is always eager to help; the love which is always happier to give than to get. Today with faith, hope, and love, let us walk in the pathway of Jesus, and live like our Lord, in whose name we pray. Amen.

Meditation: repeat three times.

Today I accept responsibility for what God has given me to do for his glory. I will trust God to control what I was never meant to, and grant me the wisdom to distinguish the difference.

Romans 12:9-21

Discussion: Christian Motivator's guide:

1). Be sure love is your incentive;
2). Pray for the people you want to motivate;
3). "Tangibilitate!"
4). Be an affirmer;
5). Focus the vision;
6). Be vulnerable;
7). Never give up;

Conclusion: repeat three times.

Today I commit myself to motivate people with love and positive information.

I will not be an agent of fear, but a channel of love.

The morning air was still, except for the myriad of bird calls from the water side, and the nearby trees. *Dreamer* lay motionless in the morning tranquility until it was rocked on the bow wave of an in-coming boat. Bruce stood up in the companionway to get a look at the wave-maker. "It's Lowell, the harbormaster," he announced. Then directing a question to no one in particular, he mused, "Wouldn't you love to commute to work in a Sea Ray?"

"Hey, Dad," his voice took on a bit of enthusiasm, "there are folks at the bakery. It must be time for breakfast, eh?" It was an invitation that didn't need to be repeated. When they had made their way up to the bakery deck, they found only one available table, which they gratefully took.

Moments later their server, who remembered them and introduced himself as Joel, told them that the traps had been a huge success. "We recycled the jugs with hundreds, maybe thousands of yellow jackets," he reported. As he pointed to the fresh traps that were in place, he went on, "We made new ones for today; the best thing is that we didn't have one complaint from the customers about the yellow jackets yesterday. The boss is really happy, eh?"

The menu he gave them was limited, but adequate, especially when they saw "Cinnamon Roll French Toast." All four ordered it. The morning was off to a perfect start.

They were almost finished with their meal when the Skipper asked, "Bubba, I haven't asked about your current project. Are you doing something that you can talk about without killing us?"

Bruce laughed before saying that he was in a boring place right now. "Our group has the challenge to fabricate a uniform jacket that will attach to all of our Microsoft Couriers. The basic idea is that we have to make something that is nearly indestructible, and in a variety of colors or patterns, that will customize the stock application." He chuckled even more. "I've been working with an ethylene monomer that has a continuously linked backbone of polymer that consists mainly of carbon atoms." The other three were staring at him in wonder; it was far more than a casual reference. Bruce waved his hand in a dismissing way, "It's pretty exotic, and we must wear hazmat coverings and breathing apparatus, because the fumes are dynamite."

"That is anything but boring, Bruce," his dad said.

"I didn't know you had to wear protective gear," Annie said.

"What a great idea to build adaptability into a top market product," Kathy added. Obviously they were each very impressed.

"I have learned the meaning of 'serendipity,'" Bruce tried to conclude this uncomfortable attention on his job. "We have found a light-weight material that is so close to bullet proof you wouldn't believe it. Because it can stop anything less than a 50 caliber round, there may be a whole new division just for body armor. And if we can find a way to increase traction, we might have a car tire that will be good for a quarter million miles, all developed while trying to find a suitable jacket for a hand-held device. I really do like my job." He adjusted his sunglasses and looked out toward the boat.

Joel brought their bill with a huge smile. It had the words, "no charge, with compliments." He nodded his head decisively, saying, "The boss really is happy to get a handle on these bees, eh?"

The Skipper started to argue with the generosity, but then said, "Thank you very much; that is more than generous. We are really glad to help the resort." When Joel turned to help the other customers, the Skipper said to the others, "We can give our own gratitude for breakfast. I'm thinking at least ten dollars a couple, and whatever tokens you may have left over from the shower." Kathy loved being called a "couple" with him. They also made their way to the kitchen to personally thank the cook for a great breakfast, and unexpected generosity. Yes indeed, the morning was off to a perfect start.

It was a few minutes before nine o'clock when *Dreamer* backed out of their slip. The Skipper had noted a small drop in the barometer for the second day. He studied the clouds to the northwest, and could see no approaching weather. The morning had a marine haze, but was nearly breathless. They would be on the diesel for sure.

"I can remember the last verse of a poem," the Skipper said quietly. "We had to learn it in a High School English class. Isn't it funny how some little shred can last through the years? The title is 'O Voice That Calls to Me', and I had an assignment to determine the source of the voice. It may have been one of my first theological challenges. The fourth stanza says, 'I hear thee and answer, O my Captain, I will aboard and quickly put to sea, for where Thou art 'tis better than in harbor, and in the breeze beside Thee I am free.'" *Dreamer* was pointed toward the front of the cove, and was increasing speed. "I've always liked that last line, 'And in the breeze beside Thee I am free.' There is a certain essence of sailing that is captured in those words." *Dreamer* was at speed, a smooth bow curl knifing through the clear water. "Who wants the helm?"

Bruce agreed that it must be about his turn. "But Dad," he asked, "how did you answer the teacher's question? What did you determine as the source of the voice?" Bruce seemed very focused on the information.

"As I recall," the Skipper mused, "I wanted to place the source as God, but didn't know exactly how that could be. I think I took a lower route identifying the spirit of discovery through exploration." He raised his eyebrows, suggesting it could have been more profound.

The Skipper pointed to a low headland just off the port bow. "That's Joyce Point, about four miles ahead. We make the turn into Teakerne Arm around it. Your course is 300°, O.K.?" Bruce gave a crisp salute and moved behind the wheel, saying, "In the breeze beside Thee, I am free." He received an affectionate head ruffle for his poetic selection.

When the Skipper said he was going below to read for a while, Kathy thought she might go with him. A second thought suggested that if she went with him, he wouldn't get to read, and she would maneuver the conversation back to that personal stuff that always made her feel uncomfortable. She decided to snuggle into the front of the cockpit, like Annie, and give some thought to the source of her aversion to a happy future.

"Is it because he is a pastor?" she asked herself. "No, he was a tourist when we first met in Victoria. I liked him, and his family, and this boat. I'm very proud of his employment. Where is the aversion there?"

"Is it because he is older?" she asked herself again. "No, he doesn't look, or act older, although he is nine years my senior. In many ways, like his enthusiasm for play, and his interest in almost everything, he definitely seems younger than me. Where is the aversion in that?"

"Is it because he is intellectual, so darned smart?" the questions continued. "No, if anything it is a turn-on for me. He seems to have a wealth of information and a thirst for more. Where is the aversion?"

"Is it because he is divorced?" she continued to ponder. "No, he seems to have understood that chapter of his life, and moved beyond any anger or resentment with comfort. Where in the world is the aversion?" Kathy watched the island slide slowly past them. The morning sun had worked its magic, wooing summer warmth all around this panorama of wilderness wonder.

"The aversion is in me, isn't it?" she asked herself the uncomfortable question. "Do I think he will somehow take advantage of me monetarily?" It was a proper question, she thought. "No, that's absurd. If anything, he will be a financial helper, however we share our incomes." She spent several moments thinking about the advantages of more monthly income.

"Do I think he will be a difficult step-parent to my kids?" she wondered. "Actually, he has shown only affection to them, and they have responded in the same way. Scott can't wait to spend more time on this sailboat." It was easy to foresee a very positive relationship between them.

"Well then," she thought, "is it because others, like mom, my sisters, the kids, will be embarrassed for me?" "What a dumb question," she answered herself. "They think he is a marvelous person. I don't know anyone who doesn't like him. I'll bet his ex even likes him." She spent several more moments dwelling on the likable nature of Norm.

"Is it because intimacy has been a problem, and thoughts of love-making are . . ." she consciously changed the subject in her thoughts. "He said he would be patient and wait until I was ready to talk about it again. I'm not ready!" She turned to Annie and began a fresh conversation.

"Annie, did you and Bruce meet at the University?" She wanted to get those thoughts out of her mind.

"Yes, we did. We were both in the engineering program. I was more on the management side, and he really excelled at research and development. He finished a year in front of me, which made my job search a lot easier. I wanted to work where he did, even though we weren't seriously dating at the time. I had some challenges, and he seemed to make them better. Did you go to a Washington school?"

"I took a detour in my senior year of high school," Kathy responded. She was grateful for the direction of this conversation. "I was a Rotary Exchange student to Holland. It was a fantastic opportunity to travel in Europe, and to be a part of three different families during the year. But when I got back, my savings had pretty much been spent, so I got a job. That's where I met Greg, who I eventually married. He enrolled at Western, so I did too. I thought I would be a CPA or something like it. We got married when I was 21, and had Scotty when I was 22. School had to be put on hold. When I was 24 I had Jenny, and Greg left us. I was glad to get a solid job in the accounting department of Starbucks. We've done well, but school was out of the question."

Annie sat up so she could face Kathy across the cockpit. "I remember you telling us just a tiny bit about that when we first met in Victoria." She was incredulous as she asked, "He never helped you with child support?"

"No, the court said he was responsible, but we never saw anything unless he was feeling real sorry for himself.

Then he would send the kids some little thing; most of the time he was unemployed. I'm proud to have been able to manage for us." She stretched out along the cockpit seat, luxuriating in the space.

CHAPTER 7:
TEAKERNE ARM
Washed in the wilderness

The Skipper came up the companionway, asking, "How close are we to the turn, Bubba?" Bruce answered that he was just about to call down, because they were approaching the point. "Yeah, I tried to read," the Skipper quipped, "but the engine made it difficult." "Was it too noisy?" Bruce asked. "Naw, it kept putting me to sleep!" They all laughed at his drowsy expression. "I'll take the helm."

Joyce Point was broken with large boulders. Caution led them to steer wide around it, even though the fathometer showed ample depth. The Skipper started a very wide starboard turn that would take them near the north side of the Arm. Several minutes passed with only the rumble of the engine and the wash from the bow.

"Dad, I don't see a waterfall. Didn't you say it was a large one?" Bruce was scanning the far shore, but could make out no point of interest. A few more minutes passed, now with all eyes searching for a surprise.

"Hey," Kathy said, pointing to the port bow. "Isn't that a boat?" As they looked in the direction she was pointing another boat came into view, and then the end of a red government dock, and then the crystal spray of the waterfall. Morning sunshine was casting a glorious halo of rainbow colors through the corona of spray it shared. The closer they got to the falls the more beautiful it grew. Taller by far than *Dreamer*'s mast, it was a sparkling cascade of fresh water that washed the rocks strewn along the edge of the Arm.

The nearer they got to the government dock, the more delighted they were with their morning plan. The entire right side was empty of visitors. "Let's do a starboard tie-up this time," the Skipper smirked. No one had pointed out that they always chose a starboard tie-up. "I think we would rather be on the outer end of the dock where there is less traffic, don't you?" When there was no reply from the crew, he understood that his question had actually been a directive. Bruce already had the bumpers over and was fixing the bowline. With no wind at all, this would be an easy landing.

A teenager in a tank-top with a red maple leaf, jumped off the boat across the dock, offering to catch the bow line, as *Dreamer* came to a full stop.

"Just drop the loop over the cleat," Bruce advised. But the cleat was a large heavy duty cleat, too large for the loop. The teen simply placed the loop over the forward arm of the cleat and adeptly took two wraps and secured the line. She grinned up at Bruce, saying, "I think that will hold." She gave a happy wave, and returned to her boat.

The Skipper pulled the transmission into reverse. "Prop walk will bring us right into the dock," he predicted.

Sure enough, as the sailboat began to ease aft, it moved to starboard, snuggling next to the dock. He hopped off to secure the stern line and get the spring line adjusted. In just that easy moment they were firmly moored. The perfect morning was still in effect.

When the diesel was turned off, the silence of solemnity again impressed the crew. Bird songs and the hissing cascade of the waterfall were the only sounds they could hear, and the thump, thump, thump of the bass jazz line from the boat across the dock. The Skipper recognized the artist. Bruce said, "I guess we are not completely in the wilderness yet."

Kathy offered the Skipper a fresh glass of tea, which he gladly accepted, and a plate of chips found their way into the cockpit. It was time to plan the rest of their day.

"Hey Dad, could you explain 'prop walk' to me. That's a term I haven't heard, but I saw it work slick."

"Sure, Brother." He was glad for the question. "There are right or left hand propellers. You can understand that two props with the same pitch, would create a strong bias to the reverse motion; as they cavitate, they create a sideward's pull. So a twin engine set-up has one right hand and one left hand prop for balance. Since a sailboat only has one prop, we get to know and use that sideward's motion as 'prop walk'. *Dreamer* has a left hand prop, which means it is easiest for us to park on the starboard side." Bruce nodded, thinking about the engineering principles.

Then, planning the use of the day, the Skipper said, "I've been thinking that we might want an early lunch, since we had the first breakfast at the bakery this morning. I want to get pictures of the waterfall, and some of the lake. Is anyone interested in taking a swim?" Bruce looked first at Annie and then Kathy.

"It will be chilly," the Skipper continued, "but this afternoon that will be so very welcome." The crew remained quiet. "Well, the waterfall is a fun shower, if you want. In the head there is a bar of soap called 'Boat Soap.' I think it would be a good idea to use that, since it's bio-friendly; that is, if you want to shower in public."

Bruce was quick to try some humor. "You don't have to take off all your clothes." Annie smacked him with her elbow, a well placed shot in the tummy.

Across the dock the side door slid open. The young lady with the maple leaf tank top stepped out on the dock and strolled toward the shore. Several minutes later she strolled back, still by herself.

The Skipper started a conversation with her by asking, "You must like Keiko Matsui."

Immediately, the young woman approached *Dreamer*. "I do. You must know her work. She was at the Paramount last summer. I got to see her show twice. Do you love jazz too?" It was obvious she was eager for a conversation. "Is the music too loud? I'll turn it down."

"It's fine for this time of day," the Skipper's smile was reassuring. "She visits Jazz Alley in Seattle at least once a year. I've heard her a couple times too."

She nodded in understanding. "Yup, my mum and dad are up at the lake again, so I crank my favorite music up a bit. They have a grant from the UBC to do some kind of study on fresh water bivalves, you know, clams. I guess I'm out of luck for any shows this summer." She was standing on the ridge at the edge of the dock, close enough that she could have stepped aboard *Dreamer*.

"How long is the study?" Bruce asked.

"Well we got here as soon as school was out five weeks ago, and we'll be back for the start in September." She had a wry smile, "I will know every plank in this dock by then."

"Don't you get some time off?" Bruce wasn't sure if the idea of an entire summer here was a good or bad thing.

"Every other weekend we go into Campbell River to do laundry and shop for groceries. It's a five hour run. Does that count as time off?"

The Skipper suddenly felt the need for an introduction. "I'm sorry. I should have first thanked you for helping with our lines." She waved her hand in a casual dismissal. "I'm Norm O'Banyon, and this is Kathy Swanson." Then pointing toward Bruce, he said, "My son Bruce and his wife Annie. We're from Seattle." She nodded.

"I'm Sherry. My folks are biologists from UBC, and we live in Burnaby."

The Skipper waited for more information, but when none came, he improvised. "We were just about to fix some sandwiches and have a picnic up at the lake. Would you like to join us?"

She studied them for a moment before accepting. She said, "The lake is good to swim in, not too cold. But the really fun thing to do is stand under the waterfall. It is usually busy in the afternoon when folks get here."

Her attention was drawn to three eagles climbing into the morning above the island. In the still warm air, their wings were busy gaining altitude. Two of the eagles had bright white head and tail; the other was all black. "That's Amelia, I call her. She's getting flight training again. I think she'll be on her own pretty soon." They watched as the trio climbed higher and higher, only an occasional chirp of encouragement to the soloist.

Four hours later a happy crowd came down the dock led by *Dreamer's* crew and Sherry, followed by Sherry's folks, Jon and June Sperry. The biologists had greeted them on their way back to the boat, saying, "We are grateful that she met some generous and proper folks. Too often there are others who would like to make friends with a lovely young woman who has nothing more to do than wait for her nerdy folks." Both Annie and Kathy assured them that Sherry had been a delight to meet and filled with information in their conversations.

Bruce chimed in, "We were impressed that she dove from the top of the rock! What is that, five meters at least? She was awesome!"

The Skipper added, "And you jumped right in too, Bubba! I was impressed."

"I didn't jump in," Bruce protested, "someone pushed me." He looked seriously first at Annie, who shook her head, then at Kathy, who also denied any culpability. "Dad, did you shove me off that cliff?"

"Hey, I wouldn't endanger my number one helper. If you hadn't cleared those rocks at the bottom, I'd be hauling up the main myself!" The Skipper shook his head to emphasize the denial.

Annie offered a solution, "Maybe because you were watching that cute girl so closely, you stumbled yourself. It might have just been an accident."

Bruce had the distinct impression that the subject should change, immediately. "Dad, did you get some good pictures of the falls? It looked like you had some creative angles."

Since there were no shore facilities at this government dock, the girls were eager to get aboard *Dreamer* and the privacy it offered. When finally all four had their turn, and were gathered in the shade of the salon, fresh glasses of Crystal Light were poured. The Skipper asked if they wanted some quiet time, or should they be about the afternoon conversation?

"When I put our topics together," he said, "today's was the one that most focused what I wanted us to get to. I suppose it could be entitled 'Love's Motivation.' But I don't want to hurry us." He looked at their faces for some suggestion one way or another.

Kathy was the first to speak, saying, "It sounds wonderful, but first I think I need some of your magic Tea Tree Oil for a bit of sunburn." Within a couple minutes the pungent fragrance of the healing ointment filled the salon, as it was applied to backs, and noses, and ears, and shoulders.

Finally, by consensus or majority vote, the Skipper felt it was time to begin. "Do you ever get frustrated with people?" he asked.

Bruce snorted with laughter, "Who doesn't?"

"I know," the Skipper continued. "Parents are frustrated by their children, and vice versa; spouses are frustrated with one another. We get frustrated with our job, or people at work." Kathy had a sudden and unwelcome recollection of the store room. We are frustrated by politicians, and pastors, which are sometime the same. We are frustrated by our neighbors, or other shoppers, or sports fans."

"When we realize that we are frustrated, we have a choice to make: do we ignore or tolerate the frustration, or do we separate ourselves from it? A third option is do we try to change it? We are really not very good at the first choice. We might tolerate it for a while, but sooner or later it will probably, by necessity, become a second or third choice. With a 50% divorce rate we know that a lot of spouses decide not to tolerate living with a frustrating mate. These days we know of a lot of employees who choose to work anywhere else but here. It's that third choice that fascinates me."

"If we know that the choices someone else is making are hurting our relationship, or hurting themselves or others, we really wish we could change them. Even if we give up our idea that we have either the right or the power to change them, we want to help them. Which brings us to more choices; we can change them through the application of fear or force, which is the manipulation in a culture of competition Mr. Branch described, and almost never works well, or. ."

Bruce interrupted to ask, "Dad, could you tell me what force might look like?"

"I think it is easiest to identify in the work community. If someone leaves their job and management chooses not to replace them, but expects the same production out of the remaining work force, that's a manipulation by force. If a work situation is arbitrarily changed in its compensation package or work hours, without the employee's input, that's force. If a contract dispute turns into a strike, that's manipulation by force. If a contract dispute cannot be resolved, attorneys or negotiators might be called in, which is often manipulation by force." Bruce nodded his understanding and agreement.

"Norm, can you give an example of fear?" Annie asked.

"I think that's the most common manipulation," he answered. "Spouses might barter at first; if you do this, I'll do that; but it can easily turn into 'If you keep doing that, don't expect to find any affection in bed tonight;' that's fear; and as soon as we discover what's really important to our mate, we have power. The possibility of withholding whatever that is, whether it's going to church, or golfing, or the opera, becomes a fear leverage. Of course, there is abuse, whether physical or emotional, and the ultimate fear is to threaten, 'If you don't do this, I'll leave.'"

"Parents are forever threatening their children with dire consequences, if the child misbehaves. Kids see through those attempts at control, by challenging the authority. There is rarely a winner in that sort of competition negotiation." When Annie nodded he continued.

"The only way to help people change is to motivate them in a culture of discovery of love. That sounds great, but how do we do it? Where can we get guidance in helping other people reach their full potential? That is the question that I wanted answered."

The Skipper smiled when he answered his own question. "The best guide for motivating people I've ever found was written by the Apostle Paul. In Romans 12: 9-21, that Kathy read for us this morning, Paul gives us the qualifications of an authentic Christian motivator. It is an inventory of our own motivational skills. As we move through them, it would help to visualize the faces of people we want to help. Would it help to hear the scripture again, in a fresh context?" When they all agreed, he asked Kathy to turn to the selection, and read again.

She was ready, this time, to read with confidence: "*Love must be sincere. Hate what is evil; cling to what is good. Be devoted to one another in love. Honor one another above yourselves. Never be lacking in zeal, but keep your spiritual fervor, serving the Lord. Be joyful in hope, patient in affliction, and faithful in prayer. Share with the Lord's people who are in need. Practice hospitality.*"

"Bless those who persecute you; bless and do not curse. Rejoice with those who rejoice; mourn with those who mourn. Live in harmony with one another. Do not be proud, but be willing to associate with people of low position. Do not be conceited. Do not repay anyone evil for evil. Be careful to do what is right in the eyes of everyone. If it is possible, as far as it depends on you, live at peace with everyone. Do not take revenge, my dear friends, but leave room for God's wrath, for it is written: 'It is mine to avenge; I will repay,' says the Lord. On the contrary: 'If your enemy is hungry, feed him; if he is thirsty, give him something to drink.

In doing this, you will heap burning coals on his head.' Do not be overcome by evil, but overcome evil with good." Her smile was one of satisfaction, and appreciation for being part of the afternoon.

"Thanks, Sweetie," the Skipper said in response. "Look at the outline from this morning. First point is: Be sure love is your incentive. 'Let love be without hypocrisy,' Paul says in verse 9. The kind of love he is talking about is the giving, forgiving, unqualified love he has received from Christ Jesus. We can't pretend to have that depth of love; it flows as a result of a profound relationship with the Lord. In reality, Jesus is the master motivator. It is from him, and how he worked in our lives, that we learn how to motivate and inspire others. He loved us when we least deserved it, and our resistance or rebellion did not dissuade his persistence in loving us."

"Jesus was more interested in our future than our past. He knew that the things we did were because of the kind of person we were inside. We couldn't change our actions until we were transformed, and that transformation didn't take place until we knew we were loved by Christ."

"The important thing to remember is that we can't change anyone!" He said it again for emphasis, "We can't change anyone. Only Christ can do that. Instead, our function is to be so filled with his love that we love others with that power. Notice that I didn't say 'copy his love.' That's what Paul meant when he spoke of hypocritical love. A hypocrite is someone who is playing a part, pretending to be what he isn't. We are hypocritical lovers when we think that on our own, we can imitate Christ's love for others. That's not our calling. We are simply riverbeds for the flow of his love." He paused for that to sink in.

"Christ's love must transform our thinking about the person we want to motivate. He wants us to see that person as a forgiven, cherished person of ultimate value. Then he wants us to help envision that person's full potential, so we can claim the miracle of change Christ alone can perform. Once that's clearly implanted in our thinking, what we say to the person and how we relate to him or her will follow naturally. So here's the hard part: do the people we'd like to motivate know how much we love them just as they are, and that our love is not something we've manufactured but comes from Christ himself?"

"To be attractive witnesses to the Good News of Jesus, we must mirror God's grace. That's why Paul says, 'Abhor what is evil. Cling to what is good.' Without being guilty of unhealthy introspection, we must ask ourselves if we are living the quality of life we want to motivate in them. Does our love for them in spite of what they do or say, make our witness dramatically irresistible? It is true, of course that people need to know where we stand. But they also need to know that we are committed to stand with them in their struggles."

"In short, our love must be expressed in unfailing friendship. Being an understanding and caring friend may well be our most Christ-like act. Remember, Jesus gave his disciples a new level of intimacy when he said, 'No longer do I call you servants, for a servant does not know what his master is doing; but I have called you friends.' (John 15:15) And to be Christ's friend means befriending others."

"Did you hear that Paul even lists specific ways to express that friendship? This is important to get right. We are to be kind in communicating real affection for the people we want to help. That means telling them how important they are to us, how much we value them, and how fervently we believe in them and their potential. We are to treat them as brothers or sisters who long for the Lord's best in their lives. Time with them is given high priority. Listening and caring about their needs honors them as persons."

"We are to be available, quick to respond to their call for help without hesitation. 'Not lagging in diligence,' is how Paul said it; he means not 'slow or pokey.' Night or day we are to be on call as truly reliable friends of those we are seeking to help and inspire." Before he could go on, Bruce again interrupted.

"Wait, Dad, isn't that way too much to ask? That sounds like a major commitment."

"You've been listening, Bubba," the Skipper said with appreciation. "It is a big-time major commitment for sure. Think about it; the people you are trying to help can be seen in the context of your service to the Lord. That carries the impact of Jesus' words, 'Inasmuch as you did it to one of the least of these my brothers, you did it to me.' (Matthew 25:40) I'd say that's about as big as it gets. The thought that Jesus may come to us in the very people we want to change, the people who disagree with us, fills us with awe.

How we respond to them is really our response to Christ. But the liberating reassurance is that he will give us the love for people that is required to motivate them. So we must be sure that love is our only incentive."

Uncharacteristically, Kathy asked, "Is that why the scripture says, 'Love your enemies and pray for those who persecute you,'?"

"Sweetie, that is right on in two ways; love is our incentive, and secondly, a great quality of an effective motivator is faithfulness in intercessory prayer." All three of his listeners signaled for an explanation. "Do you understand the word, 'intercede'? It's when a third party speaks on behalf of another person, usually in their defense. In the Bible, prayer is spoken of as anything from magic to the heights of spiritual communion with God. When a person intercedes on behalf of another, by seeking God's blessing, or healing, or nurture, we call that intercessory prayer." They nodded with fresh understanding.

"We need to spend more time talking to the Lord about a person we want to help than we spend talking to that person. As Paul put it in verse twelve, 'Rejoice in hope, patient in tribulation, continuing steadfastly in prayer.' Steadfast, consistent, prolonged prayer gives us both hope and patience. Praying for people helps us focus on what the Lord wants for them rather than our ideas of what they should do or be. Intercessory prayer is not for the purpose of getting the Lord to accomplish our vision for people, as pure as that may be. Rather, we are to allow him to show us what he wants to do in their lives."

"Does that make sense?" the Skipper asked. When three heads nodded affirming, he continued, "So often my frustration over people has driven me to pray for them. I usually begin by telling the Lord my agenda for them.

I explain how it should be. Not surprisingly, that doesn't work well. But when I commit the people to him, and ask for his vision, what I begin to see is so much greater than my wishes or notions. Then my prayer shifts into high gear. I know that what I am asking for is what the Lord is ready to give. I can rejoice in the hope that in his timing and way, it shall be so."

"But not only does prayer clarify our hopes for people, it also gives us patience in the process of trying to help them. We need not be hasty and resort to using fear tactics. At the same time we know that it is not up to us, because the Lord is at work in the people for whom we are praying. With infinite wisdom he is influencing their thoughts, creating a desire to change. As he works his purpose out in circumstances, he is arranging opportunities and preparing the way for our efforts to encourage people. Christ will be with us to love through us, to inspire the right words, and to give us strength when we get discouraged. And our prayers will lead us to the next step of being a positive and creative motivator."

"In a generation past, there was a powerful preacher in Harlem named Father Divine, who had a favorite, and often quoted phrase. He would say, 'the trouble in religion is that too many people know how to theorize, but they don't know how to tangibilitate!' He simply meant, 'Do something tangible!' For us to tangibilitate, we need to ask ourselves, 'What would communicate understanding or caring for the person we want to help? What can we do to lift some burden, meet some need, or provide some special delight?' Paul talks about 'distributing to the needs of saints, given to hospitality.' (Romans 12:13) He is asking his readers to meet physical needs and welcome people who are strangers. This is our model for all relationships."

Bruce would have asked for a fuller explanation, but the Skipper went on, "Sometimes it might mean giving financial help, or stepping in to assist in a crisis. More often it will be a sensitive, caring act that helps a person know you are committed to being a lasting friend. I suppose that could be anything from making a phone call to checking in with the person, to giving a meaningful gift, or interrupting your schedule to listen, or maybe helping with a project, or including that person in the inner circle of your cherished friends at a special event. A tangibilitating motivator is innovative. Rather than asking, 'What can I do to help?' they take the time and effort to discover what would mean the most to that other person."

The Skipper smiled at the crew, asking, "Are we ready to move on?" Again, when he received nods from each, he said, "The fourth step in motivation, rather than manipulation, is affirmation. It is the power to bless! Cool, huh? Paul goes on in verse 14 to say, 'Bless those who persecute you; bless and do not curse.' If we are to speak well of those people on the fringes of our lives who make things difficult for us, we certainly should be careful to motivate those close to us with love and not manipulate them with fear. What we say to or about a person has the power to bless or curse. And a lack of a blessing is in itself a curse."

"Hey, Dad, wait," Bruce couldn't hold back his question. "How can that be?"

"Think about it, Bubba. If we withhold praise, or a blessing, it locks a person into his or her own present stage of growth. We all need affirmation of our worth as a person and our potential to be more than we are now. Affirmation provides self-esteem and hope for their future. It is not dishonest flattery, but a communication that we are for people, and not against them. The former moves them forward, and the latter, stops them cold."

"Words of affirmation from a motivator are absolutely necessary to penetrate the layers of self-doubt and self-negation that are common. We so easily get down on ourselves and become defensive; we can understand how others would too. But when a motivator believes in us, and encourages us by the blessing of affirmation, we are able to change and grow. It is a universal principle. If it is true for us, it works just as well in others."

"An affirmer is one who has experienced the ultimate affirmation of Christ. In spite of all that they might have done or been, Christ loves absolutely. He came to live and die for us that we might know that we are loved and forgiven. And now, as reigning Lord, God with us, he constantly reassures us that we belong to him. He will never let go, and we can be a blessing to others."

"When we know that, we can become an affirmer of others even when they frustrate us. What they do cannot keep us from believing in what they can become by Christ's transforming power. Our trust is in what he will do; our only responsibility is to affirm that we love the other person, especially in their times of delight and times of suffering. Paul says, 'rejoice with those who rejoice, and weep with those who weep' (12:15). Life is a bittersweet blend of success and challenge, joy and sorrow. As genuine affirmers of other people, we are to be willing to share not only their mountain-top experiences but their darkest most threatening valleys as well. Doing this leads naturally to the next crucial aspect of motivation. Can I go on, or do you need a break?"

Annie spoke up immediately, "Oh, go on! This is really interesting to me." She was making her notes on the morning devotion sheet.

"So then, step number five: The central challenge of the Christian motivator is to help people envision what their lives would look like if committed to Christ, filled with his Spirit, and guided by his priorities for them. Our task is not to bend them to our will, or our ideas of what might be best for them. Instead, we are to ask penetrating questions that press them to evaluate where they are going in their lives, the kind of person they want to be, and the quality of relationships they want to have. Our challenge is to help put people in touch with the Master. What a person thinks about Christ, and his will, directly controls the outcome of their life. Therefore, truly creative motivators will inspire other people to allow Christ to repattern their minds in conformity with his will and purpose." Seeing Bruce's frown, the Skipper said, "Yes, that is a very large thought. This is the very heart of it! The mind of Christ is the motivating power for the reorientation of our thinking, the reformation of our wills, and the remodeling of our feelings."

"Too few Christians have discovered the gift of the indwelling mind of Christ. That's why our thinking about life is often confused, our values and priorities are so inconsistent with his, and our personalities are so far from being like him. Any effort to motivate people to change or grow that skims over the deepest need we all have, to receive more of the mind of Christ, is surface meddling that brings no lasting results."

"So often, problems and crises provide opportunities to talk with people about the direction and goals of their lives. The presence of conflict in our relationships should awaken us to be sensitive to the kinds of things we may be doing that block their response to the Lord. But any confrontation must be preceded by caring and companionship. Only then can we share with people how Christ is working in our lives to deal with problems or challenges similar to theirs. It is then that they will feel free to ask themselves hard questions about their lives. And it is only when they have come to their own conclusions about their need that we can lovingly share our hope and vision for them."

"There are just two more points to make on this subject, and I'll try to make them brief. The next step in the dynamic process of motivating people is our own vulnerability in dealing with our own needs and shortcomings. This is a tough one for me to share with the dearest people in the world to me. But I truly believe that only a person who is changing can help others change. No one has it all together. Anyone who tries to pretend that he has is disqualified as a motivator. In fact, we can reproduce in others only what we are constantly rediscovering in our own lives. And since the things that usually disturb us in others are the very things that either have been or are trouble spots in our own lives, we can readily recognize them and respond creatively."

"I believe vulnerability makes us approachable. When we are free to share what the Lord is doing with the raw material of our imperfect personalities, people are drawn to us and feel free to share their lives with us. And since the Lord is never finished with us, there is always a next step of growth we need to take."

"For example," he took a big breath, "in this one-sided discussion, I've tried to share some of the most liberating discoveries I've made about being a Christian motivator. With all my mind and heart I believe that motivating people with love is the only alternative to manipulating them with fear. And at the same time, I'm living what I believe is one of the hardest challenges of my life. As a father, a pastor, a counselor, a dear friend, there are many people I'd like to help, but I am forever tempted to bypass the first five steps of motivation based on love. It is that old 'physician, heal thyself' syndrome.'"

"I was at session a couple weeks ago, whining about our slow growth at the church. The clerk gave me a hug and reminded me that attendance is up for the first time in several years. She called me 'impatient.' And the truth is I am impatient. I get impatient with the institutional process; I often want things done yesterday. I tire of religious people who miss the adventure of exhilarating discipleship. In less noble ways, I get impatient with people who seem to repeat the same mistakes, take the same weary short-cuts. I get impatient with people who make excuses for not connecting with their faith walk, who can't seem to make obvious decisions."

"Usually my impatience is caused by inner impatience with myself. That's when I must take an extra measure of time in my prayers to receive fresh grace. The Lord is faithful: he reminds me of how patient he has had to be with me over the years. In these times of prayer I am refreshed and renewed to be a loving and vulnerable motivator of people."

"Believe me; the Lord has a way of knocking down our arrogant presuppositions by showing us what we really are. At such moments we become well aware that the kind of growth we are trying to inspire in others is also needed within our own lives. And that leads me to the seventh and final quality of a motivator; they never give up!"

"Paul concludes his list of admonitions for the Christian communicator with three negative challenges that convey a positive impact: first he says, 'repay no one evil for evil.

Have regard for good things in the sight of all men. If it is possible, as much as depends on you, live peaceably with all men.' In other words, 'don't retaliate!' For the Christian motivator this simply means that we are not to reject people who do not respond to our overtures of love. We can't write people off as long as the Lord has another chapter to write in their lives. We are to keep praying, caring, and being available. To live 'peaceably' simply means to keep the relationship going, maintaining the open channels of communication."

"Secondly Paul says, 'Beloved, do not avenge yourselves, leave room for God's activity; for it is written, 'Vengeance is mine; I will repay' says the Lord.' In other words don't play God! This brings us full circle to where we began this discussion of using fear to get what we want from people. When we threaten to punish or actually take judgment into our own hands, we not only lose our effectiveness to influence them positively, but we also provoke anger toward us that distracts people from coming to grips with what God wants to do in their lives. How does giving food and drink to our enemy heap coals of fire? It simply dissipates their anger toward us and forces them to deal with God. Our persistence in personal and practical caring for people when they seem to deserve it least can create a desire to know the Lord who is the source of our unconquerable love for them."

Looking at his watch, the Skipper gave a big sigh of relief, "And finally," he said with conviction, "Paul says, 'Do not be overcome by evil, but overcome evil with good.' In other words, don't give in to discouragement; it is sin's most powerful weapon. The five most debilitating words I can think of are, 'It won't make any difference.' That could be the theme song of underachievement. Discouragement is really a build-up of fear. Far from being the problem of a few depressed people, discouragement lurks beneath the surface in most people. I wish they could claim the five word antidote for discouragement used by effective motivators: 'Love makes all the difference.'"

"Each time we refuse to use fear to manipulate others, we overcome evil with good. Sin's program of trying to overcome good with fear is given one more defeat. Remember, we are counterculture Christians called to reverse the epidemic of fear in our world. The Lord is at work through us. Daily, he encourages us with signs of progress. We do not need to rely on fear, nor trust its outcome; and we are certainly no conduits of fear, but channels of love."

"That feels like a good place to stop, and take the offering." They were all surprised at how engaged they were in the topic. There were, of course, lots of questions. Kathy's was first.

"Norm, do you truly believe that fear is an option in our lives?" Her eyes searched his.

"You've been listening. That's great! And my answer is yes, I do; it is certainly not a necessity." He paused allowing the multiple meanings of that response to sink in. "There are terrible things that happen on our highways that cause me to be less careless. I would fear like the dickens to be involved in a crash. And I'm not wild about going to the dentist, or some of the tests my doctor must perform. I know that I am growing older, which will eventually present challenges, but none of that frightens me. My response is always mine to make."

"But there are so many real tragedies around us," she persisted. "How about . . . ?" Her lips clamped down the rest of the question. She realized it was headed in a totally negative direction.

The Skipper reached over and held her hand affectionately. "If we had time to look at more stories," he said, "there is a great one in 2 Kings 8, in which the Syrian army has surrounded the city where Elisha lives. They want to capture and kill him. Everyone is terrified. They all see the impending destruction; all that is, except the prophet, who tells them, 'Fear not for those who are with us are more than those who are with them.' In other words there are always superior resources available to us, if we just have eyes to see them. Our challenge is the reprogramming of our thought process to identify them. By the way, the story turns out quite nicely for the prophet."

Bruce brought a conclusion to the discussion by simply observing, "Dad, I had no idea Bible study could be so enjoyable. Thank you for your work in preparation. I want to be a conduit of love." Then with a growing grin, he wondered, "Do you think we have time before supper to make another trip up to the lake?"

"I think that is a great suggestion," the Skipper answered. "I'll join you in a few minutes. If I cook up some elbow macaroni, we can make a pasta salad later for supper. That way the boat will have a chance to cool off before we get back."

Kathy offered to hang out with him, saying "I've already had a little too much sun."

From the settee she watched him move about the galley. With limited space, there was a place for everything, pan, water, stove. The process looked effortless. She understood that part of his charm to her was that he rarely forced anything. For several moments she pondered the truth of that. When the water began to boil, and the macaroni was added, he came over to kiss her.

"I was hoping for that," she said softly. Standing up, she was able to press her body against his, delivering a much more direct kiss. "I was really hoping for that."

Realizing that the moment could quickly become too arousing, the Skipper guided Kathy back into the settee; he sat across from her, holding her hand. "We'd better set a good example for the kids," he said not sure how to handle the jumble of emotions that were racing through him.

Kathy was a bit flushed; or was it sunburned? She caught her breath, and tried to sound relaxed, when she was anything but. "I know I have told you what a great trip this is. It's just over the top in so many ways, and I like the scenery too." She finally managed a chuckle at her own humor. "I know that I am trying your patience. So much of what you have shared with us seems tailor-made for me. I may be one of those people who are an obstacle because I make excuses for not being more decisive." Norm tried to reassure her that he was not directing any of it toward her.

Kathy went on, "I've had a ton of thoughts since yesterday. Can I just tell you that I have felt that I haven't had much of a choice in the big decisions of my life." She gave a tremble that shook her whole body. "I was too young to fall in love with Greg. He was five years older than me, and seemed so mature. I was married and pregnant in a blink." She smiled wistfully. "In another blink I was pregnant again, and he was gone. No one ever talked with me as you have." Now the smile radiated genuine warmth. "No one ever told me that I could make any of those big decisions. I think I had a victim mentality. All I did was adjust, cope, and adjust again. Then we met." A bit of a giggle changed into her next question. "Do you remember that I thought you were the hotel concierge?" When he smiled and nodded, she continued.

"I know that the conflict within me is all my doing. You have shown me a whole new possibility. You are motivating me in love, and it's wonderful. I really want you in my life. I really want you." Her meaning was very clear to both of them. "I'm like that young eagle who is just learning to fly, but I'm afraid to be decisive. I'm afraid of heights."

He got up to take the cooking pot off the stove, and pour the pasta in a strainer. "Do you know what I would like this afternoon?" It was the sort of question Kathy halfway dreaded. When she shook her head, he chuckled and answered, "I'd like to go up and dive off the rocks. What do you say we catch up with Bruce and Annie?" He gave her a quick gentle kiss that said, "everything is going to be just right!"

"I can't believe how fun that was!" Bruce bubbled. "It looked so much higher when I just stood there. Then you dove and it seemed more manageable. What fun!" The girls had been satisfied to just watch, and take pictures, of course. Bruce was convinced that his form was Olympic, at least. The pictures might be a little disappointing for him.

The Skipper had suggested, when they returned to *Dreamer*, that supper could be done on an assembly line. "Annie, you can chop a tomato and a cucumber; Kathy can cube some cheese and cut up that deli ham. Bruce is in charge of the garlic bread, and the Skipper can assemble, and add the mayo, mustard, salt, pepper, and AP." Before the guys' hair was completely dry, they were seated in the cockpit, enjoying a summer supper with a bottle of Chardonnay.

Bruce said, "If this isn't the good life, you can sure see it from here!"

Annie asked, "What is the plan for tomorrow? Are we going to move far?"

"We are moving," the Skipper answered. "Big Bay is a salmon resort on Stuart Island. It's about three hours from here on the diesel, maybe a little more. The important thing for us to keep in mind is the tide. The last mile or so is very tide sensitive; it's called Yuculta Rapids. If we miss the high slack, we might not be able to get there until afternoon when we can ride a flood tide in."

Kathy wondered, "Can we leave earlier?"

"Good question, Kiddo," the Skipper said affectionately. "The earlier we leave the better. And you know that if you want to stay under the covers, I can get us started by myself." No one at the table thought there was a ghost of a chance of that happening.

"I'm ready to win another card game tonight," Bruce growled. "Are there any takers?"

"Do you remember how to play 'Oh Well'?" the Skipper suggested; "and what do you mean 'another'?"

When Kathy shook her head, Bruce explained that in the book of Hoyle, it's called "Oh Hell." "We bid to see how many tricks we can take in each hand. You get a bonus if you make your bid. Right, Dad?"

"Perfectly correct. And to sweeten the pot, let's say that the winner gets a Brownie Hot Fudge Sundae at Big Bay, purchased by the other three." When they nodded agreement, the Skipper said, "I have a hunger for a brownie! Let's play."

It was agreed that in fairness to Kathy, a couple practice hands were played. There was some disagreement about the rules. "No, the dealer starts by dealing only one card, and we bid who will get it."

"Just to be fair," the Skipper offered, "I'll take a handicap by dealing first."

Once started, the game took almost an hour to play the thirteen hands. There was no clear leader at hand eleven. Bruce was the leader at hand twelve, and on the final hand, the Skipper moved ahead by a mere two points.

"Ha, I have a real hunger for chocolate!" he crowed.

"Let's go two out of three," Bruce wheedled. He knew by the last lingering hint of twilight that at 10:25, it was time to turn in. He just didn't want to admit that yet another card game had slipped past him.

"How about a prayer instead," the Skipper offered. They held hands around the table.

"Heavenly Lord, we come to you tonight because we need you. We cannot work well by day without your help, and we cannot sleep well at night without your blessing. We come to you tonight, Spirit of Peace, because we love you. We want to speak to you, and we want to listen to you speaking to us before the day ends and the night comes. So come to meet us as we have come to meet you. Help us use tomorrow wisely, not foolishly; help us use it as an unrepeatable gift of life abundant, in Jesus' name. Amen."

Kathy held Annie's hand a little longer than the others. She was slow to release the day; it had been filled to over-flowing. She knew she was tired physically, but emotionally she was empowered. As they finally moved toward their staterooms, the Skipper closed the companionway hatch and turned out lights in the salon. "Oh, good the night!"

CHAPTER 8:
YUCULTA RAPIDS
Give God glory, and accept God's guidance

She lay quietly in her dark stateroom, listening. Kathy was sure that it was after 5 o'clock, but the light was dim and soft. She pulled on her sweatshirt and shorts, ruffled her hair a bit, and peeked out her door. The salon was dark, but a light was coming from under Norm's stateroom. She backed up, and closed her door softly. She would wait until she heard someone else. When the diesel kicked on she gave a startled jump. She hurried up to the cockpit to find Annie bundled under her blanket with her feet curled under her. A low marine deck of clouds prevented the morning light from finding her. The Skipper was on the dock, releasing the stern line, and Bruce was holding the spring line. A light mist had left a wet sheen on the deck.

When the Skipper stepped aboard, he whispered, "Good morning, Cutie; we have a different sort of summer morning, huh?" There were five other dark boats on the dock. It was obvious that he was trying to respect their sleep; although she wondered how quiet a diesel engine could be. He put the transmission in forward gear, and eased away from the dock. Several seconds later he eased the throttle just a bit, and *Dreamer* had separation from the snug dock. By the time they had opened a hundred meters, they were at speed, on their way deeper into the adventure.

"Hey," the Skipper said in a natural voice, "who wants some Crystal Light and Pirate Pastry?" He waited for just a couple seconds and answered his own question, "I do, I do!" Morning was surely happening, sunny or not.

Bruce said he had some reading to do in their stateroom; Annie rolled her eyes in disbelief. She made a couple snoring noises, but said she would join him. Kathy remained with the Skipper for about a half an hour before she admitted that her covers could give her some welcome warmth. The Skipper hummed, "Oh a sailor's life's for me, upon the open sea . . ." A few minutes later the mist turned into rain, and the Skipper went below long enough to find and put on his foul weather jacket and hat.

Just before seven o'clock, Kathy came up into the shelter of the dodger to offer the Skipper a cup of hot tea, and Bruce offered to take the helm so he could warm up below.

"Thanks, Bubba," the Skipper said as he relinquished his spot at the wheel. "This is called 'Calm Channel,' and this morning it is living up to its name. Can you believe there is not a ripple in sight, just rain splatters?"

At seven thirty the Skipper was back up in the cockpit with his binoculars, peering into the murky course they were on. "I may have underestimated our time of arrival.

We still have a ways to go, and I think the tide has swung around. We are beginning to struggle against the ebb."

By eight o'clock he had taken over the helm again, and was sure that they had missed the window of opportunity. "Look up the side of Stuart," he directed Bruce's attention. "The Yuculta Rapids have developed rips and white water. I think the wise thing to do would be to go over to the lee side of Read Island, and drop the hook for a while. We can ride the flood into Big Bay in time for a late lunch."

Bruce was positive as usual, "Sounds like a great plan. Maybe I can catch up on some reading." His grin was too obvious for anyone to miss. "How much chain shall I flake out?"

"We'll look for about twenty feet of depth," the Skipper replied, "but with the tide going out against us, let's put out about a hundred and twenty five, that's five red links."

As Bruce headed for the bow, he gave thumbs up. This might be a perfect way to ride out a summer rain shower.

The Skipper watched the fathometer as they eased in near the lee shore. He was sure they would be well protected in this close. *Dreamer* slowed to a near stop, and Bruce lowered the anchor to the first red link. *Dreamer* eased back as the chain was released, "There's the second red link!" and before the fifth link was over the side, they could feel the boat stop. The anchor had set in the mud and sand, but Bruce eased out a bit more chain for good measure. He snapped the safety shackle and returned to the cockpit. With an "All secure, Skipper," he joined the other three under the dodger.

"Dad, did you notice how muddy the water seems, and there are a ton of limbs or branches floating around. Do you think someone might be working up stream?"

"Could be; there hasn't been much rain down here, but maybe up on the hills there could have been enough last night for some local erosion. Anyone else want some granola?" he asked.

The boat was warm and cozy by the time the breakfast dishes were cleared. Kathy suggested, "Can we do our morning devotions? This seems perfect."

The Skipper reached into the cabinet for day 7.

Day 7.)

Beautiful, beautiful, Jesus is beautiful
And Jesus makes beautiful things of my life.
Carefully touching me, causing my eyes to see,
Jesus makes beautiful things of my life.

Morning Prayer:

Thank you Lord, for this new morning; we believe you are the Light that never goes out, the heart that never grows cold, and the hand that never stops reaching out to us. We have a powerful, positive suspicion that you have a plan for our today and tomorrow, and that this beautiful plan is unfolding exactly as it should. We will stop trying to understand, and instead start enjoying whatever you provide; in Jesus' wonderful name we pray. Amen.

Meditation: repeat three times.

Today I commit myself to motivate people with love and positive information.
I will not be an agent of fear, but a channel of love.

Romans 8: 28, 37-39

Things don't work out; God works out things!

1). How God works;
2). God uses everything;
3). Works together;
4). New every morning;
5). God's grand plan for our lives;
6). Contagious faith.

Conclusion: repeat three times.

I will boldly face the future with the sure confidence that God will work all things together for my ultimate good, and His Glory.

The salon was perfectly still for a bit, each of them savoring private thoughts. Finally Bruce asked, "Dad, do you think we could take the dinghy out and do some bottom fishing?"

"You bet, if you row." They both headed for the head, and then aft where the inflatable was waiting for them. The girls watched them glide away with high hopes, as every good fisherman would have.

The girls watched as the slow process of rigging the lines, and then dragging lures along the bottom consumed several minutes. The dinghy moved a bit further out into the ebb, and was carried a few hundred meters aft. Bruce worked to bring them back even with the boat. Finally, they moved out toward the ebb tide again but this time they dropped the fishing anchor, which held them secure.

Annie said, "I've heard Norm call you tender names, and even saw a kiss. Are you guys having a good week?" Her smile was that of a happy friend.

"I certainly am, and I think Norm is too. Now I can see how a boat trip like this could be very romantic." Her smile was just as radiant. "Seriously though, he has been so very helpful in getting my problems into a fresh focus."

What sort of problems?" Annie asked, now turned to face Kathy.

"Oh, I don't know how much I want to go into my past with you. I want you to think the best of me, and sometimes that's a challenge."

"I hope you know that I love you, and think of you as family." Annie reached over to hold Kathy's hand.

"Norm and I seem pretty right together," Kathy began. "I know I told you we were just friends, but you have seen that it is much more than that. I didn't know that we were going to be talking about fear on this trip. I might have been too afraid to come along if I had." She chuckled at her own joke. "He has helped me face some of the obstacles I have put up for protection, and he has patiently shown me a surprising depth of my abilities."

"That sounds pretty serious to me," Annie's smile grew even bigger.

"Yesterday in the boat there was a kiss that swept me . . . . ;" she wasn't sure how much she should share. "I was pretty forward, and not a little wound up. He was such a gentleman; he suggested we come up to the lake with you guys. You probably didn't know you were being used as chaperones." They both got a giggle out of that thought.

Kathy continued, "I know there are men who would love that sort of opportunity. It has been a long while since

I felt aroused passion. What I learned is that his morality is deep and solid. It makes me love him even more."

"You love him!" Annie cheered. "I knew it! You were always more than just friends. You two make such an ideal couple, and Scott and Jenny think the world of him. I can see you all as a perfect family. When you told me on the way up that . . ."

Kathy suddenly jumped up, crying out, "What's that?" Her finger was pointing up into the rapids. "Annie, what is it? Oh Annie!" She looked at the dinghy; the boys were sitting with their backs to it! Rolling and jerking along in the rapids was a large maple tree, washing directly toward the unsuspecting men, its great limbs waving like a demonic creature. "Oh crap!" She shouted! They both waved their arms and shouted warning, but to no avail.

Kathy dove for the companionway, and found the air horn in the nav station. She burst back into the cockpit, quickly giving three blasts on the horn. She did it again. Annie was screaming at the top of her voice too. The guys looked up, and saw her panicked waving. Only when she violently pointed to the approaching danger did they become aware of it. She saw Norm grab the anchor rope and begin to haul it in. The tree lurched again, rolled, closing the gap between them agonizingly fast. There was a surreal silence for a moment.

"Oh Jesus!" Kathy sobbed. "Oh Jesus, help them."

In slow motion, the tree caught them. It seemed to lurch a bit; limbs and wet leaves shook spray into the air, and partially rolled over them. It hesitated a moment, then the dinghy disappeared under the huge monster. Annie continued to scream! When she took a breath, the morning was as silent as a tomb.

The tree lurched again and the dinghy resurfaced behind it, as though the sea creature had spit out the refuse. The dinghy was empty! "O God, no!"

"We've got to help them," Kathy screamed. "Quick; go down and do that winder switch!" When Annie shook her head, Kathy said, "The one you had to flip before the anchor winder works." Annie flew down the companionway. Kathy made sure the engine was out of gear, then she turned the key. The diesel immediately started.

They both went out to the bow, only partially understanding what had to be done. Kathy saw the safety shackle, and removed it. Annie opened the windlass switch cover and stepped on the button. The chain began to clank aboard. Kathy hurried back to the cockpit remembering that Norm had said the windlass could pull in the chain, but not while pulling the boat too. She put *Dreamer* in forward gear, and listened to the chain continue to clank in. Why was everything happening so slowly? A terrible taste filled her throat.

"We've gone too far!" Annie screamed. "It's under us! We went past it!" Kathy had not taken the boat out of gear. "Damn!" Still the chain clanked in "Here it comes! It's O.K.!" A couple seconds later the anchor banged into its cradle. Kathy pushed the throttle forward and felt *Dreamer* surge ahead. She turned the wheel a bit too much and had to quickly correct, but they were closing on the still dinghy.

She said to Annie, "Get the hook thing so we can grab the line!" Now having learned how easy it is to overrun a target, she eased the throttle and approached the partially inflated dinghy from downstream. It looked like the front and middle sections had been deflated, but the back part was still O.K. She took the boat out of gear, this time. When they came alongside the dinghy, she gave a touch of reverse, then pulled the throttle off, and the transmission out of gear. She could then go to help Annie. Together they hooked the line and took it to the aft cleat, where Annie quickly took a couple turns and secured the line just in time as *Dreamer* drifted on the ebb. There was no sign of Bruce or Norm in it!

Back on the wheel, Kathy pushed the forward gear, and turned *Dreamer* to starboard. She gave the throttle a little shove. Once again it responded with power. Hardly had they started however, when the girls felt a heavy bump.

"Did we hit something?" Kathy cried out. They looked behind them to find the anchor line from the dinghy trailing on the surface, "Where's the anchor?" Annie asked. She began pulling in the empty line. They would worry about that later.

Ahead of them by about a quarter mile they could see the tree, and waving frantically from the root ball was Bruce. "Where's Norm?" Kathy asked desperately.

She began to think like someone who was driving a large sailboat. She didn't want to approach from downstream, but from the side; not the branch side but the roots, where Bruce could help. She took *Dreamer* on a big loop turning to port that should bring their starboard side in close. She could work with close. She was amazed at how clearly things seem to be happening for her. They were within a hundred meters, then fifty. She took the boat out of gear and began that long glide in. Twenty meters; Bruce was saying something to Annie. At ten meters she turned the wheel away from the tree, afraid to get any closer, but Bruce called out that she was doing fine. "Let it come on in," he said reassuringly.

It was then that she saw Norm hanging onto the tree trunk. His head was covered with blood, and his clothes were torn. Without thinking, Kathy pulled the boat into reverse and prop walked right over to the roots, where Bruce could grab the spring cleat. Then it was full stop and everything in neutral.

"Annie, open the pelican hooks on the lifelines," Bruce requested. Norm was pulling himself up, making his way to the root section. Bruce held the boat in place, grateful for no wind or chop. "Can you make it, Dad? Give me your hand. I can help."

The Skipper heaved himself over the roots, and grasped a stanchion. "Lord, that feels good," he declared.

Kathy on one side, and Annie on the other got a firm hold under his arms and heaved him aboard. Kathy noted an angry tear across the back of his hand that was bleeding; it was from the anchor line that he was still trying to free when the tree hit them. The most damage was a deep gash on his forehead, and another on the bridge of his nose; there was matted blood in his hair, but she couldn't see its source. There were nasty scratches on his neck, and both his shirt and jacket were bloody and torn. It looked like the Skipper came in second in a war. They helped Bruce scramble aboard, too.

Without thinking that she might be third or fourth in command, Kathy went to the wheel and put *Dreamer* in gear, easing away from the terrible tree. Bruce and Annie were trying to determine how extensive the Skipper's injuries might be. Straight ahead of them about a half mile, she saw a familiar sight, a red dock, and there was a boat tied to it. In her mind Kathy thought only one thing: "Help is near!" She pushed the throttle for more speed.

The folks on the dock had been watching the drama unfold near the tree. As great fortune would have it, they were Art and Bonnie, aboard "Sea Deuces." They watched

Bruce getting the bumpers over, and preparing a bow line. There must be some emergency, because the sailboat was in a hurry, and towing a deflated dinghy. At a hundred meters the power was off, and *Dreamer* started that smooth approach. At twenty meters Kathy put it in reverse, and there might be some who contend that she performed a now legendary "hockey stop." Fortunately Art was on the dock to fend off, and prevent a hard landing on *Dreamer*'s quarter.

"The Skipper is pretty banged up," was all that she could say before the tears released. She put her face in her hands and sobbed.

Art was calling Bonnie to help. Who would have guessed that strangers who had shared an evening table twice in the past week would play such a crucial role in the unfolding drama.

"The first thing we need to do," Bonnie said before she was even beside the boat, "is get these guys out of their wet clothes and into something warm. They are both at stage two hypothermia." Then she asked, "Do you have a first aid kit?" She was confident that there would be one on *Dreamer*. Kathy had regained her composure, and went to get the kit from the salon hanging locker. The Skipper was painfully making his way to his stateroom to change clothes. When Bonnie told him not to do that, he leveled a scary look, saying "I've lost some skin, but not my dignity. I'll be right back."

Bonnie, it turned out, was a nurse at the emergency room of Harborview Hospital, and the next few minutes would reveal that she was a godsend.

Both Bruce and the Skipper dropped their wet clothes in the cockpit storage compartment. Bruce had lost his topsider slip-on shoes in the accident, and his contacts when he hit the water. Fortunately he had replacements. Unfortunately, he had also been carrying his cell phone, which now was inoperative, and his wallet, which had considerable soggy Canadian money. The Skipper made his way to the dock, where Bonnie had set up her "clinic;" he wore a pair of tan shorts and deck shoes. The sweatshirt he carried would eventually cover the host of scrapes and punctures he had received. She sat him in a folding chair from their boat, and began to carefully wash his wounds with a towel soaked with bottled water. "These scratches should just have some antiseptic cream to prevent infection," she began. "We can put a butterfly bandage on this, and this," she cleaned the wounds on the back of his neck. "I think you will need stitches to repair your ear." She applied another butterfly bandage for temporary care. "You will probably need a couple here, too." She was trying to see the extent of the cuts on the back of his head. "The wounds that really need immediate care are these on your face. Your nose took a huge whack; it may be broken, and I know that this gouge on the bridge will need a stitch or two. The one on your forehead and eyebrow," she switched to a new towel, "is what worries me most. It may involve some damage to the sinuses, and inner muscles that control your eyelid." She had carefully and systematically cleaned all the damages, and placed temporary bandages where possible. "Ice on everything else will keep down the swelling. By this time tomorrow, you are going to be a colorful man with all these bruises. I've seen train-wrecks with less damage. That was such an unbelievable fluke." Bonnie offered him a couple Advil for pain.

Art finally made his presence useful; "If you leave right away, I think you can be in Campbell River in time to see a doctor this afternoon. I think the quickest way back is down

Whale passage along Read Island. It will take you about four hours. "The Skipper nodded in both understanding and agreement.

Looking at Kathy's worried face, Norm asked, "Do you know what this means, Sweetie?" His face looked ready to break into tears.

"What does it mean?" she answered shakily.

"It means I don't get a Brownie Hot Fudge Sundae at Big Bay." There was enough half-hearted laughter to break the gloomy spell on the dock.

He said to Bonnie, "Thank you. You have been an angel of mercy this morning; I can pay you in wet Canadian." She shook her head. "Or," he went on, "we can have a crab feast at our house when we get back, eh?"

"That sounds like a winner to me," Art said, offering his business card with contact information. "Just get patched up, will you? I'll get the bow line."

When they were aboard *Dreamer*, there was a moment of hesitation. The crew looked to the Skipper to take the lead, but they were unsure how injured he might be. Kathy suggested that he must be suffering a lot of shock, and should wrap up in a blanket and get his feet up. Bruce offered to fix a cup of tea. The Skipper agreed that would all be good, after he got them underway. He wanted to get a close look at that tree.

Moments later as he slowed *Dreamer* to get a good look, Bruce spotted one of his shoes; and not far from it was the tote bag, which they got with the boat hook. They circled the tree trying to find the other topsider. The Skipper replayed the furious events. He remembered the air horn warning. That was a godsend; they would have been blind-sided without it. He remembered trying to free the anchor and being engulfed in branches and leaves. As best as he could recall, the tree hit the anchor line, jerking it out of his hand, ripping the flesh. The front of the dinghy dropped under the huge weight, throwing him headlong into the chaos like a projectile. Bruce either dove or was bounced off to the side, just away from the roots as they seemed to be trailing the main part of the tree. It was noisy and painful and confusing. "I don't think I went under water," he said to Kathy, who was listening to the account. "I know I was in the water, but in the jumble of the tree, too. I think it's amazing that the oars and fishing poles stayed in the ding." It really had the feel of a bad dream. As soon as they finished a full revolution around the debris, they headed for the Rendezvous Islands and the turn toward Campbell River. The skipper suddenly felt tired, weak and shaky.

Bruce suggested that the crew each have a turn at the wheel, two bells long, (that's old school terminology for one hour.) The Skipper could wrap up in a blanket and make sure "we stay on course." Bruce said, "We could call Smitty at the marina to find out if we can get an emergency appointment at the clinic on Sunday afternoon. It might take a few minutes to do all that patching up." He went below to make the call on the Skipper's phone before his first turn on the wheel.

Once the plan was in motion, silence fell on the cockpit except for the throb of the diesel, turning at full speed, and the splash of the bow wave. Finally, the Skipper, who wanted desperately to lift the pall of gloom that had come over their trip, knew that at least he could talk to them. From his cozy corner across from Annie, he began with as much courage as he could muster, "This makes me think about the application of some of my theoretic ideas. Have I told you about my visits to the speech class at Skyline High School?" His listeners shook their heads, not completely focused on what the Skipper was trying to do. "I presented a motivation speech entitled, 'USEful Thinking.'" When he thought he could go on, he told them, "The letters stand for 'Unquenchable Self Esteem', U,S,E, full thinking. I began by telling them about an incident I had fresh out of seminary." His head felt dizzy. "I was appointed to the University Temple, as their teaching minister. My primary responsibility was the college fellowship, but I also was responsible for education for all ages. The building was enormous, almost a block long and half a block wide. I was trying to find some fresh space for the youth to use, and went into a room off the balcony." It was hard for him to concentrate, and he wondered if the others were feeling the same way. "It hadn't been used in twenty or thirty years, and was plenty large enough for some soft furniture and a sound system. The trouble began when I tried to leave the room. The door was locked. I twisted the knob, banged on it, and tried the other twist, nothing worked. I was locked in. There was no phone in the room, and in the early 70's no one had a cell phone." His head was aching and he felt a sharp pain when he lowered his chin. But he wanted to continue his distraction.

"I was in there almost an hour, trying to determine a way out. The hinges were on the other side of the door; it was the fourth floor, so I couldn't jump for it. Finally I noticed a door that went up into the bell tower; there were climbing rungs on the wall. When I think back on it, I wouldn't do the same thing again, but I did climb up the tower, out onto the roof, along the edge to the other end of the building where there was a ladder sort of thing that went up and over the red tile roof, and down onto the balcony outside the gym where there was a door with a key entry, that I had!"

"When I finally got down to the church office, shaken and completely weirded out, the church custodian happened to hear me pouring out my terrible adventure. He laughed and told me that there are no locking doors in the old part of the building, from which I had just successfully escaped. Then he led me back up to the balcony, (humiliating as that was.) He used a nail to push through to the inside mechanism, and easily opened the cursed door that had captured me. Then he demonstrated, to my ignorance, how hardware from the twenties works. 'You push it in and twist for privacy,' he instructed, 'then pull it out and twist to open the door.' I had been locked in a room with an open door!" He knew that if he went below to his stateroom he could be nauseated.

"Suddenly the words of Napoleon Hill became crystal clear: 'Anything the mind can conceive, and believe, it can achieve!' USEful thinking is addressed to the areas in which we believe the door is still locked. There are four reality laws to begin with:

> For every action there is an equal and opposite action;
> The law of averages is dependable;" He struggled to keep the memory clear.
> "Life is a stream of obstacles or opportunities, depending on how well you understand the first two;
> Choice is the power to control your destiny."

"Then I tried to help the students see that U.S.E. principles are not philosophy, but action principles." His headache had become so severe he wanted to just close his eyes.

Bruce began a slow starboard turn around the third Rendezvous Island. They were making good time.

The Skipper continued his recounting of the high school presentation.

"We can maximize every negative experience by looking for the balancing positive. Every failure plants a seed of an equivalent success!"

"We can carefully look for alternative actions trusting in the law of averages."

"Never engage in the self-destructive practice of blaming or transference. No one else is in control of your destiny!"

"Persistent problem solving is an art that grows. The more you do, the better you get at it. I tried to explain that I am not implying that absolutely everything is possible, but I asked how many of them had seen the movie 'Rudy.' At my age, height, and weight, I might not make the NBA draft, but I am equally sure that I will not accomplish what I do not attempt." He took several slow deep breaths, and a sip of tea, feeling some relief.

"Then I told the class about a Stanford Math major who was not late for his final exam, but was not there in time to hear that the two problems written on the white board were meant to relax the students as a joke, by showing an unsolvable puzzle. When he turned in his test blue book, he apologized to his professor for not getting both of the extra credit problems on the board. His test was done excellently, and one of the 'jokes', which had never been solved before, was clearly solved. He not only went on to graduate school, he is now a math professor at Stanford, because he thought it was solvable, and did. He thought the door was unlocked."

"I told them about Mattie J.T. Stepanek, who was featured by Oprah. He was fourteen years old with Cystic Fibrosis, and wrote, and illustrated, six books of love poems entitled 'Heartsongs'. Shortly before the death of this lovely young man, he said that 'life is just a measurement of time; whether short or long, it's just a measurement.' If you know the door is unlocked, it can be opened."

"I usually closed with a simple village parable. It seems a prankster came to the village chief, wishing to play a trick on him. In his hand there was a tiny bird, its beak barely poking out one side of his fist, and brown feathers sticking out the back. In a defiant voice, the prankster charged the old man to tell him if the bird was alive or dead. The chief thought about it a moment concluding that the bird was indeed alive, but if he so answered, the lad with one squeeze could change that. If the chief said that the bird was dead, the lad would simply open his hand and the bird would fly away. He thought a bit more and finally answered, 'The bird is as you will it to be.' That same conclusion is a commentary on today; it is the sum of all of yesterday's choices, and tomorrow will be fashioned in just the same way, by your choices, as you will it to be."

Before he could continue, Bruce asked Annie to take her turn at the wheel. "Our course is 175°," he instructed. "Just stay to the right of that little island ahead of us; that's Whale Passage." An hour goes by in a hurry, doesn't it?

Kathy came over to check the Skipper's bandages. She had been both listening to him, and worrying about him. "I don't know, Norm." She didn't want to dispute his theories, but was unable to clearly understand. "I can't see any positive in this accident."

Bruce sang in a western twang, "He lost his shoes, and his dinghy's flat, guess he won't be doin' that . . . . again."

"I appreciate your tender care," the Skipper said with even a bit of a smile. "Let's keep this in perspective. We had a most unfortunate fishing outing. Who would even imagine that tree carcass in July? I got some banged up, that's true, but it is not the end of the world, much less our vacation. I think all the damage is repairable, except for your shoes and contacts, Bubba."

"Dad," Bruce protested, "you're going to need several stitches!" That fact seemed pretty major to him.

"Yup, I am," his dad replied, "and the dinghy is going to need a couple of patches too." Then as though the thought had not come to him before this moment, "And by the way, what happened to that dinghy anchor?"

Kathy and Annie exchanged a guilty glance. Annie answered first, "I didn't think to pull it up when I tied the dinghy to the cleat." Kathy joined in the confession, "I was so anxious to get to you that I think I snapped it off. We felt a bump and thought I had run over something."

"You snapped it off," the Skipper said with a chuckle. "There is justice if I've ever heard it." He actually managed a crooked smile. "That damned anchor was fouled, and caused the problem. If it had come up when I tried to yank it up, we would have been drifting right along on the flood with the tree, and could have avoided it. There wouldn't have been a problem. I'm glad you snapped it off, and left him there forever."

Kathy still had misgivings about his theory for the high school class. "I can understand the law of physics that for every action there is an equal and opposite action. I just can't see one positive thing that happened this morning."

"Can't you really?" the Skipper pondered. "From my point of view I see some pretty heroic stuff. Bruce was quick to get me untangled from the limbs, making sure I didn't get dragged under water. That showed quick thinking and affection. You two ladies got *Dreamer* going, got the anchor up, and worked a very sensible process of recovery. You didn't know that we were on the tree. We might have been hanging on the dinghy, where you went first, and then followed to find us. That was about textbook recovery." Looking fondly at Kathy he continued, "We started this vacation not sure how you were going to do aboard a sailboat, and this morning you demonstrated the ability to get it started, underway, and where it needed to be, even docking, which is no cinch. I'd say that was mighty positive!"

"But we just did what we had to do," Kathy protested, near tears again. "That is hardly a balancing positive." She was still shocked to see the damage done to Norm.

"It is in my eyes," the Skipper insisted. "And Bonnie is a nurse, who has to take care of injured people, but in my eyes, she is always going to be an angel; and they will become close friends to us, I hope. That's not just a little positive." He was thinking about the tender assistance he had received.

The Skipper's cell phone rang in the salon, and Bruce dove to answer it. Moments later he reported that the clinic was closed on Sundays, but Smitty had managed to get the doctor to attend an emergency. "Her name is," he read from a scribbled note, "Dr. Tamara Roh."

Annie had been growing anxious about their course. "Are you sure I'm supposed to stay on this track? It looks like I'm going into a tight spot." Ahead of them about three miles lay a jumble of small islands and rocks.

The Skipper pulled himself up to study the area. "Yup, that's Plunger Pass. It doesn't look like it from here, but there is plenty of room. We could go around, but that takes us more toward Hariot Bay."

"Then is this island we are going past Cortez?" Bruce asked.

"Right you are, Bubba," the Skipper answered. "Just on the other side of those small islands is Whaletown; so we are closing in on Gorge Harbor. Neat, eh?" It was apparent to the crew that the Skipper was regaining some of his chipper self, at least making a valiant effort.

Kathy felt her task was to get Norm seated again, wrapped in that warm blanket, so she asked, "Did I hear you say that one of the laws is that we always have a choice in our destiny?" She smiled as he sat back into the corner of the cockpit.

"Yes, that's the fourth reality law," he replied, happy for her interest. "That is the rudder that steers our destiny."

"If I had a choice," Kathy said quietly, "I'd choose to steer around this morning, and still be at Teakerne Arm safe and happy."

"Yeah," the Skipper seemed to agree, "but time is a poor back-set driver. That's the old temptation of, 'if only.' We can say, 'If we had only started an hour earlier this morning,' or 'if only the anchor hadn't fouled,' or 'if only I had seen that rotten tree sooner and cut the anchor line.' All of which begs the point that given what we have, now we have real choices to make."

Kathy tried to think of a positive way to answer. "Well I choose to get you to a doctor, and get you patched up."

"There is a fun quote," the Skipper smiled, "that says, 'if you can only see the obstacles, you have taken your eyes off the goal.' So what are we going to do this evening, or for that matter, with the final two days of our adventure? The important thing is not what we may have lost, but what we have left to use."

Bruce wanted to be part of brightening the afternoon; with a decisive voice he announced, "I want to buy a round for the house at the Lodge during Happy Hour!" Then reconsidering the possibilities of generosity, he wondered, "If we go in early, the Sunday crowd might be light." The crew got the mood, and chuckled at his effort.

"Ding, ding, Kathy has the helm," he declared. "I think I know how we are going to get through Plunger Pass, so I'll stay back here with you." It was obvious to everyone that he had no more idea how to negotiate the channel than she did, but it was comforting to have him beside her. The Skipper may have enjoyed the moment more than anyone else.

As soon as they were successfully through the pass, the Skipper pointed back over the port quarter, "There's Whaletown, and if you look up above it, you can make out the entrance into Gorge Harbor." Then pointing straight ahead of them, he added, "There's the buoy on Wilby Shoals. We are back in familiar territory."

CHAPTER 9:
CAMPBELL RIVER II
Repair and Reaction
to Trauma

They secured *Dreamer* on the fuel dock with the Harbormaster's help, and Smitty offered to guide them to Dr. Roh's office, where she was waiting for the Skipper. There was some wry humor about a doctor waiting to see a patient; isn't it always the other way around? The reader is spared the uncomfortable details of five local anesthesia shots, and fourteen or fifteen stitches to close the angriest wounds. Doctor Tamar made extraordinarily fine stitches that would heal to hardly any telltale scarring. Since there was no open pharmacy, she also gave him a limited number of pain pills, and advised him to liberally ice the areas. Once again the Skipper expressed appreciation for outstanding care.

When the crew arrived back at the marina they found that Smitty had fueled the boat, pumped the holding tank, and moved *Dreamer* to the long dock near the entrance ramp.

"There probably won't be anyone else in tonight," he explained. "So this spot will be convenient and quiet. I called a guy who can patch the inflatable. He'll be here right after breakfast." When the Skipper offered a $20 gratuity for all the extra help, Smitty waved him off, saying, "What kind of friend would I be, accepting your wet money, eh?"

"Then come up to Dot's as soon as you close up and have a Molson with us, eh?"

Smitty offered to shake hands, but had to switch to the left hand when the Skipper offered the one without the heavy bandage. There was enough laughter to lift whatever worry they might have had.

Bruce said, "I can't remember what we had for lunch." After a short pause, he said louder, "Hey wait a minute, we didn't have any lunch. I'm starving here." It was unanimously agreed that they should head for the Lodge immediately.

Kathy asked Norm, "How are you feeling?"

"If you mean am I in any discomfort, not much. I feel fine. If you mean am I hungry too, I'd answer, I'm more thirsty. My tummy feels a little jittery." It was Happy Hour for sure.

When Bruce asked Dot if he could set up a case of Molson for the house, she countered with the offer, for that much money, even if it was wet money, she'd keep three pitchers on the bar going all evening. "O, Canada" for sure!

They had just finished their house special burger baskets when Brian and his buddy Larry came in. As usual they made their way to the pool table, loudly offering challenges to each other. When Brian noticed the Skipper, and his several bandages, he shouted "Jes . . . who did that to you,

Mr. O'Banyon? God da. .," he stuttered, "I'll knock the shi. ." He really had a limited vocabulary.

"I'll tell you friend, it was scary," the Skipper began. "We were over there in Teakerne Arm, eh? Out of the brush comes this creature, seven, maybe eight feet tall, shuffling like, hairy and brown, right at the girls. I jumped in front of him, and he lit into me." Showing Brian the stitches on the back of his head, he said, "He grabbed me in his teeth and shook me like a dirty rag, but I kicked him right in the crotch. When he bent over I smacked him on the side of the head and he went howling back into the brush."

"Oh, that's a bunch of bullsh . . ." suddenly Brian's face lit up with a grand smile. "Oh I get it. You're trying to get me to curse." He fairly radiated joy. "No way man. I gave that up for good! Hey Dot," he called to the bartender, "he's trying to get me to curse, but I'm not fallin' for it eh? I passed the test!" The crew began the applause, but in an instant the whole room was cheering for Brian's success. The young man beamed with pride.

When the pool game got fully underway, the Skipper leaned over to say to Bruce, "I remember a saying from the German writer, Goethe, 'If you treat an individual as if he were what he ought to be and could be, he will become what he ought to be and could be.' All three of his listeners nodded in understanding. Perhaps Kathy pondered it most deeply because she brought it up on the walk back to the marina.

They were walking hand in Norm's uninjured hand, a few paces behind Bruce and Annie. "I know you have said that nothing you say is ever meant for just one of us," Kathy began awkwardly, "so am I just a little insecure if I think maybe you are treating me the way I ought to be or could be?" She lowered her head thinking how tangled that thought had been. "I need to tell you that this morning when that tree crashed into you, I was terrified. I thought I was losing you. It seemed so unreal, so horrible; and then I sensed your spirit in me, showing me what ought to be done. It was like you were telling me just what to do, and how to do it."

They walked a few more steps in silence as Norm thought about his answer. "I can tell you that when I knew the tree was going to smack us, I felt really calm. I could see your face so clearly; its focus enabled me to be strong. I knew that it was only going to be a little bump, and everything was going to be O.K. You were right there with me. I think the reason I have not been upset about the accident is that it has helped me feel closer to you than ever before."

She gave a tiny chuckle, "I would never guess that getting so injured could have such a sweet effect." After a couple more steps, she continued, "But you have had a profound effect on me and several others this week."

He thoughtfully said, "I think we should all try to encourage and enable others to realize self-improvement; but we are exploring the beginning of a wonderful new life together."

"Yeah," she mused almost to herself, "I guess there is a clear line between being a helper, and a Pygmalion project."

Norm stopped so he could turn full toward her. "It would hurt me more than that maple tree did if you think our affection is anything but sincere."

"Oh, I know it is pure!" she affirmed. "I just can't match your positive enthusiasm for the future. Aren't you getting fed up with me?"

Norm leaned against her gently, and with just a bit of discomfort, kissed her. "Sweetie, I know how I feel, and it's so fine. I am patient, and know that soon something is going to click, and you will be as eager for us as well." They resumed their stroll.

A few minutes later the crew was seated in the salon, darkness claimed the surrounding hills, and muted the waterway around them. The Skipper thanked Bruce for his generosity with the pitchers of beer, saying, "I have always wanted to buy a round for the house, and haven't. Tonight you took it to a really fun level. I think Brian believes the party was for him. Good on ya' Bubba!" Uncharacteristically, he rose to give Bruce a big hug, even though he could feel a growing stiffness on his injury sites.

Bruce returned the appreciation; "Thank you for the burger supper. It was like a party, and by the way, Dot was super generous, only charging me half of what I originally offered for a case of Molson."

Kathy observed that the evening was so different than she anticipated. She thought that after the doctor's session, they would come back to the boat for quiet rest. Instead of gloomy, they did everything but "boogie down!"

Annie said, "Skipper, I remember you telling us to 'act enthusiastic and we'll be enthusiastic.' I saw that happen. Instead of being bummed out, we were having a wonderful time." She wanted to hug him but was aware of his several bruises. Instead, she just rubbed his left arm.

"O.K.," the Skipper said, "I think we are in agreement that our vacation isn't quite over. We still have two days. How would you like to use it? We could just stay here, maybe explore the north end of the island with the car. We could revisit Hariot Bay, or Gorge Harbor."

Bruce asked, "Dad, what is the Latin for 'feed?'"

He had no idea where the question might lead them, but the Skipper thought for a moment before answering,

"I think it is 'vesco,' to provide food, to feed; or 'vescor', to join in eating. Why do you ask?"

"Well, I vote for 'vesco canem!' I would love to see that huge eagle again." Both Annie and Kathy nodded in agreement.

The Skipper said, "It has been moved and seconded that we resume our vacation at Hariot Bay. Those in favor, say, 'Eh?'" It carried with a unanimous vote.

He told them that he was in truth feeling a little weary, and a bit achy. He thought that with the pain helpers Dr. Tamara had given him, he just might sleep a bit longer in the morning. "If I'm not up when you are, just knock on my door, eh?"

"Let's have a prayer to conclude this extraordinary day." He held out his good hand to Kathy. She held Annie's, who held Bruce's. It was an emergency circle.

"God, our Good Shepherd, tonight in the serenity of our boat, we give you thanks for dangers, that teach us to be brave; for suffering from which we learn patience; for pain that teaches us tenderness, and for new friends that surprise us like rainbows in a storm. Help us to remember in trying times that there is no progress without effort; no conversion without crisis; no Easter without Good Friday, no service without suffering. Trying times are times to try more faith! We are trying. You are helping. Praise the Lord, our hearts are overflowing. We whisper this prayer in Jesus' name. Amen."

Oh, good the night!

Perhaps he had rested enough, but more than likely he rolled over onto a very tender spot that woke Norm. He lay quietly listening to the beginning of a new day. The boat was still, but from outside he could hear the muted voices, probably fishermen putting their boat in at the ramp. A distant gull call and a diesel engine starting were part of the growing chorus. It was time to get this aching body out of bed and assess the damage. When he looked in the mirror, he shuddered. It wasn't the swelling that hadn't gone down as much as the bruises that were more evident. Both eyes were showing light blue hue shiners. If his heart wasn't so happy, he might actually be a little bummed out by the sight. He kept thinking about her explanation of his presence with her during the crisis. "This is going to be a fantastic day!" he thought as he carefully pulled on a fresh T-shirt.

When the Skipper returned from his shower, he found the crew sitting at the salon table. A fresh glass of tea had been poured for him, accompanied by pirate pastry. Both Kathy and Annie inspected the wounds on his head and neck to be sure the stitches were in place.

"How did you dry your hair?" Kathy asked, noting the absence of a dryer.

"It's easy," he replied, "You just hit the hand dryer, and squat down under it. I only needed two shots, to get a pretty good style, don't you think?"

They all agreed, but Kathy said, "You can hardly see the place where Dr. Roh shaved your head."

"What?" the Skipper started. His hand searched his scalp for a moment before he went on, "Oh, that's just not right!" The crew joined in a good natured chuckle, sympathizing with his distress.

"Before we go up to the Tackle Box, let's repeat yesterday's devotion." He handed the Bible to Bruce to read from Romans. It had the feel of a normal, wonderful morning.

Day 7.) (Repeated)

> Beautiful, beautiful, Jesus is beautiful
> And Jesus makes beautiful things of my life.
> Carefully touching me, causing my eyes to see,
> Jesus makes beautiful things of my life.

Morning Prayer:

Thank you Lord, for this new morning; we believe you are the Light that never goes out, the heart that never grows cold, and the hand that never stops reaching out to us. We have a powerful, positive suspicion that you have a plan for our today and tomorrow, and that this beautiful plan is unfolding exactly as it should. We will stop trying to understand, and instead start enjoying whatever you provide; in Jesus' wonderful name we pray. Amen.

Meditation: repeat three times.

> *Today I commit myself to motivate people with love and positive information.*
> *I will not be an agent of fear, but a channel of love.*

Romans 8: 28, 37-39

Things don't work out; God works out things!

1). How God works;
2). God uses everything;
3). Works together;
4). God's grand plan for our lives;
5). Contagious faith.

Conclusion: repeat three times.

I will boldly face the future with the sure confidence that God will work all things together for my ultimate good, and His Glory.

At breakfast the talk of the café was the school of Silvers that had come in yesterday. Apparently, most boats that fished late yesterday came in with nice fish. "They're hitting "blu'oochies, eh?" "I got two on a black Apex." "We limited using a red and gold plug." It seemed that any lure might be possible of success. Bruce was even more excited about fishing again than he was of the stack of blueberry hot cakes in front of him.

Minutes later, as the crew returned to *Dreamer*, they saw Smitty and another man surveying the partially inflated dinghy. When he introduced the crew to his friend Robert, he told them that he could, in fact, repair the damage.

As Robert shook the Skipper's hand, he observed, "Looks like both of you took some punishment. If I can take it to my shop, I can have it for you tomorrow. Sorry I can't do much for your nose." He grinned a playful smile.

"We're going to be out tomorrow, but if you could have it back on Wednesday afternoon, we'll be glad to have it in working shape," the Skipper countered. "The boat's heading back for Seattle on Thursday."

Robert nodded in understanding. "I don't think there will be any problem. There are two punctures that I can see, and one tear that's about four inches long. It's very doable; it'll cost $35 for the punctures and $50 for the bigger one. With tax, $136 total."

Bruce volunteered to help them carry the limp boat up to Robert's pickup. When he got back, he said, "Now I can fish from the transom easily. I think there is going to be a salmon killer back there. When do we leave?"

Kathy said, "I can see that you are your father's son; looking at the bright side of a problem."

The Skipper was ready to go, so he declared, "Let's light the fire and kick the tires!" The sun was burning off the morning marine layer, exposing clear blue skies. It was going to be a fantastic day!

They were still in the channel, making their way toward the familiar fishing spot when Bruce pointed, "Hey, look at that guy! He's got a fish on, and so does that one!" Bruce was eagerly surveying the myriad of boats that were plying the shoal. *Dreamer* had slowed to a trolling speed, and Bruce was paying out line. Smitty had told him that most of the fish were being caught at about forty feet. Bruce thought he must be pretty close to that by now.

As usual after a day of rain, the water was without a ripple, and the sun was already heating the day. The wind was absolutely calm. A couple hundred meters in front of them another fisherman jumped up with a fish on. Bruce's enthusiasm had spread to the crew; Annie had already freed the gaff hook from the storage compartment; Kathy was seated at the end of the cockpit, looking aft to see all the action; and the Skipper was carefully picking their path through the other boats, looking around as often as he could. He was sure that the smaller boats would respect a 41 foot sailboat.

After about a half hour, Kathy suggested that the Skipper get a hat to cover his shaved spots on his head. "It would be sad," she said with logic, "to make a tender place sunburn sore; or is it sorer?" She giggled at her own joke, and all the crew understood that she was finally making peace with the accident.

Bruce gave a jerk on the pole, but there was no corresponding battle. "Must have missed him. Dad, how deep are we here?" It would be easier to blame the bottom than his reflexes.

"We're just at 51 feet, but it is bouncing around from 60 to 45. You might be too deep." Hardly had the words gotten out of his mouth when Bruce gave a grunt. "Oh smack! I'm snagged on the bottom. Line was grinding off the reel as his drag grudgingly surrendered line out. The Skipper turned to starboard, trying to ease the momentum of the boat. Bruce remained certain it was hooked on some submerged obstacle, and began to speculate, "Maybe it's a ledge, or a submerged shipwreck, or a . . . Hey, Dad, it's moving!"

As *Dreamer* continued to turn to starboard, the line moved slowly forward, which a snag definitely could not do. "Bubba, I think you've hooked a dandy!"

Bruce was busy keeping steady pressure on the line, rod tip up to absorb any shock. He would crank in a bit and then feel the drag release some. It was a tug of war with twenty pound test line. One that lasted almost twenty minutes! Nearby boats became aware of the battle and courteously moved away. The Skipper tried to keep the action off the starboard quarter for Bruce's advantage, even though *Dreamer* was out of gear and drifting quietly. Twice, the line seemed to race away from the boat as the fish came toward the surface. They watched for a jump, but only saw a swirling splash.

"I think he's getting tired," Bruce finally gasped. "I know I am, for sure." Then from the dark water, they saw a large silver flash that quickly tried another dive for the depths. But the fight was gone. The salmon surrendered after just two more runs. Bruce continued to ease the line in, bit by bit, foot by foot, until he could see the size of his fish. "Oh my gosh, Dad, it's a whopper!"

The Skipper opened the pelican hooks over the transom so the lifelines could be freed. He lowered the swim ladder as Bruce eased the salmon toward the stern of the boat. There were probably many instructions that went unheard, like "easy," "not too fast!" "Can you get it?" "Just a little more." The Skipper was in position with the gaff, as the head came up near the surface. With one powerful jerk, the gaff hook did its fatal task. Norm tried to lift the fish, but had to call for Bruce's help. As the two of them hoisted the large salmon onto the boat, nearby fishermen applauded and whistled their congratulations. They would later learn at the Hariot Bay scales that the Chinook salmon weighed 41 pounds, and had they entered the daily derby, would have been in first place! They now had a reason to hurry into Hariot Bay for ice.

The Skipper asked, "So, Bruce, how's your day going?"

He couldn't answer with all the emotion he was feeling, but he did give two thumbs up!

CHAPTER 10:
HARIOT BAY II
To motivate people with love and positive information

"I love this place," Kathy whispered. They had met with the harbormaster, found their slip, filleted the fish, and fed the eagle three massive snacks; complete with photo "Oohs", and "Aahs." The store had a freezer in which they could place their fish until tomorrow; then a Styrofoam carrier would keep it frozen until they got home. A leisurely walk out to the end of Rebecca Spit gave them now another serene beach experience.

The four sat in the late morning sun, leaning against a large driftwood log. "Dad," Bruce began in a way that was now familiar to the Skipper, "where are we going next year? I thought our first trip on *Dreamer* was the absolute best, but, wow, this year tops it, I think."

"Well if fishing is in the plans, I'll make sure you are on my team." The Skipper thought for just a second; "Two salmon, and two fine trout; you have set a new family record, I think."

"Yeah, so where are we going?" Bruce was as relaxed as the morning.

"Well Bubba," the Skipper said thoughtfully, "I've wanted to go out to Barkley Sound. I especially like the idea of entering by way of Imperial Eagle Channel. With a name like that, it has to be an outstanding passage." He was quiet for a bit, then added, "Or I've been talking about going to Maui."

Kathy's stomach gave a lurch. "He's going to tell them," she thought with huge reservation. She looked away, hoping to hide her distress. "This is going to be so embarrassing!" Her anxiety rose.

"You wouldn't sail there, would you?" Bruce asked, knowing the answer.

"I have enough miles accumulated to fly free, and the Wardens have provided a place to stay. Mr. Branch has made those mental health days available. It looks to me like a perfect no-cost opportunity to get an early start on my tan." The Skipper continued to gaze at the moving tide in front of them, in spite of the troubled thoughts he was entertaining.

"Dad, isn't Barkley Sound just around the corner from Victoria, on the west side of the island?" Bruce's interest was on full alert.

"If 120 miles is just around the corner, the answer is 'yes.' I think we would need a favorable tide to make it in twelve hours, and the last half is in open ocean, which could be foggy in July." The Skipper had obviously given this some serious consideration.

"What dates should I block out for the vacation?" Bruce asked with pointed interest.

Before the Skipper could answer him, Annie said, "Speaking of blocking time out, I need to head back to the resort. The washroom is just about too far away for my comfort." She stood up, expecting Bruce to join her. They headed back at a steady pace.

Several silent moments passed before Kathy said quietly, "I was afraid you were going to . . ." Her voice trailed away.

"You were afraid I was going to share our conversations about Hawaii," the Skipper finished her sentence. "I saw the look on your face. Did you really think I would not keep my word, that I would break my promise to you?"

"No, I . . ." she couldn't finish that sentence either. "It's just that . . . well I didn't know how they would welcome the news."

Norm looked at her with new understanding. "Sweetie, that may be the heart of your hesitation. Would you like to hear what I think it is?"

She nodded her head, feeling a little too exposed for her own comfort.

"I'm not a therapist, so this is just an opinion, you understand. I think you have been hurt enough, especially by the significant men in your life, that you have trust issues, which in itself is not that unusual. We've all been damaged by the choices of others. I think you have compounded the issue, though, by having doubts about yourself. You don't trust yourself for making those major decisions, or dealing with their consequences, that could cause you great hurt. Does that make sense to you?" He waited for her to think about it for a moment or two.

Kathy smiled, saying, "Scott is always telling me that I should just make up my mind. I think I'm not decisive enough for him either. He says I argue with myself. I have a habit of telling myself why the choice I just made won't work." She hesitated a bit more before agreeing, "I think you're right."

Norm assured her, "When I think about it, why wouldn't an accountant have trouble making up her mind? She needs more information, or she needs to compare her balance with past reports, or she needs to examine other trends before she can be sure of her answer."

"Are you saying that I am more cautious than pessimistic?" Kathy was seeking a ray of hope. She gave him a playful smile.

"I'm saying that it is important for me to learn how you communicate, how you problem-solve, how you manage stress, if I want us to have a world-class relationship." His eyes twinkled as he added, "And I definitely do want that."

"Before we go back," he continued, "I want to give a disclaimer, again. This afternoon, I hope we can finish our conversations about fearless living. I want to say again that nothing about the thoughts is specifically directed to you and me."

Kathy's expression had brightened. "Now, it's my turn to ask you to trust me, again. I heard you say clearly that these are not aimed at me, necessarily. I have found them to be personally helpful, even inspiring; but I do not believe they are targeted on me." She gave him a careful hug, that concluded with a sweet kiss.

When they got back to the resort, they found Bruce and Annie in the pub patio, sharing a basket of fries and a Molson. "We've been waiting so long for you that I got really thirsty," Bruce explained.

When the Skipper looked at the menu, he realized he had been eating too well all week. Suddenly everything on the menu seemed calorically challenging. Their server suggested a fruit bowl, "The berries are fresh from the Okanagan area, pears and apples are featured with the chef's own apricot sorbet. It is really outstanding." It was an effective suggestion. Only Bruce ordered something else. "Three fruit bowls and a burger basket," he requested.

There was not a breath of breeze, nor a cloud in a piercing blue sky; the patio felt oppressively hot by the time their lunch was consumed. "I'm headed for a pair of shorts and a tank top," the Skipper declared. "And I think the salon will be the coolest spot for our concluding conversation, if you are in the mood." Nudging Bruce, he added, "No heavy breathing, Bubba."

"I wasn't sleeping," Bruce protested. "I thought you knew I was praying." They all chuckled at his humor.

The ringing of the meditation bowl helped focus their thoughts. The Skipper had a copy of Day 7 if anyone needed one. It was time to begin their final conversation by singing a now familiar song:

> Beautiful, beautiful, Jesus is beautiful
> And Jesus makes beautiful things of my life.
> Carefully touching me, causing my eyes to see,
> Jesus makes beautiful things of my life.

Meditation: repeat three times.

Today I commit myself to motivate people with love and positive information.
I will not be an agent of fear, but a channel of love.

Romans 8: 28, 37-39

Things don't work out; God works out things!

1). How God works;
2). God uses everything;
3). Works together;
4). New every morning
5). God's grand plan for our lives;
6). Contagious faith.

Conclusion: repeat three times.

I will boldly face the future with the sure confidence that God will work all things together for my ultimate good, and His Glory.

When Bruce had read the scripture again, and they had repeated the meditation phrase, the Skipper began by saying, "Lots of folks have anxiety about the future, a fear that is not just caused by the uncertainty of what may happen tomorrow. It goes much deeper than that. They buy into a heresy that is shared by many Christians. Simply stated, this belief is expressed in a trite maxim: 'Given time, everything works out.' You've heard it, haven't you?" All four nodded in agreement. "I don't believe that, nor do I believe that 'time heals all wounds.'" The Skipper gently touched the receding swelling on his forehead and bruises around his eyelids. "That is little more than a blind trust in fate. All too often we are guilty of glibly saying, 'Don't worry, things have a way of working out.' But sometimes they don't work out." Kathy wondered if this was the part Norm had said was not about them.

"Some of us feel victimized by seemingly uncontrollable events. We thank God for the good things that happen, but what do we do with the other? What about the pain and difficulties? I've heard someone say, 'Up to this point I've felt that if I was patient, things would work out for the best. Now I'm at the end of my patience.'"

He chuckled as he shared, "I almost got kicked out of a ministerial group when I challenged the man who said, 'Everything works out for those who wait. You've got to believe the Bible, right? All things work together for good.' Those of us who first learned to trust the 1611 work of the King James translation of Romans 8:28 learned it that way, 'And we know that all things work together for good to them that love God, to them who are called according to his purpose,'" he quoted from memory. "I told my clergy colleagues that God's Word is infallible, but the translators were not. My goodness, I stirred up the crowd. That King James' wording places the emphasis on things working out in the lives of people who love God. And that gave rise to the notion that given enough time, things will work themselves out. The inevitable conclusion was the development of the vague trust in eventuality, rather than God."

"In the original Greek, the order of the words in this verse puts the meaning in true perspective, and gives us a cure for our fear of the future. 'For we know that to those who love God, in all things God works together for good to those who are called according to his purpose.' Did you hear the difference? Things don't work out; God works out things!"

"That truth is the source of courage and expectation so profound that we can say without reservation: 'I will give up the vague idea that given time, things will work out. I will boldly face the future with the sure confidence that

God will work all things together for my ultimate good, and His Glory.' God *is* our future!"

"So let's begin where Paul did in his words of assurance for the Christians in Rome. God created us to receive and return his love. In Christ, he reconciled us to himself so that we could know and love him. We couldn't do that on our own. To use an old Hebrew concept, we are a chosen people by God, and called to live with trusting confidence in covenant with him. We get to see the future as a gift in which Christ accomplishes his purpose in and through us. And what is that purpose, you ask? It is to make us like his Son!"

"When we surrender ourselves, and commit ourselves to a Christ-like life, we begin the process of liberation from our fear of the future. Everything else must be secondary. No person, plan, or program can be placed ahead of this goal. When this becomes our sole agenda, Christ in us gives us the power to truly love the Father. That love qualifies us to be counted among the people Paul called 'those who love God.'"

"Christ is with us watching over all that happens to us. He goes before us to guide us each step into the future. He is beside us as our Companion and Friend, and he is behind us to gently prod us when we lag behind with caution or reluctance. Most of all Christ is in our minds to help us understand the purpose of what happens to and around us. Moment by moment he shows us that he is using the events of life to strengthen in us the fiber of his nature and character. If we come to the Lord with an open, receptive mind, he will give us exactly the insight we need to understand his deeper purpose in our circumstances. He interprets what happened the day before and inspires us to trust him for the day ahead. For anything else he gives us the quiet assurance to 'silently now I wait for thee, ready my God thy will to see, open my eyes illumine me, Spirit divine.'"

The Skipper held up the day's worksheet. Holding up one finger, he said, "That's how God works." Adding another finger, he went on, "The second crucial truth the Lord, our interpreter, wants to make plain is that he will use everything that happens to us for the accomplishment of his awesome purpose. That's what he impressed on Paul's mind and validated in the Apostle's experience."

"Excuse me, Dad," Bruce interjected, "can you explain why Paul is called an Apostle? He wasn't a disciple was he?"

"Good question; the short answer is that Saul of Tarsus, as we knew him first, was on the road to Damascus when the risen Lord intercepted him, and helped him see the new truth. Paul, his Greek name, began a journey of discovery that eventually took him on three missionary trips. Around A.D. 57, he could look back and see how the Lord had been orchestrating the events of his life. Nothing had been wasted. The triumphs and the tragedies had been used to mold the clay of his nature into the image of Christ. Paul had known success and failure, victory and defeat, acclaim and rejection."

"Only one thing could account for Paul's resiliency and his confidence for the future. The years had taught him well that 'in all things God works together for good to those who are called to his purpose.'"

"We can't face the future without fear until we are sure of this truth. Of course we may still make mistakes, bring problems on ourselves, and resist the Lord's best for our lives. But there is just no way we can face the future with confidence without the firm hope that the Lord will make the best of our efforts, and help us to grow through our failures."

This time Annie interrupted. "That sounds like you think failure is inevitable for us."

"I wouldn't go so far to say inevitable," the Skipper softened the thought, "but probable, and at least possible." His smile was reassuring that no sinister plan was implied.

"At the same time," he continued, "it is important we understand that not all of our problems are of our own making. There are times when we are victims of other people's ineptness, appetites, or simply confused motives. Our future is staffed with the full spectrum of proud, selfish, competitive, greedy humankind. Our tomorrows will be invaded by conflict and broken relationships. That doesn't sound real inviting. We can endure the people problems if only we know for sure that the Lord will help us, and that he will use even the difficulties to deepen our relationship with him."

The Skipper took a deep breath to get completely focused. "Our assurance that God will use all things for our growth, and his glory, must also extend to the realities of pain, sickness and even death. In it all, we will need to know that he is both our healer and our strength to endure. We will know his miraculous intervention and his supreme patience when we need to wait. Mysteriously, he will use our times of physical weakness to teach us to depend on him. And if we must walk through the valley of the shadow of death, he will be with us to guide us all the way. This is a really big thought! Neither the influences of evil nor the calamities of the natural world will be beyond the Lord's power to utilize for our good. He will be with us to help us overcome temptation, and to trust him in the tragedies." He knew he was repeating himself, but had to say again,

"Nothing can separate us from God or his creative purposes for us."

The Skipper held up three fingers. "You see, believing that God works all things together for good does not exempt us from the difficulties of life, but it does assure us of exceptional power in dealing with them. The way the Lord 'works things together for good' is to block us from getting into some troubles. That's the 'lead us not into temptation' part of the Lord's Prayer. God strengthens us in other troubles, and turns still others into stepping stones. Nothing escapes his loving providence. God is constantly working to increase our joys and strengthen us in difficulties."

"The Greek verb for 'works together' also means 'to work with.' God works with us in helping us understand what he is doing in and through us. We discover that it is often in life's tight places, troublesome problems, and painful experiences that we have made the longest strides in our personal growth."

"That's the confidence that cures our fears of the future. We are promised neither a trouble-free future nor one in which things just seem to eventually work out. What we are promised is that God will work all things together with creative continuity for our ultimate good. Tomorrow is under his control, and we don't need to flinch at the problems it may bring."

Holding up four fingers, the Skipper continued, "This is such a big idea that God uses everything and brings his best for us out of the worst that might happen, that it must be reaffirmed every morning or it will become dangerously commonplace to us. I have a little plaque that reminds me; each day I see it in the bathroom: 'His compassions fail not. They are new every morning; great is God's faithfulness.' (Lamentations 3:22-24) I've repeated that daily for years. Beginning the morning that way has helped me to remember that the Lord has enabled me to grow through problems, and make my most exciting discoveries while wrestling with the difficulties. That's especially true when I have been fretting about a challenge, when I wake up tense, with something I dread facing. If I am faithful and repeat that promise, I'm amazed at how often I wind up singing praises for what God has brought about rather than the worst I was imagining."

"We're about done with this outline," the Skipper said making a weary face. Holding up all five fingers he said, "The fifth crucial truth is that God has a grand plan for our lives." Looking at Bruce, he added, "No, this has nothing to do with predestination or divine control. The only way to overcome our fear of the future is to make God's 'good' our goal. God doesn't work all things together just to set us free from fear. That's a by-product of committing our lives to his plan and submitting to his agenda for fulfilling it."

"This discussion takes us full circle from where we began nine days ago. We have filled our minds with scripture, chanted positive highlights, and thought super positive meditations. We have focused on our core values. We have discovered the good, for which God works everything together, which is to make us like Christ. We don't need to fear anything that might happen to us in the future, because we belong to God, who can use everything for his plan. God never gives up on us, or on his purpose in us."

"That was Paul's conviction as he neared the end of his life in prison in Rome. We suspect the message he communicated to the Christians in Rome was what he also wrote to the Philippians. The believers in both churches were afraid. They faced opposition, persecution, and discouragement. In response, Paul shared the steadfast confidence he had for himself and for them. 'Being confident of this very thing,' he wrote, 'that he who has begun a good work in you will complete it until the day of Jesus Christ,'" (Philippians 1:6).

"The 'good work' the Lord had begun in Paul and the early Christians was the same as the 'good' for which he was working all things together: the miracle of shaping them into the image of Christ. That's his plan and purpose. What the Lord has begun in us, he will complete. All the resources of heaven and the present ministry of Christ himself are committed to assure us of victory. Once his 'good work' has begun in us, he will use all the outer trials we face to build up the inner person. God provides exactly what we need each day."

"When Billy Graham was a young man, before he started his crusades, he tells of a time when his faith was tested. He had only the assistance of a devoted wife, little money and few opportunities to preach. He says that he was in no position to help others while he himself was faltering. The situation was so desperate for him that at a retreat at Forest Home in the San Bernardino Mountains, he decided he would either give up what little calling he had for the ministry, or find a stronger base upon which to stand. He read those words to the Philippians, 'He who has begun a good work in you will complete it to the day of Jesus Christ.' It dawned on him that what faith he had was a gift of God, and that God's reserves were boundless. If he consented to receive God's gifts, his Lord was ready, willing and able to keep on giving. From that day on, he believes God has given without limit, and fulfilled what he has begun."

The Skipper looked at his watch and smiled. Their time was almost over. "How would you like to exchange your fears for a contagious faith?" He smiled broadly, pointing at his own chest. "I would for sure. Paul vividly illustrates from his own life how the Lord can use everything to help us grow, and then use us to encourage others who fear the future. He writes, 'I want you to know, brethren, that the things which happened to me have actually turned out for the furtherance of the gospel.' (Phil. 1-12). He goes on to explain that his imprisonment had given him the opportunities to lead guards to Christ and had given new boldness to the Christians in Rome."

"While Paul was imprisoned, the guards were chained to him. I suppose other prisoners thought that they were chained to the guards; Paul reversed it. It has been said that the guards had to be rotated more frequently because of the effect this evangelist had on them. They were becoming Christians as a result of prolonged contact with the fearless preacher while chained to him. The guards came to realize that, in reality, Paul was bonded to Christ. That liberating bondage made Paul the most free person in history. His faith was contagious. Even in difficult situations, the 'good work' of the Lord in Paul continued to grow. And the same thing is true for us. Our confidence is not that things work out, but that God works out things!" He clapped his hands as though announcing the conclusion.

"I'm ready for a Molson; how about you guys?"

Bruce said that he and Anne had been struggling with a decision for their future. They had considered going back to school, at least some night classes, and they might take a walk to continue the conversation, or plan a campaign to pressure another trip on *Dreamer*.

Kathy offered to exchange a Molson for a glass of chilled Chardonnay if she could hang out with the Skipper.

"Then let's share a concluding prayer." He held out his bandaged hand to Kathy, who gently placed hers under his and gave it support. Bruce and Annie joined the circle, now complete.

"Gracious God, we get it! Our fears are going, going, gone! We sense a mysterious calm, quiet, tranquil assurance rising deep within our being. This remarkable spirit of courage is over-powering. It is your very presence, working peace at the core of our invisible soul. Heavenly Lord, thank you. Our fears are gone. What a relief, in Jesus' name. Amen."

Minutes later, Norm and Kathy sat in the cockpit, watching Bruce and Annie making their way up the dock, hand in hand. Kathy quietly observed, "They are a darling couple, huh? They seem perfect together." She came around the table to sit at his left side, the one less injured, and gave him a warm kiss that lingered. "I think the same about you. You are the most perfect man I've ever met."

"Wow, thank you," Norm replied, a bit surprised by her directness. "I think we are a pretty wonderful couple, too." He knew she wanted to talk about their future, but had placed it "off limits." "When I'm with you I always feel like smiling." Now it was his turn to lean toward her with a kiss. "I think you are marvelous, and life with you would be so unbelievable."

She moved back to the other side of the table, "If I try to tell mom what we have done on this trip, it would be hard for her to grasp, I suspect. We have explored some beautiful islands aboard a fantastic boat, caught fish, ate in fun places," her smile grew playful, "and we chanted, prayed, sang, did Bible study, and had deep conversations about fear. Does that about wrap it up?"

Norm was feeling playful too, so he added, "We had a collision with a runaway Maple tree, made an emergency run to the doctor's clinic, and fell deeper in love." He noticed that her neck and ears were flushed, and realized that she must be dealing with some strong emotions.

"Are you all right, Sweetie?" He peered into her eyes, trying to understand her feelings.

"I'm just a little tired, maybe still feeling the effects of yesterday," Kathy replied. She stood up with her wine glass. "I think I'll go lie down, maybe read for a while." She didn't make eye contact with him, not wanting it to sound like an invitation to join her.

The Skipper felt an emptiness when she left. He watched a preening Loon resting on the water beside the boat. "Yes, she is a major part of my life from now on," he thought to himself.

Supper was a bit later than usual because Bruce and Annie "lost track of time." At least that was their excuse. Monday evenings the resort features an Italian buffet, which is pretty popular with the tourists, so a later time worked out nicely with no line for the dining room. Bruce offered to pick up the check since it was the last night in paradise.

When they returned to the boat, the Skipper introduced a new game. He said he was trying to win a hot fudge sundae at the Lodge when they get in tomorrow. He called his game, "forty ways to love your partner." When he explained the rules, he offered, "We each get ten cards to write a description of the way we can express love to our partner. We'll shuffle the cards and read them one at a time. You choose who wrote the card by pointing to that person, and since you can't point to yourself, there is a fail factor built in. We'll each ante a dollar to buy the sundae for whoever is the most successful at guessing."

It took several minutes for them to complete the writing phase of the game. Kathy was finished first; Annie was last. There was considerable table-talk about whether this was the G rated, or R rated version of the game.

Annie deflected that subject with, "Do you really want your dad to read anything other than G rated?" It was a fun beginning.

When the cards were dealt, Bruce turned over the top card from his pile and read: "Give a true compliment every day."

There was scrutiny of each other for a moment, and then on the count of three, each of them pointed to the person they thought wrote it. Only Norm pointed to someone other than himself. Score: them one, him zero.

Annie turned her top card over and read: "Love yourself first." Again there was a pause before fingers were pointed on the count of three. There were giggles and comments that proved this a fun game. The forty cards were shared as follows:

1). Give a true compliment every;
2). Love yourself first;
3). Serve breakfast in bed;
4). Write unexpected love letters;
5). Plant a tree together and nurture it together;
6). Send flowers for no reason;
7). Accept and love each other's family and friends;
8). Draw hearts on the bathroom mirror or shower door;
9). Kiss unexpectedly;
10). Seek out rainbows together;
11). Apologize first, and sincerely;
12). Be forgiving;

13). Remember the first kiss, and recreate it;

14). Hold hands;

15). Say, "I love you," with your eyes;

16). Let her cry in your arms;

17). Tell him you understand;

18). Drink toasts of love and commitment;

19). Do something arousing;

20). Let her give you directions when you are lost;

21). Laugh at his jokes;

22). Encourage wonderful dreams;

23). Commit a public display of affection;

24). Give loving massages with no strings attached;

25). Keep a love journal;

26). Calm each other's fears;

27). Walk barefoot on the beach;

28). Ask her to marry you again;

29). Say "yes";

30). Respect each other;

31). Be your partner's biggest fan;

32). Give the love your partner wants to receive;

33). Give the love you want to receive;

34). Share an outdoors hobby;

35). Never go to bed mad;

36). Put your partner first in your prayers;

37). Sleep in the buff occasionally;

38). Appreciate and celebrate your differences:

39). Start every day with a hug:

40). Live each day as if it's your last.

(If you were playing the game, fair reader, how would you guess the author of each answer?

The crew's attention was drawn to the dock where nearby voices were exclaiming, "I see it! There it is! It's moving so fast!" Of course they had to find out what the fuss was all about. There were seven or eight of their neighbors looking skyward. In the gathering darkness a crisp chip of light was moving across the sky. Someone nearby identified it as the international space station.

Bruce said quietly, "It's two hundred forty miles above us and still in sunshine. Isn't that cool?"

Annie asked, "How fast is it going?"

Again Bruce answered, "Nearly seventeen thousand miles an hour. It could go from coast to coast in less than seven minutes." He thought for just a moment, and then added, "The crew is travelling faster than a rifle bullet, but to them it is rock solid still. They'll be in a sleep mode pretty soon, if they're not already." He shook his head in wonder as the tiny reflection slid out of sight.

Kathy sat down on the cockpit bench so she could lean back and star-gaze. "I love being able to see the Milky Way so clearly."

Once again Bruce offered, "Yeah, there's not much city light out here to compete with them, and no clouds tonight." He pointed out the Big Dipper, and then counted five measurements of the two stars that made the front of it. Pointing to a dim star, he said, "Dad, isn't that one Polaris, the North Star?"

"Aar, right ye be matey," the Skipper said, trying to sound like an old pirate. "Just give me a tall ship, and a star to steer by."

Bruce asked, "Speaking of steering," he had no comment on the pirate voice, "where are we off to tomorrow? I'm kind of afraid of the answer." He smiled warmly, knowing that they all dreaded the end of their adventure.

"Well," the Skipper began, "I'd like us to be back in Campbell River by three or four o'clock so we can get the dinghy, and get a new fishing anchor. Then Wednesday we can clean the boat and get our stuff together. I'm not sure when the Wardens will be here, but it wouldn't surprise me if they arrive early."

"But before we go back, we have some options," he continued. "We could spend another day here, or we could cruise over to Gorge Harbor for lunch. We could give another shot at fishing on the shoal. I think that is a pretty good menu to choose from."

The spectators had all left the dock, and *Dreamer* was engulfed in deep twilight silence. "Before we let go of this day, I'd like to tell you how proud I am of us to continue our vacation of discovery after yesterday's incident," the Skipper said with obvious emotion. "I think it was a test that we all passed. Shall we have a prayer before lights out?" As usual, earnest hands sought one another until the circle was complete.

"Great and Gracious God, we praise you for this day of discovery. We have gained so much; you are helping us turn our fears around. Help us see them as a positive force for good in our lives, until we fear not that we might fail, but fear rather we might never dare to discover our potential; that we fear not that we might be hurt, but fear rather that we might never experience growing pains; that we fear not that we might love and lose, but fear rather that we might never have the chance to love at all; that we fear not that people may laugh at our mistakes, but fear rather that God will say to us, 'O ye of little faith!'; that we fear not that we might fail again, but fear rather that we might miss our greatest chance for happiness if we fail to give hope another opportunity. We tuck ourselves in tonight snug in your love and infinite Mercy. In Jesus' name we pray. Amen." They continued to hold each other's hands, knowing that the prayer was designed just for each of them personally.

Oh, good the night!

The Skipper was awakened by pain, a demanding ache in his face, and the back of his head. His hand and shoulder felt unusable. He sat up and searched for Doctor Roh's pain pills. Thirty minutes later, when he opened his stateroom door, he knew he looked pretty disheveled, but he felt better than he looked.

The crew was seated at the salon table, Kathy wearing a fresh green pair of shorts and matching top with lace trim. She was a sight for sore eyes, and the Skipper had sore eyes for sure. He told them a shower would fix him up, and he'd be right back.

A bit later, Bruce looked up from his book to say to Kathy, "I'm really glad we have shared this trip." Annie nodded her head in agreement.

"I'm glad, too, "Kathy replied. "When we started I wasn't sure I would fit in, because you were such a close family. You have made me feel like I'm really part of the crew."

Bruce made a wry face, saying, "Yeah, I'm not sure I still have first-mate status any more. Dad is very fond of you. It's like he has bloomed in spite of the accident."

Annie interjected, "I think we have all bloomed. When Nor . . . the Skipper," she corrected herself, "first started talking about changing our inner culture, I must admit I was skeptical at best. It sounded fringy. I only believed him because of the results of our first trip." She almost giggled, "Now, everything seems to be dialed in just for me. Every conversation has my address on it. I have written pages and pages in my notebook about his insights."

Kathy was about to say, "me too," when Bruce beat her to it. "I love the way he opens scripture for us. I have learned so much."

Now, she did say, "Me too! But I have so much more to learn."

The praise might have gone on, but Bruce raised his hand, listening. "He was whistling Beethoven the other day, now it's Handel, I think." Faintly they could hear his approach to the tune of "Thine Be the Glory."

His hair was still wet, but he had on a fresh sport shirt that had a bright floral print. If he didn't feel perky, at least he looked it. The Skipper poured a glass of Crystal Light, and offered them a new worship sheet. "I didn't know how many of these we would get through. We can just use what we need. By the way, the dining room is already serving stacks of hotcakes." He thought that might shorten their devotion period.

Day 8.)

Sung to the tune "O Tannenbaum":

> "We thank thee, Lord, for daily bread,
> And all thy mercies 'round us spread.
> We thank thee for thy love and care,
> For guidance in our daily prayer.
> For Christian friends, faithful, true.
> For love's unfinished work to do.
> In all we think and do and say,

Thy Kingdom come in us today. Amen"

Repeat 3X:

I will boldly face the future with the sure confidence that God will work all things together for my ultimate good, and His Glory.

Reinhold Niebuhr wrote, "O God, grant us the serenity to accept what cannot be changed, the courage to change what can be changed, and the wisdom to know the difference.

Morning Prayer:

"Great God, our Redeemer, at the beginning of this day, we ask that you make us so eager to seek the truth that no study may be too difficult for us, and no thinking too adventurous. Make us so willing to serve you and our world that no task may be too wearisome for us, and that no one may ever appeal in vain to us for help or sympathy. Make us so to feel your love for us that our hearts may return to you in wonder, love, and praise. Help us live this day boldly in Jesus' name. Amen."

Romans 12: 9-12:

Ten rules for abundant life:

1). Love must be completely sincere;
2). We must hate that which is evil and cling to that which is good;
3). We must be affectionate to one another in brotherly love;

4). We must honor one another above ourselves;

5). We must not be lacking in enthusiasm;

6). We must keep our spiritual fervor;

7). We must grasp opportunities to serve the Lord;

8). We are to rejoice in hope;

9). We are to meet tribulation with triumphant fortitude;

10). We are to persevere in prayer.

Conclusion: repeat 3X

When I feel inadequate to meet life's opportunities, I will pray for God's Holy Spirit for guidance, love, and power. I am equipped to be successful.

The crew enjoyed a delicious breakfast of hotcakes. They got underway by high tide, and fished in vain all the way to Gorge Harbor. When they were moored, they retraced their steps to the lagoon with hopes of another trout dinner. After two fruitless (fishless) hours, Norm put his fishing gear away, and found Kathy sitting in a sunny spot studying an insect.

"Come here, Norm. Have you ever seen a bug just die?" She was completely engrossed by the spectacle. "He just climbed up on that stick with his last breath. At first I thought he was just resting, or sleeping, but I touched him with this leaf, and he's dead as can be." She peered even closer. "Look, his back is even breaking open! Uhg! That's gross."

Norm sat down beside her. "I think that is a water beetle, and while I have never seen it happen, I'm pretty sure there is going to be more to his story."

Kathy was still bent over looking closely at the tan body that seemed so empty of life. "What could be more after he gave up the ghost?"

"Let's just watch for a minute." He moved his arm behind her so they could be closer.

"Oh, I have your number, Bub," she said playfully. She pressed against him affectionately. "You're doing the old, 'Let's Watch the Bug,' trick while you get all snuggly. You're not fooling me; but I'm going to let you anyway, 'cause I like it." She giggled coyly.

They sat still for several moments, each with a different awareness.

"Hey look," she whispered, "it moved!" As she watched, now spellbound, a tiny crease along the insect's back gave way to a small opening, that grew until she could see that it was only a shedding husk, revealing another life within. Unhurried and mysterious the inevitable transition occurred. She saw a new back, then part of the head. "What is it?" she wondered.

"This is a miracle," Norm answered her, just as enthralled. Moment by moment the new form was tugging its way to freedom. Finally, gossamer wings unfolded and began to dry.

"It's a Dragonfly!" Kathy bubbled with wonder. "It's so small and beautiful." There were tears in her eyes. "I had no idea this could happen." She turned to look into his eyes. "Did you know this was going to happen?"

"It was just as surprising to me," he said in a hushed voice.

She moved closer and kissed him with an eager intent. When she raised her eyes to his, she said in a broken voice, "I felt like that was me, breaking free from an old shell. I feel shaky and wonderful." She leaned her head against his chest, "Just wonderful."

They watched until the Dragonfly began to fan its wings. Then, in a heartbeat, it rose from the twig, and flew away.

"How did it know how to fly?" Kathy murmured. "The beetle never experienced that."

Norm answered, "I think that is a Higher Power sort of thing. The Dragonfly just knew what it had to do. It was created to fly, whether it knew how or not." As Norm started to stand up, Kathy gently pulled him back to her.

"That was a magic moment. I've never felt closer to God than I do right now. Thank you for introducing me to something so much bigger than I ever thought." She kissed him again, full and warm. "It was just a little bug, and so much more!"

FINALE: SEATTLE

Boldly face the future
for our ultimate
good and God's Glory.

T he crew fished at the shoals for over an hour. Bruce continued to believe there was another large salmon just moments away. Finally, they were back in Campbell River by low tide. The repaired dinghy was in place by 5:30, just in time for supper at the Lodge.

When they walked into the dining room, Norm didn't recognize any of the patrons. But as they were making their way to one of the few tables available, he heard a young man say, "Dad, they're here!" He turned to see Kurt and Donna getting up, and coming toward him.

"Hey, the Wardens are here!" he exclaimed with both gladness and a tinge of sadness, for now the adventure was over for sure.

"Holy cow, Pastor," Kurt nearly shouted, "What does the other guy look like?" Donna gave the Skipper a gentle hug, and advised Kurt to take it easy too.

"I don't know, Pilgrim," it was Norm's best effort at a John Wayne sound. "I left him face down at Church House, and he wasn't much movin'." The rest of the crew was introduced and the boys politely shook everyone's hand. The Skipper gave them the condensed version of the tree encounter.

The Warden's food had been served, so they agreed to finish their meal, and then hold two patio tables for dessert when the crew had eaten. There they made plans for the morning, breakfast at 7:30 at the Tackle Box. Since they had to be out of their room before 11:00, they would come to the boat and help with the cleaning. The holding tank had been pumped when the crew arrived, and the fuel tank topped off. By 10:30, they were coming down the dock with their duffle bags. After a quick boat briefing, which Kurt didn't need, one last look at documentation for getting back through the US Customs, there was no further reason to stay, so the crew loaded their things in either Kathy's van, or the shiny black Cadillac. Handshakes and hugs signaled the end of one adventure and the dawn of another. The crew agreed to meet at the Tea House in Stanley Park Vancouver, for a late lunch.

"Bubba," the Skipper said with some apology, "that CST will flat fly, but you must keep it inside the speed limit. It would be a bigger disaster than the Maple tree if you got stopped."

Bruce agreed, understanding the gentleness of his dad's advise. "I think I will follow you guys, since I don't know Stanley Park at all."

His dad smiled. Pointing to the Cadillac, he chuckled, "It has a voice activated GPS. Just say 'GPS on'; it will ask you where you want to go. Tell it 'Stanley Park Tea House.' I'll bet it will show you a better route than the one I know." They were headed home, for sure.

It was a little after 4 p.m. when they cleared the US Customs, and were headed south on I 5. Their conversations had mainly been reflective of the places and people they had enjoyed for the past twelve days. There were so many happy memories. "I will forever thrill to that huge eagle at Hariot Bay." "I got such a chuckle out of Brian, kicked off the pool table for cursing." "Bruce was so competitive at cards." "I'm grateful for all the work you did preparing for our discussion sessions. I learned so much." "I love my little deer necklace." "Do you remember how Smitty stood up to that loud mouth at breakfast?" "The salmon feed at Hariot Bay when we met all those other boaters." "And the shrimp from Brian's boat." "I will never forget standing under the waterfall." "You girls getting *Dreamer* going was amazing." "I'll never forget how gracious Bonnie was to bandage your wounds." Even though Kathy was driving, she reached over to momentarily hold his hand; the uninjured one. She had noticed how swollen his right hand was and how he had favored it since the incident. She was afraid there might be more damage than they first thought.

"I will always remember how included I have felt on this trip," Kathy said, about to change the subject. "I have become so comfortable with you at every meal, our walks and talks. I don't know what I'll do without them. Kisses were a gift, and I can imagine so much more." There was a sudden tear tracing down her cheek. "I can imagine . . ." she couldn't finish the sentence. "I don't know how you can put up with me. It's like I'm looking into a life that I really want, but there is no door, no way in."

Norm responded with a soft question, "Is there something keeping you out, some obstacle?"

"I think it's more like it belongs to someone else. It's not mine to have."

"Do you feel that you deserve the life?"

"Yes, but it's out of my reach."

"Is there something you must do to earn it?" Norm asked.

"No, I think about the story you told of being locked in a room that was open all the time. I think I need to talk with a counselor about some of this stuff that has not been important, until now," she paused to catch her breath, "until you. There must be a simple way to open the door." Another tear made its way unchecked down her cheek.

Norm reached over to gently pat her leg. "Sweetheart, I can see that this troubles you, and I want to help us untangle whatever is holding you back. I just want you to know that I'm on your side; there is no hurry." They watched Mount Vernon pass, and the fields of the Skagit Valley. They would be home soon.

"Hey," Norm offered, "how about taking Scott and Jenny over to Poulsbo for an overnight in a couple weeks? There is a killer bakery just across from the marina." He offered the information as though that might tip the decision. They would, indeed, be home soon.

Kathy drove to Bruce and Annie's place so they could unload the Cadillac, and say "goodbye" again. There was the promise of a dinner with cards soon; after all, they had a great salmon to barbeque. Norm put his stuff in the Cadillac and knew that he had to say "goodbye" to Kathy too, much to his dismay. She promised to call him in the afternoon, if he didn't call right after he saw his doctor in the morning. There is just no comfortable way to rend the fabric of affection they had woven over the past two weeks. He kissed her long and sweet, much to the delight of Bruce and Annie. Their adventure was complete.

EPILOGUE:

For three days Kathy had worked to clear her desk from the back log of reports she needed to catch up. Now, even though she had to spend a couple of extra hours, she was almost finished. But the printer was out of toner again and it needed to be replaced before she could print the last few pages. She just needed a trip to the supply room.

As she made her way past the empty offices, and deserted hallways, she scarcely thought about her bad experience before. But once inside the supply room, when she heard the door close behind her, it all flashed back into focus.

"What'cha lookin' for, sweet thing?" Martin asked. As before he blocked her exit, yet moved toward her. His stare was impossible to misunderstand, as he looked slowly from her feet to her face.

Kathy's initial surge of fear was almost instantly replaced with a feeling of loathing. "How many women had this creepy man victimized in this way?" she asked herself. Then, mysteriously, a calm power filled her mind. She knew she was not alone. She was empowered; and she knew what needed to be done.

"It's O.K. Martin. I just need toner again. I'll get it." She made a tiny move toward the metal cabinet and he blocked her. Again she could smell his bad breath and body odor.

"I can help you with what you need," he said. His smile widened as though he had an unusual insight of a personal conquest.

"O.K. Martin," Kathy said. "There is one more container I need from the top shelf of the cabinet." She felt him lean against her. "Can you reach that one?" She pointed toward the back corner.

His body was a growing weight against her as he moved closer to the cabinet, holding her more in his control, and obviously enjoying the moment. He was stretching as high as he could on tiptoes. "Yeah, I can get it goo . . ."

The word was cut off by the slamming metal door against his hand. "Jesus Christ!" he screamed. Kathy had spun her body, making Martin lose his balance and fall into the cabinet. Their combined weight on the door was an instant trap. She felt the soft cushion of flesh and bone. But Kathy leaned all her weight against the door. He tried to jerk his hand free but the sharp metal edge simply dug deeper into the bleeding flesh of his fingers and hand.

"This is no time for prayer, Martin," Kathy said, feeling that strange calm even stronger. "We're going to talk for a minute." She pushed on the door more determined than ever to hold him fast. He was standing awkwardly off balance on tiptoes with his hand so painfully snagged. Kathy continued with a level voice, "Martin, you might lose your job over this. You might lose the use of your fingers. What I want you to gain from this is the understanding that women, especially me, don't like what you do." She banged the door hard with her shoulder.

Martin let out another squeal of pain. "God damn, Kathy, stop!"

"Martin, do you understand me?" One more time her shoulder banged as strong as she could push, against the door.

He nearly wept, "I understand! I promise!"

Kathy said directly into his smelly face, "Martin if you ever try this again, to any woman here, I promise, you will need medical attention on a far more tender part of your body." She eased her weight off the door, not completely confident that the struggle was over. But Martin sagged to the floor. Looking for all the world like a whipped animal. He studied his bleeding hand, and sobbed.

"Martin, there is an industrial clinic just a couple blocks away. Have them stitch up your finger; that's a nasty cut; and have them x-ray your hand. I'll tell Judy that you caught your hand in a door, helping me. She'll call the clinic with the details for insurance." As she opened the door to leave, she added, "You might need to take a couple of days off to recover."

As Kathy walked back down the empty hallway, her hands and knees began to tremble. "Oh, my goodness!" she thought. "Did I actually just do that? I have something really big to talk to Norm about! We're going to have a wedding in Hawaii!"